DIRECT EVIDENCE

A Chase Adams FBI Thriller

Book 10

Patrick Logan

Prologue

EVEN THOUGH IT WAS A cool night in Las Vegas, sweat soaked the man's face. This perspiration was induced by fear as much as it was the dry air, or the fact that he'd been running for the past ten minutes.

Despite being far from the glitz and glamor that was The Strip, what every non-local thought of when they considered Las Vegas, the night sky still glittered like diamonds embedded in the mud.

"Please," he begged. "Please, I-I didn't do it—it's not what you think. It wasn't real."

His legs were rubber and his heart had grown weary from pumping so laboriously. He was not built for exertion, nor did he have experience with it. What felt to him like an all-out sprint was to most just a casual jog.

"Please."

The sweat mixed with tears now, and when one of the drops traced a line to the corner of his mouth, the man's tongue instinctively snaked out and dabbed at it.

It was salty, which was to be expected, but the mild sweetness of the liquid was surprising.

"Password. Give me the password." The man who had been chasing him spoke in a monotone voice, almost robotic. "Now."

"Y-you don't understand. This is real. I can't just—"

The man's legs buckled, and he went down. His right knee struck the pavement hard, and to avoid damaging his other leg, he pivoted upon contact and absorbed the rest of the fall with his ass. He immediately tried to rise but only managed to plant his hands and make it to an upright seated position before his pursuer was upon him.

A dark shape, an outline of a man.

A man holding a gun.

"No—no, please. Please."

"Password. Now."

"Okay. Just-just don't hurt me, okay? I'll give it to you, but you have to let me go. You have to promise to let me go."

The figure looming over him was backlit, which disguised the man's features and also made him look distinct from the background, almost like a poorly photoshopped image.

How fitting. How fitting that this seems like a simulation.

But it wasn't.

This is real, and this is where my life ends.

"Passwo—"

He gave it up. He had to—he was out of options.

But as soon as the word left his mouth, he knew it was a mistake. There was no surviving this. As a last-ditch effort, he scooted backward, but only made it a few inches before stopping cold.

It wasn't fatigue that gripped him this time. It wasn't even fear, though the man had raised the pistol and was taking aim.

It was that he saw the man's face clearly for the first time.

"Wait—it's-it's you?"

One final diamond peppered the night sky—a flash of first white then searing orange.

The last color was red—the blood that seeped from the hole in the center of the man's forehead.

And then all that was left was sheer and utter darkness.

PART I – Guilty

Chapter 1

"COME WITH ME," AGENT TATE Abernathy ordered the moment Floyd stepped through the front doors of the FBI Training Academy in Stafford County, Virginia.

Floyd was completely drained after the long trip he'd taken from Columbus, Ohio. And that didn't even consider the emotional toll of finding Julia Dreger standing over Meredith Griffith's corpse, a bloody knife in her hand.

Even after sharing more than he was obligated to with Columbus Police Lieutenant Lehner, which took upwards of two hours given the complications of the case and its links to the crimes in West Virginia, the man had no reaction.

He just stared, unblinking. Not even his large belly quivered.

Floyd had repeated the details, focusing on Cotard's Syndrome and Henry Saburra's involvement. Not only was this above Lehner's pay grade, but it was also evidently above his intelligence level. Which was fine—all Floyd wanted was for Julia Dreger to be treated fairly, given counseling and consideration prior to her arraignment. It was his opinion that the woman had acted in self-defense, despite the brutality of the crime scene. And that's what he put in his report to Director Hampton.

And now he was here, working on only a handful of hours of sleep, his mind still abuzz, his heart racing, to meet with Tate Abernathy.

His partner... who had abandoned him. Just like Chase.

Both his past and present partners knew about his PTSD, and yet they'd sent him alone to inform Meredith Griffith of her daughter's demise.

"I need to—" Tate cut Floyd off mid-sentence by wrapping his arm around his shoulder. Floyd was so angry that he was tempted to shake the other man off, but he was too tired.

"You need to come with me, that's what you need to do," Tate said sternly.

Floyd grew concerned and observed his partner. The space between the man's eyes was pinched and when Tate ran a hand through his soft brown hair, the movement wasn't particularly smooth.

Tate looked the way Floyd felt: tired, and worn out.

Had he told Director Hampton about Chase's unsanctioned participation in the Charleston and Columbus murder investigations? Had he ratted Floyd out for not reporting her himself?

No.

No, he wouldn't do that.

Floyd allowed himself to be turned and guided back out the doors he'd just passed through.

Would he?

Truth is, Tate Abernathy was full of surprises and a master at hiding them.

"Where are we going?" Floyd asked dryly. Fatigue extended to his vocal cords now.

Tate's answer came in the form of tightening his grip, anticipating Floyd's resistance.

He offered none.

Even if he had the energy, Floyd doubted it would make much difference. He was twenty years younger than his partner, but where he was thin and wiry, Tate had old-man strength.

Besides, Floyd was as intrigued by his partner's behavior as he was concerned.

Tate plopped Floyd into the passenger seat of his car, then walked around and got behind the wheel. They pulled out of the FBI parking lot and drove for about five minutes in silence before Floyd realized where they were going.

They were headed to the place that Chase had once called home.

No, not once—*definitely* more than once.

"No," Floyd said adamantly, shaking his head. "No, I don't want to go to Chase's apartment—I don't want to see her. What I need to do is speak to Director Hampton. Julia Dreger is being charged with murder. I need him to step up and do something. She was acting in self-defense, and—"

"Director Hampton's not going to do anything for Julia Dreger, Floyd," Tate informed him flatly.

"But he has to," Floyd protested. "It was Meredith's fault—you were there at the funeral, and you told me—"

"Yup, yup, I know what I told you," Tate interrupted. "And I also know you did everything you could. You submitted your report, which I looked at by the way, and I think you did a bang-up job. Now it's out of our hands. If Hampton wants to step in, so be it. If not, and knowing him I'm thinking not, well, then Julia's just going to have to put her faith in the system."

Floyd was incredulous.

Faith in the system?

"No, they-they shouldn't even charge her. It was self-defense."

When Tate said nothing, Floyd once again stared at his partner.

The man's jaw was set as was his stance on the matter.

If the dual cases in Charleston and Columbus had taught Floyd anything, it was that not all victims were created equal. And, by extension, not all perpetrators were treated the same, either. After all, Meredith Griffith was the bereaved wife of a popular and connected plastic surgeon.

Julia Dreger, on the other hand, was a prostitute and a home breaker. It didn't matter that she was the one who had actually cared for Dr. Wayne Griffith.

Floyd closed his eyes and then squeezed his temples.

"And that's why I brought you here," Tate said softly.

"To Chase's—" Floyd opened his eyes as the car came to a stop.

They weren't at Chase Adams' apartment. Instead, Tate had brought Floyd to a facility that he was familiar with.

It was also a place where he didn't belong.

Grassroots Recovery was for damaged people. It was for people like Chase Adams, for addicts, for individuals who'd lost complete control of themselves.

Not him. Not Floyd Montgomery.

Not the man from Alaska, the boy who loved trains and who used to drive people around as a chauffeur.

"No," he said forcefully. "I won't. I want to go back to Quantico. I have to speak to Director Hampton."

Tate's jaw remained set, but he was now nodding slightly. Before the man opened his mouth to speak, something Chase had said suddenly flashed in Floyd's mind.

Find what works for you. But you have to find something. You have to. It's about you being able to live without being so haunted by what you see that you find yourself descending into a pit that you can never — never — crawl out of.

Unable to meet his gaze, Tate said, "Look, this isn't like what happened to Chase. I'm not Jeremy Stitts and I'm not putting you into involuntary confinement or whatever the hell it's called. I'm just—"

"Wait, how do you know about—"

Tate held up a hand, instantly silencing him.

"Everyone knows about that—everyone in the whole fucking FBI knows about Chase Adams. But this has nothing to do with her. It's about you. Look, almost everybody in the bureau comes to see Dr. Matteo at some point or another. He's... he's good. Really good."

Tate sounded as if he was speaking from experience now, but Floyd found himself thinking not of the psychiatrist, whom he had met for his initial psych eval, or even his partner, but Chase.

Chase was an objective mess. It seemed like every step the woman took forward she stumbled three back.

And the whole time she'd been seeing Dr. Matteo.

Not a glowing report, that's for sure.

"It's up to you, Floyd," Tate continued. "But if you don't go in there, if you don't go into Grassroots right now, I'm going with you to see Director Hampton." He paused, and Floyd saw something else in the man's eyes: compassion. Only this didn't jive with what Tate said next. "I'll go with you, and I'll tell Hampton that you're not fit to be in the FBI."

Floyd gaped.

"*What?* Why would you do that?"

"Because," Tate began slowly, "because if you don't go in, then you're going to die. And I don't mean this rhetorically or as a euphemism. You will fucking die. I've seen it before. If you don't learn how to deal with the shit that we go through each and every day, you won't last another six months. I saw it with my last partner, and I refuse to see it happen with my new partner—with you, Floyd. So, there—make up your mind. And do it quick because I don't have all day."

Chapter 2

TRIGGERED BY DAWN, THE BLINDS silently rose and allowed sunlight to flood through the floor-to-ceiling windows. When the light struck Stu Barnes' cheek, he sighed and rolled onto his back.

He let the sun warm his face a little and after a few minutes, the speakers embedded in the ceiling began to play soft music. Only then did the man open his eyes, blink, then pull back his weighted duvet. After a quick stretch, Stu made his way to the bathroom, his movement activating sensors that triggered lights to illuminate the path. He urinated and then drank a glass of cold water.

Next, he slipped on his workout gear and headed downstairs. His coffee had automatically been brewed upon sunrise and he grabbed a cup before continuing to the home gym.

Today was Monday: thirty minutes of moderate effort on the treadmill, followed by a chest and triceps workout. Stu was done in just over an hour. Thirty minutes following the sweat, he was showered and dressed in a pair of dark denim jeans and a plain white V-neck T-shirt. For breakfast, he ate two hard-boiled eggs, a single slice of Ezekiel toast, and half an avocado. This was chased by a second coffee, this one including the addition of a tablespoon of organic, grass-fed butter.

During breakfast, Stu turned off the music and listened to a personalized, curated news feed of issues relevant to his many businesses. There was nothing of interest, which was a relief to him. The past month had been something of a nightmare. A previous employee of one of Stu's data collection corporations, Kevin Park, had been accused of murdering another ex-employee, Connery Sinclair. This wasn't newsworthy in and of itself, but some nosy reporter had dug up a pending civil lawsuit that Stu had levied against both men and the company they'd formed. But while they were making money from stolen technology—his technology—it wasn't worth the headache or the bad press. Stu had dropped the suit, but it was too late. His name and association with these criminals—despite barely remembering the two men—was all over the news. His image had subsequently taken a hit, which meant his financials had also been bruised.

But today? Crickets.

And that made Stu Barnes a happy man.

His schedule was light, too—just a handful of meetings, which meant that he was likely going to be able to hit up that evening's Vegas Golden Knights game in his private box.

Stu wasn't quite smiling, but his lips were definitely trending in that direction when he left his Summit Club mansion, and his good humor remained as he opened the door to his new Mercedes-Maybach S.

It faded when he heard the squeal of tires and saw flashing lights.

He was half inside his vehicle when he realized that the closest cop car, unmarked but also unmistakable, was headed not down his street and past his home, but toward his long, interlocking-brick driveway. It jumped the curb and Stu was suddenly worried that it was going to smash into the front of his Mercedes, or worse, clip the side of his knee that was still exposed.

He jumped back just as the car slammed to a halt, inches from his Mercedes' bumper.

"What the—"

Two men jumped out, guns drawn.

"Get on the ground!" the closest officer yelled. "Get on the fucking ground!"

Stu had instinctively raised his arms when he thought he was going to be run over and now he dropped his hands to his sides.

This was a bad idea.

While the first plain-clothed officer kept his pistol trained on Stu's chest, the other rushed at him.

More police cars—three? Four?—sirens blaring, followed the unmarked vehicle onto Stu's driveway, and more men with guns jumped up.

Stu had a moment to think, What the fuck is going on? before his right arm was twisted behind his back and he was shoved roughly to the ground.

Plastic zip-ties were expertly applied and then Stu was yanked back to his feet.

Bewildered, another thought crossed his mind: these aren't cops.

Despite their official-looking uniforms and outstanding police car replicas, these were thugs.

They weren't arresting him—they were kidnapping him.

For ransom, no doubt.

Stu began to struggle and started to drag his heels.

"Help!" he yelled. "Help me!"

He whipped his head back and forth and caught several bewildered looks from the uniformed impostors.

"What are you doing?" Stu shouted. "Let me—"

The man behind him raised his hands up the small of his back and Stu grunted in pain.

"Shut the fuck up."

Stu replied with another call for help but this time it was a weak, pathetic plea.

"Help?" the man in front of him, the first to point his gun, repeated. "Yeah, you're going to need it. You're going to need a lot of help." His eyes not so subtly flicked to Stu's mansion. "But I bet you can afford it. I bet you can afford a whole team of lawyers. A fucking army. And like I said, you're going to need them."

Whether it was the shock wearing off, or the man's words, Stu suddenly changed his mind. These were cops—real cops— and he was being arrested. But this revelation brought with it no overwhelming sense of comfort.

If anything, it exacerbated his confusion.

"For… for what? Why am I under arrest?"

The cop in front of him held up his hand, indicating for the officer behind Stu to stop leading him forward. He did, but the angry cop didn't lower Stu's raised wrists, and the dull ache that ran from palm to past his elbow remained.

"You hear that? He's playing the fool."

This was met with a smattering of snickers from the other officers.

"You have to tell me," Stu pleaded. "You're required to tell me why you're arresting me."

A smirk appeared on the cop's leathery face.

"Okay, okay, play dumb. Good. That means no plea deal." He made a show of looking around dramatically and then raised his voice loud enough for every cop and nosy neighbor in a half-mile radius to overhear. "Stu Barnes, you are under arrest for the murder of Jake Hollister. You have the right to remain silent…"

Chapter 3

TATE ABERNATHY WATCHED FLOYD WALK slowly up the steps to Grassroots Recovery. When the man was halfway to the double doors, he stopped and gripped the railing.

"Go," Tate urged from inside his car. "Go, Floyd, get your ass inside."

He was clenching his jaw so hard it had started to ache. He forced himself to relax, all the while silently trying to convince Floyd to go inside. Tate was an expert, second only to his ex-partner FBI Agent Constantine Striker, at convincing people to do what needed to be done. Perps had on many an occasion claimed that Tate had coerced or manipulated them, but he was by the book... mostly. And this was why he insisted on in-person meetings, whereas the rest of the world had shifted to communicating digitally.

The truth was that he liked Floyd—liked him a great deal. And it was about that time—time for him to start passing on his knowledge from years in the Bureau to someone else. Floyd fit that bill—he fit it perfectly. And what he'd told his partner was also true, albeit with a flair for the dramatic. Tate had seen many an agent go down a harrowing path and while Floyd might be too young and naive to find himself at the bottom of a bottle or addicted to pills, he was also too young to throw his life away. One of the things Tate enjoyed most about Floyd's company is that he could fuck around with the man without worrying about him taking offense. A rare quality in the age of ultimate sensitivity. But when Tate put his foot down, Floyd knew that he meant business. So, if Floyd changed his mind, Tate would live up to his word: he would go with his partner to see Director Hampton.

Then he would tell the director in no uncertain terms that it was his experienced opinion that Floyd Montgomery wasn't the right man for the job.

It was no secret that Jeremy Stitts and Chase Adams had vouched for Floyd, and this was the main reason he'd been accepted into the Academy. The man had done the rest himself — clap, clap — but both Stitts' and Chase's careers had taken unexpected turns. They held less sway now, and, besides, Tate trumped them both when it came to experience.

Hampton would listen to him, he was sure of it.

The reality was, if Floyd didn't get help, his PTSD and other holdups would grow more debilitating. Maybe not this year, or the next, but in three or four? These issues would cost either Tate or Floyd or both of them their lives.

So, yeah, if Floyd didn't open that door, this would most likely be his last day as an FBI Agent.

"Just walk up the fuckin' stairs."

When Floyd finally took another step, and then another, Tate felt some of the tension in his shoulders loosen. Motion is lotion, as they say, and Floyd seemed lubricated by these two steps. In no time, the man made it to the door and opened it.

Still, Tate watched intently. The truth was, even though they had been partners for months now, he really didn't know that much about Floyd. He'd read the man's file, of course, and he also knew what Floyd had done for Chase and Stitts before being admitted to the Academy.

But reading something and experiencing it in person were two very different things, especially for someone with Tate's talents. Usually, Tate could classify a person into one of several categories within minutes of meeting them and asking a few seemingly benign but specifically pointed questions. But Floyd proved more difficult than most. This, Tate had decided, was likely because of the man's unusual route to the FBI. To be fair, without Chase's and Stitts' intervention, the likelihood of Floyd getting anywhere close to becoming an FBI Agent was virtually zero.

And then there was Chase.

If Floyd was a puzzle, Chase was a riddle wrapped in a mystery inside of an enigma—thank you, Winston Churchill. And the two of them, despite their many glaring differences, were inexorably and inextricably linked.

But he would get to the bottom of both of them.

This, like his assertion to Floyd about the consequences of not entering Grassroots, was a promise. But as he watched, the former ultimatum became irrelevant: Floyd Montgomery set foot in the recovery center. Still, even after the doors closed behind the tall, lean man, Tate waited. This was torture for him—sitting around, doing nothing—but he endured a full five minutes.

And after those five minutes, Tate nodded to himself and finally drove off.

He hoped that the next time he saw Floyd, he could once again tease him as a friend and partner.

As he drove, Tate's mind wandered back to his last case, which, even at forty-seven years of age, almost half of which had been with the Bureau, was perhaps the most bizarre he'd ever been a part of. And that was why he needed someone like Floyd. Malcolm Gladwell might have come up with the idea that ten thousand hours were necessary to become an expert in any one subject, but Tate often wondered how many hours it took to become jaded and blasé.

Whatever that number was, he was close to it, if he hadn't passed it already. So, while others might look at Floyd's naivety as a weakness, Tate did not. To him, it was the opposite: it was a weapon in the same way that fresh eyes could infuse life into old ideas and reinvigorate a dying business. And was there a corporation that was more in need of an influx of new talent than the FBI?

Tate didn't return to his office, and while he actually had an upcoming appointment with Director Hampton, unrelated, that too was pushed to the sidelines. Instead, he drove across the Quantico campus and parked in front of the lecture hall building. After flashing his credentials to the security guard at the door, one of the few whom Tate didn't know personally, he entered the building and went straight to Lecture Hall 3.

His hope had been to arrive prior to the start of the class, but Floyd had dragged his feet—literally—and as Tate quietly opened the door, he already heard a commanding voice funneling up from the front of the room.

There were only a handful of empty seats, most of which were near the back. This suited Tate just fine, and he sidled into one of them next to a woman who looked to be all of eleven years old.

He smirked when he saw her notepad; it was like the Necronomicon, what with words extending beyond the margins of the page and intricate diagrams scribbled in all available empty space.

"Any good?" he whispered out of the corner of his mouth.

"Are you kidding me? Do you know who that is?"

Tate craned his neck forward and then alternated squinting his eyes. There was a man with brown hair at a podium, perfectly coiffed hair, bouncy yet controlled, and he was leaning on a cane as he delivered his lecture in a calm, authoritative tone.

"Oscar Wilde?"

The woman looked at him and Tate was genuinely worried that she was about to start reading from her book of the dead.

"No," she spat with disdain, "that's Jeremy Stitts."

"Ah, right." Tate sighed. "Never heard of him."

But of course, he had, and Tate Abernathy leaned back in his chair and listened to the man as he educated these young recruits on what it meant to be an FBI profiler.

And maybe—just *maybe*—he hoped to pick up a pointer or two along the way.

Chapter 4

THE CONSTANT RATTLING THAT FILLED the small interview room annoyed Stu Barnes. What annoyed him more than the sound was the fact that it was his leg making it. Or, more precisely, the noise the cuffs that were attached to each of his ankles and then passed through a welded metal loop on the floor made.

But as hard as he tried, Stu couldn't get his legs to stop shaking.

He'd been waiting for no more than ten minutes for his lawyer, for the man he paid an annual retainer of over half a million dollars, to come through the door and tell the guard to remove his cuffs and tell him, Stu Barnes, that they were leaving. And then the overpriced suit could continue saying how this was all a stupid mistake, and then threaten to sue. Stu, just happy to be leaving the Kanab County holding cell, would then dissuade his lawyer from taking any further legal action.

He would, however, release a statement through his many media outlets explaining that this was all in error and for the public to accept that cops were just people, too. Eventually, his neighbors would forget, shareholders would cease to care, and he'd be back to sleeping in his bed and waking to the sun shining on his face.

That was the plan.

Simple, surely, but that was all Stu, never a particularly creative person in the first place, could come up with given that nobody had given him any details. They took him to booking, fingerprinted him, and snapped a mug shot, which would eventually find its way on a lesser-known TMZ site, and then guided him to this holding cell.

A red light above the door suddenly flicked on at the same time a loud, archaic buzzing sound filled the room. A second after, the door opened and a man in a bespoke suit stepped in.

Stu instinctively rose to his feet and then quickly sat back down when the chains that bound his wrists to the metal table dug into his skin.

"Will—Will, thank God you're here," Stu said dryly. He cleared his throat and watched as his lawyer said something to the guard before the latter closed the door behind him. "No, no," Stu protested, "don't close the door. Get him to take these cuffs off my wrist."

Still, Will Porter. Esq. said nothing. The lawyer was approximately Stu's age, and this was far from everything they had in common. They had similar shocks of neatly trimmed silver hair and the same tall, lean frame. The major difference was that Stu had a salt-and-pepper five o'clock shadow, one that he kept even when he wasn't in prison, whereas Will Porter was completely clean-shaven.

Oh, and roughly a billion and a half dollars in net worth.

"Will, what the fuck is going on?"

Stu didn't like the silence, nor did he like the fact that Will had a briefcase with him. He liked it less when said brown leather case was laid on the table and his lawyer took up residence in the seat across from him.

"I don't-I don't understand. This is a mistake." Stu once again tried to raise his arms with the same net result: sore wrists.

Will licked his lips and finally addressed his client.

"Stu, I'm sorry I took so long—I was reviewing tapes with Detective Tolliver. I believe you met him?"

Stu shook his head.

"He was the one who made the arrest," Will explained.

In his mind, Stu pictured the short man with the mustache, the one in plain clothes who had held the gun at him and then shouted that he was under arrest for the murder of a man he never even heard of.

"Tapes?" Stu shook his head. "What do you mean, tapes? This is a misunderstanding, a mistaken identity thing." He lifted his hands again, this time more cautiously. "Will, get these fucking cuffs off me and get me the fuck out of here."

Will leaned forward.

"Stu, I'm your counsel. Anything you say in this room," he waved a finger above his head, "is privileged. It can't be recorded. That being said, I think it's in your best interest to remain calm. You don't want them knowing that you're rattled."

Stu was incredulous. No, incredulity was an insufficient noun to describe his state of mind.

Have I been transported to an alternate dimension? Have I been zapped from my home and taken to an alien planet where nothing makes sense? Where people look and sound like humans, but clearly aren't speaking the same fucking language?

"Rattled?" Will leaned forward even further but Stu wasn't about to be interrupted. "Of course, I'm rattled. I was getting into my car when these assholes came and threw me to the ground, claiming that I murdered someone I don't even know. So, yeah, I'm fucking rattled." Stu bared his teeth and pulled his hands up so hard that blood started to dot his wrists.

"Calm down, Stu. *Please*. I'm trying my best to explain what's going on here, but you need to calm down."

Stu knew Will, had known him for many years. The man was a corporate lawyer by trade, but when asked who he wanted to call, Stu hadn't hesitated.

Because any lawyer, someone who just passed the bar yesterday, could get him out of this mistaken identity case.

Besides, Will was already on the payroll.

Stu took a deep breath, closed his eyes, sucked in a huge breath, and then exhaled loudly. When he opened his eyes again, he half expected the nightmare to be over and that he would be back in his bed. Within moments, the blinds would detect the sunrise and open and he would start his day all over again. He would do the same workout, eat the same breakfast, and drink the same coffee.

Only, this time around, nobody would arrest him when he was getting into his car.

But no.

Stu was still in the musty smelling holding cell with Will Porter staring at him.

"I just want to repeat what I said: anything you discuss here today or anytime we meet is privileged. Do you understand what that means?"

Stu nodded, but the lawyer being a lawyer felt the need to explain anyway.

"You can tell me anything, and it can never be used against you."

What could be used against me?

Stu's mind raced, thinking back to all of his business dealings. Amassing the amount of wealth that he had over the years, which had ballooned from 252 million to over $1.4 billion, meant making a lot of enemies. And it also meant that not everything had been done above board.

Nothing criminal… well, nothing that criminal. Nothing this criminal.

Nothing like murder.

"I need you to tell me that you understand."

Stu looked skyward.

"I get it, I get it. Now please, tell me what the fuck is going on, Will. *Please.*"

Will took a deep breath.

"This is not a mistake, Stu. This is no clerical error and no mistaken identity. You are being charged with Jake Hollister's murder."

"Who? I—I don't even know who that is." Stu shook his head in disbelief. "I'm being framed. That's—that's the only explanation. Someone was pissed off because I bought their business on the cheap or because I put their business under. I am being framed."

That was the only thing that made any sort of sense.

But who?

Who had he pissed off that badly that they would set him up for murder.

The first two people who came to mind were the software thieves in New York—Connery Sinclair and Kevin Park. But Connery was dead, and Kevin was, for now at least, a man enjoying his freedom.

If not them, then who?

"You need to be honest with me, Stu."

Stu once again stared at his longtime lawyer and friend.

"I am being honest with you, Will. I don't know who Jake Hollister is—at least, I don't think so. The name doesn't ring a bell. But I'll one thing for sure: I didn't kill him. *Jesus.*"

There was something in Will's face that perturbed Stu.

What was it, exactly?

Confusion? Uncertainty? Perplexity?

It had to be one of them because it sure as hell couldn't be disbelief.

"Will? Why do I get the idea that you don't believe me?" Stu asked, his anger fleeing him.

"It's not my job to believe you, Stu. But if you're not—"

"Cut the bullshit. Stop with all this legal talk, this privileged information, this, 'it's not my job to believe you, shit'. You don't believe me, and I want to know why."

Will sighed and the man started to unlock his briefcase.

"You didn't let me finish. I don't know if I believe you, Stu, but to be honest, it's either I don't believe you or I don't believe my own eyes."

Stu squinted, not understanding.

"What?"

Will pulled out an iPad and turned it on. Then he spun it around to face Stu.

"Watch—watch and you'll see. And what you're going to see is you. You're gonna see yourself hovering over Jake Hollister and shooting the man in the head."

Chapter 5

"CAN I HELP YOU?" JEREMY Stitts asked, his eyes still on the papers he was collecting from the podium.

Tate, who had been sitting in the back row waiting for everyone else to leave, removed his feet from the seat in front of him. He stood and made his way down the steps toward the stage.

"Fascinating presentation, Agent Stitts. Congratulations."

This got Stitts' attention and the man glanced up at Tate. As he did, he ran a hand through his hair. Tate marveled at how every strand fell in place exactly as they had been moments ago. The FBI profiler was younger than Tate expected—having never met the man, Tate, relying on reputation alone, had assumed that Stitts would be, like him, in his late forties. Instead, he looked like he was in his late thirties. Maybe even mid-thirties, cane notwithstanding.

"You said that most killers kill for love, greed, or revenge. But I have a question for you?"

As expected, Stitts took the bait.

"Sure. Go ahead."

"Cats," Tate said simply. He waited for the next question, the one that would inevitably be, 'What about cats?', but Stitts surprised him.

"Sure. People have killed for a lot less than cats."

Well played.

He held out his hand.

"Agent Tate—"

"Abernathy," Stitts completed for him, grasping his palm, and pumping his arm.

Oh, Tate thought, he's good, he's trying to throw me off my game.

"And you're Agent Stitts."

"Just Stitts."

"Just Tate. All joking aside, I really enjoyed your class."

Stitts shoved the rest of his notes into his leather satchel.

"Thanks. And congratulations on the work you did in Columbus in Charleston."

The surprises never ended, apparently.

"You heard about that?" Tate asked, eyebrow raised.

Stitts nodded.

"I like to stay up to date on things. I may not go out in the field anymore, but I try to keep appraised of what's going on around here." He gestured towards the projector behind him which had displayed a few sparse images and words during his lecture. "I do it in an attempt to stay relevant, I guess." Stitts grabbed his cane from the side of the podium and leaned on it. "And, as complimentary as you've been, I'm assuming you weren't here solely to listen to my lecture."

"No, I'm here about something else," Tate admitted.

"*Someone* else, you mean?"

It bothered Tate that he was so surprised that Agent Stitts was this intuitive. He should have known. He should have known because anyone who had been partnered with the enigmatic and unorthodox Chase Adams as long as they had was either mentally deranged or special.

Maybe both.

In this case, Tate assumed the latter.

"That's right, but it's not about *her*."

Surprise was on Tate's side this time. As much as Stitts tried to hide his assumption that this conversation was about Chase, a tiny uptick of his left eyebrow gave him away.

"Floyd then. How's he doing, anyway? You know, I've been meaning to grab a coffee with him, but this," Stitts once again indicated his surroundings, "went from a temporary gig to ten lectures a week."

"Yeah, well, that's why I'm here. I know what you and Chase did for him, getting him in the academy, and I don't mean to take anything away from the kid. He grabbed his opportunity and ran with it. And even though he's been my partner for a few months, I get the impression that you might know him better than I."

A subtle nod of agreement from Stitts.

"I'm just going to cut the shit—to be honest with you, he's struggling. I remember my first month or so in the FBI being a grind. And I came from law enforcement—I was a beat cop for six years before applying. My first case..." Tate let his sentence trail off. His strategy had been to open up with the hopes that Stitts would feel comfortable and do the same, but when Tate started to actually recall his first case, he immediately shut down. That was something he did not want to do.

Not now, not ever.

"I know what you mean," Stitts agreed, taking Tate's silence as an invitation to speak. "My first big case involved a man with a bomb around his neck. TV crews stood around and watched, as did the ATF, bomb squad, local PD, and FBI. It didn't end well."

Tate was familiar with the case. He was also old enough to know a time when a killer could literally cross an imaginary line, enter a different State, and be completely unknown to the local cops. There was no way to communicate between departments, let alone States. Now, it was a little different with national registries, Interpol, etc., but few changes had been made when it came to interdepartmental relationships. All you needed is one cop or Agent with a short man complex and there would be more dick-measuring than crime-solving.

"That was you?"

Stitts shrugged.

"I was a junior, my first case. And it was an absolute nightmare."

"I can imagine." Tate paused. "Back to Floyd—he is struggling, and I just wanted your opinion on whether or not you think he's cut out for this gig, and I honestly mean that with zero disrespect for either you or him. I think he's a great human, Stitts, but as you know, in this job, that can be an easy flaw to exploit."

Another pause, this time mutual.

Stitts gnawed on the inside of his cheek and Tate appreciated the man actually thinking about the question instead of just blurting out an answer.

Five seconds passed, ten, and then Stitts looked Tate right in the eyes.

"Is anybody?"

Normally, Tate would've been annoyed by such an ambiguous, and quite frankly clichéd response, but he wasn't. Not from Stitts. Even though he'd known the man for a grand total of five minutes, his read on the profiler was dead on. And if Stitts had been his partner and not Floyd, there would be no need to consult with anybody to know whether or not the man was cut out for the job.

He was born for it.

"No, not really," Tate replied. For 99% of the population, seeing the things that he'd seen, the violent and despicable acts that humans were capable of, seeing them firsthand and speaking to the perpetrators, would destroy them. Eventually, it would eat them up and turn them inside out. They wouldn't be able to sleep and would inevitably resort to chemical means to just stop the images from flooding their minds.

And Tate was no different. But instead of resorting to booze or drugs, he did something different. He changed the outcome.

The problem was sleeping.

So, he simply didn't do that anymore.

"Floyd's got a soft heart, he cares... probably a little too much," Stitts continued, unprompted. "But he's also strong. Honestly? I wouldn't have recommended him if I didn't think he could do the job. Nothing I've seen since has changed my mind and that includes what he put in the most recent report."

Tate nodded. It was as good an answer as any.

"Thanks."

"No problem."

Stitts slung his bag over his shoulder and leaned on his cane as he made his way toward the door.

Tate stayed by his side.

"Do you miss it? Being in the field?"

Stitts took his time with this one, too.

"Sometimes." There was a far-off look in his eyes. "Sometimes not."

"Fair enough," Tate said. He shook the man's hand again and then made his way up the stairs and toward the student exit. He was almost to the door when the man's voice drew his attention back to the stage.

Tate had stopped moving.

"How's she doing, anyway?"

There was a moment when Tate wondered how one person could have such a strong impact on everyone she met.

But then he considered how much mental bandwidth he'd exhausted thinking about Chase Adams.

Eventually, Tate Abernathy shook his head.

"Chase is a fucking train wreck. So, by her standards, she is completely and utterly normal."

Chapter 6

"AGENT MONTGOMERY, I'M GLAD YOU made your appointment—I wasn't sure you'd show," Dr. Matteo said from behind his desk.

Floyd sucked in his chin.

Appointment? I didn't have an appointment.

He thought back to Tate's ultimatum in the car.

Did Tate make the appointment for me?

"Please," Dr. Matteo said with a pleasant smile. "Take a seat."

Floyd didn't want to take a seat. He wanted to run.

But when Dr. Matteo adjusted his spectacles and continued to smile, Floyd lowered himself into the soft chair across from the man.

"How long has it been since we first met, Floyd?" the doctor began as an obvious icebreaker.

"I–I don't know. When I f-first started, I guess." Floyd wasn't surprised by his stutter.

He was nervous, although he wasn't completely sure why.

"Right." Dr. Matteo pulled out a folder and placed it on his desk. He didn't open it. "And now you're back. Is there something specific that you wanted to talk about, or do you just want to relieve some steam? I assure you, either is fine by me."

"Actually, it was T-T-Tate who—"

"It doesn't matter to me who made the appointment, either," Dr. Matteo interrupted. Floyd got the impression that while it didn't matter, the psychiatrist was well aware of who was behind this meeting. "You're here now, so why don't you tell me what's on your mind?"

As clichéd as this interaction was quickly becoming, Floyd also felt a level of ease and comfort with this man. He recalled their first meeting and how structured it had been. A personality assessment that was also an evaluation of his potential fit in the FBI.

This seemed different.

They were, he reminded himself, both mandatory, however.

"I just—I just—"

"Take a deep breath, take your time."

Floyd inhaled and when it was time to let the air out of his lungs, the steady stream was accompanied by an equally consistent flood of words.

"The looks on their faces," he said, no trace of a stutter now. "It's the looks on their faces when I tell them that their child or sister or husband are dead. I can't get that out of my mind, and I just get stuck. It's as if I feel their grief, and I know how this sounds, whether it sounds fake or phony or cheesy or whatever, but I feel like it's my own grief. Like they're my family. And then I start to feel guilty, because deep down, they're not mine, and I haven't really lost anything."

"You can't help how you feel."

"That's the thing, Chase told me that—are we allowed to talk about Chase?"

Dr. Matteo shrugged.

"This is about you, Floyd, but if it helps to talk about Chase for a little while then I have no problem with it."

Floyd nodded.

"Well, Chase has this way of not looking at these victims as people, but compartmentalizing them as something else—I don't know what... a number? A color? Who knows? But I can't do that. I tried, and I can't. And then when I think that I failed at that, I get more nervous, and then the stutter comes out..."

Floyd took a shuddering breath and felt tears starting to well behind his eyes.

There was no judgment on Dr. Matteo's face, nor in his voice. "What works for one person doesn't necessarily work for someone else. Floyd, do you mind if I steer this in another direction, just for a moment?"

"Sure." Floyd was grateful for the interlude—it offered him time to compose himself.

"In order to help you, I need to get to know you a little better. I'm not talking about becoming friends or anything like that, I just want to know more about your interests outside of the FBI. Simple stuff."

The question stumped Floyd.

"Interests?"

"Sure, hobbies, that sort of thing."

Once again, Floyd was at a loss for words.

He really didn't have any hobbies. He worked, he worked, and he worked. That was his life.

Dr. Matteo must have noticed a change in his expression because he quickly followed up with, "Before you started the FBI, what were you into?"

"Trains."

The word just came out and Floyd cringed, thinking of how childish this must sound.

But once again, Dr. Matteo expressed no judgment.

"Trains—good, so you were interested in trains. What did you like about them?"

Floyd shrugged. He'd never really thought about why he'd been fascinated by trains, he just was.

"I don't—I don't know. I just like 'em, I guess."

Dr. Matteo adjusted his round glasses again, pushing them up his nose.

"Think about it for a moment," he suggested.

Floyd sucked in his bottom lip.

"I guess... I guess I like the tracks, the networks of tracks all over this country, and others. I-I also like the way that they seem unstoppable, especially the old trains?" He was speaking more quickly now. "Not so much the new trains, but the old ones... steam engines. They just keep on going. Don't slow down for nothing."

"Good, okay. So, you like the fact that they keep on moving forward. Makes sense. You used to have a stutter, didn't you, Floyd?"

The question came out of nowhere.

"Y-y-yes."

Floyd laughed then and a small smile crept onto Dr. Matteo's lips.

"Well, simply put, a stutter is something that prevents you from getting to your destination. In this case, the end of a sentence. You keep struggling to get through the word but can't, as if your speech train has been derailed."

An agreeable nod from Floyd. He was impressed that Dr. Matteo had managed to come full circle, to connect seemingly unrelated ideas into something cohesive.

And the man was just getting started.

"When you break the horrible news to a parent that their child is deceased you get stuck, right, Floyd?"

"Yeah."

"What would a locomotive do?"

"Wh-what?"

"What would a locomotive do? You said so yourself, you can't just hammer on the brakes and expect a freight train to immediately come to a dead stop, right?"

"I-I-I-"

"C'mon, Floyd, you're the train expert. How long would it take a freight train going at, I don't know, fifty-five miles an hour to come to a full stop?" Dr. Matteo pressed.

Floyd didn't think about the answer; it just came to him.

"Just over a mile."

"Okay, okay. So, here's what I want you to do: I want you to picture yourself as a locomotive. Not a burly inanimate piece of machinery, but something that continues to move forward, that takes a long time to slow down, let alone stop. Now, part of your job is delivering terrible news. But that's not the destination. The destination is leaving these people with this news and getting back to the investigation. That's what I want you to try. I want you to think about yourself as a locomotive that won't stop, won't even slow, until it's back in the station. What do you think, Floyd? Think you can try that?"

Floyd thought back to when he'd told Mr. Bailey that his daughter Madison had committed suicide. How he could barely make it up the apartment stairs, how all of his mental energy had been spent resisting the urge not to turn back.

By the time he told Mr. Bailey what had happened, it was all over. He had nothing left.

The idea of constantly moving forward, similar to a train, made sense to Floyd.

Whether it worked in real life was another idea altogether. But Floyd felt the weight that he didn't know had been on his chest ease a little.

"Yeah," he said, almost brightly. "I think I can try that."

Dr. Matteo nodded.

"Good. Now, is there anything else you want to chat about?"

Floyd considered this.

"Well, I know the session is about me, but there's someone else I wouldn't mind talking about…"

Chapter 7

"NOPE." STU BARNES SHOOK HIS head and leaned as far back in his chair as his shackles would allow. "This isn't happening."

Will shut off the iPad and addressed his client.

"It *is* happening, Stu."

"It can't be. This… it isn't real."

"You want to watch it again?"

"No—Jesus, no."

It was bad enough watching the video the first time. A man begging for his life while another—*not* Stu—took aim and shot him in the head. Twice. And then left with a briefcase in his hand, but not before turning and smiling—actually fucking smiling—directly at a camera mounted on the bridge.

Will sighed.

"You might not want to watch it again, but I've seen it about twenty times. Unless you have a twin, Stu, that was you."

"But it wasn't—it's been altered. Has to be," Stu protested. "This is fucking insane, Will. *Insane.* You know me. I wouldn't—Look, I've never shot a gun in my entire life."

Will raised an eyebrow at this.

"Never? You live in Vegas… you've never been to a gun range to fire off some rounds? Just for shits and giggles?"

"Shits and giggles? No. *Never.*"

Will stared at Stu long enough to make him uncomfortable.

"Why do you keep doing that? Why are you acting this way, Will?" Stu gestured toward the iPad. "You know me—and that… that wasn't me."

"I'm doing this because you keep lying to me," Will said flatly. "I'm your lawyer. If you want me to help you, you need to tell me the truth."

"I'm not lying. *Fuck.*"

Will licked his lips and set his jaw.

"You remember when you were booked?"

"It happened two hours ago," Stu said, annoyed, "so, yes, I remember it. There was this asshole cop—Tolliver, you called him? Anyway, this cop—"

Will folded his arms over his chest, which Stu desperately wanted to do himself, but couldn't.

"What did they do?"

"What do you mean?"

"Did they fingerprint you…?"

"Yes, of course," Stu snapped. "They made me strip… what are you getting at, Will?"

"Do you remember when they used something that looked like a wet nap on your hands? Particularly on the webbing between thumb and pointer finger."

Stu tried to recall exactly what had happened after being arrested. Usually, his memory was excellent. But he'd been so confused and scared…

"I think," he replied honestly. Then Stu nodded. "Yeah, I think they swabbed me or something. Why?"

"That was a gunshot residue test, Stu."

Stu suddenly knew where this was going, and his heart sank.

"Like I told you, I've never shot a gun."

"Well, I hate to break it to you, but the test came back as positive."

Stu refused to believe it.

"No. Nope, it's a mistake." He was shaking his head continuously now. "All of this—it's all a mistake. I've never shot a gun and I've never killed anyone. This is crazy. I-I-I need to wake up now. This nightmare needs to be over right *fucking* now."

Stu knew that this wasn't a dream, but that didn't stop him from lifting his arms as high as they could. When the chain caught, he just kept on pulling, drawing twin rings of blood on his wrists.

Will told him to stop.

"Stu, the cops have a subpoena for your car and your phone. They'll have another for your house in a couple of hours. Is there anything I should know? Are they going to find anything? If so, we need to get ahead of this."

The pain in Stu's wrists actually felt good. That, unlike everything else, felt *real*. Still, he lowered his hands.

"Like what?"

"Well..." Will paused.

"Don't ask me about a fucking gun. You ask me about a gun, and I'll hire someone else," Stu warned.

"Okay, what about your car's GPS? Did you go anywhere last night?"

Once again, Stu shook his head. He was doing this so often now that he was starting to feel nauseous.

"No. I didn't do anything. I came home from work, ate dinner by myself, had a glass of wine and then a scotch, and then I went to bed. I didn't leave until this morning. Until that detective grabbed me and threw me in the back of his car. By the way, I've changed my mind; when this gets sorted out, when they figure that's all just a big fucking mistake, I want that Detective Tolliver's badge."

"Forget about the goddamn cop, all right, Stu? I'm asking you as your lawyer and as your friend: are they gonna find anything incriminating in your phone or in your car?"

"No." Then Stu gestured at the iPad. "But here's the thing: I didn't go out last night and I also didn't shoot anybody in the head. That video clearly suggests differently."

Will scratched his jaw as he contemplated Stu's comment.

"Is it possible?"

"Is what possible?" Stu asked.

"Is it possible that someone faked the video? Because, if I'm being honest with you Stu, it looks like you. Exactly like you."

Stu frowned.

"Of course, it's possible. It's possible because it exists."

Will was starting to nod when there was a knock at the door. It opened and a guard peered in.

"Time's up," the burly man said.

"Time's up?" Will made a face. "I just got here."

The guard opened the door all the way and then filled the frame with his broad shoulders.

"Time's up," he repeated. "You can talk to him again tomorrow."

"No, no that's bullshit," Stu snapped. "I have a right to talk to—"

"I don't make the rules," the massive guard said.

Stu looked over at his lawyer.

"Will, tell him that this is all a mistake. You've gotta get me outta here."

"I will, just hang in there." Will looked at the guard. "When's the arraignment?"

The guard shrugged.

"No idea."

"Will?" Stu pleaded. If he'd been capable, he would have grabbed his lawyer's arm and held on for dear life.

"Just hang in there, Stu. We're going to figure this mess out."

And then the lawyer was gone.

As the massive guard began to unchain him from the table, Stu thought about his conversation with Will Porter.

And how his lawyer had warned him about lying.

But Stu had.

He had lied.

He just hoped that when the truth came out it didn't come back to haunt him.

Chapter 8

"FIX IT," DIRECTOR HAMPTON ORDERED as he thrust the report across the desk at Tate.

Tate made no attempt to grab a stack of papers. It struck him just below the chest but remained on the table.

"I've already reviewed it," he said, his voice calm and even. "There's nothing to change."

Director Hampton, whose face had turned a shade of crimson, stood, and then aggressively grabbed the report he'd just tossed. He jabbed a finger on the front page.

"You reviewed this?" A sadistic smirk appeared on the man's lips. "Half of it doesn't even make sense. Why were you in the hospital in the first place?"

Tate shrugged, refusing to take the bait.

"It's all there. Some meth head threw a bottle at me, I had to get stitched up."

Hampton was seething.

"Really? Where?" He performed a dramatic up-down of Tate's entire body. "Because I don't see any stitches."

"Did I say stitches? I meant glue. It was my ankle, and as much as I want to pull my pants up and show you some skin, HR won't allow it."

Hampton's upper lip curled, and his smirk became a sneer.

"Agent Montgomery did this—he wrote it? Maybe I'll bring his ass in here and ask him about it. I bet he won't be half as smug as you are."

Tate shrugged.

"You can do that. But like I said, I reviewed and signed off on it. And I'm the senior agent. So…"

This was a gamble, but a calculated one. He knew that if Floyd was brought in here, and the director grilled him the way he was grilling Tate, the young man would break in a matter of moments. Floyd would open up about Chase's involvement, which was something that they all wanted to avoid. She had tricked them, Tate included, into thinking that her participation had been approved and then she'd become the very center of the case.

Things would get complicated on many levels if the director found out what Chase had done.

And after his talk with Agent Stitts, Tate was prepared to go to bat for Floyd.

Which he was doing now, more or less.

Hampton slammed the papers down on the desk and then collapsed into his chair, which creaked loudly.

"If I find out—"

"You won't," Tate interjected. "You won't find out any-thing—nobody will. That's the report that Floyd wrote, and I signed off on. So, that's what happened."

The director held his gaze for a moment longer, but Tate re-fused to back down. This wasn't the first time that he had been reamed out by Hampton and it wouldn't be the last.

The director was a shark and all he had to do was smell a drop of blood and it was all over.

Tate made sure his skin was intact.

"I don't want to see another half-assed report like this, do you understand?"

Tate nodded and judging by Hampton's posture, the man expected him to rise and take his leave.

Tate didn't.

"What?" Hampton snapped.

"Julia," Tate said simply.

"Who?"

Tate indicated the report beneath the director's flexed fingers with his chin.

"Julia Dreger. Robert Griffith's widow attacked her in her home, and Julia ended up killing her. It's in the report."

Tate knew that he was treading on thin ice but if he was in for a penny he was in for a pound.

"I don't know what the fuck you're talking about."

"Sure, you do. Meredith Griffith came to Julia's house because she was sleeping with her late husband. She attacked and Julia defended herself. Meredith ended up dead."

Director Hampton's fingers tensed a little more and the pages of the report crumpled.

"And?"

"And Julia's a prostitute. I wouldn't be surprised if the DA seeks fifteen years for manslaughter."

Seeing where this was going now, Director Hampton preemptively said, "We don't interfere with local police affairs."

"Interfere?" Tate made a face and brought his hand to his chest. "I would never even think about it. I just want to make sure that she's not discriminated against. You know, some of these small towns…"

"We don't interfere," Hampton repeated.

"I just want to make sure she's treated fairly."

Now it was Director Hampton's turn to stay mum.

Tate knew that he had him. He'd planned it perfectly; Hampton had exhausted himself from the outburst and there was no fight left in the man.

He would call the DA. While it was true that the FBI didn't influence local politics or police procedures, they weren't opposed to offering a hint or a suggestion every once in a while.

After all, the only reason that they were in Columbus in the first place was because a favor had been asked.

In the future, if more favors were requested, then it might be in everyone's best interests to take suggestions to heart.

Tate slapped both hands on his knees and stood.

"Thank you," he said, and with that, he finally left the director's office.

The second he was outside, and the door was closed behind him, Tate let his breath out in a whoosh and then raised his arms and flapped them. His pits were damp with sweat.

The interaction had taken a lot out of him, as well.

Someone cleared their throat, drawing Tate's attention.

Director Hampton's secretary was staring at him. If her heavily botoxed face had been capable of expression, Tate suspected it would be a mask of confusion.

Instead, it was a mask of apathy.

"I think it's probably best if you serve Hammy decaf for the rest of the day, don't you think, Gina?"

Gina had no reaction as she turned her eyes back to her computer monitor.

Tate, knowing that he'd pushed his luck, hurried out of the building, and made his way to his car.

It was too soon to collect Floyd and too soon to hit up the bar.

It was also too soon for a new case to have come across his desk.

And what did FBI Agents do when they didn't have a case?

Paperwork.

No chance.

Tate decided to go for a drive to get a cup of coffee—not decaf, as he'd suggested to Gina, and definitely not that shit they offered in Quantico.

The best coffee in Stafford County was offered by a food cart on the eastern edge of downtown. The drive took Tate a good ten minutes, during which he thought about Floyd. He was looking forward to continuing to work with the kid as soon as he got his head on straight.

As an added bonus, Tate knew how close Chase and Floyd were. Of course, Tate was attracted to the woman—that went without saying. Not only was she good-looking, but she was smart and didn't fall for his games or his ploys like others did.

Normally, Tate could fairly easily weasel his way into someone's psyche, figure out how their mind worked, and then use that to become what they wanted him to be. Once in, it was a simple task to manipulate both their thought processes to suit his needs.

Case in point, Director Hampton.

It was more of an art than a science, surely, but if Constantine Striker was DaVinci then Tate Abernathy was Salai.

But Chase... Chase was a difficult nugget to crack.

And he liked that.

He liked that a lot.

Tate parked by the side of the road and then walked up to the coffee truck. It was unassuming, a mustard yellow booth that had wheels with rusted spokes. In addition to serving coffee, it also sold hot dogs, big fat sweaty wieners that rolled on those metal warmers.

But Tate was tired and only interested in coffee.

That was one of the consequences of never sleeping.

You are always tired.

Go figure.

"Tabir!" he hollered, waving his hand.

The Indian man on the other side of the cart smiled, although the expression was masked, and his teeth were barely visible through a thick black beard.

"Mr. Abernathy. The regular I assume?" the man said with a thick accent.

"You betcha."

Tabir poured an extra-large coffee into a white plastic cup and handed it over.

Tate held the cup in one hand as he pulled out his wallet. He laid it on the counter and was starting to open it with his free hand when he heard someone approach from behind.

"I'll take that."

Before Tate could react, his wallet was already gone.

Chapter 9

WILL PORTER HAD FILLED UP Stu's commissary. He hadn't gotten his boss out of jail, hadn't done anything else of value except for that.

And now, as Stu stood in line at the Clark County Detention Center commissary, he planned on using that money.

"Whatchu in for, Gramps?"

It took Stu a few moments to realize that the person was speaking to him.

He turned and saw a young black man with a shaved head and a tattoo above his left eye that read 'NOW' in cursive. He was wearing the same CCDC blue jumpsuit that they all wore, but his was an extra-large that seemed tight to the point of bursting, whereas Stu fit comfortably into a medium.

Immediately concerned for his safety, Stu glanced around.

Of all the detention centers in Nevada, CCDC was perhaps one of the safest. So safe, in fact, that none of the guards appeared to carry weapons other than pepper spray.

But Stu had no experience with prison. And while he hoped that he wasn't here long, he wasn't so naive to think that, based on his age, he wouldn't quickly become a target.

And that was before someone figured out who he was and how much he was worth.

The man chuckled.

"I ain't gonna hurt you. I just asked what you in for."

Stu had a hard time swallowing the lump that had risen in his throat. An idiotic idea crossed his mind.

I should tell him I'm a serial killer. A real, sick, twisted fuck.

"I didn't do anything. I was set up."

The man threw his head back and laughed, revealing a single gold incisor. It was a surprisingly pleasant sound, and although it should have been insulting, Stu didn't interpret it as derisive.

"Yeah, we's all just set up. Name's Rodrick, by the way. But everyone calls me Big Roddy."

At any moment, Stu expected to be attacked, to be jumped, to be mauled by this massive oddly mild-mannered thug or someone from his gang.

He was so paralyzed by this fear that Stu didn't say anything, and Rodrick snapped his fingers in front of his face.

Now Stu reacted.

He jumped.

"Stu. My name's Stu." He hated how meek he sounded.

Should have told him I was a serial killer.

The man laughed again.

"What's so funny?" Stu asked, unsure of where this sudden boldness had come from.

"Nuttin. Just figured your name would be something like Stu." Rodrick popped his tongue. "*Stuart.*"

"Yeah, why's that?" If this man's goal was to disarm him, it was working.

Or maybe it was just Stu's experience finally making an appearance. He was used to high-powered business discussions, cutthroat deals, that sort of thing.

Not actual cutthroat, but if the rumors about prison were true, then there were some similarities in their hierarchy structures.

Or maybe not.

What the hell did he know?

"Well," Rodrick said with a shrug. "I figured an old white dude like you had to have a name like Stu."

"Stu's an old white person's name?"

"I never met a nigga' named Stu. Have you?"

Stu had to admit, he hadn't. But in truth, he thought he'd only ever met one other Stuart in his life.

His grandfather who, before he died, also happened to be an old white man.

"What can I get you for?"

Stu turned to face the guard behind the commissary desk. It was like a budget 7-Eleven, with some items being displayed on a wire rack and many more listed on a sheet of paper taped to the counter.

All Stu wanted was a bottle of water and a pack of gum and he said as much.

"Hey Stu, they got them moon pies. I'd snatch those up because they don't last long," Rodrick informed him. "Them be like crack, you know?

Stu had no interest in moon pies, or crack for that matter, but he asked for two of them anyway. He signed for the items and grabbed his water and gum and started to walk away.

"Forgettin' your Moon Pies, Gramps," Rodrick said.

"They're yours."

"No shit." Rodrick scooped up the Moon Pies and placed an order of his own.

Stu started to make his way toward the common area, which was through a set of thick double doors.

"No, you can't go in there," the same large guard who had cut his meeting with his lawyer short informed him.

Stu didn't like to stereotype, but it was hard not to when you were a goldfish stuck in a pond full of sharks. Men like this guard wanted to make things hard for people like Stu. Anything outside these walls was beyond their control but in here, they were the boss. Stu's cash might be king in the real world, but it meant little on the inside.

And being a royal asshole was just one of the ways that this man could get even for a shitty salary and minimal benefits.

The power imbalance had most definitely shifted.

"I just want to sit in there and drink my water," Stu said, trying to come off as non-threatening but not meek.

"Misdemeanors only in there, you can go back to your cell, drink it there."

Stu didn't want to go back to his cell. It made him think about the future.

About the possibility of the cell becoming his home.

"Can't I just—"

"Go back to your cell."

Stu's experience in negotiations told him that saying anything else would either be a waste of time or even detrimental to his cause.

Clenching his teeth and squeezing his water bottle, Stu was resigned to going back to his cell when Rodrick approached.

"Is a'ight, is a'ight," the huge inmate said with something that could have been a comforting nod. The guard was a giant, but Big Roddy had at least two inches on him and ten, maybe fifteen pounds. Both were some of the largest individuals that Stu had ever seen in person.

The last thing he wanted was to see these two monsters square off, so he shrunk away a little.

But neither Rodrick's posture nor tone was aggressive.

"Hey, Boss, this fish ain't no chomo, is he?" Rodrick asked. The guard shook his head. "Why he in PC then? How he get his ass thrown in the hole?"

"He ain't."

"He got a be new booties, though, right?"

"Yep."

Stu understood one of every three words, perhaps fewer. For all he knew, the two men were conspiring to extort him.

Or rape him.

"Then why he a no-go in gen pop?"

The guard looked at Stu. Throughout this cryptic exchange, the man's hard expression did not change.

"He's on a hot one," the guard said. "That's why."

Rodrick sucked his chin in and now both men stared at Stu. Feeling uncomfortable—*more* uncomfortable—Stu twisted the cap off his water and sipped.

"He a J-Cat?" Rodrick's voice went up at the end, confirming that this was indeed a question.

"Naw."

"No shit. I'll tell you what then, Boss, if all he wanna do is drink his water, I'll be his watch."

This, Stu mostly understood. Rodrick was trying to do him a favor.

Stu didn't want a favor because favors had to be paid back.

"I'll just go back to my cell," he said.

"Nah, don't be no slug. Come wit' me."

Before he could protest again, Rodrick had his heavy arm draped over his shoulder, and just like that, the guard nodded, opened the door and the two of them stepped into the common area.

There were a couple of inmates—a half-dozen, maybe—in the room, all wearing the blue jumpsuits, but no one paid them much attention.

Stu tried to direct them towards an open table, just wanting to sit down and be alone, but Rodrick didn't allow it.

"Naw, you stayin' wit' me. I got you in here and now you owe me a favor."

Stu's heart skipped a beat.

So soon?

"What—?"

Rodrick squeezed his shoulder so tightly that Stu cowered.

"I ain't no gump, but I am a prison wolf. And you're gonna earn your keep, Gramps." Big Roddy's lips parted, revealing that now sinister-looking gold incisor. "You gonna earn it real good."

Chapter 10

TATE GRABBED THE MAN'S WRIST just as his wallet disappeared from the counter. Then he spun and got a good look at the man who dared steal from him.

He was a pale man with wide-set eyes. His broad shoulders were covered with a heavy leather coat even though it was warm out. His hairline was terrible, mostly just dark patches on the sides and wishful fluff on top.

And he was grinning.

Tate immediately let go and stepped back.

"You're late," the man hissed. His voice was dry and there was a hint of an Eastern European accent on his tongue.

"I was away," Tate replied defensively.

The man in the coat opened his wallet, pulled out two twenties—all Tate had in there—then tossed the pouch back on the counter.

"Mr. Abernathy? Is everything okay?"

The man pointed a stubby finger at Tabil.

"Shut the fuck up," he warned.

"Hey, you can't talk to me like that. He's in the FBI, you know! He'll—"

The man glowered at Tabil.

"I don't give a fuck if he's the president. You should just mind your own business. If you don't, I'll break your jaw."

Tabil looked to Tate for backup, but Tate did nothing. Ashamed, he averted his eyes. Thankfully, Tabil took the big man's warning to heart and remained quiet.

"You're late," the thug repeated.

Tate took a step backward.

"I know, Marco—like I said, I was away for work."

The man snorted and Tate got the impression that he was actually pleased that a payment had been missed.

"And now you're back. Let's go to the bank so you can get the money you owe me."

Tate swallowed hard—his Adam's apple, which was not prominent on most days now seemed to be the size of a softball.

"I'll get your money," he said, his eyes darting from side to side.

The thug nodded.

"Okay. You can get it for me tomorrow." It was a statement, not a question.

It was also impossible.

Tate had a mere two hundred dollars to his name. That wouldn't even make a dent in his debt.

But he wasn't about to argue.

"Okay," Tate nodded. "Tomorrow—"

He never saw the punch coming. There was a flap of nearly imperceptible movement as Marco's leather jacket flexed, and then a fist the size of a cinderblock hit Tate in the stomach. There was an odd delay of about a second or so before the signal from his midsection reached his brain during which everything seemed to freeze… everything except for Tate's eyes. He was somehow still able to look around. He spotted Tabil crouching behind his cart, a horrified expression on his face. He saw Marco's eyes narrowing as he put as much force into the blow as he could.

Somewhere behind him, Tate heard a dog bark—a single, high-pitched yap.

And then it felt as if he'd been eviscerated. Tate dropped not to one knee but both, sending more pain this time from his kneecaps up his thighs and hips and then culminating in his groin.

He couldn't breathe.

His diaphragm had been paralyzed and his inner organs re-arranged.

He wanted to put his arms up, thinking that this would mechanically stretch his lungs and force them to expand, but that was impossible. It was as if someone had taken a cattle prod to his abdominals.

Instead of stretching, his body did the exact opposite.

It curled into a ball and a horrible croaking sound, like a bullfrog drowning in desert sand, left his mouth.

Tate's face felt as if it were on fire, and tears streamed down his cheeks. But they weren't cooling tears, they were tears of hot magma that seared his flesh.

"Tomorrow," Marco repeated, and then Tate listened to the swish of his cracked patent leather jacket as the big man walked away.

A few seconds later, Tate's dwindling consciousness detected the presence of another person.

Tabil.

"Mr. Abernathy, do you want me to call police?" the man asked desperately.

Tate managed to raise his eyes, and through watery vision, he saw that Tabil was holding a cell phone.

He tried to shake his head, but he still had no control over his faculties.

"I call police," Tabil said with a nod. "I call police."

This motivated Tate, and somehow, he managed to lift his arm a little and reach for the man's leg.

"And I call ambulance."

"No."

Tate wasn't sure if he'd said the word or just made another one of those dry croaking noises, but either way, Tabil had already come to a decision.

Breathe, he told himself. *Breathe. Breathe, you fucking pussy.* Breathe!

And then he did.

Tate sucked in a massive, shuddering breath, and he felt oxygen flood his body.

The feeling was nearly orgasmic.

"Yes, I would like to report an assault."

"No, hang up the phone," Tate said with as much force as he could muster.

Tabil closed one eye as he looked at him.

"Hang up," Tate instructed.

Tabil stared for another second and then put his phone away.

With the man's help, Tate made it to a knee and then to a standing crouch. He spotted his coffee cup, now empty and crushed probably from Marco's size fifteen boots, on the ground and he Smeagoled over to it.

It took him three tries, but Tate finally managed to pick it up.

"Do you..." he croaked, turning his head in Tabil's direction, "Do you do free refills?"

Chapter 11

STU WAS ABSOLUTELY TERRIFIED. THIS is what he feared. This is what everyone feared.

But this was also jail. Jail wasn't supposed to be this way. Jail was for the short-term, prison was where the really bad stuff happened.

Many of the people in prison hadn't even been convicted of a crime. The last thing that someone awaiting trial wanted to do was something that would guarantee a conviction.

Something that would all but guarantee they would be shipped off to the bad place known as prison.

But none of this mattered to a man like Rodrick. A man with face tats who had been in and out of prison his whole life.

A man who had nothing to lose, a man who just wanted fresh meat for his—

"I'm fucking with you, Gramps," Rodrick said with a laugh. He let go of Stu and gave him a playful shove.

Stu was so confused and uncomfortable with what had happened that he stumbled and nearly slammed into a corrugated metal table. He dropped his pack of gum and then left it there, thinking that the blue package was roughly the same size and shape as a well-worn bar of soap.

"Relax, Stewie. This ain't ESP," Big Roddy said.

"E-ESP?" Stu stuttered.

After a quick glance to make sure no one was within striking distance, he bent down and picked up his gum, standing so quickly afterward that he nearly dislocated a hip.

"Yeah, ESP—Ely State Prison. You know, the maximum-security prison that you're going to be going to if you're convicted

of a hot one." Rodrick must've seen on his face that he was confused again because he clarified. "Murder, man. A hot one is a
murder. That's why you're here, ain't it?"

Stu wanted to deny it, it just seemed foreign—yes, I'm being
charged with murder—and, well, fake. But he said nothing.

"It's a'ight, it's a'ight," Rodrick said. He sat at an empty table
and gestured for Stu to join. Stu was grateful to rest his weak
legs. He gulped his water hungrily and watched as Rodrick tore
into one of the moon pies.

They said nothing for some time, which Stu was okay with.
He didn't understand the language here, he didn't understand
the culture, and he didn't understand the charges he was facing. But after a while, his mind started to wander, started to go
places he didn't want it to go.

And then he thought about Rodrick, about 'ESP'. According
to the veteran, Stu didn't need to worry about being raped or
sodomized, or shanked in jail, but that it would be a real concern in the maximum-security prison.

But that couldn't happen. It didn't happen to people like
him, like Stu Barnes.

Even if he was guilty, it didn't happen.

"When's your arraignment?" Rodrick said after swallowing
his second moon pie.

"I—I don't know," Stu admitted.

Rodrick raised the eyebrow with the 'NOW' tattoo above it.

"What you mean, you don't know? How could you not
know?"

Stu just shrugged. Will had asked about the arraignment,
but the giant guard had refused to answer.

Rodrick chuckled.

"Y'all got an army of suits on your side, and you don't
know." He shook his head. "Well, it gotta be tomorrow or the

next day. If it don't happen within forty-eight, they gotta cut you loose."

Stu's face brightened but Rodrick immediately dashed his hopes.

"Ain't goin' happen on a hot one, though. Don't getcha hopes up."

"Right," Stu said dryly. "What-what happens at the arraignment?"

He knew so little about the judicial process that it was shameful. But what do normal people know about it? Normal people don't get arrested, normal people don't have any experience in jail or prison. They don't know what happens, and Stu, for all of his money and business savvy, had no idea either. He knew a little bit about being sued — nobody got to where he was without stepping on some toes.

But being sued was something that lawyers did after you signed some paperwork.

Even suing someone, being on the other side of the table, was a bit of an abstract process. His altercation with Market Slice and their owners Kevin Park and Connery Sinclair was different. That was fucked-up in every sort of way, but that had been unique.

And Stu had put as much distance between himself and them as fast as humanly possible.

"At the arraignment, they'll read the charges and you enter your plea. And then they decide on bail." Bail. Stuart had forgotten about bail. "Thing is, 'cuz you in here for a hot one, they're prolly gonna take two days before y'all go in front of a judge. Before that, the DA will give all the shit he got on ya to ya lawyer, see if y'all want to plead it out."

"Plead it out?" Stu repeated, incredulous.

Rodrick shrugged.

"Yeah, man, plead it out. Most these guys," he gestured to the men in the room with them who were all pretty much doing the same thing that Stu and Big Roddy were doing: sitting around, chatting, killing time. "They just gon' plead it out. Pay a fine, probably go on parole for thirty days or some shit. Problem is, what they don' realize, is now they's got a felony on their record. That means you ain't gon' get no car loan, no mortgage, start a business or any o' dat shit."

This surprised Stu.

"Why don't they fight the charges? Take it to trial? They can't all be guilty."

Rodrick stared at him as if he was speaking in tongues.

"They ain't, but they c'aint," he said simply.

Once again, Stu's confusion was plastered all over his face.

Rodrick licked his lips, rubbed his palms together, and leaned forward.

"Here's the deal," he said. "With us niggas, the DA do somethin' called stacking. That's when they pick you up for hanging outside the local 7-11. They nab you for having maybe some coke on you or a little meth—whatever. Maybe they don't even grab you, but your boy standin' wit' ya. He's got some cash on him and then he start arguing with the 5-0 and maybe your boy pushes a cop, or maybe he don't but the cop say he do. And your boy got a piece on him, cuz erryone do. Now, they really gotchu. They drag ya ass down here and charge ya with loitering, possession, possession with intent to distribute, and illegal possession of a firearm. If you got a prior, they stack more charges—illegal possession of a firearm by a convicted felon. Like, why the fuck they do that? You get two charges for holding the same fuckin' piece?" Big Roddy sucked his teeth. "I know this one guy; he got picked up because he broke into someone's crib. Popo grabbed him for breaking and entering, but he was carrying a piece, too. Now they get him for breaking and entering and illegal possession of a gun. On top of that, he stole something—o' course he did. So, they stacked on stolen goods. Broke a window to get in, so they added destruction of property. This is all for the motherfuckin' same crime! Anyway, so, they stack all these charges, and when you go meet with the DA, and you got this fuckin' Podunk public defender who ain't even got hair on his balls yet, and he say to you, look, you can take this to trial, but they goin' hitchu with all them charges. You plead out? They toss half of 'em. The mans make it look like you gettin' a deal."

Rodrick gestured at Stu and, at first, he didn't realize what the other man wanted. But then he realized that Big Roddy was thirsting from all the talking.

He handed over his water bottle and Rodrick gulped from it. Then he wiped his mouth with the back of his CDC jumpsuit sleeve.

"But it don't end there. Even if you wanna fight it, they set bail at like five stacks, which they know you ain't got. So, you can't pay, meaning you gots to stay in this place until trial. Even if you win, then what? You missed work for at least a week and yous prolly fired. Now you broke broke, can't pay for your kids or nothing, and your life is a hot mess. Plead it out, pay a fine, or don't, whatever, but at least you keep your job. So yeah, most erryone just plead out."

Stu was impressed, not just by the man's understanding of the legal process, but by his enthusiasm. He had experience if nothing else. That was clear.

"But with you? With a hot one on your rap? Bail goin' be tight."

Stu balked.

"What do you mean, tight?"

The man shrugged.

"Maybe they not even give it to ya. I'ma be honest, you look like you gots money. And if you gots money, then they don't want to give you no bail because they know you might not show. I'll tell you what, Gramps, when you find out who your judge be, lemme know. I've seen 'em all, and they all want you to act a little bit diffy. In the end, they all hoes. You gotta be their bitch, fuckin' act the way they want you to so that they treat you good."

Stu was apparently terrible at hiding his true feelings.

"What? You don't believe me?" Rodrick said. "Watch this." He leaned back, whistled, and waved at three young black guys who were all sitting together. "Carter, getchya ass over here."

The tallest of the three men hurried over, his eyes downcast.

"Hey," Rodrick said, "What happens if you give Judge Samuel some lip?"

Carter didn't even hesitate.

"That mothafucka set the bail so high that Bill Gates can't even pay."

"And what if you act all sorry 'n shit in front of Judge Chiarelli?"

"He do this thing with his wrinkled ass face, and even though he don't say nuttin' you know what he thinkin': he thinkin' why you be all sad now, if you sad, you shouldna done in the first place."

"That's right," Rodrick said with a laugh. "All right, get tha fuck outta here."

Carter nodded and went back to his crew.

When they were alone again, Rodrick said to Stu, "See? Just lemme know who you gots, Gramps, and I'll help you out. Oh, and don't think cuz you an old cracker that things be different, you know? These judges done seen it all."

Stu thanked Rodrick, then popped a piece of gum in his mouth.

"Why are you doing this? Why are you helping me out?"

Rodrick shrugged.

"Why? I dunno… I guess cuz I just know how it goin' be in ESP. And it ain't going to be like this. Nothin' goin' be like this up der."

It was a strange, nonsensical answer, perhaps the first that Rodrick had given him since opening his mouth.

"You going to ESP?"

Rodrick looked away and took a breath.

"Yeah, prolly. Like you, they got me on a hot one. And I think I'm going down for it this time."

Chapter 12

TATE REACHED ACROSS THE PASSENGER seat and opened the door.

"Get in."

Floyd hesitated.

"Where we going?"

"Just get in the car," Tate said. "C'mon, we don't have all day."

The second Floyd sat and before he'd even closed the door, Tate pumped the gas and pulled away from Grassroots.

"Jesus," Floyd said, hurrying to buckle up. "What's the rush?"

What's the rush? The rush is I have one day to come up with an ungodly amount of cash I don't have, Tate thought. That's the rush.

That didn't sound right, even in his own head, so Tate ignored the question and changed the subject.

"How was your appointment? Clean checkup? No gonorrhea? Crabs?" his face remained stoic despite the jokes.

"Naw, it's all good," Floyd replied in a far-off voice.

"Yeah?" Tate was genuinely interested now.

"Clean bill of health." Floyd hesitated then added, "Seriously, thanks for making me go in there. I think it really did help."

"No problem," Tate said, but he was distracted now. They'd arrived in one of the seedier areas of Suffolk County and he slowed, his eyes scanning the sidewalk and alleyways. This place reminded him of Junkie's Row in Columbus. Every city had one, of lesser or greater degrees, and Quantico was no different. But he wasn't looking for just any junkie.

Tate was searching for someone specific.

"You okay?" Floyd asked. The seriousness in his partner's tone caused Tate to look over at him.

"I'm fine. Why you asking?"

Floyd made a face and shrugged.

"Sorry," Tate said, realizing that he was being unduly harsh. "I've just been having one of those days."

"You eat something bad? Something didn't agree with you?"

It took Tate a few seconds to realize what the hell Floyd was talking about. He looked down at himself and realized that he was hunched, and his shoulders were rolled forward. He still felt the impact of the blow to his stomach. His abs were knotted and tight and he couldn't seem to draw a full breath.

"Oh, yeah, gas station sushi. Does it to me every time."

Tate did his best to assume a more natural posture and then went back to staring out the window.

He spotted a face peek out from a particularly grimy alley before ducking back into the shadows.

"What are we doing here anyway? What are you looking for?"

Not what, but who, Tate thought.

"This is a local drug hangout. Pushers and pimps, that sort of thing. They all hang out here."

Floyd shrugged.

"Okay, so… what are we doing here? Did you grab another case while I was seeing Dr. Matteo? Something local?"

"Nope," Tate said, popping the 'p'. "Nothing like that."

Floyd sighed and he rubbed his eyes.

"Then what—"

Tate cut him off by suddenly pointing at a kid with a shaved head. His pants were nearly at his ankles, and he held his crotch as he strutted.

"I know you didn't come from law enforcement, have no experience with it. You literally skipped basic math and went directly to calculus. And let me tell you something, Floyd, calculus is fucking hard."

Floyd's upper lip curled.

"What? Can you speak plainly for once? I have no idea—"

"There!" Tate slammed on the brakes and jumped out of the car.

"Tate?" Floyd cursed and followed his partner onto the street. "What the hell are we doing here?"

"Learning basic math," Tate shouted over his shoulder.

The wannabe thug heard Tate and craned his head over his shoulder. When he saw who it was, his eyes went wide, and he hiked up his jeans.

Then he started to run.

"Shit!" Tate yelled. He pointed down an alley. "Go that way! Floyd, go that way! Cut him off!"

Floyd held his hands up.

"What are—"

"Just go that way!" Tate swore. "Cut him off!"

He waited for Floyd to finally start to move, before chasing after the thug. It didn't take long to catch him; his pants were like a parachute, slowing him down. In truth, Tate didn't mean to shove the much younger and smaller man to the ground, but the man's gait was incredibly awkward, and their feet got tangled.

And as Tate was going down, he decided that it was in his best interest to go down on top of the other man.

"You been hiding from me, Frankie," Tate said, pinning the man's arms to the ground beneath him.

He shot a glance over his shoulder. Floyd was nowhere to be seen.

"I ain't been hiding, Tate. Now, let me the fuck up."

"Quiet," Tate hissed. He moved the man's thin wrists together, over his head, and pressed them down with one hand. Then Tate used his free hand to start rifling through the man's oversized pockets.

"What the fuck, man?" Frankie protested. "It's been slow, I ain't—"

Tate pulled a thick wad of bills, held together by a blue elastic band from the back pocket of the man's jeans.

"Slow my ass." He let go of Frankie's arms and wagged the stack in front of his face. "Is this what you call slow?"

"I need that. It ain't even mine."

Tate sat up, then got to his feet and brushed off his knees.

"That's the first true thing you've said to me."

He slipped the bills into his own pocket and Frankie sucked his teeth.

"What the fuck? You don't understand, that—"

Tate suddenly reached down and grabbed the man by the collar and pulled his slender upper body off the ground.

"No, you don't understand. We had a deal. You give me ten percent of your take and let me know when any big deals are going down, and I don't haul your sorry ass to jail each and every morning. That's the fucking deal. And you haven't paid up recently, which means, you're not upholding your part of the bargain. So, I'm keeping this cash."

Frankie's face started to turn red, but before he had a mind to protest, Tate shoved him back down.

The young man grunted when his shoulder blades smacked off the cracked asphalt.

"Ten percent," Tate hissed. "Ten—"

"Tate! Everything okay?"

Floyd, breathing heavily, appeared at Tate's side.

"I'm fine." Tate brushed himself off again, this time surreptitiously adjusting the stack of bills in his pocket. "Perfectly, a-okay."

"A-okay? This motherfucker just robbed me," Frankie cried, making his way to a seated position. "This corrupt motherfucker robbed me."

Chapter 13

"**WHY YOU LOOK SO SHOCKED,** Gramps? You tell me you're in here for a hot one, when I tell you the same, you look like you just shit your pants."

Stu was tempted to correct the man. He hadn't said anything about why he was in here, Rodrick had asked the guard.

"I get it, it's cuz you didn't actually do nobody, right? Falsely accused?"

Stu nodded ever so slightly, and this made Rodrick laugh.

"You wanna know somethin' funny, Gramps?"

"Sure," Stu replied dryly.

"I didn't do mine either." Rodrick made a grandiose gesture, indicating everyone in the meeting area, including the kid who had come over earlier. "But that's what erryone in this room would tell ya. Difference is, if you's tellin' the truth, then so am I."

Rodrick let this hang in the air as if begging Stu to challenge them, which he had no intention of doing.

Even though the reality of being caged had set in, the entire scenario was still surreal. If someone had told Stu two days ago that he would be in jail, sitting in a blue CCDC jumpsuit across from a six-foot-five black man with a tattoo on his face telling him his life story, he would've thought that he'd accidentally switched his micro dose of psilocybin for fentanyl.

But here he was, and Stu didn't see any other options at the moment other than just going with the flow.

"You wanna go first, or me?" Rodrick asked. Stu wasn't really sure what was being proposed, so he said nothing. The big man sighed. "Look, Gramps, if you go down for the hot one you didn't commit, you better get used to listenin' and telling stories. Because that's all we do. People whine about how they got fucked by the system, how dey black and that's why they's in here... day in, day out, they run their mouths. And when they all outta stories of they own, they just tell other people's stories. By the end of yer first year on the inside you've heard them all—and I mean, all. The only way to stop hearin' 'em is to start tellin' 'em some of yer own." Rodrick grinned and interlaced his fingers. "So, you wanna go first, or should I?"

Stu mulled over the man's words and then shrugged and started to speak. He'd been told that he was a good storyteller, that this was one of the skills that had helped him turn his business from low nine figures to ten. But his wasn't much of a story.

"There's a video," Stu said, eyes downcast. "There's a video of someone who looks exactly like me shooting one of my employees in the head. Twice. I don't know this guy—never met him. I don't do the day-to-day thing with any of my companies..."

Rodrick stared at him.

"That's it?"

"That's it," Stu admitted with a shrug.

"You cappin', homie. That can't be everything. What about disclosure?"

"Haven't seen it yet. That's all they told me. I've seen the video though, and it looks like me. Like, *a lot*."

"Aw, shit," Rodrick said, a slight grin appearing on his face as he leaned backward in the hard metal chair.

"What? I didn't do it. I know it looks like me, but it's gotta be a fake."

"Now, not that." Rodrick waved Stu's comments away. "It's just, they must really have it out for you, Gramps."

Stu's eyebrows knitted.

"Why's that?"

"Because they holdin' on ya, waiting until the very last moment to show you what they got on ya. I wouldn't be surprised
if tomorrow right before your arraignment you get a visit from
the DA offering you a deal at the same time, they show you
what they got. They tryin' to sweat you, confuse you, and overwhelm you. They keep you locked up in here until the twenty-
third hour then spring errything on ya. It's called being in the
cooker. Just surprised they doin' to you… normally they only
pull out them bush league tactics for niggas like me."

Rodrick was smiling, but Stu wasn't.

He was angry.

"But here's the thing, Gramps, whatever deal they offer you
tomorra, it goin' be der six months from now before your trial.
They tell you it ain't, but it will. And it'll get better, too. Like I
said before, Gramps, ain't nobody wanna go to trial. Trial cost
money and time and ain't nobody got neither a' dat. That just
ain't the way things work."

Stu tucked this information away, making a mental note to
bring it up with Will Porter.

"What about you?" Stu asked. "What's your story?"

Asking Rodrick about his case was good etiquette, inside jail
or elsewhere. But Stu was genuinely interested. Fact was, walking cliché or not, Big Roddy was an interesting man.

"I got a call." The smile fell off Rodrick's face as he began to
talk. "A homie said they was in trouble and needed a pick him
up. So, that's what I did, I got into my whip and picked 'em up.
They jumped in the car and just told me to go. Drove right into
a roadblock. I did the right thing, the thing that every black man
is told to do when the po-lice is on ya: put ya hands on the
wheel, look straight ahead, no sudden movements. I ain't
gonna lie, Gramps, I got a few convictions on my record, but
nothing major. But my boy… well, they dragged his ass out the

car. They found a piece on him and some cash. They say he capped someone and robbed them, then called me for a pickup."

Rodrick stopped and Stu waited for the man to finish his story.

But that appeared to be the end of it.

"That's it? And for that... they charged you with murder?"

Rodrick shrugged.

"I mean, they prolly goin' knock it down to manslaughter, but yeah. They says I was the getaway driver. And it don't matter that I ain't never pulled the trigger. My mans was robbin' someone and all parties be guilty of all crimes during the commission of a felony."

"Did anybody put you at the scene?"

"Naw."

"What about you friend? Did he—"

"I dunno what he say, but it don't really matter. Thing is, erryone be all tough and they say they ain't never gonna snitch. But when a suit tells you you goin' away for life? You tweet like a motherfuckin' bird. Trust."

"But was your car spotted at the scene?"

"Naw, I wan't der."

"And you know nothing about this robbery or shooting?"

Rodrick shrugged.

"I know nuttin'."

"Who's this other guy?"

"I know him from the hood. Motherfucker got a rap sheet longer than Santa Claus' list."

Rodrick was playing a role—in here, they all were. He was the tough guy, the one who saw jail as just part of life.

But Stu heard something in the man's voice. He wouldn't go as far as to say it was fear, but it was close.

More like regret.

Rodrick, who had been looking off to one side, suddenly clenched his jaw and popped his knuckles.

"Anyway, that's my story, and that's why I'm goin' away for a long, long motherfuckin' time, Gramps."

Chapter 14

"**I'M GONNA ROB YOU OF** your freedom in a minute, Frankie," Tate warned, shooting the man on the ground a death stare.

Floyd was confused by what was happening. Tate had gone from forcing him to see Dr. Matteo to taking him on a field trip that he got the impression was supposed to look spontaneous and random but was anything but.

Even Tate's bizarre mathematical analogy didn't fit. On many an occasion, his partner had told him directly then sometimes you were better off if you came to the Bureau without a background in policing. That way you didn't bring your baggage and biases with you.

"Whatever," Frankie grumbled. Tate continued to glare at the skinny man, who could have been anywhere from fifteen to thirty-five years of age, as he struggled to get to his feet. "Can I go now?" He hiked up his pants, which were large enough to contain three of him. "Can I fucking go?"

"Yeah, just keep your nose clean."

Frankie flipped them off, hiked up his pants, and sauntered away.

"What was that all about?" Floyd asked as they watched the man go.

"I thought he was someone else," Tate said. "Anyway, he didn't have anything on him. Come on, let's go."

Floyd was even more confused when he got back into Tate's car.

"Who did you... who did you think he was?" Floyd asked.

Tate started the engine.

"Nobody."

"But you—"

Tate's hands tightened on the steering wheel.

"Look," he said sharply, "I was just trying to teach you a les- son on the basics, alright? Just forget about it. It was stupid."

Tate was a master of disguise. Floyd knew this better than most. The man had an uncanny ability to ascertain very quickly what he needed to become in order to obtain whatever it was he wanted: be it information or a confession or just gossip.

This made Tate, the real Tate, a very difficult man to read. You never knew if what you were seeing at any given moment was the real Tate.

But this... this tightly wound, and slightly manic version of his partner seemed genuine. Paradoxically, it also seemed noth- ing like the man Floyd knew.

Or thought he knew.

Floyd decided to push the issue a little more than he nor- mally would.

"Right, just so we're c-clear, you thought that instead of looking into new cases, we should drive around looking for what? Junkies? That guy back there—Frankie, or whatever— what would you have done if you did find something on him?"

"What anybody would do: call the cops."

The response was so bizarre that Floyd found himself unable to continue with the conversation.

"Tate, c'mon. What's going on? You send me to Grassroots and—"

"There, right there." Tate pointed out Floyd's window. "You see that guy?"

Floyd followed the man's finger, which was aimed at a young black kid sporting a wife beater and low-hanging jeans. Not as low as Frankie's but close.

"Yeah," Floyd said hesitantly. "I see him. What about him?"

"I'll go right for him, you dart down the alley like last time, in case he runs."

"Tate—" Before Floyd could finish the sentence, his partner was out of the car again. "God dammit."

He followed—he had no choice.

Instead of wasting his time sprinting down an alley, which, he was fairly certain, would not allow him to cut anyone off, Floyd decided to hide just out of sight and watch.

This is insane, he thought. *What is wrong with Tate?*

He'd never seen his partner act so irrationally.

After his conversation with Dr. Matteo, Floyd felt good. Much better than this morning. He was actually excited about getting back to work. No, maybe not excited, but at least not dreading another case as he had been.

Now… *this.*

Just keep the train moving, he instructed himself. *Imagine the wheels turning, imagine you can't be stopped.*

Tate shoved the black man to the ground, *hard*, and then barked something that Floyd couldn't make out.

As he was reminded several times already, Floyd had little experience with shakedowns. But this looked off to him. It looked aggressive and unprovoked. Still, he hung back and continued to observe.

When Tate pulled a handful of bills out of the kid's pocket, who only cursed but did nothing to defend himself, Floyd, experienced or not, knew that this wasn't normal.

That it was wrong.

Before jamming the cash into his own pocket, Tate looked around and Floyd quickly ducked out of sight.

After three breaths, he glanced out of the alley again. The kid was on his feet now and Tate was pushing him in the chest, gesturing him to move along, which he reluctantly did. Like Frankie, this kid also offered Tate a middle finger salute as a parting gift.

Floyd stepped onto the sidewalk.

"He wasn't carrying, either?" he asked loudly.

Tate was startled by his presence but quickly composed himself.

"Naw, he wasn't."

Tate wasn't stupid and Floyd had never been any good at hiding his emotions. Tate could see it all over his face: Floyd had seen what had just gone down.

This realization didn't make the decision of what to do next any easier, however.

Do I call him on it? Or do I just let it go?

If this morning hadn't happened, Floyd wouldn't have hesitated. He would've said, *"What the fuck are you doing, Tate? I saw you rob that kid!"*

But things had changed. Tate's ultimatum, well-meaning as it had been, had made it clear that while the FBI considered their relationship a partnership, there was definitely a hierarchy in play.

Just as Floyd made up his mind, and was about to break the uncomfortable stand-off, Tate's phone started to ring.

This broke the tension, and he quickly answered it, grateful for the interruption.

"Yeah? Is everything okay?" Tate said, turning his back to Floyd as if that would somehow block him from hearing. "Really? But she's okay?"

Pause.

"It's early. She never has an episode this early."

Pause.

"Okay, okay, I'm coming. Just stay there until I arrive."

Tate hung up the phone and tapped it against his palm.

When he turned around, Floyd's hard stare was met with wide, soft eyes.

It was at that moment that Floyd realized he really had no idea who this man before him was.

Who are you, Tate?

"Floyd, I'm sorry. But I really have to go."

Floyd, more lost than ever, just stood there and nodded.

"I'm sorry," Tate repeated. To his credit, he really did appear distraught. "Can you…"

"Yeah, I c-can get back on my o-own. Just go," Floyd urged.

Tate didn't need further encouragement. He was already on his way back to his car. When the man drove past him, he didn't so much as glance in Floyd's direction.

Just keep the train moving. Don't stop. Don't ever stop…

Chapter 15

IT WAS IMPOSSIBLE FOR STU Barnes to fall asleep that first night in the Clark County Detention Center. It was impossible for Stu Barnes to fall asleep the second night, as well.

Not only was his mind racing with his upcoming arraignment and the possibility that he would be denied bail, but he'd been conditioned to sleeping on a hundred-and fifty-thousand-dollar Hästens mattress, pure silk sheets, cooling pillows, in a temperature-controlled room, and swathed in complete blackness.

Everything about his cell in CCDC was literally the complete opposite. People were shouting all the time and when they weren't shouting, they were crying. And then they were shouting at whoever was crying to shut the fuck up. There was weak yellow light coming from bulbs spaced every dozen or so feet in the corridor outside his cell and his mattress was wafer thin.

Forget cooling pillow, Stu had something that was nearly as flat as his sheet to rest his head on. And the sheets... they were clean.

That's it. That's all he could say about them.

Stu figured that he'd passed out for a grand total of two hours from lights out to lights on. And before he'd been able to take a single bite of his breakfast—no eggs here, just different colored gruel—the big guard who never seemed to be off-shift tapped him aggressively on the shoulder.

"Lawyer's here," was all he said.

Stu abandoned his meal and followed the guard out of the mess hall and down a series of interconnected corridors and hallways. He wasn't sure whether the jail had been designed this way on purpose—to make it as difficult as possible to get from one location to another in case the inmates tried to escape or if there was a riot—or if the place had been continually expanded over time and the different sections were added piecemeal.

After numerous turns, they stopped in front of one of a dozen identical square concrete meeting rooms. The guard cuffed Stu, not to the table this time, thankfully, then opened the door and ushered him inside where Will Porter was waiting.

"Fucking hell, Will. Two days, really? Tell me you got some good news," Stu said.

"Why don't you take a seat." Will indicated the chair across from him.

Stu shook his head.

"Naw, I don't want to sit. Tell me what's going on?"

During the vast majority of the wasted time trying to fall asleep, Stu's mind had been occupied by dark thoughts. But occasionally, something bright attempted to creep in.

Like the idea that the charges would be dropped, and that someone would realize just how insane this was all was.

Because he didn't do it.

Stu didn't kill anyone.

This foolishness quickly evaporated when he saw the grim expression on his lawyer's face.

"Okay, fine. Stu, I just got disclosure this morning—we're set to stand in front of the judge in an hour. They're offering you a plea."

"A plea?" Stu couldn't believe it. This was exactly what Rodrick had said would happen.

Everything from making him sweat to providing disclosure as close to his arraignment as possible, to offering him a plea deal.

"Yes, a plea. And it's not a good one, either. But this is how things go. It's a negotiation and they were just opening the lines of communi—"

Stu stiffened.

"No plea."

"Stu, as your lawyer—"

"Yeah, I get it, you're obligated to pass on the information. But I don't care. I'm not taking a plea. Not now, not ever. I don't care whether they offer parole or time served. The only thing I'm willing to accept is an apology."

Will sighed.

"I figured you'd say that."

The man got up and walked over to the door. He knocked on it once and the guard opened it.

"Wait, Will? Where are you going?" Stu was suddenly concerned that he'd somehow offended his lawyer and the idea of being abandoned took hold. "Will?"

"Come with me."

Stu followed the guard and Will down another hall.

"Where we going?"

Instead of answering, Will gestured toward another conference room, this one much larger than the first. Inside, were four men. Stu recognized one as Detective Tolliver, the man who had arrested him. The middle-aged man with shifty eyes beside the detective wearing a cheap brown suit and cheaper haircut was probably the assistant district attorney.

The two men on the other side of the table, wearing expensive suits and expensive haircuts, were a mystery.

"Those are the two best criminal law attorneys in Nevada," Will informed him. "They're here to help."

He said this with an air of pride, thinking that this would help ease some of Stu's anxiety. If anything, it did the opposite.

The idea of two strangers, exceptional legal counsel or not, in charge of what very might well be the rest of his life was terrifying.

"You're—you're gonna stay with me, right?"

Will looked at him and nodded.

"Of course. I'll be by your side the whole time. Now, Stu, when we go in there, you don't need to say anything at all. The ADA and the detective want one thing: for you to take the deal. They'll say whatever they have to, to make that happen. You just sit there and listen. Afterward, we can talk about what they said—when they're gone."

"Yeah, I get it." Out of habit, Stu reached for the door handle.

"Don't touch it," the guard barked, and Stu pulled his hand back as if he'd been electrocuted.

The guard maneuvered his way in front of both Stu and Will, accidentally on purpose bumping into the former, and then used a key that looked like it belonged in a 90's video game to unlock the door. The big man never took his eyes off Stu as Will placed a comforting hand on his shoulder and led him inside the room.

"Remember what I said," Will whispered in his ear. "Just listen."

Chapter 16

MARGUERITE MET TATE ON THE stoop of his house. The woman's coffee and cream-colored features, typically smooth, were uncharacteristically pinched.

"Is she okay?" he asked, sliding by the diminutive woman.

"She's fine now. She had an episode, but she's okay. I put her in bed."

Tate nodded and stepped into the front hallway.

Marguerite followed.

"Rachel? Rachel?" he called softly as he made his way upstairs. His eyes traced the mechanical track that followed the contours of the wall.

Once, Rachel had had a fit on the main floor. Even after it passed, the girl had been so exhausted that Tate had to carry her to the stairlift. This was no easy task, and Tate was a hundred and eighty pounds.

Marguerite weighed barely half that much.

Moving slowly, not wanting to frighten or surprise Rachel in the rare case that she was still awake, Tate passed the bathroom and went straight for her room.

The door was slightly ajar, and he paused in the hall to collect himself. He couldn't remember the last time that she'd had an episode this early in the day.

They were much more common at night. Sometimes they happened twice.

Tate put his hand on the door, pushed it open wider, and peered inside.

Rachel was lying in bed, her short brown hair splayed on the pillow. The sheets had been tucked up to her armpits and her thin, pale arms lay draped over top of them. The girl's wheelchair was tucked and folded off to one side.

Even though her green eyes were open, Tate knew that this was no guarantee she was awake.

"Rachel?" he asked softly.

She blinked and her eyes lazily drifted toward him.

"Hi, sweetie," Tate said as he entered the room. He leaned down and kissed her on the forehead. Her skin was cool and clammy, as it always was after one of her episodes.

"Did you come straight from work, Daddy?" Rachel offered him a weak smile.

"Yeah, straight from work."

Tate lay down beside his daughter, using his arm to prop her head up. She was so thin, so frail. Before the accident, Rachel had been a swimmer, and like all swimmers, while they were in good shape, they always carried a little bit of body fat to help with buoyancy.

Now Rachel was all bones.

"I'm sorry for making you come home."

"Don't be silly."

Rachel took a deep breath—just speaking was difficult now and Tate didn't press her.

As they lay there in silence, his eyes drifted to the framed photograph on top of the dresser. It showed three people, three happy people: Tate, smiling broadly, Rachel offering her classic lopsided grin, and Olivia, smirking.

When Tate saw Olivia, he felt a pang in his stomach, unrelated to Marco's punch.

It wasn't his favorite picture of his wife. It wasn't even close. But there was something about Olivia's eyes in this photo that captured who she really was, as much as a photograph was capable.

They were big, brown, and wide, and even though you could see a shimmer in all three of their eyes, there was something about Olivia's that just seemed to glow brighter than either Tate's or Rachel's.

"I was thinking of Mom," Rachel said softly. Tate nodded and felt a tingle in his lower eyelids. "I was thinking of Mom when I started to shake. I don't know—"

"Shhh," Tate hushed her. "Shhhh."

The doctors had told them both that it was good if Rachel talked about what preceded one of her seizures, but Tate rarely gave the girl a chance.

It was too hard for him. And today, he had too much on his mind.

Floyd had seen him; he was sure of it. The man was perhaps the worst liar in the history of the FBI, perhaps in any law enforcement department in existence.

He'd seen him take the money from Jabari. And that meant that there was a good possibility that his partner was now on his way to tell Director Hampton. And there would be no talking his way out of this one. Tomorrow, he might be out of a job, seniority, or experience or not.

And then how would he be able to pay Marco back?

The real question was why had he picked up Floyd in the first place? Why not just go and take Frankie's and Jabari's money alone?

Floyd would have found his way from Grassroots to Quantico.

Was it because he wanted to be caught?

There was a common misconception in the public that serial killers left clues behind because they wanted to be caught. In almost every case, this wasn't true. After all, a serial killer liked to kill, and options were limited to one in solitary confinement.

But there was some relief to be had when you were found out. Some of the pressure of dealing with everything alone was alleviated, even if the end result was negative.

At least someone else knew.

Tate stayed completely still for upwards of ten minutes, his eyes locked on his wife's image.

"Rachel?" When there was no answer, he looked at his daughter.

She was sleeping soundly now, her chest rising and falling.

He would've stayed there for the rest of the day just watching her sleep when he noticed movement in his periphery.

Marguerite was standing in the doorway.

He brought his finger to his lips and then kissed Rachel's forehead. Moving as slowly as possible, he pulled his arm out from beneath her head and then slid off the bed.

Only when the door was closed behind them, did Tate address Marguerite.

"I know you don't like to be called at work, but it was a bad one, Mr. Abernathy. She was screaming and shaking, and I was afraid she was going to swallow her tongue."

"Don't worry about it. You did the right thing." But despite his assurances, Marguerite's face didn't change. "What's wrong?"

The woman looked down at her feet.

"Mr. Abernathy, I hate to do this, but it's been nearly a month now. I know that things have been difficult for you and for Rachel, but I have my own family to support."

Tate winced.

Payment—Marguerite wanted to be paid. And she deserved to be paid. Without her, Rachel would be stuck in a home somewhere.

Day in and day out, the woman looked after Rachel, helping her with her schoolwork, preparing her meals, helping her use the bathroom. And despite the woman's current request, Rachel and Marguerite's relationship was much more than simply transactional.

Rachel loved Marguerite, she'd said so on many an occasion, and the feeling was reciprocal.

Without her, both Tate and Rachel would be lost.

"I know," Tate said. He reached into his pocket and pulled out the money he'd taken from Frankie and Jabari.

Money that was supposed to go to Marco.

And it was a lot less than he'd first thought. The thing about drug dealers and wanna-be thugs was that they always carried small bills. Made it seem like they had more money than they actually did.

He counted out three hundred and twenty dollars, more than half of what he'd taken, and offered it to Marguerite.

She hesitated.

"Are you sure?"

Marguerite was well-versed in his money troubles. The fact was, the FBI didn't pay all that well and Rachel's medical bills and the lawyer fees had quickly eaten through all of Tate's and Olivia's savings.

But even after things had settled, Rachel being unable to look after herself meant that there was a constant financial burden for Tate to deal with.

That's where Marco came in. Temporary loans at a high price.

"Take it, please," he urged.

She was reluctant but eventually took the cash.

"You can go back to work now," Marguerite said.

The truth was, Tate didn't want to go back to work. It wasn't just the fact that he was pretty sure he was fired—he'd switched his phone to silent before entering his house—but he wanted to be here, with Rachel.

"You know what? I think I'll stay. Why don't you take the rest of the day off," Tate suggested. Marguerite started to shake her head, but Tate insisted. "No, seriously. Take the day off."

"Thank you, Mr. Abernathy," Marguerite said. She knew him well enough to know that when he made up his mind about something the likelihood of him changing it was almost always zero. "Thank you."

After Marguerite left, Tate went back into Rachel's room. This time, he elected for the chair beside the bed and watched her sleep.

It was barely noon, but he knew based on the way his daughter twitched and sighed in her sleep that tonight was going to be a bad one.

Which meant, once again, Tate wouldn't be sleeping at all.

Chapter 17

THE TWO LAWYERS STOOD AND introduced themselves to Stu when he entered the room. The ADA and the detective waited for him to be seated before they did the same.

"My name is Matthew Lombardo and I'm an assistant district attorney for the state of Nevada," cheap suit man said. "And I believe you've met Detective Ben Tolliver."

The detective scowled at the mention of his name, but Stu paid him no heed. If his business dealings had taught him anything, it was that anger only led to one of two things: indecision or bad decisions.

Clearly, the two men had expected a reaction because when Stu did not oblige there was a hesitation on both their parts. Eventually, the ADA ran a hand through his hair, for which the inspiration had likely been that of a Lego man, and he cleared his throat.

"I'm sure your lawyers have instructed you of your rights, but I think it's prudent that we repeat them to you now." Matthew nodded at the detective, who derived far too much pleasure in reciting his lines. When he was done, Detective Tolliver asked if Stu understood.

Stu said he did, and that, on the advice of Will Porter, were the only words that left his mouth while the ADA and detective remained in the room.

For a while after this charade, nobody said anything. Detective Tolliver was too busy setting up his props to worry about speaking. He laid out a series of photographs, taking great care to ensure that they were perfectly spaced. The first was of a man—him, or so they claimed—standing with a gun in hand, aiming it at Jake Hollister who was seated, his palm outstretched in front of his face. The next was a close-up of Jake's face, post-shooting. There were two clear bullet holes, one almost directly in the center of his forehead, the other closer to the right temple. The man's tongue hung out of his mouth and his eyes showed his whites, which Stu found to be more obscene and disturbing than the damage from the bullets.

This setup was clearly meant to shock him, and it worked. Stu had never seen a dead body before, not like this.

He'd never seen anything that upset him so viscerally, but he refused to give the detective any satisfaction.

The next photograph featured a list of coordinates and addresses that meant nothing to Stu. Then there was the GSR test result.

Pleased with himself, Detective Tolliver made one final adjustment and then sat down and crossed his arms over his chest.

This collection of images told a story, but just in case Stu had a problem following the narrative, the ADA finally broke the silence.

"Means, and opportunity," Matthew Lombardo said with the theatrics of addressing a group of jurors during closing arguments. "That's what we have here. Means," he indicated the GSR test, "and opportunity." Matthew brought his thumb down on the GPS data, while at the same time raising the index finger on his other hand. "But, in reality, we don't need any of these. Because we have these."

Using the pointer finger of each hand, Matthew Lombardo pointed at the close-up image of Jake's skull and the image of Stu hovering over him at the exact same time.

"Mr. Barnes," he continued, still pointing at the photographs, "we know that your car drove to the location of the murder based on the GPS data we obtained from our search warrant. We also know that you fired a gun within the last four or five days—this was confirmed via GSR test. But none of that matters because—*because*—we have a videotape of you, clear as day, shooting and murdering Jake Hollister."

This last sentence hung in the air and Stu felt his entire body tense. All of this had been faked, of course, and he'd been set up, but Stu couldn't help but appreciate the compelling nature of the young ADA's argument. Deep down, he knew he'd have a hard time convincing his mother, God rest her soul, of his innocence, let alone a group of jurors.

Like before, the ADA and detective expected something from Stu—an outburst? Staunch denial? Admission of guilt?—but he just sat there, staring intently across the table.

Detective Tolliver's expression, which was always, and perhaps perpetually sour, became positively acerbic.

The ADA was unfazed.

"In spite—*in spite*—of this overwhelming evidence, we are willing to negotiate a plea deal, Mr. Barnes. The details and specifics are outlined in the document in your representations' possession. But, quite simply, we are willing to downgrade the charge from first to second-degree murder. Now, in the state of Nevada, a second-degree murder charge typically brings a sentence of 15 to 30 years, with a minimum of 10. But—but—this deal is contingent on you telling us where the murder weapon is."

I can't tell you where the gun is, asshole, Stu thought. *Because it's not mine.*

"Nothing? You've got nothing to say for yourself?" Detective Tolliver barked.

"Where's your motive, Detective?" Will said, ignoring the man's questions. "You talk a lot about means and opportunity, but why would my client, who is the majority owner of Happy Valley Gaming as well as nearly a hundred more companies, want to kill an employee? A coder? Hmm?"

Detective Tolliver's face started to turn red, but the ADA cut in before the man could verbalize his anger.

"Don't worry about motive. We have the videotape."

"Right, well, we will discuss your plea deal in private and get back to you."

"Fucking rich prick," Tolliver grumbled under his breath as he collapsed back into his chair.

"Mr. Lombardo, please tell the detective to—"

"My apologies," the ADA said, cutting Will off. "Just so that we're clear, this deal will be available for three hours, right up until Mr. Barnes' arraignment in front of Judge Davenport."

"And afterward?" one of Stu's other lawyers asked.

The ADA shrugged.

"We'll see."

Matthew nudged Detective Tolliver and the latter collected the photographs with far less care than had been used setting them up. Then the two men rose, nodded, and left without further pomp and circumstances. As soon as the door closed behind them, Stu let out a deep breath.

"It's okay, relax," Will said, gently rubbing Stu's back. "They're posturing. The deal's not going anywhere."

"What about the GPSand—"

It was the younger of the two criminal lawyers, the man who had introduced himself as Colin something who spoke up.

"Mike and I have all of these documents in our possession. There will be plenty of time to go through them after the arraignment. But first, we need to discuss the—"

Stu shook his head.

"No deal."

Colin cocked his head. Clearly, Will had prepped him on Stu's position regarding a plea deal and was therefore unsurprised by the preemptive reply.

ALREADY DEAD 91

"I understand. As I said, the deal isn't going anywhere. In three hours, we will stand by you when you state not guilty in front of the judge. However, Mr. Barnes, I—"

"Stu."

"Right, Stu. I've tried dozens of high-profile criminal cases and negotiated pleas for at least three times that many. And while proving guilt is the burden of the prosecution, jurors are human. And humans love stories." Colin waved a manicured hand over the table where the photographs had been moments ago. "I won't lie to you—Detective Tolliver and the ADA tell a compelling tale. Now, Mike and I will tear their evidence apart, I guarantee it. Every shred of data or evidence will be second-guessed, interpreted, and questioned. But the story... the story is something that we will have a difficult time dissembling. In my experience, the best way to combat the ADA's narrative is to come up with an alternative one. One that is equally as compelling as theirs."

Stu sucked in his bottom lip and nodded.

Innocent until proven guilty was an interesting concept in theory, but the reality was that Stu was going to be on trial. Jurors recognized that this meant not only did the cops think he was guilty, but that the DA or, in this case, the ADA, thought that there was enough evidence for a conviction.

If that didn't bias the twelve people sitting on hard wooden chairs and taking notes for hours on end, then Stu didn't know what did.

A silent exchange occurred between Colin, Mike, and Will. The latter stood and helped Stu to his feet.

"But for now, we just need to get you in front of the judge. Get yourself cleaned up and we'll see you in an hour, okay?"

Stu, who was still somewhat shell-shocked, nodded. He knew that ruminating on all of the evidence that the State had on him was pointless—he hadn't even been able to look at the so-called email exchanges—but it was hard not to.

GPS, GSR, email, video, photo evidence.

Why? *Who?*

The guard opened the door and Will said something that Stu didn't hear. He repeated it, but Stu was already being led away.

Who would do this to me? Who?

And how?

"Hey, Gramps."

Stu kept walking.

"Gramps!"

He finally looked up. Rodrick was also leaving an interview room and upon seeing Stu's expression, the man lowered his voice.

"Your arraignment's set, huh?"

"Yeah," he said dryly.

"This aft?"

"Three hours."

Rodrick sucked his teeth.

"I told you, they ain't givin' you no time. Who da judge?"

Stu, still in a daze, couldn't remember.

"I... I dunno."

"Whatchu mean you don't know?"

"I mean, I think they said his name was... uhh... Daven... Deven..."

"Davenport?" Rodrick offered.

"Yeah, Davenport."

"Sheeet, he a tough mothafucka," Rodrick said, his expression and voice suddenly serious. "A real tough cracka. He like to see you all pouty 'n shit. Remorseful. Gramps, when you go in front of that judge, you tell him yous sorry."

"But I didn't do it," Stu said softly.

Big Roddy grinned and his gold tooth glinted.

"Ain't nobody in here did nothin'. You just tell that gray-haired motherfucker yous sorry for taking up erryone time 'n shit. You do that, Gramps, and you get bail. You don't—hell, then you better stock up on dem moon pies cuz my co-counsel ain't goin' be free forever."

Chapter 18

FLOYD THOUGHT THAT THE WALK back to Quantico would provide him with some clarity.

It didn't. If anything, time just served to muddy the waters.

On several occasions, Tate had stretched the rules to get the job done. Everyone's heard the story of the beat cop who illegally stops someone and searches the car when they knew it's loaded with drugs by citing a broken taillight. Hell, maybe they even facilitate the smashed plastic.

Drugs were a plague, but plagues take time to work their way through a population. The impact of a serial killer was a little more immediate.

As such, some of their actions as FBI agents were left to their own discretion and even more were justifiable with a positive outcome. Yet, Tate had not overtly or blatantly broken the law, at least not to Floyd's knowledge.

Until today.

Assault and robbery.

Why?

And, perhaps more importantly, what was Floyd supposed to do about it?

He'd been walking for about ten minutes when he realized that he'd made it back to the location of the first incident, the one that involved Frankie in his ridiculously oversized pants.

Comically large. Obscenely—

It was as if just thinking about these jeans made them appear.

Frankie was standing half in and half out of an alley. The thug spotted Floyd first.

"Naw, I ain't got nothin' for you," he said. "That asshole Tate already took everything."

Tate already took everything.

Tate.

They knew each other.

Floyd had no idea what this meant. Did this mean that they had a relationship? He could never picture the two as friends, but maybe Frankie was a confidential informant?

Or was this familiarity indicative of something even more sinister?

Did Tate regularly come here and rob people? So often that they knew him by name?

It seemed ridiculous but someone like Frankie couldn't exactly go to the cops and report that a rogue FBI Agent was stealing his illegal contraband or cash acquired from the sale of said drugs.

Then what?

Floyd felt goosebumps form on the back of his neck and felt his scalp shrivel. The stress was getting to him.

And it was threatening to take over.

No, he scolded himself. *Just keep going. Like a freight train, just keep on going. Choo-choo!*

Floyd licked his lips and swallowed in an attempt to moisten his suddenly dry throat.

"Every—" He coughed. "Everything?"

Frankie scowled, and he jammed his hands into his pockets. His pants hung so low that this required him to hunch over a fair amount.

"Don't lie to me," Floyd warned.

Frankie tried to look tough, but he was only a kid. And he was scared, too.

"Fuck, I mean, I gave him more than ten percent, that for sure."

It clicked then.

Ten percent.

What he'd witnessed wasn't a robbery but some sort of arrangement.

Ten percent... for what?

Floyd wanted to feel relieved that Tate wasn't just a thug himself. A thug with a badge and a gun and the abilities of a chameleon.

But he wasn't.

"I ain't giving you nothing, though. That ain't the deal."

The change from *Tate took everything* to *I'm not giving you anything* was not lost on Floyd. It was, however, irrelevant. The only thing Floyd wanted was information.

Tate had said that he came out here to teach Floyd some math, but that had been a lie. It hadn't been about educating Floyd at all.

It was about Tate—Tate and a payday.

A series of fireworks went off inside Floyd's brain.

Tate's letting these men deal their drugs for percentage of the take.

That's why he felt no relief; Floyd wasn't sure which scenario—Tate the simple robber or Tate the extortionist—was better.

"How long?" he asked, unsure of what else to say.

"What?"

"How long has this been going on?"

Frankie, hands still in his pockets, lifted his pants a little as if preparing to bolt.

"I ain't saying anything else. You ask Tate if you wanna know more."

Keep the train moving.

Floyd stepped forward and not so subtly brought his hand to the gun on his hip. Frankie noticed and when Floyd asked the question again, he reluctantly answered.

"Two years. But that's all I'm saying. If you want—"

"Get lost."

"What?"

"I'm not as accommodating as my partner. Either you take off now, or I'll a-arrest you where you stand."

Frankie took a read of his face, muttered something incomprehensible, then disappeared down the alley.

Staying true to Dr. Matteo's advice, Floyd kept moving. He kept moving until he was all the way back at his office computer, sweat soaking the back of his shirt in the shape of an inverted Christmas tree.

He knew that Tate had been in the FBI for seven years. At least two years ago, he'd started extorting local thugs for cash.

Two years was a long time.

Two years was more than double the time that Floyd had been with the FBI. At this juncture, he was inclined to just shelf what he knew. After all, Tate wasn't just his superior, but he was a mentor to him.

So, what if the man broke the law? What difference did it make? It wasn't like he was hurting good, hard-working people. In fact, with just a little mental gymnastics, leaping a pommel horse of rationality as opposed to performing an entire floor routine of complicated reasoning, Floyd could see a positive to what Tate was doing.

But that was the old him. This was the new *Choo-Choo* Floyd. He pressed on.

The first thing Floyd did was perform a brief review of all of Tate's FBI cases going back two years or so, hoping to find some connection between his partner and Frankie or the other guy or just drugs in general.

He came up empty.

The most notable case was Tate and his then partner Constantine Striker's arrest of the notorious serial killer dubbed The Sandman, but the impact of this case affected Con much more deeply than Tate.

And for good reason.

Floyd switched his focus, leaning more toward Tate's personal life rather than professional. This proved slower going, owing to his partner being exceedingly private. So far as Floyd could tell, he had no social media presence at all.

Still, he found it. Eventually, Floyd found what he was looking for.

Near the back of a local newspaper, almost as if written as an afterthought, a filler for empty space, Floyd discovered the inciting incident that indeed, occurred almost exactly two years prior.

A devastating accident that had permanently changed the course of Tate and his family's lives.

But now that he'd found it, what was he to do with this information?

What would Choo-Choo Floyd do now?

Chapter 19

WHILE STU BARNES WAS STILL dressed in the same CCDC uniform and his hands were still handcuffed in front of him when he entered the courtroom three hours later, he felt like a new man.

He felt ready—he felt ready to put this nightmare behind him.

Two guards led Stu to a table that was already occupied by his cadre of expensive lawyers, including Will. The table across the aisle was occupied by ADA Matthew Lombardo and another man who looked like a clerk of some sort.

"All rise, the Honorable Judge Davenport residing."

The judge entered from a rear chamber and climbed up to his chair which was elevated on some sort of platform. Judge Davenport typified his profession: paunch, jowls, gray hair, and icy stare.

He took a seat and then instructed everyone to do the same. As the judge proceeded to describe the charges, Stu couldn't help but think of what Rodrick had described as 'stacking'.

There was the first-degree murder charge, of course, but there was a litany of others, including possession of a firearm without completing a background check, illegal discharge of a firearm, and a number of more obscure criminal charges that seemed irrelevant given the murder rap.

"Will the defendant please stand," the judge said without looking up from the papers in front of him.

A still shackled Stu rose but kept his head respectfully bowed.

"Defendant, how do you plead for the charges?"

The judge looked up and his eyes met Stu's. There was an unforgiving hardness in the look.

Judge Davenport didn't care whether the man on trial was worth a dollar or a billion.

"Not guilty, your Honor," Stu said, trying to sound confident. He wasn't sure he succeeded.

The judge continued to stare at him for several seconds as if trying to silently persuade him to change his mind.

"All right. Next up, bail. Mr. Lombardo?"

The bailiff motioned for Stu to sit but he elected to stand. He wanted to be toe-to-toe with the ADA when they made their argument against him being released. But when both the judge and the bailiff frowned at this, Will gently tugged on the side of his shirt and Stu reluctantly took a seat in the hard wooden chair.

"Your Honor, the defendant has been charged with first-degree murder. This was a heinous, premeditated act that involved shooting an unarmed man twice in the head. We have video evidence of the defendant murdering Jake Hollister. We have GSR from the defendant's hand confirming that he fired the weapon and GPS data revealing that the defendant's vehicle was at the scene of the crime. Given the damning nature of this evidence, we believe—"

"Your Honor, there is no motive for this crime. My client—"

"You will get your chance, Mr. Porter. Please, do not interrupt again," the judge warned. "Mr. Lombardo, please go on."

The assistant district attorney cleared his throat before continuing.

"We believe that because of the volume of evidence against Mr. Barnes combined with his extensive wealth, he is not just a flight risk but him fleeing the country is almost guaranteed." The ADA paused almost as if daring Will to interrupt, but Stu's lawyer only offered a disapproving grunt. "Mr. Barnes has the means of hiring a private jet or a yacht or any other conceivable method of transportation and fleeing the United States at a moment's notice. It is for these reasons, that we request bail be withheld."

Stu inhaled sharply. This was expected, but it still stung. He'd been adamant about not taking any deals, but he knew that a prolonged stay behind bars while awaiting trial would test him.

"Now it's your turn, Mr. Porter," the judge said. His face, heavily lined as it was, was unreadable.

"Thank you, your honor. Now, despite the prosecution's claims, this is far from a cut-and-dry case. With his legal enterprises, my client has amassed considerable wealth and has employed hundreds of hard-working Americans. The one thing that the prosecution failed to mention is a motive. Because there is no motive. No motive that would risk all of my client's lifetime of hard work that—"

"We have a clear motive in this case, your Honor. We—"

"Mr. Lombardo, you had your chance. Please, do not interrupt." The judge's tone during his admonition of the assistant district attorney was considerably more aggressive than with Will, and this brought a tiny smile to Stu's lips. "Go on, Mr. Porter."

"Right, well, I would just like to point out that while the prosecution views my client's wealth as a quote guaranteed unquote flight risk, we interpret this very differently. His status ensures that he will be present to stand trial. Mr. Barnes fully intends to continue to run his businesses and oversee his more than 500 employees in the tech industry, while on bail. He is a public figure, and thus the idea of him fleeing the country is just ludicrous."

Judge Davenport scribbled something on a sheet of paper.

"Thank you, I have reviewed the evidence and arguments." As the judge spoke, he glared at Stu. "And I'm ready to make my decision."

Stu knew what that decision was. He knew it in his heart. Judge Davenport was going to deny him bail and he was going to be locked up, stuck behind bars for how long? Six months? A year? Two? Before going to trial. His life would be destroyed. His businesses sunk. And worst of all, Stu knew that the deal would always be looming, dangling like a carrot or a moon pie after the store had just run out.

To a man who owned an island, the ground was just land. To a man stranded at sea, a bog was a little slice of Heaven.

"Your Honor," he unexpectedly blurted.

Remorse, Rodrick had told him. *Be remorseful, even if you didn't do it.*

"What are you doing?" Will hissed out of the corner of his mouth.

The judge raised a gray eyebrow.

"Yes?" And that was the invitation Stu needed.

"Sit down," Will warned, but he ignored his counsel.

"I just want to apologize," Stu began. "I didn't do what the prosecution is accusing me of doing. I am not admitting guilt. I did not kill Jake Hollister. I've never killed anyone. But I do understand what a burden this trial will be on everyone involved, including the lawyers, the jurors, yourself, and, perhaps most importantly, Jake's family. I just wanted to express my regret and apology for this strain on the system and for taking up everyone's time."

By the end of the truncated speech, Stu felt like the words meant something. He'd spoken them off the cuff, and they weren't perfect by any means, but he was genuinely sorry. Mostly for himself because he was innocent and had been set up, but also for Jake. He didn't know Jake Hollister, but Stu could think of very few legitimate reasons why someone deserved to be murdered, execution style.

The judge scribbled on his paper again.

"My decision," the man said, speaking painfully slowly, "is to grant the defendant bail on several conditions."

That was all Stu Barnes heard. The judge continued to speak but the blood roaring inside Stu's head made it impossible to hear anything.

I'm out, he thought. *I'm getting out. Thank you, Rodrick—I owe you infinite moon pies. Thank you, thank you, thank you.*

This overwhelming feeling of gratitude lasted all but thirty seconds.

Then Stu's analytical mind to over.

Part A was accomplished.

Now onto Part B.

Colin Sachs, the high-priced criminal law attorney who had said and done basically nothing for a fee that, while not yet established, was likely to be astronomical, looked at Stu.

This was a reminder of a look. A reminder that they still had work to do.

Back in the interview room, Colin had said that they needed to come up with an equally if not more compelling narrative than the DA's to sell to the jurors.

And Stu was inclined to agree. The reality as he saw it was that to prove he didn't kill Jake Hollister they had to find out who did.

Fuck the burden of proof. This was his life they were talking about.

But was Will up to that challenge? The man was good, and he was a friend, but he was also getting up there in the years. Try as he might, Stu couldn't picture Will combing the streets for evidence, digging deep into whatever leads they might un-cover, forgoing food, sleep, family... everything to make sure Stu didn't rot behind bars.

And if Will Porter wasn't up to the challenge, Stu knew someone who was. And if she wasn't, well, he'd had saved her twice.

And now, it was time to call in a favor.

It was Chase Adams' turn to save him.

PART II – Nothing is Real

Chapter 20

"Do you believe in God, Brian?" Chase Adams asked as she held the small white pill up to eye level.

Chase knew the answer to this already. No matter what Brian Jalston said now, no matter how many times he might have gone to the prison chapel or prayed while lying alone in his cell, Brian did not believe in God.

The only person that this extreme narcissist believed in was himself. And Chase knew that once Brian ate this pill, there would be nothing stopping him from doing what Father David had done, or Madison, Kylie, Brook, and Victoria.

Shortly after Brian Jalston consumed Cerebrum the man would see the light. And then he would take his own life.

That was what was going to happen, and Chase was determined to watch.

"Eat the fucking pill, Brian," Chase hissed when he refused to answer a question.

"I'm not eating shit," the man drawled, easing off the gas pedal.

"You will," Chase promised. She pushed the gun into the back of Brian's seat, reminding him that she was the one in control.

The man chuckled.

"Naw, I won't."

Chase had pictured this going differently—she'd imagined something cleaner. Brian was going to fight her, of course, he was, but eventually, Chase envisioned breaking the man down. He'd eat the pill and she'd get out of the car, send him on his way. Somewhere down the road, just far enough for Chase to be out of danger but close enough to witness, Brian would yank the wheel hard and veer off the road.

Then he'd smash headlong into a light pole, effectively ending his miserable life and putting a stop to the decades-old nightmare that continued to haunt Chase Adams.

But if that didn't work, then she wasn't opposed to taking a more direct role in the man's demise.

Chase raised the gun and put it to Brian's temple.

The barrel must've been cool because he inhaled sharply.

"Eat the pill, or I'll shoot you," she said. Her lack of intonation surprised even her. Such a calm demeanor for such a loaded threat.

"I don't think—"

Brian's words were cut off by the screech of tires. Chase's first thought was that this was a tactic by the recent parolee to send her flying into the front seat, but then she spotted another car pulling in front of them, sending up a cloud of dust.

The pill flew from her hand and bounced off the windshield before landing somewhere on the floor, but Chase's main concern was making sure that as her body was launched forward, she didn't pull the trigger.

Her shoulder banged hard against the passenger seat, and Chase was momentarily wedged in the opening between the front and back seats.

She expected Brian to go for the gun, but he didn't. Instead, he opened the door and jumped from the car.

"Fuck!" Chase swore.

After pulling herself free, she followed Brian into the hot sun.

"Stop!" she screamed, planting her feet and taking aim at Brian's back. He was moving quickly and was a much smaller target since his recent weight loss. "Stop!"

In her periphery, Chase saw the door of the dark car that they had nearly T-boned open and a man get out.

He was thin, black, and had a mustache. He was also holding a gun, but this weapon wasn't pointed at Brian Jalston.

It was pointed at Chase.

"Terrence?"

"Put the gun down, Chase," the man ordered.

Chase kept her aim on Brian who had since slowed and was starting to turn.

"I'm serious, Chase, put it down."

Brian was looking at her now. The fucker was smiling at her, and his expression was so different from that of Terrence Conway of the Tennessee Bureau of Investigation that it was jarring.

Chase's hand began to tremble.

Just pull the trigger. Pull the fucking trigger and be done with it.

But she couldn't.

She'd killed Timothy Jalston. Slit his throat.

But the man had been in the process of raping her. She would have killed Brian, too, but his brainwashed harem, which included Chase's late sister, Georgina, had used their bodies to shield and protect him.

Chase hated Brian. Hated him more than anything, but she couldn't shoot him.

Not like this.

"I—" she broke and finally lowered the gun. "He's gonna take her, Terrence. Brian's going to take Georgina." When

Brian's smile became a lecherous grin, Chase suddenly felt her strength returning. And her resolve. She raised the gun again. "You'll never have her."

"Chase," Terrence said softly. "There are other ways to do this."

"Really?" she spat. "Like what? Put my faith in the system? The same fucking system that let this piece of shit out of prison after only a few years? After what he did? I won't let him have her, Terrence, I won't."

Terrence nodded subtly.

"I know."

The man's calmness during this time of unparalleled emotion and stress seemed to transfer over to Chase.

She didn't just lower the gun this time but holstered it.

"After this?" Brian held out his arms. "After you held me at gunpoint? Who do you think a judge is going to side with? The little girl's psychotic aunt or me? Her father?"

Chase squinted against the sun to get a better look at Brian.

Does he want me to shoot him? Did he swallow Cerebrum when I wasn't looking?

"That never happened," Terrence intoned.

Brian, whose focus had only been Chase at this point, glanced over at Terrence and glared at the man.

"What?"

"You heard me," Terrence said. "None of this happened. You're going to get back in your car and collect your wives and go about your merry way."

"And why would I do that?" Brian asked with a sneer.

"Because if you don't, I will make your life very difficult," Terrence promised. "Me or one of my men will be stationed outside of your house every single day. We will follow you everywhere you go and the moment you slip up, and you will, because everyone does, I'll be there. This time, there won't be a deal. This time, I'll put you away for life. So, why don't you just get the fuck back into your car and drive away."

Brian was angry. His face was red and there was an ugly vein in the center of his forehead that had started to pulse.

But for all of his bravado, the man knew that he was beaten.

"I'll see you in court," the man said as he passed Chase who made no effort to move out of his way.

No, you won't, Chase thought. No, you fucking won't.

Brian peeled away and when the dust cleared, Chase looked at Terrence.

"I meant what I said. I won't let him have her."

There was a deep sadness in Terrence's eyes.

"I know. But there are other ways to do this, Chase. There are other ways, and not all of them end with you behind bars for the rest of your life."

But most of them do, Chase thought, but didn't say. *Scratch that, almost all of them do.*

Chapter 21

TONY METCALFE'S HEART WAS RACING. Sweat soaked his cheap dress shirt, making it cling to his back and underarms. His balls were also sweaty, which made him walk with an uncomfortable bowlegged gait.

Come on, come on, get a hold of yourself. Keep it together. This is your chance. Your only chance.

This wasn't hyperbole. Tony had been shocked when he'd been granted an interview at Happy Valley Games, a subsidiary of AI Integrations. He'd only applied on a whim, and even then, he'd relied on the courage imbued by half a case of PBR.

The position required a computer engineering background, which, of course, Tony did not have. In fact, he didn't have any formal training at all.

That didn't mean that Tony didn't know his worth. He was the best software engineer in Nevada. Maybe even the country. He just had a knack for programming, something he'd done for over fifteen years, ever since he was a little boy.

To him, the code was like lyrical prose—it was like reading poetry.

Tony loved it.

But love only got you so far. You couldn't go to the bank, deposit love, and use it to pay your mortgage.

Best programmer or not, this was Tony's chance. Someone had clearly made a mistake at Happy Valley Games. Someone in HR had just assumed that he had a degree from LSVU or somewhere else—Stanford, MIT, or Berkeley.

But now that didn't matter. All he had to do was get in the door, then he would show them.

So long as he didn't melt into a puddle of mud beforehand, that is.

The building that housed Valley Games was impressive. So much so that Tony felt embarrassed pulling up in a cab and asked the driver to park a few blocks away.

Then, the Nevada heat hadn't been a consideration.

Not, it most certainly was.

Valley Games was a massive, twenty-story glass monstrosity which reflected so much sunlight that Tony was surprised it didn't cause passersby to erupt into flames.

There you go again, Tony. Letting your mind run away from you. Focus… focus… FOCUS! You can't fuck this up like last time. You can't.

That was just a shitty little job at a shitty little company that made disposable games for your cell phone. *This* was Valley Games.

This was the creator of the most realistic and popular metaverse ever made.

And Tony wanted to be part of it.

Hell, that's what Tony wanted more than anything else.

He straightened as he walked toward the front doors, ignoring the chafing on his inner thighs.

The inside of Valley Games was surprisingly understated. It was a video game company, which meant that there was a plethora of computer stations and a touch of mandatory RGB rope lighting, but it didn't seem like the monolith it was from the outside.

It was comfortable and cozy. Instead of hard plastic or wooden chairs in the lobby, there were beanbags.

Maybe a little cheesy, maybe trying a little too hard, but comfortable, nevertheless.

Tony was waiting in the entrance, taking this all in and allowing the air conditioning to do its work, when a man approached him.

"Jake Hollister," he said with a perfect grin. Jake had shaggy blonde hair, and instead of a suit, he was wearing a black T-shirt and dark jeans with white running shoes. Classic comfortable chic. "I'm the head programmer here at Valley Games. Now, Tony—it is Tony, right?"

"Yes," Tony said, swiping his palm on his pants to dry it before shaking Jake's hand. "Tony Metcalfe."

"Thought so." Jake suddenly turned serious, and Tony thought the worst. He'd been intercepted and was about to be told that there had been a mistake, that he wasn't qualified, and they were sorry, and blah, blah, blah. "Look, I know that you were supposed to meet with HR for an interview, but… I'm going to be honest. I hate HR, with their rules and all that nonsense. I just want to know one thing, Tony: can you code?"

Tony was taken aback and said nothing, even as Jake slipped an arm over his sweaty shoulders and guided him deeper into the building. They passed a large glass desk behind which stood a pretty woman with almost natural red hair tied up in a bun that contrasted with her pale features.

"Morning, Janice," Jake said cheerily.

"Good morning."

Tony gave the woman a polite wave, and she repeated the greeting to him, as well.

Jake led them to an elevator and finally took his arm off Tony's shoulder, for which he was grateful. He imagined Jake's forearm just dripping in his sweat.

The elevator pinged and they got inside.

Jake pressed 16.

"It's a short ride, but maybe you can tell me a little about yourself, Tony?" Jake asked when the doors closed.

Tony cleared his throat.

"Now, I-I don't have any formal education, but I have been programming for years. We're talking about starting with Turing and then Visual Basics… yeah, all the way back then. I've done everything from working on websites to making my own games. There was even—

Tony stopped himself.

He was about to say that he'd created the base code for one of the most popular mobile games of the last ten years.

Before they fucked him. Before that piece of shit company had bent him over and fucked him right in the ass.

Took everything. Gave him nothing.

Jake waved a hand dismissively.

"I know about your accomplishments, Tony, and your history. You sent us all that stuff, remember? Let me ask you something else… what do you know about Happy Valley games? Have you ever traveled into the multiverse?" Jake said this last part with an air of an afternoon game show host.

"O-o-of course. I have a subscription to Happy Valley games… I-I-I love the multiverse.

"So, you're a fanboy?"

"I-I-" Tony didn't know what to say. He didn't want to come across as too eager, but he didn't want to insult the lead programmer either.

"Oh, come on." Jake rolled his eyes. "Tell me what you really think. I'm not soft, I can take it. We want people who have ideas for improving the metaverse, not yes men. It's a fickle business… one day we're on top, the next, another company puts out a better, more realistic, multiverse, and our membership tanks overnight. So, Tony, I'm going to ask you this just once: what's wrong with our multiverse?"

Oh, shit. This is a trap. I've walked into a trap.

If he hadn't been dripping with sweat already, Tony's entire body would have broken out in a slick, greasy coating.

What do I say?

"Tick-tock, Tony. Tick-tock." Jake laughed and pointed at the digital display telling them what floor they were passing.

They were on eleven now.

He had to say something. He *had* to.

This was his chance.

His *only* chance.

"The uncanny valley," Tony blurted. This was the truth. This was the problem with Happy Valley Gaming and all the other multiverses he'd tested.

Jake looked at him.

"Go on."

Fuck it, Tony thought. *I'm just going to roll with it. It's too late to take it back now, anyway.*

"The faces of the NPCs, you know? The non-playable characters? They look good, but not real enough. Like they just... well, they make me uncomfortable. Hell, even the other players, their faces? They're not right, either—they're too good to be robots but not good enough to be human. It just makes you cringe a little, and that takes you out of the multiverse. It's supposed to be completely immersive, you know, like, it's supposed to make you forget what's real and what's just a game? But it's those faces and reactions... emotions..."

Jake stared at him with an intensity that Tony didn't know how to read.

Then the man burst out laughing.

"I know what the uncanny valley is, Tony, my man!" He slapped Tony on the back, which made an awkward sloshing sound. "But you *nailed* it. Fucking nailed it. I'm like you, I want to be so invested in the game that it's more real than real, you know? That's what I want. But we can't do that with these characters with plastic features and—" he pointed his fingers in front of his face, one going to the left, the other to the right, "—wonky eyes when your virtual reality wife is supposed to be sad. Or horny or I don't know, dead! So, can you help us? Tony Metcalfe, ye of no formal education, can you help us break through the uncanny valley?"

Tony stiffened.

"I can," he said confidently. Then he repeated the claim. "Yes, I can."

Jake smiled again, revealing his perfectly white teeth. The elevator chimed and the doors opened.

Standing in the doorway was a man with silver hair and a deep tan. He was in his mid- to late-fifties, Tony guessed.

"Ah, what timing!" Jake said cheerfully. "Always one for the theatrics, hey, Stu?"

The silver fox grinned.

"Who's this?" he asked, indicating Tony with his chin.

Jake stepped to one side and waved his arms.

"Stu Barnes, CEO of Happy Valley Gaming, meet Tony Metcalfe, the man who is going to finally help us break through the uncanny valley."

Chapter 22

CHASE HAD PLENTY OF TIME to think about what had tran-
spired with Brian during her flight from Nashville back to New
York.

Would she have killed him? If Terrence hadn't shown up
when he did, could she have really shot and killed an unarmed
man? Even if said unarmed man was responsible for so much
of her, and others', suffering?

No.

Maybe.

What wasn't in question was whether Chase would have fed
Brian the Cerebrum if she hadn't dropped it.

That was a hard yes.

But now the pill was gone. As were Terrence and Brian.

Chase pulled into Louisa's driveway but didn't get out right
away. She could see them inside, Louisa and her two boys,
Brandon and Lawrence, and of course Georgina. They were
playing some sort of game together and laughing.

They were happy.

This made Chase angry, and it also made her want to turn
around and leave, to just go home. Maybe she'd grab her drone
and fly through the fields, zoom through the flowers, and just
let—

"No," she said out loud. "*No.*"

It made no sense to run. If she ran, Brian would be able to
gain custody of Georgina uncontested. And then what?

Chase couldn't even fathom what the monster would do to
her.

There was a custody hearing in two weeks. Chase would either be there or wouldn't. In either case, Georgina would be by
her side.

Louisa, who was miming either something terribly inappropriate or acting like an elephant glanced out the front window and their eyes met. To her credit, Louisa barely missed a step. She just kept going with the routine.

I don't deserve her, Chase thought.

And she really didn't. Louisa had been through nearly as much as she had. Like Chase, she'd been taken by Brian and Tim and had gotten away.

Louisa hadn't left a sister behind, but she was haunted by demons, as well. But whereas Louisa had put most of her bad habits behind her and had thrown herself into her family life instead of just cycling from one coping mechanism to another, Chase continued to struggle.

It wasn't fair.

It wasn't fair to Louisa.

Chase made up her mind and got out of the car. Louisa must have noticed because she opened the front door and Georgina rushed out.

The girl was smiling so hard that her cheeks were like cherries when she embraced Chase.

"I missed you," Chase said. She hugged her niece so hard that the girl grunted with discomfort. "I missed you so much."

"I missed... you... too," Georgina managed. She wriggled free.

"Welcome back, Chase," Louisa said from the doorway.

"Thanks." She put her hand on Georgina's head. "Let's go inside."

Louisa's house was larger than Chase's but not by much and it shared the same homey feel.

Brandon and Lawrence both said hi, and Chase tousled their blond mops.

"How's school?" Chase asked Georgina as Louisa poured her a cup of coffee.

"It's school," Georgina said, rolling her eyes. "How do you think it is? *Booooring*."

"So boring," Brandon parroted.

Chase laughed. This was good. Boring was good. Excitement was bad. Excitement meant that someone found out who Georgina really was.

"She's doing great," Louisa said, noticing the change in Chase's face. "Really. I spoke to both her teachers, and they only had good things to say about little G."

Chase spent the next twenty minutes catching up with her niece, which proved difficult. Prying information from the girl was perhaps as challenging as getting a suspect to admit their guilt.

This too was also normal.

Chase did manage to learn about some of her friends and her classes, including her Science teacher, Mrs. Bina, who was categorically meaner to Georgina than any of the other kids.

When it was clear nothing else was forthcoming, Chase hugged Georgina again and told the kids to go on, to go play.

"How are you doing, Chase?" Louisa asked when it was just the two of them.

Chase was dangerously close to telling her friend the truth. She almost blurted that Brian Jalston was out of prison, that he was seeking custody of Georgina, and that she'd been so incensed that she'd put a gun to the man's head.

But where would this outpouring of truth end? Would she tell Louisa how one of Brian's wives had tried to kill Chase, but then, in a twist of fate, sacrificed herself to save her?

Would she offhand mention that this poor soul could have been either one of them if they hadn't gotten lucky and escaped?

No.

Chase refused to give in.

Louisa had put this behind her, and bringing up the man's name alone might be enough to send her back to the dark place that had landed her in Grassroots to begin with.

It wouldn't be fair. Knowing that Brian was free would haunt Louisa.

"I'll be honest with you," Chase lied — she had no intention of telling the truth. At least, not all of it. Not nearly all of it. "Things aren't great. No — no, it's not that, it's not drugs."

"But you're not gonna tell me what it is, are you?" Louisa swirled her coffee.

"Not now," Chase admitted. "The last case... well, it was tough. Really tough. And now?" she sighed. "I hate to do this. I really, *really* hate it. If there is another option — "

"Did you practice the speech?" Louisa asked with a smirk. "It sounds rehearsed."

Chase had.

"I'm trying to be serious here, Louisa."

Louisa became serious.

"I know you are. And I know what you want. The answer is yes. It will always be yes, Chase. *Always.*"

Chase looked at her coffee, suddenly feeling ashamed. She'd rescued Georgina from Brian Jalston only to hand her off to someone else. The comparison wasn't fair, of course, but it still felt wrong.

"Why?" Chase asked, eyes still locked on her drink.

"Why? Because she's an amazing kid, Chase. You know, I always tell Brandon and Lawrence that I don't want them to be perfect, that perfect is boring, and making mistakes is fun. But when they act up? When they push things too far? Georgina is the one who brings them back to earth, who helps them regain control. And they look up to her—I know, silly, right? But they do. She really is a great kid. And she has you to thank for that."

Chase scoffed.

"Me?" She shook her head and finally raised her gaze. "That's ridiculous. All I do is run away. You're the only one I can count on. Without you... I... I..."

Chase's emotions threatened to get the better of her and she aggressively wiped her cheeks.

Louisa came over and comforted her.

"You're a good person, Chase. You just have to forgive yourself."

Chase's fingers on her face were wet now.

"Thank you," she whispered.

Something that Brian had said echoed in her mind.

Who's looking out for you?

Chase hadn't known how to answer that until now: Louisa.

She hugged her friend tightly for several minutes before finally letting her go.

"Two weeks," she said.

Louisa nodded.

"Take care of yourself."

Chase left without saying goodbye.

It would've been too hard otherwise.

Two weeks was all she needed. In two weeks, she would either come for Georgina and they would head to Nashville for the custody hearing together, or Chase would grab her niece and run.

Chapter 23

HAPPY VALLEY GAMING WAS LIKE no other company that Tony Metcalfe had ever worked for, of which there had been many. Nobody cared that he didn't have a fancy degree—no one even asked him about it. All they cared about was productivity.

More than that, he liked the people, and they liked him.

But the real prize at HVG was Jake Hollister. The man was smart and one of the best programmers that Tony had ever met. Not only that, but Jake was able to quickly identify what people were good at and let them have at it. In other companies, being new meant that you would have to perform the tasks that nobody more senior wanted to do, mainly debugging endless lines of code.

But not at HVG.

At HVG Tony was pretty much left alone and allowed to work.

And he was good. But his problem was a big one.

The uncanny valley.

After a hard day of work, when people came home, slipped on their virtual reality goggles, and grabbed their controllers, they were transported into a different world: the metaverse. The irony was that the more like the real world that the metaverse was, the more people enjoyed the experience despite it being designed as pure escapism. There were tens of thousands of people who populated HVG's metaverse, known as one of the most realistic, and they were physically located around the world. But the metaverse was vast, potentially infinite, and that required an equal number of participants. In time, Jake and the rest of the HVG crew were convinced that with millions of players, the world would be self-sufficient. But if you were a shift worker who decided to slip on your VR gear just before lunch while most other people were working? It could be an empty, lonely place.

Enter the non-playable characters, the NPCs. New AI tools, especially large language models, have made these computer-generated characters more believable and made their dialog generative, intuitive, and interesting, but there was still the problem of the uncanny valley. This pertained to the models that people used to represent themselves, which were infinitely moddable, but gamers had more patience when dealing with other players as opposed to NPCs.

HVG's NPCs weren't half bad. Tony thought they were actually some of the better ones out there. When he was playing and came across these characters, he would initially think that these were other real players. But invariably, something would be amiss, and he would clue into the fact that these were actually NPCs. It had something to do with their expressions. They were good, but not great. Everyone has heard of the creepy guy whose smile doesn't quite reach his eyes. For normal people, a smile wasn't confined to just lips or cheeks, it spread everywhere, to their eyes, hell, even their ears moved.

And when Tony realized that the character wasn't a real person, that he'd been almost duped, it made his skin crawl. Gamers like him got uncomfortable and when they got uncomfortable, they didn't want to play anymore.

And that was the challenge that Tony faced. Make the NPCs so real that no one could ever tell the difference.

This was more crucial for HVG than for the other companies that had their own multiverses because their business model relied on it. Whereas others charged a membership fee, it was free to play HVG's platform. Instead of charging players directly, they relied on sponsorships and in-game product placement, coupled with optional character 'upgrades'. They also sold digital land to companies and players alike.

IRL, you didn't pay to live, you paid to stay alive. That was HVG's platform. And when people got squirrely from the uncanny valley and logged off, HVG stopped making money.

"Hey, Tony, you doing okay?"

Tony pulled his headphones off and rubbed his eyes.

"Yeah, fine," he told Jake, who was resting on the partition that offered him some semblance of privacy.

The truth was that Tony was exhausted. Today had been a long day—fourteen hours and still going. This was coming on the heels of an eighteen-hour session fueled by energy drinks and Grappleberry vape juice.

"Any progress?"

Tony felt a pang of guilt and an inclination to lie. They were treating him so well, paying him even better, and what did he have to show for it?

An elevated heart rate and a mechanical keyboard that was starting to fail.

"I'm trying, Jake, I really am. I'm attempting to control all twenty individual muscles of the human face independently and then map emotion data obtained from these psych textbooks on top of them?" he sighed. "I don't know. Sometimes it looks great, but other times…"

Jake scratched his chin as he nodded.

"You dropped in yet today, Tony?"

Tony's eyes immediately went toward the VR goggles and controllers on his desk.

He tried to think about the last time he'd loaded up. Two days? Three? Had it been a week?

He couldn't remember.

"You should try it," Jake said with a shrug. "Maybe you'll get some ideas. You know what they say? All work and no play..."

"Maybe you're right. Thanks."

Jake saluted him with two fingers and then left the open-air cubicle.

It wasn't uncommon for half of the forty or so software engineers on the sixteenth floor to be in the metaverse at any given time. But the idea of gaming during work time, for research or not, made Tony a little uncomfortable.

This didn't apply now, however. At just after two in the morning nobody but Jake was around. HVG didn't hold normal office hours. They were a results-oriented company, and nobody cared if you rolled in at six am or noon so long as you got your work done.

Somewhere tucked in the dark recesses of his mind, Tony knew that his behavior was bordering on obsessive.

He also knew that the same thing had happened at his last job.

The job with those pricks who had stolen his game and given him nothing.

Nothing.

But this was different.

HVG was different.

The metaverse was different.

It wasn't just a game. It was another life. A *better* life. The great equalizer.

IRL, everyone started at different levels. Some were lucky and had rich parents, others were born in a ditch to a crack-addicted mother and no father in sight.

But in the game, in the metaverse, everyone started at zero. And that was the true American dream. Work hard. Move up.

It didn't matter who your parents were, what school you went to, where you got your degree from—hell, it didn't even matter if you had a degree.

All you had to do was put the time and effort in and you could succeed.

You could win.

Tony would do what he promised. He would build a bridge across the uncanny valley, and he would help create a metaverse that was indistinguishable from reality.

When Tony had been a young boy, he'd read something that had blown his mind and changed the trajectory of his life forever. It was what had gotten him interested in computers and computer programming. It was the simple theory that if you believed it was scientifically possible, maybe not now, maybe not in a hundred years, but eventually, for a computer to create a universe as complex as our own, then it follows that it could create an infinite number of said universes. In the future, a more advanced being could create such worlds on their supercomputers with the ease of someone doodling in MS Paint on their eight-year-old IBM Thinkpad today.

And if that were true, then what are the odds that this world, our world, was the only real one?

Effectively zero.

And if that wasn't meta, what was?

Tony was smirking when he picked up the VR goggles. And he was smiling a smile that reached his eyes and activated all twenty facial muscles when he dropped into the metaverse.

Chapter 24

USE. ABUSE. WORK.

Those were Chase Adams' three outlets. Dr. Matteo had identified them instantly, and he had made Chase aware of them. But this self-awareness came at a cost.

Knowing what you were addicted to could help you avoid them. It could also drive you to them.

After leaving Louisa's, Chase didn't go home. Instead, she drove to New York City, a place she hadn't been in a long time.

A place that brought back mixed feelings.

She drove through some of the seedier neighborhoods, slowing as she passed the darkening alleyways. The memories conjured by these locations surprisingly had nothing to do with her time as an NYPD Detective. Instead, she was reminded of Seattle.

Chase had always wanted to be in the FBI because she knew that they had the best chance of finding her sister. But she was continually turned down by the bureau with them repeatedly citing her lack of experience. So, Chase became a cop, taking the first job she was offered: a NARC in Seattle.

This was during the time that the opioid crisis was just starting to peak. Her superiors, trying, and failing miserably to stop the trend, realized that Chase's special talents could be put to better use than sniffing out marijuana on the street.

Mainly, her youth and attractiveness.

Chase had been on the job for less than a year before it was suggested that she go undercover.

The FBI wanted experience, and that's what Chase got... in the worst possible way.

On several occasions—no, more than several—Chase's addictions had nearly cost her her life.

Chase trained her eyes straight ahead.

But that was all in the past.

Wasn't it?

Her cell phone rang but the number wasn't programmed into her phone, so she ignored it.

Chase was thinking more and more about running. There was some truth to the adage that you can't run from your problems, but sometimes a change of scenery—maybe of names, too—was all you needed.

A fresh start... people said that, too.

It would be hard on Georgina, especially now that she was established and going to a regular school.

But she'd get over it. She'd have to.

The issue was money. Chase still had some stashed away, but her hospital bills had taken a huge bite out of her savings.

As she drove, Chase subconsciously reached up and massaged the spot near her collar bone where Bridget, who had been suffering from induced Cotard's Syndrome, had tried to murder her.

The sick woman had come close. But Chase was nothing if not resilient.

She'd survived much, much more than a knife nicking her carotid.

Almost all of her money had come from playing online poker. Seattle PD, the NYPD, and the FBI for that matter were known for a lot of things, but not their competitive salaries.

Chase had recently tried to get back into the game, but things had changed. It was considerably more difficult, especially at the higher stakes. The other players, if they were indeed players and not bots, just didn't make mistakes. Using game theory optimization, they seemed to make the best possible decision in all scenarios.

That meant that someone like Chase, who was more of a 'feel' player, would get lucky every once in a while, but like more chance-based casino games, you would eventually lose to the odds.

Odds were king.

She needed money. Lots of it. Enough to go somewhere—

Her phone rang again and even though she didn't recognize the number, she saw that it was coming from a Nevada area code.

Chase pulled over to the side road and answered.

"Hello?"

"Chase?"

Like the number, Chase didn't recognize the voice, either.

"Who is this?"

"It's Stu. Stu Barnes."

Chase fell silent as she pictured the handsome man in his sixties. And then she started to contemplate the coincidence of thinking about poker and the man who had staked her into a deadly game calling her at that very moment.

"Chase? You there? I'm in trouble. I'm in trouble and I need your help."

The seriousness of the man's voice dashed silly notions of coincidences.

"Yeah, I'm here. Tell me."

Chase listened intently as Stu told her about being charged, about the evidence against him, and him adamantly stating that he was not guilty.

While their interactions were limited, and often blurred by consumption, Chase knew Stu to be a lot of things.

Trusting, generous, and confident came to mind.

Murderer did not.

When Chase spoke next, it was with two things in mind: one, she owed him. She owed this man a lot. Two, he had money.

A lot.

"What can I do?"

"My lawyers… they're not optimistic. They say the evidence—Chase, they say evidence can bury me. The only chance we have is to find out who really killed Jake Hollister. That's the only way they think I'm going to go free."

With Stu's financial resources, Chase knew that he could afford to hire the best PIs in Nevada—no, *all* the PIs in Nevada.

And yet, he was calling her.

Why?

As if reading Chase's mind, Stu said, "I don't know who to trust—except for you. I can trust you, Chase. And you… well, I know that you won't stop until you find out who did this."

Chase closed her eyes.

"Will you help me?" Stu asked.

Chase wasn't well versed with Nevada law, but she thought that sixty days was a reasonable time frame from arraignment to trial. Probably on the short side, but still, she didn't have sixty days.

She didn't even have thirty.

Chase had two weeks.

"Chase? Please."

Chase's eyes snapped open.

"I can do it. I can help, but I can't do it alone. There are a couple of other people I need to bring in. Is that going to work for you? I trust them."

Stu cleared his throat.

"If you trust them, then, yeah, I have no problem with that. I'll cover all expenses, of course, and—"

"Just send me your address. We need to start yesterday."

Chase hung up before either of them could contemplate just how strange this entire conversation had been.

Then she made another call and a man answered on the first ring.

"Floyd? It's Chase. I need your help."

Chapter 25

IT WASN'T LIKE BEING TRANSPORTED into a different world. It was like being transported into the same world... only different. How, exactly, Tony couldn't say. It definitely wasn't the lack of realism. The HVG metaverse was indistinguishable from reality. As Tony Metcalfe stood outside the HVG headquarters he was awestruck by how much the building looked like it did in real life. The glass was so perfectly reflective that Tony thought he could feel the sunlight heating his skin.

Someone had made some major upgrades.

The inside of the building was equally as detailed as the outside and Tony quickly felt the barrier between reality and the game dissolving.

This is amazing, he thought. He looked down at his hands and turned them over, marveling at how lifelike they were.

"Good morning," a pleasant female voice said.

Tony glanced at Gina who was standing at her post behind the glass desk.

"M-morning," he said hesitantly.

Feeling slightly disoriented now, Tony got into the elevator and hit the number 16. When the doors opened moments later, he was surprised to see Jake waiting for him, a wide grin on his face.

"Jesus," Tony said. He reached out and grazed Jake's cheek with his fingertips. "You seem so real."

Jake's smile faltered and he pulled away.

"Because I am real."

"No, seriously, Jake, I can't even tell that this is the metaverse. The changes, like, it must have—what? What's wrong?"

The corner of Jake's lips had turned downward.

"Remember the rules," he reminded Tony in a whisper.

Tony was instantly remorseful.

"Of course, of course. I'm sorry."

And then he mentally checked off the three golden rules of the metaverse: one, always stay in character; two, no killing other characters; three, you can only be one character at a time. No swapping out characters on the fly.

There were, of course, other rules, but these were buried in the terms of service and pretty much ubiquitous for all massively multiplayer online games: you had to be 18 to play, no hate speech, no overtly sexual behavior, and basically anything offensive could get you reported and suspended or even banned.

"What are you doing here so late, anyway?" Jake asked.

"Working on that problem, you know?"

Tony was hesitant to say exactly what the problem was because it fell in a strange gray area. In the metaverse, people had jobs, just like in real life. There were cops, judges, even computer programmers. But rarely was there a computer programmer working on the actual game while they were in the game.

It was a bit of a mind meld.

Jake cleared up this discrepancy pretty quickly.

"Uncanny valley? Any development on that?"

Tony shook his hand.

"As I said earlier, I'm trying everything. I'm pulling data from the HVG archives from their other games, trying to figure out what worked and what didn't. The real sticking point is getting from here," Tony put the blade of his hand on his nose just below his eyes and then raised it over his head, "to here. Nothing seems to work to connect the eyes to the mouth, you know?"

Jake nibbled on the inside of his cheek, which was something he'd never seen his boss do before.

It made him nervous.

"No, no, there is progress. I'm making progress, things are getting better, but it's just gonna take—"

Jake waved a hand.

"I know you've been working your ass off. Don't think that your long hours aren't being noticed, either. They are. But burnout is a real thing, Tony. You should think about taking a little break. Nothing huge, just a little time off. Refresh your mind."

"You're still here," Tony pointed out.

Jake smiled.

"Yeah, but I'm not *reaaally* working."

Tony was intrigued.

"Tell me more," he pressed.

Jake appeared to wrestle with this for a moment before he shrugged and led Tony over to his desk.

"It's a work in progress," he said excitedly. "Kind of a passion project that's outside the purview of what we do here at Happy Valley. But if you promise not to say anything…"

Tony crossed himself.

"I swear."

Jake was clearly conflicted, which only made Tony want to see what his boss was working on even more.

"Jake, I won't say anything. You can trust me."

Jake assessed him with one squinted eye and then glanced around nervously. Tony did the same, but their apprehension was unwarranted; just like in the real world, at this hour, HVG was practically empty.

It was just the two of them.

"All right," Jake said, unable to keep the excitement from his voice. "It's a new kind of metaverse."

Try as he might, Tony couldn't keep the disappointment from his face.

A new metaverse? What's wrong with the old one?

"No, *no*," Jake held up a finger, "this is different. You know the rules we talked about earlier?"

Tony nodded.

"Yeah, the three golden rules."

"Well, what if there was a metaverse with only *one* rule?" Jake put a hand on Tony's shoulder and squeezed. "And this one rule is, you get a single chance, that's it. When it's over, it's done."

Tony glanced up at his boss.

"What do you mean?"

"What I mean, is that you get to create one character and that's it. When they're toast, they're dead, or they're stuck or whatever, you can't play anymore."

Tony wanted to share his boss' enthusiasm, but he was too tired to fake it.

"Uhh, I dunno, they tried that with hackers in Call of Duty. People get banned and they just make a new profile, get dummy phone numbers and they're back in a few days."

Jake's smile grew.

"Not if we have a hardware lock."

"Hardware lock?"

"Yeah, it's complicated, but in order to play in this metaverse, you need to grant the program access to your GPU, CPU, and peripheral serial numbers. You can't fake those. It registers them with you and your character. We're also working on some pretty advanced biometrics so that you can't even get a new computer and try to run it on that, you'll just be locked out."

Tony had heard rumors of technology such as this, but in the past, it had been linked to software and was designed to help prevent piracy. This was a different use entirely.

"Okay, but why does that matter? Why is it so important that you only get one chance?"

"Because of the beta," Jake informed him.

Tony still wasn't getting it.

"Beta?"

"Okay, okay." Jake exhaled loudly and he looked around again. "Between me and you, I had some people try out an early version of this metaverse—beta testing, you know? Like, *real* early. I just wanted to see if they liked it, liked the idea of it, if there was a market for it, that sort of thing, before I put all this work in. I told them that this was different than the HVG metaverse, that this was a world where they could do whatever they wanted. And I granted them anonymity just to appease any concerns they might have. Tony, get this: they loved it. They fucking loved it." Jake's eyes sparkled now. "Yeah, they were reserved at first, but then I told them to look inward and reminded them that this was a world where they could fulfill their deepest, darkest desires and fantasies. Once they got the hang of it, Tony, you're not going to believe the amount of time they spent online."

Jake inserted a pregnant pause here.

"How many hours?" Tony asked, brow furrowing.

Jake shook his head.

"Not hours. *Days*. They stayed logged on for *days*."

Tony scoffed.

"C'mon."

"No, I'm not kidding. The average daily play time was twenty-four hours. Twenty-four hours of straight gameplay was the *average* time spent per day. Tony, this is ridiculous. The average *session* time? Like, the amount of time between when they dropped in and when they finally logged off? Twenty-nine hours."

It was ridiculous but also impossible. Even the HVG metaverse numbers, and they had the best numbers in the genre, weren't close to this—not even a quarter as high.

"I know, I know, but I double-checked. I ran everything twice, three times. Five, ten. I checked and checked. One person played for eighty-eight hours without even a single pause."

"That's insane. And it's not a glitch?"

Jake laughed.

"Yeah, insane. And, no, not a glitch." He cocked his head. "But it didn't last."

"What happened?"

"The thing is it was fun for a while. It was mad, like, it de-generated into some pretty gnarly shit, crazy shit, but then people would get into these situations and just quit. They'd start a new character and do some other shit and then quit again." Jake finally let go of Tony's shoulder and scratched his chin. "Tony, let me ask you something: why do people like to go skydiving?"

"I have no idea."

This was the truth: Tony preferred to spend his time in front of a computer. Jumping out of a plane with only a parachute on your back made no sense to him.

"C'mon, play along."

"Because it's fun?" Tony suggested.

"Right and..." Jake waved his hand in a little circle.

"It's... dangerous?"

Now, Jake pointed at him.

"Right, it's dangerous. There's a consequence, you know? Like, you could die. Rare, true, but you *could*. That adds to the allure, the excitement. That's what I think went wrong with

Cerberus version one. There were no consequences… if you got into a fight or—okay, I'll give you a real example. There was this one guy who started hunting people in the city, like pure Rambo-styles? It got crazy. He was literally decapitating people in the street. Covered in blood and gore. Well, as you might expect, the cops, mostly NPCs, eventually circled in and he just quit. Started again. And that's when I knew that I had to make some consequences, to add an element of danger. Hence the hardware lock. Tony, if we can get this up and going, it's going to be huge. *Huge*."

We, he said 'we'.

Tony's heart was racing, and his throat was suddenly dry. Jake was onto something and if his numbers were even half as good as he claimed, he was onto something massive. His eyes fell on the VR goggles lying on Jake's desk and he subconsciously started to reach for them.

"Is it—"

Jake stayed his hand.

"No, it's not ready. Cerberus v2 isn't even in beta, and it's only me who goes in there now. But it's good. Really good, Tony. Graphics, environment, everything is better in this version. When it's ready, I'll let you try it. But… there are some kinks."

Ah, there it was.

"Oh, yeah, right. I'm working on it."

Jake wasn't interested in the uncanny valley just for the HVG metaverse but for his own creation.

For Cerberus.

And it made sense. In the HVG metaverse, having a secretary smile at you and look a little off in doing it was one thing— it didn't necessarily make you want to quit. But if you were

Rambo decapitating NPCs in the streets and they didn't seem to care?

That wouldn't be fun at all.

No consequences, as Jake had said.

Sure, his boss had also used the term 'we', but there was something implicit that went unsaid: you conquer this problem, Tony, you fix the uncanny valley, and you're in.

If that happens, then we're in this together.

This is going to be massive, Tony thought. *Way bigger than that stupid fucking cell phone game.*

"I'm going to figure this out. I'm going to—"

Something that Jake had just said resonated with Tony and he paused.

I told them to look inward and reminded them that this was a world where they could fulfill their deepest, darkest desires and fantasies...

"That's it," Tony said softly, and Jake raised an eyebrow.

"Now, I'm the one who's lost."

"I think I know how to solve it," he elaborated. "I think I can solve the uncanny valley."

Before Jake could answer, Tony Metcalfe reached up and tore the goggles from his face.

And then he started to work on his idea with unrelenting fervor.

You won't be disappointed, Jake. Hiring me was the best thing that you and Happy Valley ever did. We're in this together.

We're in Cerberus together.

Chapter 26

"**THANK YOU SO MUCH FOR** coming."

Stu was clearly uncertain whether a hug or a handshake was appropriate in this instance. Chase was all hugged out and even though her 'voodoo' had become less common and intense, and perhaps even compromised by Cerebrum, she didn't really want to test this theory with skin-on-skin contact.

She opted for a simple nod.

"We should probably get started right away," she said, maintaining an air of professionalism.

As she spoke, Chase peered over Stu's shoulder and looked into the man's formidable home. At the same time, Stu glanced past her.

Chase was searching for a team of lawyers, while Stu was trying to identify the 'others' that she'd promised to bring along with her.

Unfortunately, Stu came up empty.

Things with Floyd just hadn't gone according to plan.

No—that was an understatement.

Things with Floyd had gone terribly. He was still pissed. Very pissed at her for sneaking onto the last case and lying to him.

Thinking of the Cotard's case triggered a numbness near her throat and Chase massaged her collar bone to try to get the feeling back. The stitches were healing well, but there would be a scar.

Add it to the list.

"Come in, come in." Stu led her inside his mansion, taking a final glance behind her before closing the door. "This is Will Porter, he's a long-time friend and part of my legal team."

The man who offered his hand held a striking resemblance to Stu. So much so, that they could have been brothers. Chase offered him the same courteous nod as she had Stu, avoiding his outstretched palm.

When she introduced herself, she did so as Chase Adams, being conscientious not to mention the FBI. She didn't say she was a friend, either.

Chase settled on acquaintance.

Next came Colin Sachs and Mike Portnoy, who were typical suits. According to Will, they were also the brains of the defense, even though for the most part, they elected to remain relatively quiet and stay in the background.

Chase got the impression that they weren't keen on her involvement.

She didn't care.

Will, however, was very open. He almost seemed relieved by her presence. After introducing the other lawyers, the man waved a hand over stacks of evidence piled on a marble countertop.

"This is all of the disclosure."

Chase gave it a quick once over.

"I went through the important stuff you sent me while on the plane." She turned to face Stu. "It's pretty damning."

Stu screwed up his lips and nodded.

"I know. *I know.*" The second iteration was spoken with more gusto. "But I didn't do it. I didn't kill anybody, Chase." Stu reached over and opened the first file. Inside was a photograph of the deceased, Jake Hollister. Stu angrily motioned toward the image. "I don't even know who this is."

The DA had an entire timeline set-up, with individual pieces of evidence to justify each step. It wasn't what Chase would call 'iron-clad', but it was far from a weak case.

And the video evidence… that was the most damning. Jurors loved videos.

Stu was fucked.

After a long exhale, Chase thought of what to do next, of how to get started. This had occupied most of her mind during the flight, but she hadn't come up with anything concrete.

Stu tapped Jake's photo absently then shut the file.

That was the answer, of course.

Chase didn't believe that this man, someone who had once held her while she wept, was capable of murder.

But she had to know for sure.

Two things were still holding her back, however: one, the visceral revulsion that she felt when she'd touched the corpse *in the morgue in Columbus.*

"I do not eat, for I am dead. I do not sleep, for I am dead. I do not bathe, for I am dead."

Even thinking about it now was enough to cause her hackles to rise.

Two, what would she do if her vision told her that Stu was lying? What would she do if she uncovered that Stu had actually murdered Jake Hollister?

There was only one way to find out.

"Stu, we're going to get you through this," Chase said, moving closer to the man.

And then she awkwardly took Stu's hand between hers.

"Please… don't hurt me. Please."

The bridge was well-lit, but the man's face was oddly shadowed.

The gun… the gun…

Chase let go of Stu's hand. She was forcing it. There had been a flash of something, a smattering of stars maybe, or maybe not. The problem was, she didn't know what this meant. It could be that her ability was gone, or it could be that Stu was innocent.

Well, that was a lot of help.

Chase realized that all four men were looking at her now, queer expressions on their tanned faces.

If you think that's weird...

The pressure was on. Of all people Stu could have called or hired, he'd gone with her. And Chase had no fucking idea what to do. Everything about this was foreign, from the luxurious kitchen in which they stood, to having three lawyers to deal with, to not being here in an official capacity...

There was one common thread, however.

"Can I see that? The folder?"

Stu passed it over and Chase opened it.

A body. That was the thing that this case had in common.

Jake Hollister...

He looked more like a frat boy with his blond hair and prefect teeth than a computer engineer.

But he was still dead.

And Chase worked well with the dead.

We're going about this all wrong... we need to learn about Jake and why he was targeted and not Stu.

The man's death wasn't random. There was no doubt that Stu had been set up, but this struck Chase as two birds, one—two—bullets scenario.

"Who was he? Who was Jake?" she asked absently.

"Jake Hollister was the lead software engineer at Happy Valley Gaming," Will answered. "A company that Stu owns and is also the CEO."

Stu threw his arms up.

"CEO! I visited the place once! That's it. A business adviser told me to expand into the VR realm. I barely remember the place let alone what they do."

"Well, Jake's the key to figuring this thing out," Chase said. Now she was the one tapping the photo. "We need to go to Happy Gaming or whatever—what? What's wrong?"

Both Stu and Will were frowning.

"That's gonna be a problem," Stu said. He teased up the leg of his slacks, revealing an ankle monitor. "In addition to $10 million bond, I'm not allowed to leave my house."

Chase cursed.

"Well, that's going to—" Someone knocked loudly on the front door. "You expecting somebody?"

Stu shook his head and then cowered just a little when the knocking continued. Will made a move toward the door, but Chase stopped him.

She had a hand on the butt of her gun—FBI or not, she always carried it with her—when she pulled the door wide.

"What the hell?" Chase took two steps back. "What are you guys doing here?"

Chapter 27

Fueled by Adderall and energy drinks, Tony worked throughout the night. At some point, Jake must've left because when Tony saw him again, he was wearing a different shirt and pants.

"You have to see this, Jake—you *have* to," Tony said excitedly, licking his lips between each word. Jake's eyes wandered briefly to the stack of empty cans on Tony's desk, and he subconsciously scooped them into the garbage. Several fell on the floor, but he made no move to pick them up.

"You been at it all night?"

Tony nodded enthusiastically.

"Yeah, yeah—but I-I-I think I did it, man."

"Did what?"

"It was—it was like what-what-what you said when you were talking about—" Tony caught himself and lowered his voice. "You know, the special project. Anyway, you were talking about looking inward."

Jake scratched the back of his neck. He looked confused and more than a little uncomfortable.

"I said that?"

"Yeah, you did. Check it out." Tony spun his chair around but went a little too far and had to adjust to center himself with his keyboard and screen. He clicked a few buttons and two images of his face appeared side-by-side on the monitor. "One of these is an actual video of me, the other is CGI. Look the same, though, right?" He didn't wait for a response. "Now, watch."

First, the version of Tony on the right started speaking—*I love Happy Valley Gaming*—when that was done, the left said the exact same thing.

Tony, beaming now, spun around.

"Which is the real me, Jake?"

Jake didn't hesitate.

"The left."

Tony snapped his fingers.

"Correct," he said with a smile. "But how'd you know?"

Unlike his previous reply, Jake took his time with this one. But this delay evidently did not translate into increased insight.

"I—I'm not sure. I think maybe the mouth is different?"

Tony shook his head.

"It's not. Watch."

This time, Tony covered the top half of the screen, everything from the nose up, with a sheet of paper and replayed the videos.

"Yeah, they are the same," Jake concluded. "So, why—"

"Now, watch this." Tony pulled up two more videos and played them in succession. They were similar to the first, but instead of saying *I love Happy Valley Gaming*, they said, *I am the uncanny valley*. "Well? What do you think?"

Jake leaned closer to the computer monitor and asked Tony to play both video games again.

"They're the same," he concluded. "I don't notice a difference."

"Do they look strange?"

"No, they look normal. And identical."

Tony laughed a giddy laugh.

"You're right—they are identical. But I never said those words."

"I don't get it."

"They're AI—I never said those words. It's all fake."

"No way."

"Yes, way."

Jake nudged Tony so that he could get even closer to the screen.

"Play them again."

Tony did and they were no less impressive this time around.

"I-I don't believe you," Jake said, crossing his arms over his chest. He watched Tony closely as if trying to pick out differences between the man's real face and the supposedly digital version.

"Watch this."

Tony quickly swapped the videos of himself for one of Jake Hollister.

He pressed play.

"Tony Metcalfe is the best computer programmer in the whole world!" AI Jake proclaimed with a smile.

When Jake didn't say anything, Tony looked at his boss. The uneasy expression on the man's handsome face inspired doubt.

"It's—it's not good?"

Jake shuddered.

"No, it's incredible. It's a perfect deep fake. How did you— how did you do it?"

Tony's excitement returned and he licked his lips again.

"It's mostly in the eyes, right? The eyes and the tiny muscles around the eyes are a bit off for most of these models. It's also the details in the irises or whatever, it's the micro dilations, the way that the human tracks an object… to be honest, Jake? It's a host of other things, too, but I'm not really sure what. I just developed a program that analyzed hundreds of hours of data and use that as the basis for the model."

"Hundreds of hours of data… from where? From whom?" Jake asked.

Tony laughed again. The sound was high and tight, a clear indication that the stimulants were starting to wear off.

"That's the beautiful part. It's from you. It's a video of you."

Jake's patience was wearing thin and his arms, which were still laced over his chest, tensed.

"I don't have hundreds of hours of video."

"Ah, but you do." Tony picked up the VR helmet off his desk. "From here."

"Tony, I'm not—"

"Right, sorry. Last night, when you said to look inward, I thought about how the helmet tracks your movements, right? Well, there are actually a bunch of infrared cameras that are constantly scanning and recording your face and your eyes as you look out into the metaverse. At first, I thought, there's no way that this data is stored, but it is. I found it. It's recorded. So, I just used my program to develop a model based on hundreds of hours of your data. But here's the beauty of it, I can access data from every single person who has dropped into the metaverse. We're not talking hundreds of hours, but millions. It'll take some time but with my program and HVG data? We can make NPCs that no one will ever know are fake."

As a joke, Tony played the video of Jake saying he was the world's best programmer again.

But Jake wasn't smiling. He wasn't rejoicing in the discovery, either.

"You've been up all night?"

Tony didn't understand the question. Who cares if he'd been up for a month? What he'd done was about to change everything. It would solidify the HVG metaverse as *the* metaverse.

Not to mention what it could do for Cerberus.

"Tony, you look like you need some rest. Why don't you head home, take a shower, a nap. Come back tomorrow."

Tony frowned.

"What?"

"Go home, Tony."

"I don't get it... this is what you asked for." Tony's voice began to escalate. "What *everyone* asked for."

Jake unfurled his arms and dropped a hand onto Tony's shoulder.

"Look, you did great, you really did. But now you need a rest. I'll sit on this... it's not going anywhere. And when you come back, we can look at it with fresh eyes, okay?" He gave Tony's shoulder a patronizing squeeze. "Seriously, this is great. But you need to sleep."

Tony looked at the computer screen, then back at Jake.

Was he missing something? Why wasn't Jake more excited?

"I—I guess."

"That's right. Now, go on. Get some sleep, you deserve it."

Maybe it was exhaustion or just the come down from all the stimulants, but for some reason what Jake was saying started to make some sense.

What was the harm in waiting another day? When he was fresher, they could put a presentation together and share this discovery with everyone.

In the end, it didn't really matter whether this was what Tony wanted or not. Because before he knew it, Jake had led him to the front doors and now he was looking back at his own warped reflection in the polished glass of HVG headquarters.

Chapter 28

"YOU DIDN'T THINK WE'D LET a little lady do this all on her own, did ya?" Tate Abernathy said with a grin. Chase saw Floyd standing behind his partner, but he refused to meet her eyes. "So, what are we up to?" Tate said, brushing by Chase and entering Stu's home. "Just keeping another billionaire out of jail, is that right? Wouldn't want another Epstein on our hands?"

"Who are you?" Will Porter snapped. "Mrs. Adams, this—"

"Tate Abernathy, FBI. And the shy guy outside is Floyd Montgomery, also FBI. But we're not here, officially, of course." Tate looked over his shoulder at Chase and offered her a wink. "Just helping out a friend."

"I don't know what you think—"

"It's okay," Stu said, calming Will's temper. "They're with Chase."

Sort of…?

Chase couldn't believe that Floyd had shown up. And he'd brought Tate, no less?

"Stu Barnes, Will Porter, Colin Sachs, and Mike Portnoy."

As Tate saluted the lawyers and repeated his name, Floyd entered the mansion, still not looking at Chase.

"Floyd, I didn't mean to—"

"It's fine," Floyd hissed. Clearly, it wasn't fine. But he was here, and that was something. "Stu, it's good to see you again."

Stu and Floyd shook hands.

"Oh, you two know each other?" Tate said. "Where'd you meet? Plenty of Fish?"

Stu and Floyd looked uncomfortable but only Chase knew this wasn't because of the crude joke. It was likely because the two men were thinking back to when they'd first met... to searching for what they'd then expected to be Chase's corpse.

Instead, they'd found her alive—barely—dressed only in her underwear, her bruised and battered body lying in an abandoned gravel pit.

There'd been enough heroin coursing through her blood to kill a horse. Fortunately, it was just shy of the lethal dose for a lifelong addict.

"Right, well, thanks for coming. Let's get started," Chase said, trying to change the subject. This wasn't about her. This was about helping Stu stay out of jail. With this in mind, she spent the next ten minutes outlining the case against him, including showing them the images that Detective Tolliver had shown her.

When she was down, Tate whistled because, well, he was Tate.

"Damn. That's a lot of evidence."

"My client is not guilty," Will said abruptly.

Tate was a good two inches taller and ten years younger than the lawyer. But the latter refused to be intimidated.

"Are we doing that?" Tate asked, shaking his head ever so slightly.

"Doing what?" Will demanded.

"That, *my client is not guilty*, stuff," Tate said in a faux British accent. "If we're going to get hung up on technicalities, formalities, practicalities, and professionalities, finding out what really happened is going to be hella difficult."

"I understand," Stu said. And then he addressed his lawyer. "Will, I trust Chase. And if these are her friends, I trust them, too."

"They're FBI. They work for—" Will started to protest but Floyd interjected.

"We're not here officially." He finally looked at Chase. Glared, more like it. "This is completely off the books. Both Tate and I took some personal days."

"I will make sure to compensate you for—"

Now Tate cut Stu off.

"We'll work out the details later. First, because you are 'not guilty'," he framed the term with air quotes, "we need to find out who is. And that starts with learning more about the victim."

Chase wasn't surprised that Tate had come to the same conclusion she had—in fact, she would have been concerned if he hadn't—but the speed was impressive.

"That's exactly what I was saying," Chase agreed. "Stu, is it possible to log into employment records remotely? Do you still have access to Happy Valley Gaming computers, servers, that sort of thing?"

Stu was about to answer but then Will grimaced, and he addressed his friend instead.

"What? What is it, Will?"

Will sighed.

"Well, unfortunately, there is a clause in your contract, in most contracts, really, at least at the C-level, put in place after the whole #metoo movement that—"

"I thought time was of the essence, here?" Tate held his palms out and craned his neck forward.

Will stiffened.

"It is. We're moving as—"

"Then stop fucking talking in riddles," Tate snapped. "Just tell us what you mean."

The lawyer's face turned scarlet, but Stu encouraged him to continue.

"Fine," Will said petulantly. "Stu, you're still CEO of AI Integrations, the parent company of Happy Valley Gaming, but you've been suspended indefinitely. The board has stripped you of all authority and they've revoked your access to the building and your company accounts have been frozen. Nothing personal, just business."

Chase couldn't tell whether Stu was upset by this removal of power or because their job just became exponentially more difficult.

"Can we subpoena employment records, then?" she asked.

"On it," Colin Sachs said from the kitchen table. "Request has been submitted but it will take time."

"He speaks—I thought he was just a statue," Chase heard Tate grumble under his breath. She couldn't help but smile. "What if we went in with our badges, you know? Would they let the FBI into the building?"

"But we're not with the FBI," Floyd reminded Tate.

Tate rolled his eyes.

"Right. Not officially."

"To be honest, I don't know if it will help. I've been doing a little reading on the detective who arrested you?" Will said.

"Tolliver," Stu offered.

"Yeah, Tolliver. Well, he has a reputation for slamming pretty much anyone who steps out of line with obstruction. Seems he has a cozy relationship with the ADA, too, and they actually go through with some of these charges."

Tate looked at Chase.

"Translation?"

Chase was prepared to answer but Will did the honors.

"I'd bet that Detective Tolliver told everyone at Happy Valley to keep their mouths shut. If they start yapping, they're likely to spend the weekend behind bars."

"Hardly seems fair," Tate remarked without venom. "What does Happy Valley do, anyway?"

"Make games, but their flagship product is their realistic metaverse," Will replied.

"What do you know about the metaverse, Floyd?" Chase asked.

The man's face said it all. She'd hoped that being as young as he was that Floyd would have some experience with the altered reality simulation, but she'd forgotten where he'd come from.

"Is it for porn?" Tate asked and Chase shot him a look. "Kidding."

"I think Tate and I should head over to Happy Valley. Even if they're averse to speaking to us, might still be things we can discover about Jake. Floyd, why don't you stick around with Stu and Will and take a deeper dive into the metaverse," Chase suggested.

Floyd held her gaze for a moment, then shook his head.

"The w-way I see it, the main piece of evidence against Stu is the videotape. That's the m-most d-damning. And it can't be a coincidence that both Jake and Stu work for an AI company and the video is clearly faked. I'm going to go check out the location where the shot was taken from, see if maybe it was tampered with."

This was a great idea, but Chase was concerned.

"Alone?"

Floyd's upper lip curled.

"It's the middle of the day and I'm an FBI Agent—I think I'll be okay," he said, clearly insulted by her insinuation.

While the man's false bravado helped him save face in front of Stu and his cadre of lawyers, it did nothing to quell Chase's apprehension. Before she could argue, however, Tate whispered in her ear.

"He's in therapy."

"What?"

Tate cleared his throat.

"I said, while Chase and I are talking to some geeks and Floyd is looking into the cameras, can you suits figure out what the hell this metaverse thing is all about?"

"Yeah, sure," Will said through pursed lips. "I'll see if we can get a computer engineer or programmer to help us out."

They were nearly at the door when Tate stopped and held up a finger.

"Oh, but if there is porn? I get first dibs, alright?"

Chapter 29

TONY COULDN'T SLEEP. HE WASN'T sure why he thought that it would even be remotely possible.

The metaverse was the great equalizer.

It was also the future.

In a few years, the idea of leaving one's home to experience anything will be as foreign as going shopping in an actual store. You want to watch the Vegas Golden Knights play hockey? Put your goggles on and you can sit anywhere you want in the arena. What about a concert? A private concert with the Weeknd? Sure, on demand.

Sex... that was the big one. The porn industry drives computer innovation and the metaverse was like one giant orgy.

The one drawback was that it just wasn't real. Under certain circumstances, *specific* circumstances, usually involving psychedelics, you could trick your body and mind into thinking that VR was a new type of reality.

But most of the time, there was a nagging voice in the back of your head that just wouldn't shut up and stop reminding you that no matter how pleasurable the experience was, it simply wasn't real.

Tony poured himself a glass of whiskey.

That was before.

That was when the uncanny valley was something that nobody had been able to cross.

Until Tony Metcalfe had come along.

As he sipped his drink, Tony closed his eyes. He pictured Jake Hollister's face and heard his boss say the words: *Tony Metcalfe is the best computer programmer in the whole world!*

This is wrong, Tony thought. He opened his eyes and drank what was left in his glass. *We shouldn't be sleeping now. We need to be working. We need to be telling people about what I've done, what I've accomplished.*

Tony grabbed his VR helmet off his desk and slipped it over his head. Then he slid his wrists through the controller wrist straps and booted up. There were three seconds of loading time, during which he was visually stimulated by a rotating HVG logo and a brief ad about some new digital watch that you could purchase in-game.

Then he was in.

Happy Valley Gaming headquarters looked as impressive in the metaverse as it did in real life.

Indistinguishable, in fact.

Tony entered through the front doors and glanced at Gina behind the glass desk.

He smiled at her, and she smiled back.

"Good afternoon, Tony."

"Good afternoon to you too, Gina."

Tony used his ID card to unlock the subway-style turnstile and then took the elevator to the 16th floor. As usual, the place was buzzing with activity. After saying hi to a few friends, he wormed his way to Jake's desk.

The man was seated in front of his computer with his back to Tony.

"Jake?"

Jake turned. He'd been grinning but when he saw it was Tony, the expression vanished.

"Tony? I thought I told you to go get some rest."

"I can't sleep. I was thinking about what you said, about coming back to the uncanny valley tomorrow, but why wait? The faster we get to analyzing the footage, the faster we can make real changes to the metaverse."

Jake screwed up his face.

"What's wrong?" Tony said, his frustration mounting. "This is an incredible discovery. I thought you'd be happier. Wait—wait, you don't believe me, do you? You don't think I did it? You don't think that I managed to figure out the uncanny valley?"

"It's not—"

"That's it, alright. Jake, put your goggles on. I'm not cappin'. Trust."

"Tony, it's not that."

"Yeah, right. I get it, I get it. You don't think that me, Tony 'Nobody' Metcalfe, with no formal education, who got screwed out of millions in residuals from my last job, could figure out how to fix this problem." Jake tried to interrupt but Tony wouldn't let him get a word in. "Listen, I knew y'all would be skeptical, but I put a piece of code in the game already. Just a little tester to make some of the NPCs more believable. It won't be perfect yet because this is based on your data only, but... Jake, put the goggles on, and let's test it out."

"Tony. I'm sorry, but—"

"Try it!" Tony urged. "If it's not good, on God, I'll go to sleep, I promise."

Jake looked like he was about to complain, but Tony was already hurrying toward his desk.

"Drop in, Jake!" He put his VR helmet on. "Drop in!"

Three seconds later Tony was outside HVG headquarters again. He hurried through the front doors, once more said hello to Gina, and then found Jake by the elevators.

"Jake?"

Tony scanned his card to unlock the turnstile, but it beeped and the LED display flashed red. He tried to push the metal bar, but it didn't budge. He flashed his card again with the same result.

"Jake?"

His boss finally acknowledged him.

"I'm sorry, Tony. The thing is, there is no recording of facial expressions, eyes or nose or anywhere. HVG doesn't record anything from the metaverse. Period. It's in the TOS."

Tony frowned.

"No, it's there—it's recorded. All eye-tracking data. I found it and I used the data to create the video of you."

Jake shook his head.

"There isn't. I know because I'm the one who wrote the eye-tracking software code. *Nothing's* recorded. So, I don't know what you think you found or what you think you managed to create, but you didn't just stumble upon a solution to the uncanny valley hidden in some data recordings. C'mon, be real."

Tony couldn't believe his ears.

Or his eyes.

He squinted at Jake, paying particularly close attention to his micro-expressions.

"Wait? Is this some sort of joke? Are you an NPC?"

"Tony, I'm being serious."

And Jake looked it. He also looked real.

Tony Metcalfe is the best computer programmer in the whole world!

He swiped his card again, but it was apparent that his credentials had been blocked.

"I'm sorry, Tony, but we're going to have to let you go."

Tony's forehead broke out in a cold sweat. This was all too familiar to him.

"No," he stated flatly.

"I'm really sorry, I am, but we have a pretty solid honor code here at HVG. And we can't have someone telling lies. That'll compromise the team. You know how it is, just a little bit of bad code can ruin an entire program."

Tony growled and he reached for Jake, but the man simply backed up.

"No! Not again! This can't be happening *again!*"

Chapter 30

"THANKS FOR COMING," CHASE SAID. "I appreciate it."

"It was Floyd," Tate replied. "He convinced me."

Chase doubted it.

"Stu, he's a…" She let her sentence trail off.

What was Stu to her? A friend? Not really. An associate? That didn't quite work either.

One of many to whom she owed a favor was most accurate. It just didn't seem right to say it out loud.

"You don't need to explain anything to me. We might not know each other that well, Chase, but I know Floyd. And if he says you's good people, then you's good people."

Chase scoffed.

"Yeah, I don't think that's how Floyd would describe me."

"Caught me in a lie," Tate said with a grin. "Anyways, I just had to get away." He paused and Chase thought that what he said next was authentic. "You ever just need to get away, Chase?"

Every damn day.

Chase bit her tongue and an uncomfortable silence settled over the car. If Stitts had been beside her, the rest of the ride to Happy Valley Gaming would have remained quiet. But Tate wasn't Stitts.

"That's what this whole metaverse thing is all about, isn't it?" Tate said. "Getting away? Becoming someone else, somewhere else? Reminds me of The Matrix, remember that movie?"

Chase nodded. She knew exactly where this conversation was going but was helpless to stop it.

"Blue pill or red pill?" Tate mused. "You know that some people believe that the world we live in—the actual world, not the metaverse—is just a simulation? I'm not talking about the

Area 51 nutjobs either. Smart people. If that were the case, how would you know? How could you ever tell the difference?"

"Product placement?" Chase suggested with a shrug.

Tate laughed.

"Ha, yeah, Red Bull cans showing up everywhere as our almighty deity tries to stay awake while programming another terrorist attack."

Chase glanced over at Tate. He was staring out the window as he spoke, and she noticed a softness to his face that hadn't been there before. The man had a square jaw, a five o'clock shadow, bold features, but there was more to Tate Abernathy than good looks.

There was pain.

And that, Chase recognized almost immediately.

"Are you—"

"This is it," Tate said suddenly, pointing out the window.

Chase followed his finger.

Happy Valley Gaming was a four-story building seemingly made entirely from huge slabs of reflective glass. The expansive parking lot held dozens of cars, and as they parked, Chase noted that most were of the mid-luxury variety: BMWs, Audis, Teslas.

"Looks like Happy Valley is doing alright without their CEO," Tate remarked, clearly noticing the same thing.

Chase reached for the door handle then stopped and looked at Tate one last time before getting out into the hot sun.

"How do you want to handle this?"

Tate didn't hesitate.

"Absentee CEO accused of murdering trendy computer programmer? I think it's pretty obvious how to play this. You want me to lead?"

"Yeah, I'll sit back." Chase didn't mind playing second team this time around. She had much to learn about the metaverse and something was telling her that anything she could glean about the artificial world would come in handy later.

"You bring your badge?"

Chase reached into her pocket and pulled it out. Tate produced his own.

"See? We're bonding... now you're not the only one pretending to be on official business."

"What about Detective Tolliver?" Chase asked, remembering what Will had told her about the overzealous detective threatening to charge people with obstruction. She was pretty sure that the lawyer was referring to civilians, but the law applied to them as well.

"Local cops, real scary," Tate mocked.

As they walked toward the front of the reflective building, Chase noticed that Tate's posture was different. He was hunched forward a little.

"You okay? You're walking funny."

"Gas station sushi," he said. Chase had heard this line before but couldn't quite remember from where.

She let it go. They both had their secrets and Tate's digestive issues were none of her business.

The sliding glass doors opened as they approached, revealing a polished interior that Chase had imagined almost perfectly in her mind: an expensive frat house vibe, with too many TVs, too many computers, too many lights.

"Welcome to Happy Valley," a cheerful woman with short brown hair and freckles across her nose said cheerily. "How can I help you?"

Tate, now stern-faced, flashed his badge and Chase followed suit.

The woman's smile faltered when she saw the FBI insignia. "We're investigating Jake Hollister's murder." Her smile was gone completely now. "Did you know him?"

"Yes, of course. He was—" The woman looked skyward. "It's so strange speaking about him in the past tense. But Jake was great. Like, really great. Everyone will tell you that. I can't believe it—and the CEO? He did this? *Why?*"

Tate put an end to the woman's rambling.

"That's what we're trying to figure out. Did you know the CEO?" Tate's tone was hard and his use of 'CEO' instead of 'Stu' or 'Mr. Barnes' was deliberate.

"Never met the man. Like, ever. To be honest, I didn't even know who he was until—well, until this happened. I just thought—I just thought that Jake was in charge." She sniffed and brought a finger to her nose. As odd as the woman's behavior was, Chase thought it genuine. "And now—"

"What can you tell us about what Jake was working on?"

"Working on?" the woman said. Her eyebrows were finely tattooed, and they did a little dance up her forehead. "The metaverse. That's pretty much all we do here. But if you want to know specifics, I can't really help with that. I just work the front desk."

"Who worked most closely with Jake?" Tate continued.

"I'm not sure."

As Tate continued to ask questions that didn't seem to be going anywhere, Chase looked around. In addition to the TVs on the walls, she counted seven security cameras.

"Who worked under him, then?"

"That's… look, Happy Valley isn't like other companies. We have a pretty flat, like, org chart? There aren't any what you would call 'bosses' here. We are united in a common goal and are all working together to improve the metaverse."

Chase rolled her eyes. This was starting to sound more like a promotional brochure than an FBI inquisition—*unofficial* inquisition.

"You said that Jake was in charge," Tate noted.

"I know, I know. I guess technically he was the boss, but he didn't act like one."

"Right," Chase said. "Now, I get that there's no real boss, but is there someone with a little more authority that we can speak with?"

Out of the corner of her eye, she saw Tate look at her, but she kept her eyes trained on the woman's fine eyebrows.

"I'll call up."

As the secretary reached for the phone on her desk, Chase pointed at one of the security cameras, the one she was most interested in.

The one that was trained at a turnstile that looked more ornamental than a real security feature.

"We're also going to need your security footage."

"Not without a warrant."

The man who had spoken strode through the turnstile. Following closely behind him was the second half of the 2-for-1 Brook's Brothers' suit sale.

"We're with the FBI," Tate said, flashing his badge.

The man didn't even give the laminated card a cursory look.

"The security tapes were delivered to Detective Tolliver. If you want them, I suggest you ask the detective."

Chase frowned. She could only play second fiddle for so long.

"And you are...?"

"Legal."

Of course—*fucking lawyers.*

"Detective Tolliver didn't mention the FBI's involvement in Mr. Hollister's case," the second suit said.

"Right, well, here we are," Chase said cheerily. "Instead of making things difficult, why don't you just get us the tapes?"

"We have fully cooperated with LVPD in every way possible. However, due to the nature of our business, downtime must be limited. If you require anything from us or Happy Valley Gaming LLC, please contact Detective Tolliver."

"Why—"

Tate slid in front of Chase.

"Thank you, fellas."

He looked at the secretary who was holding the phone a foot away from her ear. As if just remembering that it was in her hand, she startled and hung it up.

"I'll walk them out."

Legal shot her a look but didn't say anything. They just stood there in a classic lawyer pose as the secretary unnecessarily led them to the automatic sliding doors.

"I can get you the tapes," the woman whispered when they were out of earshot of the two lawyers. "But not here. Everything is recorded here, and we've all been told not to speak to anyone about Jake."

"You want to meet at a bar or…?" Tate asked in an even quieter voice.

The woman looked almost appalled by the suggestion.

"A restaurant?" Chase offered.

The woman glanced over her shoulder. This idea was even more offensive, it seemed.

"No, no way. Not a real place."

What the fuck?

Seeing the look on their faces, the woman clarified, "The metaverse. I'll meet you in the metaverse after I get off work."

Chapter 31

"FIRED? Y-Y-YOU'RE JOKING."

"I'm sorry, Tony. This is no joke," Jake said.

"Mr. Metcalfe, please come with us."

Two rectangular men in matching outfits appeared out of nowhere.

"What the fuck is going on here?" Tony whined. He refused to believe that this was real. This *couldn't* be real.

HVG was different. They wouldn't fuck him out of the prestige he deserved.

They weren't like those other guys.

"Please, Jake, c'mon. I'm not lying—you saw the video."

Softness graced Jake's eyes for half a second, then it was gone.

"I saw a pretty good AI video... I guess? That's all I saw. I told you, the data you said you used just doesn't exist. HVG does not record the metaverse."

Tony gaped.

"It does! And pretty good? Really? That video—"

"Just get him out of here," Jake instructed the two security guards. "Tony, you'll receive your final paycheck in the mail."

"The *mail?*" Despite everything, Tony found this particularly insulting. Snail mail? Who used snail mail? Definitely not HVG, creator of the most immersive metaverse experience. And definitely not the man who had finally bridged the uncanny valley. "I don't get mail. I don't get *fucking* mail!"

The security guards passed through the turnstile and grabbed him roughly by the arms. Tony instinctively began to struggle, but they simply lifted him off his feet.

"Jake!" he shouted as they started to carry him toward the door. "Jake!"

But Jake didn't care. Jake never cared.

He just wanted Tony's code. That's all they ever wanted.

"Jake!"

The elevator pinged and a man with silver hair stepped out. He had a serious expression on his face. Jake immediately addressed him, and he nodded.

I know him… I know that man. Who is he? Who is he?

They neared the front desk, which was unoccupied for what Tony thought was the first time since joining the company. During the day, anyway. The pretty and peppy Gina was nowhere to be found. There was, however, a white, HVG-branded VR helmet sitting on top of the glass surface. And that's when Tony remembered: the good-looking man with the silver hair was none other than Stu Barnes, HVG's CEO.

Rage filled him to his core.

"You… stole… my… *code.*"

Tony broke free. He wasn't sure if he'd bucked or wriggled or simply slipped from the security guards' grasp. All he knew was that one second, they were holding him and the next they were not.

Tony snatched the VR mask and sprinted back toward Jake and Stu who were now deep in conversation. He was only aware of the fact that he was yelling something.

Neither man paid him any attention.

Even when Tony hurdled the turnstile and leaped at Jake, the two men failed to acknowledge him.

Tony was used to it—this had always been the case. His whole life, Tony Metcalfe had been ignored. All anybody ever wanted was to steal from him.

"You guys used me!" he shrieked. Now Jake had an expression of sheer amazement on his face. But it was too late. Tony was already on him. "You stole my code!"

All he could think about as he brought his hand gripping the VR helmet back was that once again, he'd been exploited.

But this time he vowed that they wouldn't get away with it.

"It's in here!" Tony swung the heavy mask in an exaggerated arc. It connected with the side of Jake's blond head and the man crumpled. "I solved it!" Another blow. "I did it! I solved the uncanny valley!" Blood sprayed his arms, but Tony kept on swinging. "I did it and you stole it from me!"

By the fifth strike, Jake's head had been reduced to a pulpy mess. All Tony could see was red and a smattering of pink. But even as he lifted the now mangled piece of electronic equipment, all cables and shards of plastic, his rage persisted.

The security guards were vaulting the turnstile behind him, but Tony had his eyes locked on Stu, who was cowering by the elevator, reaching behind him, and jamming the elevator call button repeatedly.

"You!" Jake hissed. He lumbered forward, blood dripping down his elbow, onto his hand, and then what was left of the VR mask. "You will pay. You'll—"

Something smashed into his back, sending Tony rocketing forward. Just before his head collided with Stu's sternum, he heard a loud, ear-piercing beep and then his entire field of vision went red.

Chapter 32

FLOYD WAS NO LONGER ANGRY at Tate or Chase. A cross-country flight did wonders for dissipating anger.

But he was confused. *Very* confused. Air travel, apparently, did not bring clarity to erratic behavior.

In truth, he hadn't even meant to tell Tate about Chase's call. His intention had been to confront his partner about the two robberies. But Tate was a master deflector and instead, the conversation had gone very differently than Floyd wanted.

"I have to talk to you about something, Tate."

"Right. Is this about the head doc? Because—"

"No, not about that. I mean, not r-really. It's more about—"

"Let me guess? Chase?"

Pause.

"Why d-do you—"

"She's been on my mind lately, too. She called, didn't she? What did she say?"

Pause.

"Sh-she wants help. N-n-not a case, but a favor to a friend—in Nevada."

"Nevada? Shit, I could use a vacation. Get away from this crazy place. How about you?"

And the next thing Floyd knew they were on a plane, Tate conveniently "sleeping" the entire time to avoid any relevant conversation. It wasn't until seeing Chase in Stu Barnes' elaborate foyer that Floyd realized that he'd been duped. Tate knew that he'd seen the confrontations with Frankie and Jabari, and Chase knew he'd come.

It wasn't a good feeling, despite being used to it by now.

Just keep the train moving.

Floyd double-checked the coordinates on his GPS and then pulled over to the side of the road. It took him all of thirty seconds to locate the camera that had captured Jake Hollister's murder. On the opposite side of the street was a *U-Lock-it* self-storage facility. Floyd got out of his rental and looked at the facility, hands on his hips.

U-Lock-it was surrounded by a twelve-foot chain link fence, with an additional foot of razor wire looped at the top. A seemingly vacant guard booth with a white and red striped barricade blocked the vehicle entrance.

It was there that he spotted the camera. It was angled in such a way that it captured the driver who pulled up to the barricade, but in the absence of a car, it had a clear view of the bridge on which Floyd presently stood.

No, not exactly… more like *here*.

There was a dark stain on the pavement that either the CSU hadn't tried or had been unsuccessful in removing. Oblong in shape, maybe eighteen or twenty inches at its widest point.

This is where Jake was killed, Floyd thought. *This is the exact location where he took his final breath.*

Floyd inhaled deeply himself and then looked around, unwilling to let his mind fixate on morbid thoughts.

Choo-Choo.

The camera and the stain… something about the way they lined up seemed odd to Floyd. He moved first five feet to his left and then back to the stain and then five feet to his right.

If Jake's murder had happened outside of that ten or maybe twelve-foot radius, then it would have been compromised. A few more feet and it wouldn't have been captured at all.

Coincidence?

Floyd didn't have the same aversion to the idea of a coincidence that Stitts had, but he'd been around enough to know that the more complicated a case, the less likelihood of things just 'happening'.

And to him, this seemed almost certainly staged.

With a self-affirming nod, he headed across the street. The barricade was designed to stop cars only, and he ducked beneath it. After observing the maybe two-dozen squat, garage-style storage units, Floyd walked over to the main glass enclosure with a paper 'OFFICE' sign hanging in the door.

A bell chimed when he stepped into the cramped room, which reminded him of a miniaturized old-school motel lobby. There was a single orange plastic chair beside the door and a cheap laminate countertop separating the employees from the patrons. In addition to the computer monitor on the counter, there was another mounted in the corner of the room. Displayed for all parties to see a quad-screen of four different video feeds, one of which was of the front entrance.

An interior door at the back of the room opened and a man stepped through. He'd clearly just finished eating something as he swallowed and then slapped his hands to rid his palms of crumbs.

"Can I—" he looked at Floyd with a pair of wide, hooded eyes. "LVPD?"

Floyd shook his head.

"FBI."

The man appeared impressed by this.

"This about that murder, right?"

Floyd nodded, grateful that he could get right to the chase.

"Were you working four nights ago?"

"Yep." The man hooked his thumb at the door from which he'd just stepped through. "Right back there."

"Did you hear the shots?"

The man sucked his teeth.

"I already told the cops—"

"Then you won't mind telling the FBI, will you?"

"Yeah, okay," the man relented. "Sure—I ain't got nothin' to do anyway. I was working that night. It was late, maybe two—

" Two eighteen, Floyd thought, recalling the time stamp on the security video, "—in the morning. I hear two shots—bam, bam—and I rush outta the back. I seen a man on the ground—

" he pointed at the monitor, "—bleeding from the head. I look out the window, up and down the street, but I don't see nothin' else. Nothing. Just the guy on the ground. Then I called the cops. That's it, that's all she wrote."

Floyd put himself in the man's shoes, going over what he'd just been told. It made sense until it didn't. If this guy had come out immediately after he'd heard the shots, then he couldn't have missed the executioner. In the video, Jake had been killed point-blank.

On a bridge.

A bridge that had high guard rails protecting cars and pedestrians from what was at least a twenty-foot drop to gravel below.

There was nowhere for the killer to go.

Except...

Floyd's eyes focused on the security camera display. One of the four cameras was pointed between the rows of storage units.

"I'm going to need a list of everyone who's renting a unit here. I'm also going to wanna see the v-video footage from four nights ago. All four cameras."

The man reached beneath the counter and produced a massive ledger.

"I can help you with the first request," he said. "But not the second."

Floyd immediately thought of a warrant and said forcefully, "Why's that?"

"Because," the man replied, flipping through the pages, "none of that footage is kept locally. It's all stored at corporate... just like I told LVPD."

Okay, so no warrant needed.

"You wouldn't happen to know where the *U-lock-it* head office is located?"

"No, that's not it." The man waved a hand in the air. "Not *U-lock-it*—this here's all owned by one of them 'brella corps."

It took Floyd a second to realize that the man meant umbrella.

"And before you ask, 'cuz I know you gonna, the company that owns this place is some artificial intelligence rig, if you can believe that. AI something or other."

Chapter 33

"THEY REALLY STOPPED YOU FROM entering the building?" Stu asked.

Chase swirled the coffee in her cup and let the man's words linger. The disbelief in Stu's voice was telling. People with power loved to think that they were indispensable. But most often, the machines that they've built, or more likely inherited, to generate untold wealth was just that, a machine. And, as with most machines, a cog can break or be removed, a gear can be out of true, but things just keep on moving forward. Sure, there might be momentary slowdowns while cogs are fixed or replaced, and lubricants are sprayed over the individual parts.

But the money never stops.

"I would say, strongly discouraged from entering the building," Tate offered. "Security says that if we have questions, we should talk to your buddy Detective Tolliver."

Stu scowled.

Not wanting to get sidetracked, Chase brought the conversation back.

"What about discovery? They have to send us anything relevant, right?" Her eyes naturally drifted to the folders on the counter. "Where are the video files? The security footage? We should be able to track Jake Hollister's movements on the day of his murder."

"We received some video footage," Will informed them. "But the thing is, LVPD and the ADA are only sending us what they deem relevant. In theory, if there's something on the security footage from the Happy Valley Gaming lobby that might point toward another suspect, they're supposed to hand that over. *Supposed to*, being the operative term. The burden of guilt is on them, and we're given all of their evidence to analyze and refute."

"Except we all agree that that's not going to be enough," Tate stated. "We need to find another suspect."

Will nodded.

"Right. I can put in a petition for additional footage from HVG and, in all likelihood, a warrant will be—"

"Too long," Tate interjected. "Look, I understand that your trial isn't going to be for another six months at least, but in my experience, the longer things take, the staler they get. Videos get misplaced, lost, deleted. People forget things, even important things."

"And you have a job to get back to," Stu pointed out. There was no disdain in his voice. The man was simply stating a fact.

"We have jobs to get back to," Tate corrected.

Chase got the impression by his tone that Tate was about to ask for money, in a subtle and respectable manner, no doubt, and decided to cut that off at the knees.

This wasn't about money. This was about returning a favor, of balancing the scales.

She considered this.

Well, putting a dent in the debt, in any case.

"Do you know the secretary at Happy Valley? I didn't catch her name, but she's cute, mid-twenties, light brown hair?" Chase asked.

"No idea," Stu replied with a shrug. "I think I went there once, maybe twice? It's just part of my portfolio. They made me interim CEO but that was just to boost credibility, I guess."

"Jake was the one in charge," Tate said, repeating what the secretary had told them.

Chase sipped her coffee, and another question came to her.

"What about the metaverse? You spend any time there?"

Stu frowned.

"No." He paused. "I mean—when I first visited Happy Valley, they wanted to show me what it was all about. They had an avatar set up for me and I just put on the gear, walked around a little, and said hi. It was a little strange."

"Do you still have the gear?" Tate asked, glancing at Chase out of the corner of his eye.

"I think so." Stu looked suspicious now. "Why?"

During the ride back to Stu's mansion, Tate and Chase had talked briefly about the secretary's offer to meet them in the metaverse. Both were apprehensive and noncommittal, admittedly because it was such a foreign concept.

Deep throat in the deep web. No, that wasn't right. The fake web?

Fake world?

"The secretary was shut down by legal," Chase told Stu and Will, the latter having moved even closer, his lawyer ears now perked. "But she told us that she liked Jake and I think she wants to help, but she's afraid of losing her job. She claimed that she could get us the security tapes from HVG, but I don't know."

"Steal them?" Will asked.

"It would make them inadmissible," Colin Sachs, he of few words, added.

Tate made a face and rolled his eyes.

"She said she could get them for us," Chase said plainly. "Never said how, only said where."

"Where?" With his lawyer act down, Will was very poor at hiding his emotions.

"The metaverse," Stu answered.

"That's right. The metaverse," Tate confirmed.

"Is that legal?" Stu asked.

Will looked at Colin and then Mike. All three lawyers shrugged.

"I'm not sure."

"How much are you paying these clowns, again?" Tate asked.

Will got his back up.

"I'm a corporate lawyer, Mike and Colin are criminal lawyers. We aren't experts in cyber security laws."

"I'm a corporate lawyer," Tate mocked, using a nasal voice to imitate the man.

"Relax! Everyone just relax," Stu nearly shouted. "We're on the same team here." He looked at Will first. "If we need a cyber security lawyer, hire one." Now, he turned to face Chase and Tate. "In the meantime, if this secretary wants to talk in the metaverse, I say let's do it. I'll go in just in case there are legal ramifications."

Will looked ready to protest but Tate beat him to it.

"Not a good idea."

Will's nod confirmed that, for once, the two men were in agreement.

"Why not?" Stu demanded.

"Because she liked Jake Hollister. Really liked him. She might be willing to help us, the FBI, because she thinks we're helping Jake. But if she sees you, I don't think she's going to be as willing," Chase said.

"Then who?" Stu asked.

"Do you even have the equipment?" Will countered.

Without saying another word, Stu left the room. Everyone was silent until he returned less than a minute later with something that resembled the goggles that Chase wore to fly her drone. Only these had handles and cables and tentacles.

A mechanical Cthulhu of sorts.

After Stu set it down on the table, Will, herself, and Tate just stared at it as if it was going to come to life before their eyes.

This is where Floyd is supposed to come in, Chase thought.

But Floyd still hadn't gotten back yet.

Something to be worried about? Maybe…

"So? If not me, then who?" Stu asked again.

Chase wasn't going anywhere near the thing. She'd had enough out-of-body experiences to last a lifetime—no, a dozen lifetimes. Putting another lens between her and reality wasn't a good idea.

"I'm—I'm not sure of the legality of all of this," Will said, scratching the back of his head.

"Pussy," Tate muttered under his breath as he reached for the goggles. "I'll do it."

He put the goggles on, but they were crooked and covered his nose. He looked so absurd that Chase laughed out loud.

"Am I… am I doing this right?"

Chapter 34

"WHA-WHA-WHAT'S HAPPENING?" TONY STUTTERED. "Wh-what's going on?"

There was no reply. There was only the red screen in front of his face. Even the ambient sound from the HVG headquarters lobby, that strange echo of nothingness in large open spaces, was missing.

Then that obnoxious, shrill beep came again, this time accompanied by a black message in the sea of red: *You have been banned from the Happy Valley Metaverse.*

"No," he cried. "No *fucking* way."

Tony had broken one of the cardinal rules of the metaverse. He'd killed Jake Hollister.

Cursing, Tony removed his mask and blinked rapidly, waiting for his eyes to adjust to the real world.

But when they did, Tony found himself in exactly the same place he'd just been.

"What's happening?" His throat was so dry that the words were almost painful to speak.

Tony was back in HVG, only there were no security guards lunging at him. There were no gawking employees with wide eyes and wider mouths, either.

Most importantly of all, Jake Hollister wasn't lying on the floor, drowning in a puddle of his own blood.

With unsteady strides, he entered the elevator—it was open, as if Stu had called it but vanished just as it arrived—and then made his way to the 16th floor. There, he found Jake, with his back to Tony, the VR helmet firmly affixed to his head.

Tony looked at his own metaverse gear, which he held in his hand. Now, it was as if all the moisture in his throat had somehow migrated to his forehead. He struggled to put the helmet on, his skin was so slick with sweat.

There was no change; the message was still there—*You have been banned from the Happy Valley Metaverse*—and no amount of button mashing made it go away.

All he saw was that message and the red. Red, like the blood that had leaked out of Jake's smashed head.

"No, please..."

"Tony? You okay?"

Tony removed the useless goggles and saw that Jake had done the same with his. The man was looking at him, his head cocked, one eye partially squinted.

"You okay?"

Tony saw a flash and Jake's concerned face was replaced by a blood-splattered mess. When he blinked again, the real Jake was back.

"I-I-I—" That was all he could manage.

"You don't look so hot. Too much caffeine... and how long have you been going at it, now? Eighteen, nineteen hours straight?"

"Twenty-six," Tony corrected. He swallowed what little spit he could generate. It felt like razor blades going down.

Jake's eyes went wide, and Tony couldn't help but notice the contrast between this and... *before*. Eyes bulging now, eyes forced from their sockets before.

But that couldn't have been before. That wouldn't make sense. That had to be... after?

"Tony... seriously, go home. Take a day off. You've earned it."

"I-I-I-I know, but my code... we need to get it into the game. The sooner—" he dry coughed, "—the better."

"Your... your code? I'm not sure what code you're talking about." Jake smiled, showing off his big white teeth. He gently squeezed Tony's shoulder. "C'mon, buddy, go get some rest."

Tony slunk away from the man's grasp.

"The code... the code from the eye-tracking data? The uncanny valley?"

Jake rubbed his lips together and raised an eyebrow.

"Eye-tracking data? You really need some sleep, my boy. Happy Valley doesn't track any data." He made a face and held his hands out like some politician saying their catchphrase. "Whatever happens in the metaverse, stays in the metaverse!"

No—He knows. *He knows what I've done, he knows what I've accomplished, and he's trying to take it from me.*

Tony recalled Jake conversing with the silver-haired CEO.

Oh, Jake knew alright. But this wasn't his doing. The mandate to screw Tony out of his money had come from above.

"Right, of c-course," he said with a weak smile. "You're right—just tired. Also, I seemed to have gotten locked out of the metaverse. Think I can use your admin status to get me back in?"

As he said this, Tony casually reached for Jake's goggles.

"What'd you do? Trigger the—" The man's jovial expression disappeared when he caught sight of the red glow coming from Tony's eyepiece. "Shit, that's not—that's not a dev error, Tony. That's a—what did you do?"

Tony laughed but the sound came out all wrong. It was tight and unpleasant.

Grating.

"Nothing—*ha*, nothing. Just—j-j-just let me just use your admin status to reinstate me."

Jake made no move toward his headset.

"Tony, what happened?"

"Nothing." Another one of those terrible laughs erupted from his mouth before he could catch it. "Just reboot my username, Jake. C'mon!"

Jake rolled his chair so that he blocked his gear now.

"I don't think so," he said flatly. "I don't know what's going on with you lately, but you're not being yourself. I highly recommend you get some sleep. We can talk about what rules you broke in the metaverse when you're fully rested."

"Highly recommend..." Tony couldn't stop laughing now. This was all so fucked up. "It was just a mistake—*ha*. Get me back in. Come on. Back in."

"No, I'm not—"

"Get me the fuck back in, Jake!"

Tony aggressively reached for the man's headset.

"What the fuck, Tony!" Jake leaped to his feet. He was a good two inches taller than Tony, but the man was lean whereas Tony had meat on his bones.

I can take him. I can take him and smash his fucking head in.

"Go home. And that's not a recommendation. That's an order."

"An order, really?" Tony laughed right in his face now. "Why do you want me to leave so bad, Jake? So you can just pretend that my code 'didn't work' like last time? That it doesn't 'exist'?"

"Last time? What the—"

"Just give me the fucking goggles, Jake!" Tony planted a hand in the center of Jake's chest and shoved.

The force generated by the shove was not commensurate with the ensuing damage. As Jake staggered, his left heel struck something hard—a printer? Paper-shredder? Garbage pail?—

and he twisted awkwardly. He started to fall, and Tony lunged for the goggles. His hand grazed one of the controllers but before he could grasp it, somehow, like Jake, Tony also tripped.

The two of them went down together, with Tony landing heavily on top of the smaller man. There was a loud crack followed by a sickening wet crunch, but Tony still managed to come up with the goggles.

He immediately went to put them on but stopped when he saw that the glass display inside the helmet was shattered.

"No! Fuck, Jake! *No!*"

But Jake didn't answer, at least not verbally. His reply, if you could consider it one, came in the form of spasmodic twitching in both legs.

Tony dropped the worthless goggles and glared down at Jake.

The man's right ear was pressed against his shoulder with his neck fully extended. Blood was leaking from said ear and the twitching, which had started in Jake's feet, migrated up his body like the shudder of a skyscraper during an earthquake. When it got to Jake's head, the spasms had become a full-on body-rocking seizure.

"What's happening?" someone yelled.

"Jake? What the hell happened?"

"Call 9-1-1!"

Tony walked backward and almost tripped again.

"It was an accident," he said softly.

One of his colleagues grabbed his elbow.

"What happened, Tony?"

"It was a fucking accident," Tony gasped.

Amidst the now-increasing panic in the office as others began to understand the severity of Jake's injuries, Tony heard the elevator ping.

"You! You told him—" Tony was looking at the elevator but pointing back toward Jake. "You told him to take my code, to pretend that it didn't work! *To steal from me!*"

Stu Barnes didn't justify this with a response—his type never did. Why would they? They were better than everyone else.

More important.

But the man did smile.

Stu gave Tony Metcalfe a half-assed knowing smile before everything faded to red.

Chapter 35

TO FLOYD, STU'S CASE WAS looking more and more like a setup. He knew Stu Barnes, which was one of the reasons why he'd come so willingly to help Chase after she'd nearly cost him his job, and the man wasn't stupid. Many different types of people fell into money, including idiots, morons, and criminals. But Stu was none of these. It was no secret that he'd gotten his start with inherited coin, but shrewd investments had more than 10x'd his net worth.

This made the reality of this case, of Stu murdering an employee in plain view of a camera affixed to a building that he owned, no less, dubious.

But it also made things considerably more complicated and inspired a host of interrogative words, including who, how, and why.

And jurors didn't like complicated. Complicated was difficult to follow. They preferred clean and simple, and, invariably, someone would bring up the courtroom buzzword Occam's Razer.

Quite frankly, they liked video evidence.

Shaking his head in frustration, Floyd entered Stu's home and found himself bearing witness to a bizarre scene. Chase, Stu, Will, and the two other lawyers whose names he'd already forgotten, were all sitting with their elbows on the large kitchen table, their necks craned forward.

They were staring at Tate who looked like a supervillain from a low-budget sci-fi movie. Well, maybe *super*villain was a bit of an overstatement. More like bungling villain, what with the awkward way he was waving his arms around. In his hands were circular controllers, with wires that connected to the headpiece.

"What in the—"

"Shh!" all three people at the table said at once.

"Okay, geez." Floyd backed toward the fridge and Chase rose to meet him.

"Tate is in the metaverse," she said matter-of-factly. Floyd just stared at Chase until she elaborated. "We got stuffed at the gaming office—legal blocked us. The secretary wanted to tell us something but would only do it in the metaverse. Hence the getup."

"Ahh."

Tate mumbled something incomprehensible.

"What about you?" Chase asked. "How'd it go with the camera?"

Oh, how easily the circuits established from old patterns could be reactivated.

Floyd wanted to be pissed at Chase, had every right to be pissed.

But he wasn't.

"You know the building Jake was killed outside?"

"The storage place?"

"*U-lock-it*, yep. Wanna take a stab at who owns it?"

Chase crinkled her nose.

"No way."

Floyd nodded.

"Our man Stu. They have a bunch of cameras—not just the one—and I tried to get footage from the night of the murder from all of them but—"

"They shut you down, too?"

"No, not really. I mean, maybe? According to the guy working there, all recordings are stored in some big corporate machine. I thought that maybe Stu could access them, but based on your lack of success, I guess not. I did, however," Floyd pulled out his phone and showed Chase a series of images, "obtain a list of the people who rent storage units."

He went on to explain to Chase his theory that, in the absence of a vehicle in the video and the employee's claims, the real murderer might have run into *U-lock-it*.

"Except Stu's car was there," Chase reminded him. "According to the GPS data, anyway."

"I don't—I don't get it," he admitted. "Why was Stu there? Why was Jake there?"

Chase said nothing. It was clear, by her intense focus on Tate, that the woman's mind had drifted.

This angered Floyd more than it should have.

Keep moving forward, his brain urged. *Choo-Choo.*

But sometimes even a train was forced to back up.

"Chase... you left me. You lied to me, then left me."

"Hmm?"

Floyd grabbed Chase's arm. He had her attention back.

"Why did you lie to me?" he hissed. "Why did you l-leave me? Chase, I had to v-v-v-v-visit... just—just why?"

It didn't matter that Floyd hadn't managed to get his question out. They both knew what he was asking.

Why did you make me go to see Meredith Griffith to tell her that her daughter was dead? You know my issues with that.

A deep sadness crossed Chase's face.

"I'm sorry," she said simply.

"That's... not an a-answer. What did you have to do that was s-s-so important?"

Chase opened her mouth as if to elaborate, but then Floyd saw an expression he was unfortunately familiar with. Tight lips, knitted brow.

Classic, stubborn, no-nonsense.

"I'm sorry, Floyd. I really am. I should have never put you in that position."

But I did because I had to. And it worked: we stopped Henry Saburra from turning those sick girls into murderers.

And I would do it again.

This, like Floyd's question, went unspoken and understood.

Tate suddenly pulled the mask off. He was grinning from ear to ear.

"Shit, this is *amazing*. It's so real. Chase, you have to try it."

"No chance," Chase said, walking away from Floyd. "You find out anything?"

"Oh, did I ever," Tate replied, still smiling. "That woman? The woman we met at the front desk? Her name is Beverly. She might be a secretary in real life, but in here—" he tapped the mask, "—she's a redhead who goes by Gina. Anyways, Bev said that at Happy Valley Gaming they encourage people to work on their own projects on company time. And Bev—"

"Can you please stop calling her Bev?" Chase snapped.

Tate's smile waned.

"That's what—okay, whatever. *Beverly* said that Jake was working on another metaverse. Something much darker."

"What about the security tapes?" Chase probed.

Floyd thought that her brevity could be attributed to her feeling badly about what she'd done to him.

Petty as it was, that made him a little warm inside.

As did seeing Tate, normally the one in charge and responsible for barking orders, being so openly chastised.

"They're in here," Tate said, tapping the device a second time. "In the metaverse."

"I don't understand," Will Porter said. "The real tapes or the meta... tapes?"

"Yeah, I don't get it either," Floyd admitted.

Tate, who had all of five minutes experience in the metaverse, sighed as if he were Sam Altman forced to give a lecture to Luddites.

"The tapes exist in the cloud, right? Online?"

Mostly nods from the group.

"Well, Beverly said that she can access the tapes through the metaverse—the actual security tapes from Happy Valley Gaming. And that's what she set me up with in here. I have my own private viewing booth." Tate grinned and winked at Floyd.

Floyd frowned.

"Is this real?" Chase asked, looking to Stu for an answer.

"I… I guess? Like I told you guys, I'm no expert."

"Okay, fine," Chase continued. "Review the tapes, Tate."

Tate saluted Chase and fumbled with the mask.

"One more thing," Chase said before he managed to get the device righted on his head, "ask Bev if there's a way to access video footage from *U-lock-it* in the east end? Apparently, Stu, you own that, too."

"Really?" Tate said.

"Really."

"Okay, I'll ask. Work my charm."

"*U-Lock-it* is part of AI Integrations?" Stu asked after Tate was once again teleported elsewhere.

"So the employee says," Floyd answered.

"I'll double-check on that," Will offered before passing the task onto Colin Sachs.

While he didn't share his partner's open distaste for lawyers in general, Floyd agreed with Tate's opinion that they'd been relatively useless up until this point.

"Stu, you have a printer here?" Floyd asked.

"Yeah, somewhere in my office, I think."

"Alright, I'm going to send you a list of names, can you print it out and see if any look familiar?"

"Yep."

When Stu left the room to search, Floyd addressed Chase and Will in a hushed tone.

"This place... Stu's got security cameras, right?"

Will looked around and then pointed at a small device located in the corner of the room, high above their heads.

"Okay. Well, Stu claims he never left the house the night Jake was killed, right?"

"Yes," Will said hesitantly.

"Well, let's check the footage to see—"

"It's not working," Stu said as he reentered the room. "Printer's not working." He looked up and must have seen something on their faces. "What? What's going on?"

Because it had been Floyd's idea, it was his responsibility to pass the information along. But he didn't answer, and Stu's frustration bubbled over.

"So, I have to tell you everything, have to be completely transparent, then when I leave the room for a minute, you guys are whispering about me? That's bullshit. Fucking bullshit. How many times do I have to say this? I didn't kill anyone. Not Jake Hollister, nobody."

Floyd glanced at Chase. He was surprised that she hadn't spoken up yet and was even more shocked when it didn't appear as if she had any intention of doing so.

"We were—"

"Floyd," Chase warned.

"No, it's fine. He called us here; he wants us to help. So, let's keep him in the loop," Floyd said, sternly. "Stu, you said you didn't leave the house the night that Jake was killed, is that correct?"

"I was right here at the table."

"Okay, so let's check your security tapes and prove it."

All eyes were on Stu. If the man faltered, even for a moment, it might be more telling of his guilt than any video evidence.

He didn't so much as blink.

"I can't believe you didn't think of that," Stu said accusingly to Will. Then to the rest, "Let's do it. Let's look at those tapes because I swear to you, I didn't leave the house."

Chapter 36

TONY WAS SO ANGRY THAT he almost threw his VR headset. He couldn't believe it—it had happened again.

He'd killed Jake again. But this time, it had been an accident. They had to know that. The *metaverse* had to know that.

And yet, when Tony calmed down enough to put the goggles back on, he was still locked out. He tried his username and password and was informed that his account had been blocked.

"This can't be happening," he whined. He tried to access his account again and again, but there was no change.

He was out.

The man who had managed to crack the code of the uncanny valley had been denied access to his own fucking game.

This time when Tony removed his goggles, he tossed them onto his desk. There was an audible crack, which drew the attention of someone close to him.

"Everything alright, Tony?"

Tony was too shocked to answer.

He was alone… wasn't he?

Squeezing his eyes didn't make the person go away.

"Tony?"

He was back in his office, back in his makeshift cubicle with those chest-high mobile dividers because of course he was.

"Fine," Tony answered, his eyes still closed.

But he wasn't fine.

"Tony?" The man beside him, Paul or Peter or something like that called his name again, but Tony didn't acknowledge him this time.

He just stood and glared at Jake's back, his face so hot that it felt like there were pins and needles in his cheeks. And his hands… they were balled into tight fists.

Tony started to move toward Jake. He weaved through the dividers but when he got near his boss, he stopped.

No. You don't want to do this.

But he did. Deep down, though, Tony knew that this wouldn't solve his problem. His problem wasn't with Jake.

It was with someone higher up.

It was with Stu, the man at the top. The man with the sleazy smirk and fake tan and hair plugs who had made Jake lie to him, to tell him that they hadn't used his code or that it wasn't good enough or that it didn't even exist. Like anyone would believe he made it up! Him, Tony Metcalfe, the creator of one of the most popular cell phone games in the past three years.

Fucking laughable.

Tony must have actually laughed then because Jake lifted his legs and swiveled around.

"Hey... what's up?"

Tony flexed his fingers straight and sucked in a shuddering breath.

"Tony?"

He said nothing, just turned.

Where is Stu Barnes?

A man like him, he would be on the top floor. He had to be. That's what all CEOs needed: to be above everyone else. Physically and psychologically.

And to smile down upon them all.

"Hey, Tony, we need to talk about something," Jake called after him. But Tony was on a mission now, a mission to find Stu Barnes.

And when he found him, the man would lie. Because that was what men like Stu did. They lied and they forced people

like Jake to lie to people like him. They made them do it. Because for them, the metaverse wasn't about creating the most
realistic, most enraptured, most encompassing experience ever.

It wasn't about the uncanny valley, either.

It was about the almighty dollar. It was always about
money.

When Tony made it to the elevator, his lips were tacky. He
tried to moisten them with his tongue, but it just stuck to his
lower lip.

He reached for the elevator button but was startled when it
pinged, and the doors opened before he could push it. Tony
stumbled backward and found himself staring at the ever-smil-
ing Stu Barnes. But he wasn't alone. HVG's CEO was flanked
by two square men.

Security guards, probably, but Tony had never seen them
before.

Despite wanting to say something, despite having mentally
prepared for this moment, Tony was tongue-tied. It was the
man's creepy fucking smile.

"Mr. Metcalfe, we need to talk."

Still smiling. *Always* smiling.

Tony, his heart racing now from fear and not rage, took a
giant step backward.

He bumped into someone, and a small gasp escaped his lips.

It was Jake. The man had snuck up behind him.

"Just… just leave me alone…" he sputtered.

Jake grabbed him by the shoulders.

"Hey, buddy, you okay?"

"Mr. Metcalfe?"

"No… you're lying… you're *all* lying…" Spit flew from
Tony's lips. "You're *fucking* lying!"

Jake held his hands up.

"Just calm down, we... uhh... we just want to talk to you."

Tony shook his head violently.

"You don't want to talk, you want to lie!"

"Tony, I don't know — "

"You took it... my code..." he whined. "My cooooode..."

"What?" Jake looked genuinely confused, which only enraged Tony further.

How can he pretend that he didn't know? How can he be so convincing? He's ruining my life's work and he... and he acts like this?

They were going to cut him off. They were going to make millions off his discovery, maybe even billions.

And he'd once again be left in the lurch, seeking work with no education, no references, no...

Tony didn't even realize he was striking Jake. Had no idea until a gout of blood splattered the bridge of his nose and dripped into his left eye.

Then arms were on him, yanking him off Jake's body.

Tony struggled, but the two men holding him were strong and they spun him around.

And there was Stu Barnes. Grinning Stu Barnes.

And then, *red.*

Red.

RED.

You have been banned from the Happy Valley Metaverse.

Chapter 37

"I DON'T UNDERSTAND," STU MUTTERED. "How can it all be blank?"

Chase watched as Floyd flicked through several of the videos, which were arranged by date and time. They'd already reviewed all the videos from the many cameras in the house from the day Jake was murdered to the present day. They were blank. All blank. Just a black screen.

"I didn't—I didn't delete them," Stu said defensively.

Chase didn't think he did. But someone had. And if Stu hadn't left his home the day that Jake Hollister was murdered as he said, then it would make sense that whoever was behind all this would destroy his alibi.

Which meant that someone had either broken into Stu's home or into his system.

"Go back further," Chase instructed. "Go back until you find something. Focus on the camera at the front of the house. Who knows? Maybe we get lucky and see someone trying to break in."

Floyd did as she asked, but his expression suggested he wasn't hopeful. Truthfully, neither was Chase. If the person who set Stu up had managed to fake the video of Jake's murder, then breaking into his home to delete his cloud-based security footage seemed pedestrian.

Chase averted her eyes from the computer monitor and rubbed them. She was far more tired than she should have been, given the fact that it wasn't even six yet—nine her local time, and eight Nashville time. But to say that the day had been emotionally taxing would have been a dramatic understatement. First, Nashville and that piece of shit Brian Jalston. Then, New York and Luisa and Georgina.

Now, Vegas and Tate and Floyd and Stu.

She glanced over at Tate who still had his face wedged in the helmet, living in the metaverse reviewing Happy Valley security footage.

The more she watched him, the more curious she became.

Chase wondered what her psychiatrist Dr. Matteo would think of the metaverse. Was it still considered living in the moment, which he seemed to encourage ad nauseum?

"Here, I think I've got something," Floyd remarked.

No longer was the video feed just a black screen, but instead, there was a clear image, crystal-clear, of the interlocking bricks on Stu's driveway.

"This is three days before Jake Hollister's death," Floyd said. He let the footage play, and they all watched a whole lot of nothing. Just the sun beating down on that expensive, custom brickwork.

"What are we—"

Floyd cut Chase off.

"Just watch." A few seconds later, the screen flickered and then went black. "This is the moment when it goes dark. All cameras, all around the same time."

"Roll it back, and slow it way down," Chase said.

They watched again but saw nothing new this time around. Just a sporadic digital stutter, then darkness.

"Looks like there's a short or something," Will Porter suggested. "Malfunction."

"I don't think so," Chase countered. "Floyd, can you do frame by frame? I think I saw something in the bottom corner."

"Sure."

"There!" Chase nearly shouted and Floyd froze the image.

She leaned forward and pointed at a dark spot on the screen. It was a different angle than the stripes and was more reflected. It didn't look like part of the glitch.

"What is that?" Will asked.

It was Stu who answered.

"That looks like my car. Part of the hood."

Floyd jogged the video back and forth a few frames.

"Yeah, I think you're right," he said. Then Floyd dramatically pulled back from the computer. "Stu, do you have a Bluetooth speaker?"

"A Bluetooth speaker...?"

"Yeah, you know, a wireless speaker?"

The annoyance in Floyd's voice brought a grin to Chase's lips.

"Sure, hold on."

Stu rushed over to the family room and grabbed an expensive-looking speaker off the mantle. He handed it to Floyd who took out his phone while continuing to ask questions.

"Where were you coming back from, by the way?" Floyd asked, clearly trying to connect his phone to the speaker.

Stu's face underwent a series of convolutions.

"I'm not sure. I can't remember. It's been a crazy last few days, but—"

"You have a calendar?" Floyd interrupted, still fiddling with the speaker.

"Yep." Stu took out his own phone.

Chase was strangely proud of Floyd. She was also annoyed at him for not bringing her into the loop, but he looked more like a battle-hardened FBI agent than a young boy from Alaska with an affinity for trains.

"Here... it says I had a car appointment. Oil change. That's probably what I was coming back from."

Floyd set the speaker down.

"Can't connect. You said the printer wasn't working?"

Stu nodded.

"Yeah, that's right. Wouldn't connect."

"What are you thinking, Floyd?" Chase asked.

Without answering, Floyd rose out of his chair and asked for Stu's car keys. The man handed them over and then, still with this annoying shroud of secrecy, Floyd made his way to the front door. Chase and Stu followed while Tate just waved his hands around like a blind person trying to find a rare gem amongst hundreds of shiny stones.

Colin and Mike stayed on the phone, doing lawyerly things, which Chase had come to learn was mostly racking up billable hours.

"Let me show you something," Floyd said as he led them outside. The sun was still high in the sky, but it wasn't nearly as warm as it had been earlier in the day.

Floyd used the key fob to unlock Stu's Mercedes. Then he got in and ran his fingers along the dash, beneath it, searched through the center console, and then reached all the way beneath both front seats.

His lips remained pursed the entire time.

"What are you looking for?" Stu asked.

Still no answer.

Is he doing this on purpose? Chase wondered. *Is he doing it because this is something I would do?*

Shaking her head, she watched Floyd get out of the sports car only to immediately drop onto his hands in a push-up position.

What the fuck, Floyd? I don't tell you what I see when I touch a body because of the time I have no idea what's real and what's not.

Stu lowered himself to the ground as well, but Chase refused to buy into this charade. Instead, she crossed her arms over her chest.

Floyd grunted as he extended his arm beneath the car, and then they all heard a metallic click. When he pulled his hand out, he was holding a rectangular device that was about the size of a cell phone, only it didn't look like any brand that Chase had ever seen.

"What the hell is that?" Stu asked, taking a step back as if it might be an explosive device.

Floyd flipped the black object over in his hand. If it was a phone, somebody in QC was going to be fired: there was no screen or keys. It was completely devoid of features.

"This," Floyd said, a grin still plastered on his face, "is the reason why your printer and Bluetooth speaker won't work. It's also the reason why your camera stopped recording the second you pulled into your driveway."

Chapter 38

TONY WAS LOST. HE WAS surrounded by darkness and blanketed with a foul smell. Groping blindly, his outstretched hand struck something that toppled. It made a loud metallic clink followed by a wet splat. He immediately drew his hand back to his chest.

Still blind, still confused, he stood, then took a step forward. Now his foot struck something, several somethings, but at least these he recognized: empty cans. He cursed, and wondered why everything was so dark, why—

Tony's train of thought was derailed by the realization that he was gripping something in each hand. He also felt something pressing against the sides of his head.

I'm still wearing goggles, he thought, *and I'm still holding controllers.*

There was a strange disconnect between this thought and reality, almost as if it wasn't something he was feeling so much as a string of code instructing him of these facts.

He dropped the controllers, and they swung at his sides, just below his knees, suspended by the cables that led to his headset.

His shoulders were stiff and sore and removing the mask required more effort than the simple act should have.

Three blinks and his vision cleared.

Tony almost put the mask back on.

His place was an absolute sty. The cans that he'd sent spinning across the floor were a mixture of beans and energy drinks. There were other containers, too, dozens of others of various sizes. Most of these were empty, licked clean, but some still had microwaved food clinging to the sidewalls.

Tony grunted with disgust.

The smell was probably the worst part. Most of it was coming from the garbage, a sickly-sweet odor like condensed milk left out in the sun, but some of it was also coming from him.

He didn't want to look down, his stomach warned him not to, but eventually, the urge was too great to ignore.

"Oh, god."

Tony was never particularly concerned with style. Every day at Happy Valley, he wore pretty much the same thing: jeans and a plain T-shirt, not always dark, but he shied away from bright colors, white in particular. But his clothes were always clean.

Why he was wearing a pair of oversized track pants and a pale green sweatshirt that was ripped in several places and frayed at the hem was as mysterious as the origins of the multitude of stains across the chest and waist.

Why am I wearing this disgusting outfit?

Tony waited for an answer that never came. He remembered going to work and…

He drew a blank.

What the hell?

He was about to tap his forehead to encourage his memory to return, but the brown stain he noticed on his first two fingers convinced him otherwise.

Thinking the worst, Tony cautiously sniffed his hand from about a foot away from his nose.

Thank God. It's only food.

The relief was short-lived. He still didn't know where he was exactly, why it was so dark, and how he'd gotten here.

There was a single bare bulb above him, but it wasn't of the LED variety and emitted only a weak orangey glow.

He needed sunlight and fresh air.

About eight feet behind him, Tony noticed a rectangular window at shoulder height. It was covered in blackout curtains and with stiff legs he walked over to it and pulled one of them aside.

"Fuck," he moaned, letting the thick fabric go immediately. The sun was harsh and offensive. It blinded him, and Tony was forced to squint as he tried again, this time using his forearm to shield his face.

He'd hoped that seeing the outside would trigger his memory, but it didn't. The view wasn't inspiring—he saw pea gravel and the side of what he thought was an apartment building—and even the bars on the window, which he quickly learned prevented it from being opened in addition to being a theft deterrent meant nothing to him.

Where am I?

The light did bring more of the room into focus, but this was an undesired effect.

He'd been sitting on a worn and dirty armchair and the mess was far more extensive than Tony had first thought. The empty cans and microwavable containers weren't just confined to the vicinity of the chair. The sea of garbage was pretty much everywhere—Tony could barely tell that the floor was made of untreated plywood. Plywood that was now irreparably stained.

He lifted his eyes, trying to take everything in.

Happy Valley paid him well and he lived in a small, but serviceable one-bedroom apartment in a decent neighborhood on the outskirts of Las Vegas.

Why am I here?

Then he saw it.

The wall across from the chair was completely covered in newspaper articles. Tony, his throat suddenly parched, moved toward the collage.

Some of the articles were older, but most were recent. It wasn't all newspaper articles, either; roughly a third of the pages stuck to the wall with clear tape were printouts from a website.

But, at least on first blush, they all seemed to have one thing in common: they featured Randy Milligan's name or smiling face.

Randy Milligan, the CEO of PopTop Games.

Randy Milligan, the man who had stolen Tony's game and went on to make millions from it.

Randy Milligan, who had lied about Tony to pretty much anyone who would listen, telling them that he was a below-average programmer, thus pretty much making him unhireable.

Tony's lips pulled back in a snarl, revealing his teeth.

Just seeing the man's smug face was enough to get Tony's heart racing.

"Fuck you," he cursed.

On the opposite wall, Tony saw a cheap door that someone had tried to paint but they'd obviously used the wrong type because it was peeling off in huge sheets.

He grabbed the door handle and pulled it open, needing to be out of there, needing to rid his lungs of foul air. But the hallway Tony found himself in didn't smell all that much better. The maroon carpeting was worn and musty as if it had gotten wet at some point and nobody had bothered to deep clean it.

Where am I? He wondered for what felt like the thousandth time. And while there was still no definitive answer, Tony couldn't overlook the obvious.

He'd been sitting in the chair. He'd been wearing his VR helmet and holding the controllers.

The brown smudges on his fingers looked suspiciously like the contents of several of the empty cans.

And the wall… the wall featured Randy Milligan, the man who had stolen millions from him.

Tony started walking. With every step, his muscles loosened, and his gait became more natural.

His snarl didn't change, however.

Tony wasn't sure where he was, but he knew exactly where he was headed.

Randy Milligan had found out what happened when you screwed Tony Metcalf out of code.

Now it was Jake Milligan's and Stu Barnes' turn.

Jake's voice suddenly piped up in his head and Tony started to laugh.

Tony Metcalfe is the best computer programmer in the whole world!

Chapter 39

"IT'S A BLUETOOTH SCRAMBLER," FLOYD said, turning the device over in his hand. "I'm no expert, but basically while this thing's on, Bluetooth is not going to work."

Stu suddenly snapped his fingers.

"You know what? Coming back from the garage I remember my phone wouldn't connect to the car."

Floyd held the scrambler up.

"This explains it. Your cameras work on Bluetooth, so someone just put this on your car and once you pulled into the driveway, they lost connection."

"And I lost an alibi."

Chase followed Floyd and Stu back inside.

"I turned it off, by the way," Floyd said, setting the device on the counter. "Security system should come back on soon."

Something was niggling at Chase.

"Stu, how did you know to go for an oil change?"

Stu made a face.

"What do you mean?"

"Was it on your calendar or do you have a personal assistant?"

"No PA. Something just popped up on the dash telling me it was time."

"Hmm," Chase said.

"What are you thinking?" Floyd asked.

"I'm thinking that if someone was good enough with computers to fake the video, then they'd probably be able to hack into Stu's car to tell him to get an oil change."

Stu looked uncomfortable now and Chase had to remind herself that even though this was a very rich man, he was still a civilian. The idea of being manipulated and targeted so specifically had to be alarming.

"Stu, what garage did you—"

"Gordon's. I always take it to Gordon's."

"And you don't have someone do this for you?"

Stu shook his head.

"No. I always do it."

Chase leaned over and picked up Stu's car keys from the counter where Floyd had placed them.

"Hey, Tate," she said loudly. The man turned his head in her direction.

"What's up?" His voice was even louder than hers. "What's going on?"

Chase looked skyward.

"Want to go for a drive?"

"Can't." Tate tapped at the helmet he was wearing. "Still reviewing footage. This is amazing."

Chase was starting to get annoyed with the man continually being awestruck by the technology.

"You finding anything out or just enjoying yourself?"

Tate raspberried his lips.

"Enjoying myself... I'm working here. Haven't seen anything yet other than a bunch of computer nerds."

Chase frowned and shook the keys in her hand.

"What about you, Floyd?"

Floyd shrugged.

"Sure, I'll go for a ride."

"What do you want me to do?" Stu asked.

Chase wasn't sure. Normally, she wouldn't want someone charged with murder involved at all. Especially a civilian. In this case, however, Stu should have had access to what they needed—HVG security footage and contacts at the company. But that had all been shut down.

At least through official means.

"Can you think of anyone at Happy Valley who would be willing to talk to you?"

Stu sighed.

"I don't... I'll try."

So far, the man had been holding up fairly well. Better than most. But now the weight of the situation was clearly pressing down on him.

Stu's features were drawn and there were dark circles beneath his eyes.

"Don't worry, Stu. We're going to figure this out," Chase said. But at the last second, she looked away.

***

Gordon's was a busy garage, with multiple bays full of luxury cars that were either on lifts or in the process of being hoisted onto lifts to be worked on. Chase parked Stu's car in front of one of the open bay doors.

"I'll have a chat with reception, you look around. They probably have security cameras somewhere."

Chase walked toward the entrance without waiting for a reply from Floyd. A bell chimed when she opened the door, and she shook her shoulders out.

A car garage wasn't the place to be a bully. Here, she needed to implement Tate's technique: to adopt a different personality completely.

"Hi," she said cheerily.

The man behind the counter was wearing blue coveralls and the backs of his hands were smeared with grease. The skin on his face was thick and red.

"How can I help you?" His voice was equally weathered.

Chase cringed dramatically.

"*Welllll*, this is going to sound weird, but I just started working for my boss and after I dropped him off, his car started to make a funny noise." Chase indicated Stu's car through the window. "At least, I think it just started? Anyways, he *loooves* his car. Is there a way to check if it was something that I did or if it was there all along, you know?"

The man suppressed a chuckle.

"I can take a look at it. We're busy now, but—"

"Can you just tell me if the car has any, like, history of ticking? It goes tick, tick, tick, every time I press the brake. It would make me feel *sooo* much better to know that it wasn't something I did. He brings it here for oil changes."

"What's the tag number?" the mechanic asked, his eyes drifting toward the window again.

"Oh, geez, I—"

"Never mind. I know that car."

As the man's large fingers attacked the keyboard, Chase twisted her shoulders forward, trying to release some of the tension. She didn't know how Tate did it. Being fake was physically and mentally exhausting and all Chase was doing was some lowkey flirting with a mechanic.

"No, no, no record of any ticking sound. But I do see here that Mr. Barnes' car is due for an oil change soon. As you can see, today isn't the best day but—"

"What?" Chase was so surprised that she dropped the act. "What do you mean, it's due for an oil change."

The man pursed his lips.

"Yeah, an oil change. Last one was nearly six months ago."

This couldn't be right.

"Are you sure?"

"Yes."

"Can you double-check? I mean, it's just that the last person who worked for my boss said that they brought the car in for an oil change last week."

The mechanic didn't look at his screen.

"Don't know what to tell you, lady, if the Maybach-S had an oil change, it wasn't done here."

Somebody was lying. Chase didn't like to stereotype, but this man who typed with just two fingers didn't strike her as someone capable of manipulating video footage of Jake's murder.

Not to mention why would he?

That meant one of two things: Stu was mistaken, or he was lying. But why would he lie? To further convince them of his innocence?

That didn't make much sense. Stu had to have known that Chase would investigate and discover the lie.

"Thanks," she said out of the corner of her mouth.

"Hey, you, uhh, you wanna book that oil change for later in the week? Hello? *Hello?*"

Chase left without turning. She didn't go to the car, however, and instead walked into one of the garage bays. A quick rundown revealed eight cars and eleven mechanics. All of the latter were white men, save one black male. All were wearing blue coveralls and all had grease smeared somewhere on their skin.

Floyd, who had been speaking to the only black mechanic spotted her, hooked a chin, and then came over to her side.

Bullying hadn't been the play inside with the man at the computer. But now that Chase knew what she wanted, what she needed, it was time to go back to her bread and butter.

She pulled her badge out and held it high.

Raising her voice, she said, "My name is Chase Adams and I'm a special agent with the FBI. Which one of you can get me the security footage from four days ago?"

Behind her, the door from the lobby leading directly into the garage opened, and the man that Chase had just spoken to stepped through.

He looked at her badge and then scowled.

"FBI? Really? I don't like being lied to."

"That makes two of us. But I'm still going to need to see that security camera footage. And I'm going to need to see it now."

Chapter 40

THE HEAT COMBINED WITH TONY'S exhaustion made Happy Valley Gaming look different from how he remembered it. It was still a glass building, but it was no longer as reflective as a placid body of water. It had ripples and waves, tiny imperfections in the glass that scattered the light in unpredictable directions. It also appeared shorter somehow, but Tony chalked this up to the haziness of the sweltering air and the fact that every time he tried to look up, his eyes started to water.

It was hot outside—*very* hot. And Tony hadn't had anything to drink in hours. His sweatshirt was soaked through, and his face was coated in a layer of thick, oily sweat.

It didn't matter how many floors there were, anyway—ten, sixteen, or a hundred.

He just had to get to the top.

He shuffled across the parking lot, keeping his head low so that his greasy hair covered most of his face. In his condition, it would be a miracle if they even let him inside the building. But they had to. Once he revealed who he was, they had to.

Tony's fall from revered programmer, the man who had single-handedly bridged the uncanny valley, to what he was now—despicable, disgusting, just a step up from vagrant—was unprecedented.

One day… one day after being fired and this is what he'd become.

Tony reached the door and was about to open it when he raised his eyes and peered through the glass.

Then he froze.

Gina was gone. The cute redheaded secretary who had said hello to him every single day since he started working at HVG was no longer behind her desk.

Had they fired her too? Why? Because she'd been nice to him?

It was an irrational thought. After all, the brunette behind the desk now, which, like the building itself seemed smaller than usual, could have just been standing in for Gina, who might have been sick or was just taking a personal day.

Tony swept his hair back from his face and stepped into the air-conditioned lobby. The air was so cool that it shocked his system and sent waves of goose pimples shooting across his flesh. He shivered but kept moving, heading for the turnstiles — no, not turnstiles.

The turnstiles were gone.

What the fuck?

The turnstiles Tony was used to had been swapped out for new, plastic partitions, the kind that opened in the middle and allowed you to walk through. The card readers, small metal boxes on round supports were the same, but this didn't matter because he didn't have a card anyway. They had confiscated that when they had fired him.

Or that's what he thought, anyway. Tony couldn't remember much of what had actually gone down, only that Jake had been grinning with his horse teeth and Stu —

"Excuse me?" Gina's replacement hollered after him. "Sir?"

Tony ignored her and approached the vertical plastic sheets. "Can I help you?"

Out of habit, Tony tapped his pockets but of course, there was no card there. He tested the plastic, tried to separate the two halves, but they were solid and didn't move.

Tony had been clenching his jaw and he forced himself to relax. Then he attempted a smile as he turned around to look at the secretary.

She had followed him halfway across the foyer.

"Hi, I need to speak to Stu," he said calmly. The woman didn't recoil but she had started to lean back a little.

"Oh, Stu," the woman appeared surprised by the request, and she tried to guide him toward the front desk. Tony didn't. "Well, sir, I can make you an appointment—"

"Appointment? No, I work here," Tony stated. When the secretary leaned back even further, he softened his approach. "What happened to Gina?"

"Gina...?"

Despite the woman's words, Tony could tell that she knew exactly who he was referring to.

"Yeah, Gina," he said impatiently. "You know, the redhead who has been working here every single day since I started?"

The woman cocked her head and batted her eyes.

"I'm sorry, but I'm not sure who are you referring to."

Tony stepped toward the woman. His skin felt hot again.

"Why are you lying? Why are you—"

There was a ping, a sound that Tony recognized immediately, and he spun back around.

It was Stu Barnes stepping from the elevator. And for once, the man wasn't smiling. Flanking him were two men—the lawyers, not the security guards, although they looked nearly identical to Tony. They weren't wearing suits, though, but business casual attire.

"Sir, if you come with me, I can book you an appointment." To her credit, the secretary was trying hard, but it was a lost cause.

"Stu!" Tony shouted, waving his hand.

Stu Barnes stepped through the plastic partition, which opened automatically when approaching from the other side.

"Can I help you?"

Yeah, you're not smiling now, are you? Tony paused. *Why aren't you smiling?*

He had come up with an entire dialog, a narrative, which he'd rehearsed in his head hundreds of times as he slogged through the heat to get here.

But now that Stu was in front of him, and he wasn't smiling? Tony forgot everything.

"I-I need my job back."

"I'm sorry?"

"No, like, I-I need it. My job. I need it back. I-I—"

The two men who had accompanied Stu out of the elevator moved into more protective postures.

"I'm very sorry, but I really don't know all the employees. I might be—"

"Why are you lying?" Tony's voice was high and tight.

"Excuse me?"

"You're lying! You're *fucking* lying! You stole my code! I solved the uncanny—" One of the men stepped forward and reached toward him. Tony slapped his hand away. "Don't you fucking touch me," he nearly shrieked. "You stole my work just like Roger!"

"Listen, buddy, you're going to have to leave," the same man who Tony had just swatted at said.

"Roger...?" Stu said, still engaging him despite obvious discouragement from his lawyers.

"Roger Milligan! Don't pretend to not know him. CEO of PopTop? He stole my code. And now you've done the same!"

Stu's expression which had been one of concern, softened a little.

"Look, I am the CEO here, but, admittedly, I have spent very little time at Happy Valley and my understanding of what people do here is minimal. If you have a legitimate gripe, I can set you up in a meeting with someone who knows the business—" Stu snapped fingers and turned to the man at his side. "What's his name?"

"Jake."

"Jake?" Tony repeated the word out of disgust, but this went misinterpreted.

"Yes, Jake…"

The lawyer filled in Stu's blank.

"Hollister."

"Right, Jake Hollister. I can get you a meeting. But you can't come in here dressed like that and yelling. That's not—"

"Why are you pretending not to know me?" Tony squealed. "You're a fucking liar! A thief and a *liar!*"

Tony reached for Stu's throat with both hands but didn't even come close to touching the man. Both of the lawyers anticipated the assault and grabbed him at the same time.

This triggered something in Tony's dehydrated brain: a flashback. In the vision, he was being hauled out of HVG by two square men, much larger men than Stu's lawyers. Men who looked identical to one another.

And like in the present, he was overcome with rage.

"Make sure you get this man some water," Stu said. "And give him some transit fare, if he needs it."

"Fucking bus money?" Tony screamed. He was being dragged now and Stu was walking briskly toward the front door. *"Bus money?* That's what you're offering me?"

No answer from Stu as he slipped outside. Tony bucked as he watched the man get behind the wheel of a slick Mercedes.

"Take it easy, bud. Take it easy."

Tony ignored the lawyer.

"You're going to pay," Tony hissed. "Like Roger paid. You're going to pay just like Roger."

Chapter 41

CHASE SHOULDN'T HAVE BEEN SURPRISED but she was.

There was no security footage for the days that Stu claimed to have gotten his oil changed at Gordan's. The man whom she'd lied to in the lobby was the head mechanic and also the manager and while he was not impressed by her deception, he did his best to be helpful. The issue was, simply, the man wasn't; he could not, for the life of him, explain why that day was the only day when the cameras didn't seem to be working.

"Does anyone remember seeing the car in here?" Chase shouted over the ambient garage sounds. "C'mon, it's a black Mercedes-Maybach for Christ's sake."

Most of the men shook their heads.

Apparently, serving a clientèle that included high rollers and Vegas performers meant that one could travel in relative anonymity even when driving a car that was worth nearly a quarter million dollars.

"Oil change, last Wednesday?" Chase continued to press. "Anybody?"

Nobody spoke up and she cursed under her breath.

They were wasting their time here.

She turned to the mechanic.

"I'm going to need a list of your employees."

The man nodded and disappeared back into the lobby. Chase dismissed the other workers and watched them closely, trying to pick up some sort of tell.

Was it one of them? Was one of these men responsible for murdering Jake and framing Stu?

Why?

It didn't make sense and there was no way to tell.

The mechanic returned and handed over a printout that had grease smudges on it.

"Here, hope this helps."

It probably wouldn't—the person they were looking for either didn't work at Gordon's or, if they did, identifying his name amongst the others would prove impossible.

Still, the mechanic had been as helpful as he could be, which Chase didn't deserve, and she thanked him.

Then she dragged Floyd back to Stu's car.

"I'm tired. So damn tired."

"Me too," Floyd admitted.

"Did you book a place to stay?" she asked as they made their way back toward Stu's mansion.

Floyd shook his head.

"Naw, just hopped on a plane. Stu has enough rooms—"

"Probably best if you get a hotel room," Chase suggested. She didn't think that Stu was dangerous, far from it, but if he was convicted it wouldn't look good for three FBI agents—well, two current and one ex—to have been staying at his home before the trial. "I'm at the Juniper Inn, just up the road. Nice place. I'm sure Stu will cover the costs if you and Tate want to stay there."

"*Hmm.*"

This response was starting to bug Chase nearly as much as being referred to as 'ma'am'. She pulled into Stu's driveway, put the car in park, and then aggressively turned toward her friend. It was time to clear the air once and for all.

"Floyd, when I—"

"Why do you care so much?" the man interrupted.

Chase recoiled as if Floyd's words were the equivalent of a physical assault.

"Excuse me?"

"Why do you care so much about Stu Barnes?"

"He's a—"

Once again, Floyd refused to let her answer.

"I get that he saved you. And I know all about what happened in Vegas. But still," he shrugged, "you come all the way out here to help him out of a bind? Why?"

This wasn't the question, of course. The real question was the one that Floyd wasn't asking.

Why do you care so much about Stu, but so little about me?

Chase sighed.

Just tell him. Tell him about Brian Jalston, about him getting out of prison and seeking custody of Georgina. He'll understand.

True, but then he'd also be burdened by another issue and Floyd had enough on his plate already.

"I'm not... I'm not good for you, Floyd," she admitted. Chase glanced out the windshield and at Stu's mansion. "After this thing with Stu is done, I'll leave here. Maybe I'll get a Christmas card or something from him on my birthday. And if I'm ever in Vegas, I'll look him up." This time, when Chase wished he'd interrupt, Floyd allowed her to continue. And she did—reluctantly. "But with you... we're connected. And the more connected we become, the more dangerous it is for you. The worse..." She closed her eyes, thinking of the way she used to be, how she would risk anything to get a fix. "Look, it's better for you if I stay away."

Floyd stared at her for a long time without even blinking. But Chase was unaffected by the man's shock. Despite her harsh words, it felt as if a weight had been lifted off her shoulders. Chase wasn't the most introspective of people, but she knew that she was toxic. Brad had also known it—he'd taken the first and furthest job offer he'd gotten and packed up and left. Took Felix with him. Stitts knew it, too. And Floyd... he was too innocent to be corrupted by her.

"You're a coward."

Chase felt all the air being squeezed from her lungs as if there was a vice wrapped around her midsection.

"Wh-what?"

But the word fell on deaf ears. Floyd was already out of the car and hustling toward Stu's front steps. She chased after him, but he made it inside before she could even get close.

And as soon as she stepped over the threshold, Chase was back in FBI mode.

"Anything?" Stu asked desperately.

Floyd was the one who answered.

"Sorry, security footage was wiped, probably used the same device as the one on your car. Worse, they have no record of you even being there."

"But I was," Stu protested. "I *was*."

"Did you get a receipt?" Floyd asked.

Stu frowned.

"No receipt. They have everything on file, they usually just bill my card. I-I—"

"It's alright," Chase said, trying to calm the man. She pulled out the list of employees and passed it to Stu. He was so frustrated that he snatched it from her. "Recognize any of these names?"

Stu quickly scanned the list.

"I-I don't know. I don't think so." Stu raised his eyes from the paper and stared at her. "Do you think the mechanic was the guy who put that scrambler thing on my car? Do you think—"

"Maybe. Do you remember what he looked like? The man who changed your oil?"

She knew the answer to this, too, but had to ask.

"I mean—I mean, he looked like a regular guy," Stu stammered. "A mechanic, you know?"

Chase nodded. All you saw at Gordon's were blue coveralls and grease smears. Stu was becoming deflated, and the feeling was contagious.

"Tell them about Isaac," Will lowered a cup of what looked like coffee from his lips. "Stu?"

"Isaac?" Chase asked, unable to keep the excitement from her voice. They were desperate and everyone knew it.

"Yeah, Isaac Lomax. VP of software at Happy Valley. I reached out like you asked and he's willing to talk. He's the *only* one who's willing to talk."

"You know him well?"

"No, not really. Met him once or twice. Talked on the phone before we bought Happy Valley. But he said he'd talk to me."

"When?"

"Tonight."

Chase considered this and then shook her head.

"No, not tonight." She glanced down at his ankle. Even though Stu was wearing slacks, she could see the bulge of the ankle monitor beneath. "Does he know about that?"

"No—I don't think so."

"Okay, set up the meeting for tomorrow. Breakfast. Somewhere busy."

"I can't leave, Chase. I—"

"You're not going. I am." Nobody protested, not even Floyd, so Chase changed the subject. "Tate? Did you hear anything we said?"

"What?" The jackass still had his head jammed in the VR helmet. "Chase? That you?"

For fuck's sake.

"You find out anything?" she asked in a tone just shy of a yell.

"No—I mean, other than the fact that—fuck, hold on." Tate removed his mask and stretched the skin under his eyes. Then he blinked long and slow. "Jesus, that's disorienting."

"Did you get anything from the security footage at HVG?"

"No, not really. He left late the night he was killed alone, pretty much the same time as every other night. This Jake Hollister worked a lot. I mean, he practically slept at the office. Especially in the days leading up to his murder."

"What was he working on?"

Tate shrugged.

"No clue. I only have footage of people coming and going. Maybe this Isaac guy can clear that up?" Tate lifted his chin toward Will. He had a red line around his face from where the mask was too tight that reminded Chase of the ring that little kids would get around their asses when they sat on the toilet for too long. "You have a picture of this guy?"

So, you did hear, Chase thought. *What's your game, Tate?*

Will spun the laptop around and showed them Isaac Lomax's bio from the Happy Valley website.

"No shit," Tate said. He tapped the VR helmet. "Isaac's in here. He spends a lot of time talking to Jake. Secrets, you know?"

Tate picked up the mask, clearly intending on putting it back on.

"Maybe you should take a break," Chase suggested. "I know I need one."

Tate lifted one shoulder.

"*Mehhhh.*"

"Well, I'm going to get some food," Chase said. "Stu, you reach out to Isaac and change the meeting to tomorrow morning. Ten-ish. We'll meet here before that. Early"

And then Chase left, daring someone to tell her to stay.

No one did, not even Floyd, and this, for some reason, made Chase a little sadder than she'd been when she'd stepped inside the mansion.

Chapter 42

TONY DIDN'T GO HOME. THE two men who escorted him out of Happy Valley told him to go home, but he didn't.

Sure, he pretended that that was where he was headed, but he declined a cab, which those assholes even offered to pay for, and set off on foot. When the two men went back inside, he watched Stu Barnes leave in his fancy car from hiding. This wasn't a particularly easy task, given the fact that the Happy Valley Gaming headquarters was essentially a mirror in the desert. There was a single, large tree on the east side of the building, offering a paltry amount of shade for a picnic table that only an insane person would use during the day. Probably some HR mandate.

Tony hunkered next to it, pressing his back against the trunk, his eyes trained on the front of Happy Valley.

And then he waited.

And waited.

And waited.

Time had a curious way of operating in the desert, especially for someone who was dehydrated and on the verge of heat stroke. Several times, Tony, in a state of mild delirium, had risen with the intention of heading home, or going anywhere to get a drink of water, but his body had rejected the idea.

He dozed instead and when he awoke sometime later, the sun had set, and the air had cooled.

It was late when Jake finally emerged from the building. Past midnight, certainly, but beyond that, Tony was unable to be more specific.

Despite having his head down, Tony could see the fatigue reflected in the man's posture. His shoulders were rounded, his chin down as if his head had become too heavy for his neck.

Tony felt similar pain throughout his body, but his extended all the way to his lower back.

Grunting, Tony wriggled up the tree trunk until he was standing. He was forced to ignore the pain and break into a half-jog to catch up with his ex-boss.

"Jake?" Tony said when he was within a dozen feet of the man. "Hey, Jake?"

Startled, Jake turned around. The way his eyes darted, and he licked his lips furiously was a clear giveaway that his nerves were shot from too much caffeine and Adderall.

"Y-yes?"

Yes? What kind of question was that?

"Don't 'yes' me," Tony snapped. "You know what I want—you stole my code."

Jake took a step backward.

"What? I don't know what you're talking about."

Oh, he was good. Who knew Jake was an Oscar-level actor to go along with a lying, thieving bastard?

"Don't act dumb with me," Tony sneered. "I broke the valley, and you stole the code. Then you fired me. I want back in."

"Buddy, I-I don't know what you're talking about."

Tony snarled and reached for the man, but his muscles were weak, and his movements labored from sitting in the hot sun all day. Jake easily stepped out of range.

"I'm going to call the cops," Jake warned. He looked toward Happy Valley, but they both knew that nobody was going to come out and save him. "You come anywhere near me, and I'll call the cops."

He was lying. Jake wouldn't call the cops because then he'd have to explain the stolen code.

"Let me back in!" Tony screamed as he lunged.

Jake was exhausted, but Tony was in far rougher shape. Despite having the element of surprise on his side, Jake easily side-stepped his attack while at the same time delivering a surprisingly deft sweep kick to Tony's ankles.

He was airborne and then he fell.

Hard.

Tony's chin smashed off the pavement and his teeth gnashed together with such violent intensity that the front two broke in half. He screamed and blood filled his mouth—from his lips? His tongue? Where is the blood coming from? Tony was only passively aware that one of his elbows had taken what brunt his chin had selfishly neglected to absorb.

"I didn't want to hurt you, Tony—I didn't. But you're not supposed to be here!"

Still emitting a prolonged croak originating from somewhere deep inside his belly, Tony managed to raise his eyes to look at Jake through tear-streaked vision.

True to his word, he'd pulled his cell phone out and pressed it to his ear.

"You stole my code..." Tony tried to say, but his words were wet with blood.

"No," Jake muttered. "No, no, no... this is all wrong."

"You stole it!" Even to Tony, this sounded wrong—*you shhhtole etch.*

"9-1-1, what's your emergency?" Tony heard the words even though the phone was still against the side of Jake's head. "Hello? 9-1-1?"

Jake hung up the phone. His face looked different now. He was more angry than surprised now.

"There was no code, Tony! Cerberus isn't about code—it never was. It was about you! Just leave it alone. Please, just leave it alone."

Blood dripped down the back of Tony's throat and he sputtered and coughed. When he'd recovered, Jake was already getting in his car.

"No!" Tony moaned.

As he watched Jake drive off, he rolled onto his back, spat off to the side, and stared up at the crescent of a moon. Running his tongue over what was left of his two front teeth, Tony realized that the missing portions were exactly that shape: crescent.

Jake had told him that this wasn't about his code.

But it was.

It was always about the code.

Leave it alone? Really?

When he started working at HVG, Tony had thought that Jake and the company were different.

But they weren't.

They were just like PopTop Games. Just like Roger Milligan.

Happy Valley, PopTop, Stu Barnes, Roger Milligan, Jake Hollister.

They were all the same. All the *fucking* same.

They'd stolen from him, both claiming that he was a liar that his code didn't exist that he was a nobody that he was worthless that he didn't exist.

Tony slowly began to peel himself off the pavement, wincing at the pain in his elbow. His sweatshirt had grown tight over the joint, which had ballooned to three times its normal size.

A plan began to form in his head. A delicious, delightful plan. An ironic plan.

A beautiful plan.

They claimed his code didn't exist, that he didn't make any code. Perhaps it was time to make them pay for something they didn't do.

When he finally managed to stand at his full height, Tony looked at the moon again. Then he smiled, marveling at how his teeth looked like the moon. For now, anyway. But things change. In a day or two, a week, maybe, the moon would be full.

But Tony's teeth would still be crescents.

And his code would still be gone.

Chapter 43

FLOYD HAD NEVER BEEN A big drinker. He hadn't attended college and during the time when others his age were out getting wasted, he was too busy working for his uncle to spend many nights out on the town. It wasn't just a lack of opportunity, however, but also the fact that his debilitating stutter meant that he really didn't have any friends to party with.

This was the primary reason why after only three beers during a rather mundane and pedantic dinner with his past and present partners, Floyd was well on his way to being drunk.

After imbibing a fourth beverage, he was all the way there.

When the check came, Chase was the first one to reach for it.

Floyd waved a hand at Tate.

"Hey, why d-don't you pitch in?"

Tate, who had drunk more than him but was much better at tolerating his alcohol, frowned.

"I'm cash-strapped at the moment."

"Yeah, right," Floyd said with mock laughter. "Cash strapped, my a-ass."

Tate shot daggers at him.

"Relax," Chase said, offering them both a curious look. "I'll just pass it on to Stu."

And the man would gladly pay it. All Floyd had to do was mention that he didn't have a place to sleep, and Stu had called the Juniper Inn where Chase was booked, just like she said he would. Floyd had asked for his own room, but Tate insisted they share. Because, of course, he did.

Choo-Choo, Floyd.

"I'm tired," Chase proclaimed, a sentiment shared by all. "I think I'm going to head to my room."

They said their goodbyes and Floyd, stumbling a little, followed Tate who kept on rambling about how realistic the metaverse was. He'd borrowed the VR equipment from Stu and was itching to drop back into an alternate reality.

Tate used the electronic keycard to unlock the hotel room door and held it open for Floyd.

"You know what I'm thinking?" Tate said, a large grin spreading across his face. "I'm thinking that fucking in the metaverse would—"

"What about f-fighting?"

Tate stopped smiling.

"What?"

Floyd flopped onto the bed. He put his hands behind his head and closed his eyes.

"I mean, can you find some l-lowlife drug dealer to beat up and s-s-steal his money in the m-metaverse?" Floyd's words ran together but they were still comprehensible.

Or so he thought. But when no reply came, he opened one eye and turned his head to face Tate.

The man's jaw was tight, as were the muscles in his neck.

"It's not what you think, Floyd."

Floyd sputtered a laugh.

"Oh, yeah, it was about teaching me the ropes, right? Learning how things on the s-s-street work? L-like, how to r-rob people?"

"No," Tate snapped. "Well, yeah—that learning the streets shit was a lie. But you don't..." he allowed his sentence to trail off.

"I don't, what? Understand—yeah, sure, little Floyd with his l-little problems, doesn't understand big k-k-k-k-kid issues. I'm so sick of hearing that. You and Chase are the same. You won't get it. Really? Why don't fu-fu-fucking try me, then? Huh?

Goddamn it, you two f-f-f-f-f..." Now it was his turn to end his sentence prematurely, although likely for very different reasons. But when he noticed that Tate's hands had become fists, he managed to get his stutter under control and said, "What, you gonna hit me now? Just so you know, I don't have any money to s-steal."

For some reason, Floyd's inflammatory remarks, designed to incite, had the opposite effect. Tate's lips transformed from a thin, tight line, to a smirk.

"You're wasted, bro. Sleep it off."

"Whatever," Floyd grumbled. He closed his eyes again and flipped onto his side. "What am I even doing here?"

Helping a friend, a tiny voice in the back of his head told him. No, that's not right. *Helping a friend of a friend... a friend of a friend of a friend... Choo-Choo, the train has stopped at the station. Last stop, everyone out!*

Floyd must have dozed off because he barely heard the hotel room door open. He turned in that direction, but the alcohol had made his movements languid. The door closed just as Tate left with the case containing the VR equipment in hand.

He turned his head straight.

Fuck him and fuck Chase, was the last thought Floyd had before slumber took him.

That night, he dreamed of a train. As per Dr. Matteo's advice, the locomotive kept on moving and wouldn't stop. Floyd was in the conductor's chair, and he was wearing an old-timey black and white striped hat. Ahead, there was a fork in the tracks and at the helm of a train that would, could not be stopped, Floyd had to choo-choose which way to go.

And on each of these tracks stood a person. Chase was to the right, hands on her hips, her strange greyish-white hair blowing in the wind. On the left, Tate massaged his mustache with one hand.

Old and new. Past and present.

It's time to *Choo-Choose*, Floyd.

It's time to *Choo-Choose* whose side you're really on.

Chapter 44

IT WAS EASY. TOO EASY.

Tony already had a gun, a piece he'd picked up a few years back when there had been a rash of burglaries in his neighborhood. The Bluetooth scrambler he purchased in Broward County using cash. The location that he planned on using was poetic, to say the least. It was also convenient. While Tony's access to anything HVG related had been revoked, the *U-lock-it* facility was owned by the same parent company, Stu Barnes' company, and they used similar cybersecurity software. But unlike the Happy Valley Metaverse, which, thanks to his help, was nearly impossible to hack into, nobody put much effort into securing the security footage from a storage facility in the middle of nowhere. The same could be said of the cameras in Stu Barnes' home.

Finding the man's address had been easy, as had been hacking into his router. Creating the deep fake proved to be a bit more challenging, especially because the timing had to be perfect, but he was Tony *fucking* Metcalfe.

And, according to the man himself, according to Jake Hollister, *Tony Metcalfe is the best computer programmer in the whole world!*

The hardest part would be luring Jake to the storage facility, especially because the man would be on edge from their 'encounter'.

Tony rubbed his tongue across his broken front teeth.

Cerberus... last night, Jake mentioned Cerberus again.

His secret project. The one he claimed that once people dropped in, they couldn't help but stay there.

A world with no rules except for you only get one chance. Controlled chaos... but controlled by whom?

That's why Jake was so desperate to improve the quality of the NPCs, to make them more real, more lifelike.

There was potential there and Tony knew it. There was a market for chaos. It was sold in brightly colored cans, paraded in the streets under different flags, professed in Reddit threads that resembled manifestos.

Tony also knew that anything created under Happy Valley's roof, or by a HVG employee, whether it was a side gig or on your own time, would eventually become their property.

Like his fucking code.

Jake had been hush-hush about Cerberus for a reason.

Because he didn't want to share. Not with HVG and after he'd gotten what he'd wanted out of Tony, not with him either.

This gave Tony an idea. He didn't have time to create an entirely new identity, so he modded someone who already existed, hijacked their profile, so to speak. Someone with money and clout, someone who had already expressed an interest in the metaverse. Then all he had to do was start probing, lightly at first, inquiring about novel developments and applications.

Looking for something new and unique to buy.

And Jake took the bait, hook line, and *motherfucking* sinker.

The corners of his lips curled upward, and Tony raised his eyes from the gun that lay on the crotch of his soiled sweatpants to the wall across from him.

The wall was covered in articles and printouts and photos and handwritten notes.

There was Roger Milligan, smiling during his announcement that PopTop hadn't just exceeded but had *shattered* quarterly earnings estimates just as he was in his obituary photo.

Tony didn't linger on these. His main focus was two more recent images: Jake Hollister and Stu Barnes.

The Roger Milligan situation hadn't gone as planned. Not even close. Tony had fucked almost everything up and he'd nearly gotten caught.

But things would be different this time around.

Someone *would* get caught for Jake's murder.

But it wouldn't be him.

He'd also get the password he needed, the master password to the metaverse that only Jake Hollister possessed. Tony would drop in, grab his code, and pull it out. Then he'd sell to the highest bidder. Maybe he'd even take Cerberus as his own, sell that, too. Why not? It was his code that made the thing any good if it was good. And instead of Happy Valley or PopTop reaping the rewards this time around, it would be him.

Tony tightened his grip on the gun, never taking his eyes off the two photographs of the men who had screwed him over.

"Yeah," he whispered. "It will be me this time. For once in my fucking life, it will be my time to shine. And everyone will know exactly what Jake Hollister already knows."

Tony cleared his throat, ran his tongue over his chipped teeth, and using his best impression of his ex-boss's voice, he shouted, "*Tony Metcalfe is the best computer programmer in the whole world!*"

Then he started to chuckle.

Chapter 45

CHASE HAD CROSSED THE PERNICIOUS line between being exhausted and not being able to sleep. Worse, fatigue had caused her thoughts to blend into a twisted Salvador Dali creation.

Brian Jalston, Floyd, Georgina, Stu, the metaverse. Cerebrum, the pill that made non-believers take their own lives, briefly played a starring role.

At least Georgina was safe—for the time being, at least. Louisa would protect the girl with her life but if the courts came calling... what would she do then?

Chase was sitting on the corner of her bed, twisting the sheets in her hands.

It won't come to that. I won't let it come to that. If I have to, I'll run.

Unlike Floyd, who was apparently pissed at the entire world, she hadn't overdone it with drinks at dinner. Only two pints, and they were commercial low-ABV garbage. What she wanted now was a nice scotch. Something smoky. Something cask strength that would settle her mind and help her sleep.

Having made up her mind, Chase left the hotel room and stepped into the night. While it wasn't quite stifling as it had been earlier in the day, it was still warm enough. Vegas was strange like that. Most everywhere she'd lived, from Seattle to New York, had distinct seasons, which were reflected on a smaller scale during the day. It was cool in the morning—spring—warm during midday—summer—then cooler in the evening—fall—and cold at night—winter.

But not Las Vegas. Las Vegas was either sweltering hot or just plain regular hot.

Chase was so wrapped up in this inane line of thinking that she didn't immediately realize that the man standing with his forehead pressed against the vending machine was Tate.

He was standing completely still, one hand gripping the handle of a case, the other hanging limply at his side.

"Tate?"

When the man didn't react, Chase considered that perhaps it wasn't Tate. She walked closer to get a better look.

"Tate? You okay?"

Fearing that he'd had a stroke or heart attack, Chase rushed toward him.

"Tate!"

She grabbed the man by the arm and spun him around, prepared to catch him if he fell—a stupid idea, given that Tate outweighed her by at least fifty pounds, probably more. But he didn't fall. Instead, he finally turned to look at her.

There was a deep sadness in Tate's eyes. Real pain that Chase recognized. Pain that seemed strangely familiar.

This is the real Tate, she realized. Not the person he pretended to be, the one who jokingly asked for her autograph, or who got great pleasure out of grossing out and teasing Floyd.

"Shit, are you okay?"

Tate shuddered, a minor convulsion, and then he offered her a weak smile.

"Yeah, fine. I think they put cheese on my burger. Damn lactose."

Chase let go of the man's arm.

"Don't do that."

Tate rubbed his mustache.

"Do what?"

Chase wasn't sure why she'd said what she had. Tate's business was Tate's business. She barely knew the man. But as much as she wanted to blame her actions on exhaustion, Chase knew there was another reason why she'd challenged him.

It was because of what she'd seen in his eyes. She saw the same look every time she looked in the mirror.

"Lie. You can lie to Floyd—hell, I lie to him, I lie to protect him all the time, but you don't need to do that to me. I don't need protection."

Tate tried to smile but this attempt was even more pathetic than the first.

Chase grabbed his arm again, gently this time, and eased him in the direction of her room. They said nothing until they were in her room and Chase, desperately wanting a smoky scotch, settled for two mini bottles of Jack Daniels from the fridge. She didn't bother with glasses, just tore the tops off before handing one to Tate and keeping one for herself.

Tate plopped himself in the room's only chair, while Chase opted for her usual position on the bed, free hand flat this time instead of wrapping her fingers in the thin sheet.

She said nothing—neither of them did. They just sipped their whiskey in silence.

Only when they were done with their first bottles and Chase had retrieved two more, did Tate finally say, "I lied to him."

The sadness had returned to his features.

"Floyd—I lied to him. And I hate that I did. He's a good kid—I mean, you'd know better than I, but…" Tate paused to collect his thoughts. "There are some things that he doesn't need to know. Some things that I shouldn't have exposed him to… aw, fuck. I just—I don't know why—"

"I was addicted to heroin," Chase blurted. "I was working undercover as a Narc for Seattle PD and shit happened. Got in too deep and took my first hit to save face but also to escape. And then I couldn't stop. I fucked everyone and everything just to make sure that I could get another hit. That was the only thing that mattered."

If Tate was shocked by her admission, or even surprised by it, he never let on.

What the fuck are you doing, Chase?

She didn't know whose voice that was, but she recognized the one that followed.

It was Dr. Matteo.

Live in the motherfucking moment.

Well, minus the *motherfucking* part.

"I was trying to forget. My sister," now Chase faltered as a flood of memories stole her words. Flashes of her sister with her bright orange hair, looking so much like her niece, like little Georgina. "She was taken, kidnapped. And I couldn't find her. No matter how hard I tried, I could not find her. And heroin just offered me something that nobody or nothing else could: the ability to forget. The ability to forget about what happened to her, to us. It wasn't just the high, either, although that was potent. It was that when I was addicted the only thing that mattered was getting more smack. And that meant I couldn't think about anything else... including my sister."

Tate nodded and finished what little whiskey was left in the plastic container. Then he folded his hands on his lap and sighed.

"A couple years back, my wife and daughter were in a terrible accident. They were coming home from this event, a celebration for my daughter who had just finished competing in a swim meet. She was sixteen. They left the event around nine in the evening. It was raining out, really raining, and for some reason, they tried to beat a red light. They swerved and hit another car. The man in the other vehicle didn't make it and my daughter was paralyzed." When Chase saw the tears streaming down the man's cheeks, she finished her drink and walked over to him. She placed a comforting hand on his shoulder. "My wife... she was fine, but she was also drunk. She was arrested and I spent every dime I had getting help for my daughter and trying to keep my wife out of prison. I failed at both. Wife is serving fifteen years, daughter can't walk, and the night terrors she suffers from keep us both up every night."

Chase leaned into Tate as he sobbed.

"Every dollar I make goes to helping my daughter... I work to pay for her to be looked after during the day."

Chase got the impression that there was more to this story that, like her, Tate was omitting certain details, but that was okay. She also had the sense that this is the most the man had shared with anyone in some time.

"Sometimes," Tate continued after a handful of shuddering breaths, "I let drug dealers peddle their shit with immunity if they pay me a cut. They're going to do it anyways. But I limit how much they can move and where and I use the cash to—"

Chase lifted Tate's chin.

And then she kissed him. Maybe it was the man's vulnerability or maybe it was the fact that she could finally relate with someone with pain that cut nearly as deeply as hers.

Or perhaps what she felt was less refined and more carnal in nature.

Tate kissed her back. His mustache tickled her upper lip, but this only made her lean into the kiss, her tongue slipping from her mouth and into his.

Tate grabbed the back of her neck and pulled her tight. They kissed hungrily, both desperate, both needing to feel something other than pain.

For all of his macho talk, Tate was too polite, too reserved. That changed when Chase grabbed his hand and placed it on one of her breasts. It was as if she'd flicked a switch in him—Tate tore her shirt off, unhooked her bra, and then squeezed her nipple between thumb and forefinger, instantly making it hard.

Chase gasped.

This was painful, but it was a good kind of painful.

Tate pulled his face away and made wet trails with his lips and tongue from her collarbone to her breast, before finally taking her nipple into his mouth.

Moaning softly, Chase reached into his pants, felt his hardness, and began stroking him.

They barely made it to the bed.

Chase finished first, gasping, panting, raking her nails down Tate's back as she came. A few seconds later, Tate followed suit, shuddering as he collapsed on top of her.

It was the best sex Chase had since… well, for as long as she could remember.

After he'd caught his breath, Tate rolled onto his back. For Chase, sleep came quickly. For him, not so much. At some point during the night, Chase awoke to find the bed empty beside her.

But Tate hadn't left her. He was sitting in the chair, Stu's VR goggles attached to his head.

We all have our addictions, she thought incomprehensibly, before turning onto her side. *Some are just more deadly than others.*

PART III – Cerberus

Chapter 46

"NO, NO, NO," TONY MUTTERED, shaking his head. Greasy strands of hair, like overcooked spaghetti, stuck first to his right then his left cheek.

Things had gone perfectly until they hadn't.

Stu had been arrested for Jake's murder even faster than Tony could have hoped. But then they'd let him out again.

Bail.

They gave *him* bail.

Tony couldn't believe it.

I should have left the gun. I should have just left it.

His initial plan had been to lift Stu's prints off his car and place them on the gun that he'd used to kill Jake. But the stupid mechanic with the wrinkly face kept on coming around, rushing him. Tony didn't have time to pull a usable print. He'd barely had enough to install the Bluetooth jammer and that thing was magnetic.

So, he'd kept the gun.

No court would have let Stu out on bail if the murder weapon, with his prints on it, was found at the scene.

But it was too late now.

Tony's eyes drifted to the gun in his lap. Even though two bullets had been spent, it felt strangely heavier now. Like a lump of ore.

He casually slipped his finger onto the trigger and ever so gently ran his finger across it.

Eyes closed, he pictured Jake Hollister on the ground, whimpering, holding his hand up in front of his face.

The other times that Tony had killed his boss, watching the fear in the man's eyes as he realized that he was about to die, that for once, he had no control over the situation, had been the most satisfying part.

This time around it had been different, because this time Jake had given him the master password and much, much more.

And that had made Tony smile.

But the best part? The best part was when Tony stepped into the light and Jake finally saw who it was.

The man thought he was meeting with someone interested in buying Cerberus, the cloak and dagger circumstances necessitated by the fact that most, if not all, of the chaotic new metaverse, was owned by Happy Valley Gaming. The investor didn't care—after all, possession was nine-tenths of the law. And Jake had promised to wipe all traces of the development of Cerberus from HVG servers.

But, of course, there was no investor.

There was only Tony Metcalfe—*the best computer programmer in the whole world!*—with a gun and a vendetta. And when Jake realized that…

Tony licked his lips, reveling at how high the corners had extended up his cheeks.

Yeah, that was the best part.

Hands down.

At some point during his reverie, Tony had shut his eyes. He opened them now, and the grin dropped off his face.

There were new people pasted to his wall now. Three of them.

A skinny black kid, a man in his forties with a mustache and brown hair, and her.

The grin threatened to return, more lascivious this time, and Tony licked his lips as he thought about her. She had strange hair, gray, nearly white, even though he doubted she was even in her thirties. Short, five-three on a good day, with a small but athletic frame. A runner's body, maybe. There was something about her, about the way she moved. This woman did not take shit from anyone.

Tony felt himself getting hard.

It had been easy to identify the two men. They were both FBI Agents: Floyd Montgomery and Tate Abernathy, respectively. One a vet, one a rookie.

Figuring out who the woman was had taken more digging. A lot more. Somebody had done a decent job scrubbing her from the Internet and had almost succeeded in eliminating her presence entirely. But life was easier to erase than death, and Mrs. Chase Adams was already dead. Tony had uncovered a charming obituary for Chase that had been issued in the Times, which had either been missed or someone had deliberately left it online.

Either way, it was a mistake.

Chase Adams was very much alive. My god was she ever.

Now Tony was as hard as the gun in his hand.

His eyes drifted from the photograph of Jake on his wall, now defaced with a giant red X, to Stu Barnes. He'd crossed this man's face out, too, but that had proven a tad premature.

Tate's and Floyd's faces had no markings on them—yet— but Chase's image, a photograph that Tony had taken himself outside Stu's home, was circled multiple times.

"Oh, Chase," Tony moaned. He released his hold of the gun and grabbed his VR gear. "Chase, Chase, Chase."

What an ironic name, he thought. *Chase*.

He slipped the goggles over his head.

But the thing is, I don't have to chase you, Chase, because I have you right here.

The screen lit up before his eyes and the word '*CERBERUS*' in front of a gnashing three-headed dog appeared.

Jake had given him so much more than just a password.

He'd given him Cerberus.

And in the process, Jake Hollister had unwittingly transformed Tony Metcalfe from the best computer programmer in the whole world to a God.

Chapter 47

"**WERE YOU UP ALL NIGHT?**" Chase asked when she rolled over and saw Tate still sitting on the chair, goggles still on his eyes.

Tate didn't answer so Chase sat up. She was naked but didn't bother pulling the sheet up to cover her breasts. There was no need. Even if she was bashful, which she wasn't, Tate couldn't see her with his eyes, and his mind was stuck in the metaverse.

"Tate? Were you up all night?"

Tate cleared his throat.

"Yeah, couldn't sleep. Might have found something."

Chase stood, completely naked now, and walked to the bathroom to start the shower.

"Like what?" she asked over her shoulder, hand extended as she tested the water temperature.

"Not sure yet," Tate admitted. "I'm going to keep on looking."

"Careful—you stay in there any longer, and you'll forget which world is the real one."

"Naw," Tate said, with a chuckle. "Not after last night—that was real."

Chase rolled her eyes and stepped into the shower. As the water and soap cascaded over her, she thought about last night. Tate was right, what had happened between them was real.

It was also the first time in a long time, maybe since meeting Brad, that she didn't hate herself or the person she'd just slept with.

Why was that? Was it because she actually had feelings for Tate? He wasn't her usual 'type', although to be fair, he was handsome in a traditional way and Chase had never been all

that discriminating. Sometimes a dick was just a dick. Could it
be that she felt something for him, then? Was that even possible? Last night notwithstanding, she'd spent—what? A total of
twenty hours with the man? Thirty, at best?

Chase knew firsthand that not all hours were created equal
just as she knew that what Tate had shared with her was something that he hadn't even hinted at with those he spent months
with, like Floyd.

Or was it simpler… was it that they were two broken people
and together they came close to a mended whole?

Chase rinsed the soap from her hair and scolded herself.

Why are you even thinking about this? It was just one time; it was
just a fuck.

Chase distracted herself by coming back to the case, and her
upcoming meeting with Isaac Lomax, the one man in all of
HVG that agreed to speak with Stu.

Would he have any insight into why Jake was killed? Or by
whom?

Chase turned off the water and got out of the shower. She
wrapped a towel around herself and leaned into the room.

"I've got that meeting with Isaac this morning, you want to
join?"

Tate finally pulled off the headgear and stretched his eyes.

"Love to, but I gotta ask Stu about something I saw on here."

Chase waited for the man to elaborate but when he didn't,
she shrugged.

"Okay." She looked at the door. "What about Floyd?"

Something that wasn't quite a scowl but close to it, appeared
on Tate's face.

"He probably needs a little more time to sleep it off. I'm
gonna need his lip-reading skills soon, though."

Chase nodded and then stretched. She wished that she'd gone for a run this morning as planned, but she'd been exhausted and had slept in.

It was almost eight in the morning.

"I'm going to get going."

"Sure."

Chase dressed quickly, with the intention of leaving before things became awkward.

She was almost home free—hand on the doorknob, car keys wrapped around a knuckle—when Tate said, "Chase... is this over?"

She tried her best not to cringe.

Well, is it, Chase? Was this just a one-night stand? Or something more?

"Chase?"

She shrugged and opened the door.

"Sorry, can't think on an empty stomach."

***

Isaac Lomax was a fidgety, nervous man.

Chase was early for the breakfast date—Isaac had reluctantly agreed to change the meeting time—but Isaac was earlier still. Instead of sliding into the booth across from Happy Valley's VP of software, Chase elected to sit at the bar and order a coffee. Then she watched.

Isaac sat with his hands on the table, his long fingers interlaced. Like her, he had a coffee in front of him, but he didn't drink it. Several times, he took out his phone, checked the time, and looked for a text that never arrived, before putting the device back in his pocket.

Chase waited until 8:30 when it appeared as if Isaac was ready to leave before, coffee in hand, she sat wordlessly across from him.

"*Uhh*, excuse me?"

Chase reached into her pocket and flopped her badge onto the table. This got the reaction she wanted. Those three letters—FBI—made everyone nervous. It was one of the very few perks of the job.

"You look like you're waiting for someone."

"What—what?"

"No, not what—who. Mr. Stu Barnes, am I right?"

Isaac Lomax looked as if he was attempting to swallow a burr.

"Am I in trouble here?"

Chase shrugged.

"That depends—did you kill Jake Hollister?"

If the man had been drinking his coffee instead of just staring at it, Chase had no doubt that he would have spat it all over both of them.

"What? No. No. Isn't Stu—"

"Well, that's the thing. Stu said he didn't do it, either. And, well, I just happen to be a good friend of the man. So, who am I more inclined to believe?"

"I-I-I didn't do anything." The man's nose wriggled. "I-I-I didn't."

Chase sighed.

"If you keep repeating the same thing, I'll just have to take you down to the station," she bluffed.

"No, I—I just—"

"Take a deep breath, Isaac. Drink some coffee."

Isaac did the former, not the latter. Probably for the best. This man was twitchy enough without caffeine.

"Okay, feel better? I'll make you a deal: you answer my questions, tell the truth, and I'll walk out of here. Alone. You lie, even once, and we leave together. That work for you?"

The burr had become a softball.

"Okay. So, you said that Stu killed Jake, right?"

"No, I mean, that's what—"

Chase silenced him with a wave.

"I'm not accusing you of anything. But you're right, that's what everyone's saying, aren't they? Stu murdered Jake. Let me ask you another question: why? Why would Stu want Jake dead? He doesn't even know the man."

Isaac sucked on his top lip. He looked like he was about to burst into tears.

"Remember what I said. You tell the truth, or I take you in."

Isaac reached into his pocket with a trembling hand and pulled out a piece of paper. It was worn and appeared damp—likely from sweat.

"I found this. I… don't know what it means."

Chase took the paper and unfolded it. It appeared to be a series of email exchanges between Jake Hollister, and someone named Jeremiah Thuring. Chase quickly scanned the text. Jake and this Jeremiah were apparently negotiating the sale of something called 'C'. The last message was from Jeremiah, and it outlined a meeting time and place: outside the *U-Lock-it* the night Jake was murdered.

Chase reread this last message to make sure she hadn't imagined it.

"Shit." Chase exhaled. "Why didn't you give this to the police?"

Isaac's upper lip flopped out of his mouth with an audible 'plop'.

"I just—when Stu—it was encrypted, okay?" Isaac rubbed his forehead hard enough to leave a red mark behind. "After Stu called me, I tried to get into Jake's emails, see what he was working on? But he'd received nothing in the last week or so."

Chase, not understanding the man's hesitation, shrugged.

"So?"

"Well, I don't know about the FBI, like how emails you receive or—"

"Just get to the point, Isaac."

Isaac's cheeks turned nearly as red as his forehead.

"Right, well, in our business, we get hundreds of emails a week. There is only one reason why Jake's inbox would be empty."

Chase finally caught on.

"Someone deleted the emails."

"Yeah, but all HVG communications are backed up. Encrypted but I got in. Wasn't really supposed to... legal said—"

"What's 'C'?" Chase interrupted.

"That's the thing, I have no idea."

Chase pursed her lips.

"Jake is selling something called 'C' and you, VP of software, have no idea what it is?"

Sweat beaded on his forehead.

"No, I swear, I have no idea."

"Isaac..."

"I swear!"

"Was Jake working on anything that started with a C or...?"

"That's the thing," Isaac's face pinched, "Not at all. His project, most of our projects, were the metaverse. No C in metaverse. It's technically called the Happy Valley Gaming Metaverse, or HVGM, or just HVG, but—"

"You're rambling."

"I'm sorry, but that was the only thing that I could find that Jake was working on. His entire team was focused on the metaverse."

Chase frowned. She didn't want to believe the nervous man who was shaking like a leaf, but she did.

"Let me ask you something else."

"Yeah, okay, sure."

"Is it possible to alter surveillance footage? Like swap faces in a video in a way that whoever is watching it wouldn't be able to tell the difference?"

"Like a deep fake?"

Chase wasn't sure what that was, so she said nothing.

"Yeah, of course."

"Could *you* do that?"

Isaac hummed and hawed.

"Hypothetical for Christ's sake."

"I could do it. If words were spoken it would be a little more difficult, but swapping out one person for another isn't all that hard. If I had time to prepare, I bet I could even do it live." There was a hint of pride in the man's voice.

"Who else could do it?"

"I mean, lots of people, I guess. There are—"

"At Happy Valley? Who else at Happy Valley could do what you said? Change video footage on the fly? Could Jake?"

"Sure. Anyone on his team, really."

"And could you trace this? Like, figure out who did it?"

Isaac laughed.

"No, it doesn't work that way. If they're good enough to make the deep fake, they're good enough to hide their tracks."

Chase committed this to memory then finished her coffee and stood.

"That's—that's it?" Isaac asked, suddenly nervous. He was leaning away from Chase as if expecting her to pull out a pair of cuffs and slap them on him.

"No, that's not it." Chase was amused by this man and let him sweat for several seconds.

"What? What else?" His words were barely more than gasps.

"I want you to keep digging. I want you to find out what 'C' is and call Stu when you do." Isaac nodded. "And I want you to stick around. Don't leave the city, understand me?"

Chapter 48

TATE FELT GUILTY. HE KNEW this was unjustified — not only had his wife been behind bars for close to two years, but they'd also discussed this possibility, and she had given him the okay before going inside. But as he made his way toward Stu's — without Floyd, who had continued to sleep, and snore, while Tate had showered and dressed — the guilt gnawed at him.

If it had just been a random hookup at a bar, Tate was certain that these feelings would quickly pass. But this... this thing with Chase, no matter how brief, felt different.

Tate replayed the last night's events and his heart rate quickened, just a little.

This felt like it had with Robyn. It felt real. It felt important.

Years ago, before the accident, his then partner Constantine Striker had spent considerable time teaching him how to manipulate suspects by reading subtle cues, minor changes in body language, slight differences in inflection, facial tics, mannerisms, when and how they interacted with others. It took considerable observing and practice, but eventually, noticing these things became second nature. Soon, Tate's ability to predict how people would react to different sceneries and different interrogative approaches had become almost legendary in the Bureau. Take Martin, the cook at the homeless shelter in West Virginia, for instance. Within seconds, Tate knew exactly how to approach the man to extract the most information. This proved to be an invaluable skill for an FBI Agent and all the credit went to his maligned ex-partner. But it wasn't until after the accident that Tate started to implement these techniques in his own life in a sort of reverse-engineered way. Not to get ahead at work — to be fair, this wasn't something he was particularly interested in—but to disguise his own feelings, to prevent himself from lashing out at the inane and unoriginal comments people would make following the accident.

So sorry that your daughter is now a cripple… what a tragedy.

It's a shame that your wife is in prison… she was convicted of vehicular manslaughter, really? Bum rap, yeah? I mean, was she really that drunk?

What was he supposed to say to this?

Yup, yup, I agree, absolutely tragic… it was just one little mistake. Seems unfair.

Or was he supposed to go the other way?

Robyn done did a bad thing, I ain't gonna support her no mo'.

The real issue was that nobody understood. Not in a philosophical or emotional sense, but in objectivity. They weren't working with all the facts.

Only three people could do that: himself, Rachel, and Robyn.

But being a chameleon was addictive. After people stopped talking about the accident and its repercussions—much sooner than he expected, by the way—it just became a part of his every day. Play a character, extract information, move on to the next mission.

Truthfully, it wasn't that unlike being in the metaverse.

Eventually, however, Tate had pretended to be someone else for so long that he feared his genuine self had become lost or muddled at best.

And then Chase came along. Sure, he knew about her. Most agents in the FBI did. While her issues with addiction weren't openly discussed, everyone was aware of them. She was a unique and polarizing figure. The misfits revered her and the self-righteous loathed her. Regardless of sentiment, if Chase hadn't been as good at her job as she was, she would have been let go within her first week.

But no amount of gossip or rumor had prepared Tate for Chase.

When they'd first met in the diner, he'd been acting. Chase had seen through him instantly, even though she hadn't called him on it. And Tate likewise knew that she was acting, too.

Last night was different. Tate had opened up, not all the way, and so had she.

For the first time in maybe a year, Tate had been himself, and rather than making him feel ashamed or self-conscious, Chase had made him comfortable.

And Tate wanted to feel that way again.

Then maybe you shouldn't say stupid shit like, Chase... is this over? he scolded himself. Fucking idiot.

Tate pulled up to Stu's mansion, grabbed the case with the VR setup inside, and walked to the door. It opened before he had a chance to knock.

Will Porter held it for him, looking surprisingly fresh—Tate doubted the man had left last night. Regardless of how annoying Tate found the lawyer, it was clear that he was dedicated and loyal. The other two lawyers, the supposed experts, not so much; they were suspiciously absent.

"Agent Abernathy," Will said with a nod.

"Mr. Porter, esquire," Tate shot back as he passed the man.

Stu was sitting at the kitchen table, a coffee in hand. While his attire matched Will's demeanor, his face told a different story: everything about the man's clean-shaven face appeared drained.

Like Chase, Tate had come to the conclusion that Stu was no murderer. Also, like Chase, he was convinced that Stu was holding something back.

Something that Tate thought he'd discovered in the metaverse on the HVG security tapes.

Something important.

Something that Stu should have told them.

And it was finally time to challenge the man on it.

"Good morning," Stu said with a subtle nod.

"Not really," Tate replied. "I mean, it was a good night, no doubt about that, but morning? Not so much."

Stu stared at him quizzically and Tate placed the VR case on the table and began unpacking it.

"So, Stewie, when were you going to tell us about the man you had thrown out of Happy Valley?" Tate asked the question offhand, not bothering to even glance at the man.

"Pardon?"

"Oh, you know," Tate remarked passively, "the mangy dude who came up to you in HVG who you had your security team throw out of the building?"

Now, Tate looked at Stu. Looked him right in the eyes.

"The same man Jake got into a fight with in the parking lot... the man who left with his face covered in blood and his teeth looking mangled like a Brit with a meth addiction? That guy? Ring a bell?"

Chapter 49

FLOYD DIDN'T FEEL GREAT. THE good news was that he didn't feel terrible. The one benefit to not drinking that often is that your tolerance was quite low, and it only took a handful of drinks to get drunk. Hangovers were less intense because your liver had fewer toxins to clear out.

What pissed him off more than the mild headache and dry mouth, was the fact that he was alone. Tate had clearly come and gone—there was a damp towel on his bed—without saying a word. Floyd could recall some of their exchange from the night prior, which had been far from complimentary, but Tate was a big boy, and their relationship was in a place that he thought it could handle even some malicious ribbing.

Maybe this is just another teaching moment, Floyd thought glumly. *One that involves him taking our car and stranding me here.*

Asking Chase for a ride wasn't something that he was keen on doing—he was still pissed at her, too—but that wasn't even an option: her car was no longer in the parking lot, either.

Feeling no need to rush, Floyd took his time showering and getting ready for the day, then went to the motel lobby for a coffee and a stale Danish. He drank the former, had a single bite of the latter, and then tried to hail an Uber, which proved surprisingly difficult. This was strange; they weren't technically in Vegas, the hotel was located on the outskirts of Clark County, but they were roughly ten miles from the taxi/Uber/Lyft capital of the world.

This perturbed him so much—as was the case with hangovers, so much as a loud sneeze was sufficient to piss one off—that Floyd asked his driver about it when one of them finally showed.

"You guys on strike, or what? It was nearly impossible for me to get a ride."

The driver, a young man in his mid-twenties with what Floyd would describe as a trendy mullet, said, "Yeah, we have a fantastic union." He laughed. "Naw, we are busier than ever."

"Then why did everyone keep canceling on me?"

"If I had to guess, it's where you're going."

Where I'm going?

It took Floyd a couple of seconds to understand what mullet-man was saying. In fairness it wasn't where he was going—Stu lived in one of the nicest areas in the state—but who he was going to see.

He hadn't paid any attention to the media since arriving in Nevada, but he supposed that Stu's indictment was a big deal. People got off on seeing those they were envious of fall from grace.

And Stu Barnes, a super-rich white man? He was the perfect target.

Just as they pulled up to Stu's place, a thought occurred to him, and his eyes drifted to the camera hanging below the rear-view mirror.

Aw, shit.

Both he and Tate had taken personal leave—a week, with the possibility of an extension—mentioning nothing of Stu Barnes. If Director Hampton found out that they were here, not quite impersonating but also not denying that they were on FBI business, there would be repercussions. Perhaps not that serious for Tate, given his history and seniority, but for Floyd? It could be significant.

"What are you, anyway? An investigator or something like that? A lawyer?"

Floyd got out of the car and as he closed the door, he said, "Just a computer nerd."

As he approached Stu's mansion, Floyd just knew that the man in the Uber was snapping pictures of him.

Fuck it, take all the pictures you want.

He found Stu and Tate sitting at the kitchen table while Will was hovering over the counter. Chase was nowhere to be found, which Floyd didn't find surprising.

"We should think about closing your gate," he said as he made his way over to the coffee machine. "It's only a matter of time before the media starts showing up and I don't know if it's a good look for two current and one ex-FBI agent to be holding hands with an accused murderer." His words had the desired effect; Stu's eyes grew larger. "I mean, if we want to keep our jobs."

"I wouldn't worry about that," Tate said dismissively.

"You wouldn't, but I—"

"You shouldn't worry about it either."

This was Tate's way of saying that he had Floyd's back. Comforting, definitely, but Floyd was still pissed at his partner.

"Thanks for the ride, by the way." Floyd turned from Tate to Stu. "I'm billing you for the Uber."

Stu was confused by the strange dance.

"Yeah, of course. I'll cover all expenses. I'll just write you a check, just let me know."

"Well, you arrived just in time," Tate said, seamlessly changing the subject.

Floyd wanted to stay angry, but they simply didn't have the time.

"You find something online?"

"You'd be so proud," Tate said, rising to his feet and walking across the room. "Not only did I find something in the metaverse, but this old man managed to take a screen shot and even print it. All by myself, I did, I did!"

Well, if there was time for Tate to act like an idiot, maybe there was time for him to remain pissed.

"What did you find?"

Tate grabbed a sheet of paper from the printer.

"Just that our boy Stu here got into a fight with some absolute greaseball who waited outside for Jake who rearranged the man's teeth."

"What?"

Floyd tried to look at the printout, but Tate childishly hid the printed image from view.

"I told you, this happened more than six months ago!" Stu protested. "It wasn't a fight... couldn't have been a fight. I don't... I don't remember."

"Mmm, hmmm," Tate said, and then dramatically flipped the page around. "Maybe this will jog your memory."

Floyd, coming in on the story halfway through, had no expectations of Stu's reaction. But Tate clearly hadn't expected the man to instantly recoil and go as pale as a sheet.

"That's... that's the mechanic!" Stu proclaimed. When nobody reacted, he added, "The mechanic! That's the guy who changed my oil at Gordon's!"

Tate blinked.

"You sure?" He held the image closer, but Stu was already nodding emphatically.

"Yes—he had his hair up in a bun, and I guess it was longer, but that's him. I'm positive—those teeth. I remember thinking at the time that it looked like his front two had been perfectly broken, almost as if they'd only grown out halfway and then stopped."

"Shit," Tate said with an exhale. "Do you know who he is, though?"

Stu's face was answer enough but just in case this wasn't clear, he said, "No idea. I don't know his name or who he is. All I know is that he was my mechanic, he's the one who changed my oil."

"Great," Floyd said. "So, we have no name and no—"

"His name is Jerimiah Thuring," a voice said from the doorway. Everyone turned to look at Chase who, at some point, had stepped into Stu's home without anyone realizing it. "And he's the person who really killed Jake Hollister."

Chapter 50

"THURING? REALLY?" FLOYD SAID AFTER Chase recounted what Isaac Lomax had said.

"Yeah—Thuring. Why do you say it like that?" Chase asked.

"I dunno... it's just, Turing was the grandfather of computer programming. I find it strange that this guy's name is so close. Turing, Thuring. Did you look him up?"

"Didn't get a chance. I was—"

"Got him," Will interrupted, waving them over to his laptop. The instant Chase saw the image on screen, she knew that Isaac had either manufactured the emails or that the person offering to buy 'C', whatever the hell that was, wasn't Jerimiah Thuring.

"C'mon," Tate said rolling his eyes. "That's our guy? He doesn't even look strong enough to pick up a gun, let alone pull the trigger."

Chase had to agree. While there was no age listed beneath the photo, the emaciated old man, purported to be a 'technology investor', looked as if he'd already died, twice, and had been propped up with a boom and winch for the photo. She suspected that the only technology Jeremiah was interested in purchasing were things that could keep him alive for a few more seconds.

"I mean, I'll reach out," Will said, but it was clear by his tone that he was as skeptical as Chase. "See if there's any connection."

"Just gentle probing," Chase said. "Don't want to tip him off."

"Yeah, gentle," Tate repeated. "A strong wind might send this guy into the afterlife."

Chase sighed. It seemed like every break that they got in the case just led to another dead end.

"I asked Isaac about the security video if someone could fake it? He said, yeah, pretty much anyone at the company could do that."

"Being capable of altering the video and proving that it was altered are very different things," Will said. He had his cell phone pressed to his ear. "Hi, I'm looking for Jeremiah Thuring?" Will put up a finger and backed away from the counter. "Yes, I'm interested in pitching an idea…"

Chase turned to Tate.

"Any luck gaining access to the *U-Lock-it* security footage from Brittany?"

"Beverly," Tate corrected. "And no. I asked but she has no idea where that might be stored. Stu, you sure you don't remember this guy, the mechanic, coming up to you in the HVG lobby? Any idea what he might have said? I'm going on the assumption that he's the guy behind all this."

Chase thought it a safe assumption. The fake mechanic who had placed the Bluetooth scrambler and accosted Stu in the lobby had to be involved.

"I don't. I mean, the more you talk about it the more I think I remember, but…" Stu let his sentence trail off.

"There's no audio?" Floyd asked.

Tate shook his head.

"No, just video. And they're angled in such a way that you can't see their lips. But," Tate held up a finger, "the one from the outside? Late at night when Jake and our mystery man get into it? You can see their lips then. Floyd, you wanna drop in and see if you can tell me what they're saying?"

"I can give it a shot."

"Let's try."

As Tate started to unpack the VR gear, Will returned, a frown on his tanned face.

"So, that's not our guy," he said. "Jeremiah Thuring has been in the hospital for the last week."

"Hospital or morgue?" Tate asked as he placed the VR helmet on Floyd. For some reason, it looked even more ridiculous on the younger man than it had Tate.

"Funny," Will shot back with an expression that indicated he did not find this funny at all.

"All right, you're all set. Good luck." Tate tapped Floyd on the head and then addressed Chase, Stu, and Will. "You know what? I was just thinking. I watched the security tapes in the metaverse, right? Stu, can the tapes be altered there? Like, can they be changed in the metaverse?"

Stu shrugged.

"I don't know. As I said, I'm just an investor—I don't know how any of this stuff works. The CEO position was temporary."

"But your company is called AI Integrations, isn't it?" Tate challenged.

Stu was starting to get frustrated.

"A board decision, not mine. Wanted to keep us relevant. You think Warren Buffet knows everything there is about the companies in his portfolio?"

Tate didn't hesitate.

"Yeah, I certainly do."

"Well, I don't, alright? I don't know—"

"Calm down," Chase said. "We're on the same side."

"The wrong side," Will remarked. "We're not getting anywhere."

Chase shot the man a look.

"We're doing the best we can. It's not like you or your lawyer buddies are doing anything productive other than padding your wallets. Where are they, by the way? F. Lee and Bob Shapiro? Expensing a mimosa breakfast?"

Tate stepped between them, going from annoyed himself to the voice of reason.

"Relax. I wouldn't say that we've made no progress. We're pretty sure that meth teeth is our guy and we know that he probably faked the video. We also know how he nuked your alibi with the Bluetooth scrambler. That leaves the GSR and car GPS. I'm guessing that if our guy hacked the car to get you to go in for a fake oil change, altering the GPS system wouldn't be that hard."

"You're absolutely sure you haven't shot a gun in the past few days?" Chase asked Stu.

"That's not something I would forget."

Chase had a retort on the tip of her tongue, but she held it back.

"Stu," Floyd said loudly. He raised his head in their direction, but with the mask, he was looking off-center. "Did you shake the mechanic's hand at any point?"

Stu pondered this.

"Yeah, I did—he left grease on my palm. Why?"

A goofy smile crept onto Floyd's lips.

Stu thought about this for a moment and then nodded.

"Yeah—I remember because his hands were black with grease, which I only noticed afterward."

Floyd was beaming now.

"That's why you tested positive. Mechanics, welders, people who work with paper… they can all test positive for GSR even if they've never shot a gun. He transferred the residue to you when he shook your hand."

"Shit," Tate grumbled. "This asshole planned the whole thing out."

"So, we know the *how*, *when*, and *where*. But we still don't know the why or the who." Stu paused as if contemplating his own words. "We should do a background check on all Happy Valley employees past and present. Maybe there was a perceived slight or something."

"That's one hell of a slight," Tate remarked.

Chase picked up the picture of the man Tate had printed out.

"Can we run this through facial recognition software?"

"Like I said—"

"Yeah, we get it," Tate cut in. "You're no expert. But your company clearly was."

"And I don't have access—"

Once again, Tate didn't let Stu finish.

"Hire them," he suggested with a shrug. "Use a fake name and hire your company to look into this guy."

It was risky—if their suspect worked for Happy Valley and they put in this request, it would tip him off—but it could be worth it. The man might make a mistake, might slip up. He'd planned this thing out to a T and if all of a sudden, things weren't going according to plan if he was worried about being sniffed out, he could get nervous and do something stupid.

"Do it," Chase instructed, and Stu nodded at Will who went back to the computer to get started. "Let's just hope that it doesn't lead to another dead end. We're running out of time here."

Chapter 51

THE METAVERSE WAS DISORIENTING AT first. The frame rate took a few minutes to get used to, but the hardest thing for Floyd was adjusting to having pale hands.

Well, he thought, *if I ever wanted to know what it was like to live as a sixty-something-year-old white billionaire, this is my chance.*

Floyd tilted his head and caught his reflection in the computer monitor in front of him. Then he brought his fingers to his face, pulled his eyelids down, looked into his eyes, ran the pad of his index and forefinger down the thin lines that flanked his mouth. Next, he touched his hair. It was fine and smooth, and he wondered briefly if you had to wash and condition it in the metaverse.

Do you have to bathe here? Do you need to brush your teeth? Go to the bathroom? Eat?

Feeling overwhelmed, Floyd closed his eyes for a moment, relishing the comfort that darkness brought, then opened them again. Within minutes, everything just became normal. Almost too normal, and the appeal of this fake world was starkly apparent.

Even though he was in Stu's avatar, he could easily imagine himself as his own character in the metaverse. It would be him, but different. Maybe he'd be ten pounds heavier, more muscular than rail thin, and there was no way he'd have a stutter. His PTSD? Gone. No need for Choo-Choo Floyd. In the metaverse, he could be his best-imagined self.

Focus, he chided. *Focus, Floyd.*

The possibility of becoming lost here was real, and if time hadn't been such a pressing issue, Floyd would have gladly explored this world.

But not now. After they kept Stu out of prison, perhaps.

In the metaverse, Tate had set up the fake Stu in front of a computer, somewhere in HVG, Floyd assumed, and the security footage was paused at the moment that Jake exited the building. It was dark out and the time stamp indicated that it was just after two in the morning. Head down, a tired-looking Jake Hollister was walking briskly toward the parking lot when a figure appeared from down the side of the building. He was disheveled, with long, greasy hair and he was dressed in clothing that was dirty. The camera was aimed at the back of his head, but this newcomer must have said something because Jake stopped and turned.

Jake appeared surprised at first, but this quickly transitioned to suspicion. Their argument quickly became heated and then the unsub made an aggressive move, attempting to grab Jake. Jake avoided the lunge but when the man tried a second time, Jake delivered a textbook, and unsuspecting, sweep kick, knocking his feet out from under him. The man's face struck the ground with violence, sending blood pooling into his mouth and shattering his front teeth.

Floyd was grateful there was no sound, but he flinched upon impact nonetheless, his brain manufacturing what the speakers did not. He ran the tape back several times focusing in on the men's lips as they spoke.

You stole… mode.

That wasn't right.

He slowed the tape, using Stu's hand to turn the dial in the metaverse.

Not mode… code.

You stole the code.

Jake then followed this with something along the lines of 'I'm not sure what you're talking about', which angered the other man.

Fired? Did the other man say that he was fired?

Floyd wasn't sure about this, but then Jake threatened to call the police. That was fairly clear and made sense when, after the man's face had been smashed, he pulled out his cell.

With all the blood, it was impossible to tell what the man on the ground was saying but Jake…

There's no code. Serpents no code… never was. It's you. Leave me alone. Leave me alone.

That was the gist of it, but it wasn't right.

Floyd jogged the video back several times refining what Jake was saying.

There's no code. Serpents isn't about code. It's you. Leave me alone. Leave me alone.

Again.

There was no code. Serpents isn't about code — it never was. It's you. Leave me alone. Leave me alone.

Floyd said the words out loud, trying to figure out what was wrong. *Serpents.* That was it — or, that *wasn't* it.

No, not serpents.

Surface?

Surface was close but there was an extra syllable at the end, a vowel followed by an s, he thought.

Surfaces?

That wasn't it, either. There was no hard f.

Floyd relaxed his mouth and looked skyward. Something came to him then, something Chase had said.

Jake was selling something that started with a 'C'.

No, not *surfaces.*

It had to start with a 'C'.

It took Floyd maybe two dozen tries, but eventually, he saw the corners of Stu's lips rise into a smile in the reflection of the computer monitor.

He'd figured it out.

He knew what 'C' was.

Floyd just had no fucking idea what any of it meant.

Chapter 52

CHASE HATED WAITING AROUND. ABSOLUTELY loathed it. But there really wasn't anything she could think of to do. She'd spoken to Isaac Lomax, Floyd was lost in the metaverse trying to read lips, Tate was helping Will look through employee records and hire Stu's own company to run facial recognition software on the broken-toothed mechanic, which left her and Stu sitting on their hands.

Chase considered going back to Gordon's to interrogate the other employees, but she doubted that that would lead anywhere. What were the chances that someone would remember a new 'worker' with busted teeth? Even if someone recalled a new guy in overalls who strangely hadn't been announced or introduced, what were the odds they'd give him up? Chase had seen several of the mechanics adorned with classic prison tats—mostly letters across the knuckles, and at least one on the face—and the no-snitch code extended to life outside the clink. It wasn't as if Chase could make them talk either, given her unofficial capacity, let alone the fact that she technically wasn't FBI anymore.

So, she was stuck doing nothing while Stu got closer to being put away for life, if not the needle, and Brian got closer to taking Georgina.

Chase hadn't thought about her niece in some time—*you throw yourself in your work, you use, or you have sex*—and now that she had, she couldn't get the image of the smart, red-haired girl out of her head.

"You okay?"

Chase had been staring at her hands and now she glanced up.

It was just like Stu to ask about her wellbeing when he was the one facing the death penalty.

I can't believe that I thought this man was capable of killing someone.

She shrugged.

"Been better."

"Been worse, too," Stu remarked. It wasn't meant as an insult, but a reminder that things could always be worse.

Chase wasn't interested in reminiscing about her hitting rock bottom.

"How about you?"

Stu shrugged.

"I don't know. To be honest, the worst part is the why. Why does someone hate me this much? I'm not naive, I understand why people would dislike me. But to go this far? It seems personal."

There was no denying what Stu said.

"When I first got here, you said you didn't know Jake Hollister, that you'd never met him before. You said the same thing about the mechanic. But we know you met Jake at HVG and the guy with our suspect attacked you."

"Attack is a pretty strong word," Stu remarked.

"Still."

He sighed and rubbed his eyes.

"I didn't remember them. I still don't, not really. Chase, I mean, I saw the footage and I kind of remember the man coming up to me in the lobby and I kind of remember speaking to Jake when I visited Happy Valley, but I deal with so many different people all the time. Employees, investors, people who are just angry because I have so much, and they have so little. When someone, maybe Will or maybe it was you, asked me who would want to do this to me? I thought about..." the man suddenly had a far off-look in his eyes. "Well, I made some business decisions long ago that I'm not super proud of. Nothing that would deserve this, but people were mad. I thought about them, I thought about an ex-girlfriend… I dunno, I thought about someone who had to be just livid at me to do something like this. I didn't think about two people I met once or *maybe* twice."

Chase didn't reply, mostly because she was personally aware of several sociopaths who had gone on killing sprees for something as little as a look, a perceived slight. In this new, snowflake era, the simple use of an incorrect pronoun was sufficient to send a ripple through the internet wide enough to incite extreme violence on both sides of the pond.

But Stu's comment did get her thinking. What kind of person were they looking for? Given the meticulous planning that this sort of murder and frame job required, their unsub wasn't a run-of-the-mill psychopath. And the deep fake Stu Barnes video wasn't just proof that their man was computer literate, but also that this was personal. Could it be related to something that Jake had been working on at Happy Valley and trying to sell? 'C', whatever the hell that was? Isaac Lomax had been nervous, making it nearly impossible for Chase to tell if he was lying about anything. Did he know more than he was letting on?

Why didn't you shake his hand, Chase? Why didn't you try to use your 'voodoo' on him?

Chase tried to push this thought from her mind, but it refused to go away.

You could go to the morgue, examine Jake Hollister's body. Maybe that will give you some clues.

But over time, over the past six months or so, Chase had become increasingly skeptical of her special skill. It had become unreliable and sporadic. Had she gotten a read on Tate when they were naked, their bodies intertwined?

No.

Something must have shown on her face because Stu suddenly grew defensive.

"I'm sorry, Chase. I didn't mean to suggest that you weren't working hard enough. I know you're doing all you can. It's just—"

Chase stopped the man's apology by shaking her head.

My voodoo...

The word, not the skill, had given her an idea.

Stu was wrong, she wasn't doing all she could.

"You know what? Give me a sec," Chase said, backing out of the room. She walked down a long hallway adorned with oil paintings that looked expensive. When she could no longer hear Will and Tate, she pulled her phone out and scrolled through her contacts.

At the very last moment, she felt her nerve waning.

How long has it been since I've spoken to him? She wondered. Six months? A year? And now you're calling to ask a favor...

Deep down, she knew he would answer, knew that he would drop everything and take her call. And he would help, too, because that's what he did.

The issue was that, once again, Chase felt guilty. After all, Tate wasn't the first partner that she'd slept with.

"Fuck it," she whispered and clicked send.

As predicted, FBI Special Agent Jeremy Stitts answered before the first ring had finished.

Chapter 53

"NOTHING," TATE GRUMBLED AS HE leaned away from Will Porter and the computer. Happy Valley had an exhaustive list of current employees, complete with headshots, but no one came close to matching the man who had accosted both Stu and Jake, teeth or no teeth. For a significant fee and a promise to scour the Internet, they'd gone ahead and commissioned Happy Valley to run facial recognition on the man, which required signing about a half dozen disclaimers and legal agreements that not even Will read. But this would take time, and, for the moment, it left them exactly where they'd started.

Tate's frustration, not just with this case but compounded by his issues back home, had left him anxious. So much so, that he even debated utilizing FBI resources to aid in their search. He could log into a remote server and run the man's image through the FBI's mugshot database, which included images that Happy Valley probably wouldn't have access to. The only thing that stopped him was something that Floyd had said earlier. When Tate had initially heard about Chase's affluent 'friend' being charged with murder, his thoughts had been twofold: payday and no way. The former still looked accurate but the latter? Guilty or not, if tried today, Tate wouldn't bet on Stu coming out a free man. Which meant that Floyd was right. The unofficial involvement of two current and one ex-FBI Agent on this case wasn't a good look. Tapping FBI resources to help said man would make for a PR nightmare.

Tate sighed and toyed with his mustache with his thumb and forefinger.

The longer they went without making any real progress, the more singular his goal became: money. It felt dirty. It felt wrong. But that was the truth, and the truth had a strange way of avoiding Tate Abernathy.

And as uncomfortable as it would be to ask Stu for money given his contribution, any of theirs, really, including the harem of lawyers, was minimal, Tate would swallow his pride and do it. Because he didn't want to take another one of Marco's devastating punches to the stomach. Because he needed to keep Rachel comfortable.

"I'll tell you what, Stu," Tate began quietly. He glanced at Floyd, but the man was lost in another world, and he doubted that with the ear buds in, the man would be able to hear anything. He knew that Chase wouldn't care, knew from the stories about her that she was more concerned with finding out the truth than her own wellbeing, but even if she'd been a stickler for the rules like Floyd, she'd since left the room.

"Yeah?"

"If Happy Valley comes up empty, I'll access the FBI servers, see if I can get a hit there."

Stu gave him an approving nod.

Was that a ten-thousand-dollar nod? Tate couldn't help but wonder. Or a, 'thanks, bro' and a slap on the back nod?

The man had stated that money wasn't an issue, and if it were Tate in his shoes, then all of his personal wealth was a fair exchange for staying out of prison for the rest of his life and/or avoiding the needle.

Tate immediately scoffed at this idea.

Personal wealth? What personal wealth?

"You okay?" Stu asked and Tate realized that the man was still staring at him. He must have looked like a lunatic having an entire conversation in his head, complete with scoffs, frowns, chuckles, what have you.

"I'm fine," Tate said, now observing Stu the way the man had been eyeing him. This was the moment, he knew. "Actually, you know what? There is one thing that I wanted to talk to you about."

Stu straightened, his posture becoming professional. He knew what was coming and he didn't shy away from it.

Was that a good sign? Or was this just the start of a negotiation?

"Sure, why don't we go—"

"I think—I think I've found s-something," Floyd suddenly exclaimed as he tore off his headgear.

Tate winced at the intrusion and then felt bad for his reaction. To make up for it, he hurried to Floyd's side.

"What is it? What did you find?"

Now, it was him being professional. Well, as professional as Tate could muster.

Floyd smiled broadly.

"I think I know what our g-g-guy was after."

Chapter 54

"IS FLOYD OKAY?" JEREMY STITTS asked.

Chase was taken aback by the question—and a little hurt. After so long, the man's first question wasn't about her but Floyd?

"He's fine," she said sharply.

"Are you—"

"Fine, too," Chase replied preemptively.

Stitts exhaled audibly and Chase was suddenly at a loss for how to continue.

How are you or how have you been or any other facsimile, would come off as disingenuous or, worse, trite. Yet, Chase also knew that Stitts wouldn't be the one to break the silence. His opening line—*Is Floyd okay?*—was already more than she'd expected without prompting. Stitts... the master of uncomfortable silences.

She eventually settled on, "How's the leg?"

"Peachy. Running a marathon this weekend."

"Yeah? Is Piper running with you?"

Stitts chuckled.

"Are you kidding me? That dog is the laziest thing on earth. Barely wants to lift his leg to take a piss."

"Well, he is officially retired, so can you blame him?"

Another laugh from Stitts and Chase joined in. Their relationship had never revolved around humor, but it wasn't until this moment that she realized how much she'd missed her ex-partner, laugh or no laugh. They'd been through a lot, more than most, high and low times—he'd taken a bullet for her, and they'd had sex, both of which had contributed to Stitts moving on.

"What about you?" Stitts said and it took a moment for Chase to realize what he was asking.

"Me? I'm not exactly retired," she said, trying not to come off as too serious. "More like taking an indefinite hiatus."

"Right," Stitts said, and Chase was happy to still hear joviality in his voice. "So, you were calling to see how my leg is doing?"

"Yeah... *aaaaand* now that I have you on the phone, I wonder if I can pick your brain on something—purely for research purposes and purely hypothetical, of course."

"Purely and 100% bullshit, you mean. But I aim to serve. This wouldn't, pray tell, have anything to do with a criminal profile, would it?" Chase started to answer, but Stitts wasn't done yet. "Particularly one involving a handsome man in his sixties who is charged with murder and two off-duty FBI Agents lending a hand?"

Chase balked.

"What? How did you know?" Stitts didn't answer—not that she'd expected one. "Right, you're a profiler. But, like I said, this is purely hypothetical."

"Well, to be honest, Chase, I expected this call from Floyd, not you."

Chase grinned.

"But you did expect it, meaning you're familiar with this absolutely fictional scenario?"

A short pause.

"Why don't you tell me what you know, and I'll slap some criminal psychology 101 to your words? That work?"

"Perfect." Chase agreed and then told Stitts about the elaborate lengths that their unsub had gone to, to frame Stu. When she was done, Stitts didn't say anything for a good thirty seconds. Chase knew that the man was thinking and didn't interrupt his train of thought.

"A plan that elaborate, that orchestrated, is indicative of deep-rooted resentment. To kill someone is one thing, to kill someone and plan to frame another is something else."

"Who's the main target here?"

"Both. Jake—*uhh*, I mean, Joe and Steve. You said that their interactions with the unsub were limited?"

"With Steve, for sure, maybe just one visit," Chase confirmed, keeping with the alliterative fake names. "Not sure about Joe, but we think that their interactions were minimal, as well."

"Well, this crime doesn't strike me as a, 'he didn't say thank you after I held the door for the man,' type of slight. This is something bigger. What you've described is classic, paranoid-schizoid behavior. That, coupled with the highly sophisticated frame job, makes me think that this wasn't your guy's first kick at the can."

Chase raised an eyebrow. They'd been so focused on Jake and Stu that they hadn't considered this possibility before.

"You think he's killed before?"

"I don't know—maybe. I'm no expert when it comes to the tech world, but what I do know is that some of these guys are on the spectrum, and often morality gets pushed to the side in favor of productivity and profits. Someone with the characteristics we described might take this too far, too literally."

"Sounds like pretty much every industry."

"Yeah, no kidding. But tech is unique. If this guy has committed a similar crime in the past, I suspect it'll also be tech-related," Stitts suggested.

Chase exhaled loudly.

"Anybody ever tell you that you're pretty good at this pro-filing thing?"

"Naw, just a hobby. But there is one more thing, Chase. If I'm right about this profile, then you need to be aware that these paranoid schizophrenics often jump from one idea to another, fixating on a certain industry or idea... or person."

There it was, Stitts being Stitts—trying to protect her from everything, even hypothetical unsubs who had no idea who she even was.

"Yeah, sure, I'll be careful. Always am. What about you? Seeing as you're so good at this profiling thing, maybe you should think about becoming a field agent, you know? Hunting down bad guys. Ever thought of that?"

"Yeah, that's exactly what the FBI needs. A gimpy man in his forties and his lazy-ass canine chasing America's Most Wanted."

"What about an ex-heroin addict with zero regards for rules and a wanton penchant for self-destruction?"

Chase's words hung in the air, seeming to cling to the invisible threads that linked their phones across state lines. But it wasn't an uncomfortable silence, nor did Chase perceive it as one designed by the man on the other end to get her to talk more, to extract information from her. It was just the natural comfort of two old friends and one-time lovers enjoying their company, even at a distance.

"I miss you, Chase," Stitts said suddenly.

"I miss you, too."

And now the silence was uncomfortable.

Does he want me to say I want him back? Wait... want him back? Are we talking partners again? Partners...

Chase could think of two distinct meanings.

She chewed her bottom lip.

"When I'm in town, do you want to—"

Tate suddenly busted into the hallway, his face red.

"Floyd found something—Chase, you're going to want to hear this."

"Is that... is that Agent Abernathy?" Stitts asked.

Chase nodded at Tate.

"I'm sorry, Stitts, I have to go," she said, ignoring the man's question. "Thanks for your help."

She hung up and followed Floyd back into the kitchen.

"What is it?" Chase asked, thoughts about partners of any capacity long since gone from her mind. "What did you find?"

Chapter 55

"CERBERUS," FLOYD SAID WITH A little flair.

He didn't get the response he obviously wanted.

"The fuck is that?" Tate blurted. He looked to Chase who just shrugged.

"In the video, Jake says," Floyd continued, "There was no code. Cerberus isn't about code—never was. It's about you!"

Still not the reaction he expected.

"What?" Tate balked. "What the fuck is Cerberus?"

It was Stu who answered.

"Cerberus is Hades' pet dog—three-headed dog, to be more specific." Everyone waited for Stu to elaborate, and eventually, he said, "You guys skip Greek mythology or what?"

"Wasn't high on the Academy's required reading," Tate replied.

Stu frowned but continued.

"Cerberus, the three-headed dog, is responsible for keeping souls that have been banished to hell from escaping. I think the dog was eventually slain by Hercules, but I could be wrong on that."

"Cool lesson," Tate said, clearly annoyed now. "But what does this have to do with Stu? Or Jake?"

Nobody had an answer.

Every time they uncovered something about this case, something that should be a great reveal, they got no closer to figuring out who was actually behind all of this.

"You didn't happen to kick any mutant dogs recently, did you?" Tate asked Stu.

The question was ignored.

"What's this about code?" Chase said.

"Cerberus isn't about code—never was. It's about you!" Floyd repeated. "Something like that, anyway.

Chase internalized this, then said, "I just spoke to a friend who has experience with profiling."

Tate knew that she was referring to Stitts and wondered why she didn't address him by name. He also noticed that while she was looking at everyone else in the room, she seemed to be avoiding eye contact with him.

"He doesn't think that this is the first time that our unsub has done something like this."

"Like what?" Stu asked, suddenly sounding concerned. "Framed someone? Or murdered someone?"

Chase shrugged.

"To be honest? Probably both. Will, do you think you can search for any connection between Cerberus and recent accidents or deaths? Maybe something also related to computer programming?"

Will looked skeptical, a sentiment shared by Tate—it was a broad task to say the least—but the lawyer addressed the computer without complaint. They all waited, to his obvious discomfort, for him to look through the first few Google search results.

"I dunno," he said, sounding dejected. "Lots of stuff here about Hades, and death, but... I mean, I can keep looking but I... I..."

"Waste of time," Tate mumbled. "What about the Happy Valley face recognition search? Can you add Cerberus to the parameters, or whatever?"

Again, Will nodded and his fingers clacked away at the laptop.

"Done," he said after just a few moments. "I think. I added an additional search, just so—" he was interrupted by the sound of an incoming email. The man's eyebrows lifted as he looked at the screen. "Shit, they found something already. Two things, actually. Hold on." Tate, Floyd, Chase, and Stu moved to get a better look. "Pinged right away. Happy Valley employees Jake Hollister and Isaac Lomax working on Cerberus, a new type of metaverse."

Chase inhaled sharply.

"Isaac and Jake? Wait a second, if 'C' is Cerberus then that fucker lied to me." Tate put a hand on her shoulder, but she shrugged him off. "He knew all along what 'C' was. When was that article from?"

Will leaned into the computer.

"Three years, give or take."

"Three years?" Chase shook her head. "The timeline is all messed up. Jake was supposedly selling this thing the night he died."

Tate, worried that they were about to get sidetracked with the why when the who was most important, said, "What about the other thing? Did they find a match for our guy?"

Will cocked his head.

"Yeah... his face pinged from a newspaper article. Here it is: *Randy Milligan, CEO programmer for PopTop Games found dead of an apparent suicide.*"

Tate felt his heart rate quicken.

"Another software CEO dead? What else does it say?"

Will clicked the trackpad and then pulled both hands back from the laptop as if it had suddenly become hot.

"What's wrong?" Chase asked.

"I dunno—the email. It's gone."

"What do you mean it's gone?" Tate inquired.

Will replaced his hands on the keys and then moved around his inbox, before going to the trash, then the junk folders.

"It's not here. I—what the hell? The email with the two hits was here and now it's gone."

Tate had seen the email with the two hits, but his mind had wandered when Will had mentioned the CEO.

"I don't get it. Did you delete it?"

"I didn't do anything! Just clicked on the link to see the article and now it's gone," Will protested.

"Check again," Chase said.

Will did, but it was still gone.

"How the hell—" Will was interrupted by the whoosh notification of an incoming email. He quickly opened it and read it out loud. "*Thank you for your interest in Happy Valley's services. Unfortunately, we are unable to complete your request at this time. You will receive a full refund for any purchases.*"

"What the fuck?" Tate blurted.

Chase suddenly stiffened.

"That asshole Isaac," she muttered. "He knows… he fucking knows." Now, instead of avoiding him, Chase was looking Tate directly in the eyes. "He told me that someone erased Jake's emails and that he didn't know what 'C' was. He was lying. He was involved and must have seen your request. He deleted it and now he's going to make a run for it. We need to get to Happy Valley, *now.*"

Chase started to move toward the door and Tate, still not one-hundred percent sure what was going on, but driven by her conviction, went with the woman.

"You think he's going to run?" he asked.

"You should have seen this guy. He was nervous as all hell. He doesn't want a confrontation and now that he knows we're—"

"Wait!" Stu shouted after them. Chase slowed, as did Tate, but neither of them turned. "Just wait! I have someone tailing Isaac. Give me a second."

What?

Tate stopped abruptly and whipped around to glare at the silver-haired man, ready to tear a strip off him—so much for transparency—but he was already on the phone. Chase felt the same way; her eyes were blazing into Stu.

"He's leaving?" Stu said. "I don't—okay, hold on." He lowered the phone. "My guy says that Isaac just rushed out of Happy Valley. What should he do?"

"Follow him," Chase said without hesitation. Stu started to bring the phone back to his ear, but Chase suddenly rushed forward and tore it from his hand. "Just follow him," she barked. "Tell us where you're headed, and we'll meet you there. Don't engage."

Chase kept the phone on and in her hand as she pointed at Tate.

"Come with me."

"What about me?" Floyd asked, coming off rather petulantly.

"Look into the suicide with the other CEO. Tate and I are going to have a chat with Isaac Lomax."

As Tate hurried to stay by Chase's side as they once again commandeered Stu's Mercedes, he couldn't help but smile. He knew that Chase telling him to come along had nothing to do with the night they'd shared.

It was to protect Floyd.

And that meant only one thing: they were going to have more than a chat with Mr. Lomax. This served Tate well because roughing up Frankie and Jabari had done nothing to quell the pent-up hostility that he felt buried deep inside his gut. A gut that was still bruised from that prick Marco's fist.

If things got physical, Tate knew exactly whose face he would be picturing before he drove his knuckles into it.

Chapter 56

CHASE'S INSTRUCTIONS TO THE UNNAMED man on the phone to simply follow Isaac Lomax had gone unheeded. There was a black Chrysler parked diagonally up the driveway of a typical Las Vegas suburban home so that a Tesla couldn't exit.

Chase brought Stu's Mercedes to a screeching halt not quite blocking in the Chrysler, but definitely making it more difficult for the driver to leave in a hurry. The second that she got out of the car, the Chrysler driver's door, which had heavily tinted windows, opened.

Chase instinctively put a hand on the butt of her gun.

"He tried to run." The man who had stepped out of the car was large, easily six-four, and thick across the chest. His biceps were so large that his dark skin was lighter in spots as if the muscles beneath were nearly pushing through. As she got closer, Chase saw that he had a tattoo above one eye that read 'NOW'.

"I told you to just follow him."

The huge man just shrugged.

"He tried to run. I didn't hurt him none."

Chase looked through the rear window of the Chrysler and while she could make out a slim outline in the backseat, the heavy tint made it impossible to know if it was Isaac Lomax. Without asking permission, she opened the door and peered inside the vehicle. True to his word, Isaac didn't appear to be harmed, at least not in the physical sense. He was, however, extremely frightened.

Behind her, Chase heard Tate introduce himself to the big man, who called himself Big Roddy.

"Mr. Lomax," Chase said, making the split decision to flash her badge even though she'd introduced herself previously.

Anything to add to the man's unease and to make him think that this—forcible confinement by one of the lesser-known Wutang Clan members—and what was to come, was above board. "Chase Adams, FBI. I believe we've already met."

"Agent Adams." Isaac's eyes looked huge behind his round spectacles. "I didn't do anything! This guy, he just—"

"You lied to me," Chase interrupted. "You know all about Cerberus."

Isaac groaned. It was as painful a sound as Chase could remember hearing. Then the man looked at his hands, the long digits of which were intertwined on his lap.

"I'm sorry."

"Me too," Chase exclaimed. "Out of the car. Let's have a little talk inside."

She stepped back and Isaac dejectedly exited the vehicle. Head hung low, he walked up to this house, the door of which Chase now saw hung open. At any point the man could have told her to fuck off, that he wasn't doing anything she said. If he did that—worse, if Isaac threatened to call the police, then she was going to be put to some very difficult decisions. In the past, Chase wouldn't have hesitated in breaking certain laws to protect or defend her friends. Things were different now. She had Georgina and Brian was coming for her.

Just how much Chase was willing to risk to keep Stu Barnes out of jail was thankfully not put to the test—not right now, anyway. Isaac just shambled into his house and Chase followed. When she reached the doorway, Tate hurried to her side.

"I told Big Roddy thanks and that we won't be needing his help anymore." Chase looked over Tate's shoulder and saw the man with the 'Now' tattoo over his eye nod and get into his blacked-out Chrysler. He expertly maneuvered around her car and slowly drove out of sight. "But I doubt he's going to listen," Tate said, reading her expression. "Big Roddy said that—"

"Can you please stop calling him that?"

"What the hell do you want me to call him? He said his name is Big Roddy and I wasn't about to argue. Anyways, he said something about owing Stu. He might back off while we're here, but I doubt he's gone far."

"Hmm," was all Chase could think of saying. They'd clear this up with Stu later. This, and a lot of other things. She was grateful that Rod? Rodrick? Rodney? Rodford? Had intercepted Isaac, because not only would finding the man be a pain in the ass, but the intervening time might have brought him to his senses and caused him to lawyer up. Right now, however, Isaac believed that he was about to partake in a legitimate FBI interview. And who was Chase to tell him any different?

Isaac Lomax slumped at his kitchen table, an old, wooden round thing with four chairs that could only have come from one of two places: his grandmother's house or a flea market. Like in Roddy's car, his head was down, his long fingers rubbing up against one another as if trying to turn two pennies into a nickel. Chase gave Tate a quick nod, then she took up residence in the ancient wooden chair across from the man. She didn't say a word until after Tate returned with a glass of water and set it in front of Isaac. Adrenaline always made you dehydrated, and this was no exception. The most adrenaline Isaac probably experienced prior to today was rescuing Princess from Bowser. Being cornered by a giant black man with face tatts likely put his adrenals into organ failure.

The man took a polite sip of the water then threw manners out the window and chugged the contents of the glass. Tate promptly refilled it. This time, Isaac sipped twice and then stopped.

"Why did you lie to me, Mr. Lomax? You said you had no idea what 'C' was—but you knew. You knew about Cerberus because you worked on it with Jake, didn't you?"

Isaac nibbled on his upper lip which made him look like an English Bulldog.

"*Used* to," he said in a mere whisper. "I used to work on something called Cerberus with Jake, but that was a long time ago."

Chase grinned. She had him, and everyone in the room, including Isaac, knew it.

Chapter 57

IT DIDN'T TAKE WILL LONG to find several articles pertaining to the late Randy Milligan. According to nearly all of reports, Randy Milligan had been a well-loved man. At the ripe age of twenty-four, he started a software company that specialized in creating addictive mobile phone games. His company, PopTop Gaming, had a couple of minor hits but real success didn't come to the breakout game Captive Carnage.

It was rumored that the game, which was a tower defense clone with zombies attacking a cemetery and then a funeral home, pulled in a whopping $50,000 a day in optional upgrades. This made it even more surprising when the multimillionaire was discovered in his palatial home, a single gunshot wound to the side of his head. The more he read, the more Floyd became suspicious that this was a suicide. However, after what the papers deemed an extensive investigation, it was concluded that the wound had been self-inflicted. There was no apparent motivation for the suicide, and it was eventually chalked up to the trials and tribulations of being young and rich. There were recreational drugs found at the scene and these were tacitly mentioned. After Randy's death, PopTop had been purchased by a group of anonymous investors.

Floyd, who considered himself a graduate of the Stitts theory of coincidences, felt that something was off. CEO of a successful software company dead by gunshot? True, Jake wasn't a CEO, but he was the lead programmer. Were the two cases related?

The real question was why this particular article had been flagged by their facial recognition search. Floyd had only caught a quick glimpse of the inset photograph of Randy Milligan, but the man looked nothing like the guy in the security footage from HVG.

"Any idea why we got a hit on Randy Milligan? What does it have to do with our unsub?"

Will shrugged and Floyd realized that he was the only member of law enforcement left in the room. He crossed his arms over his chest as Will searched for more articles about Randy.

Why did I get left behind? He wondered bitterly. *Why did Chase take Tate with her instead of me?*

But he already knew the answer. It had everything to do with the fact that when Floyd had woken up to take a piss in the middle of the night, he'd been alone in the room.

His attitude had sufficiently soured now, and the last thing Floyd wanted to do was stand around watching someone else search the Internet. He was about as useful as the table upon which the ThinkPad sat.

His mind began to wander, and Floyd wondered if perhaps there was no link between Randy and Jake. Stitts didn't say that coincidences never existed, only that they were rare. And Floyd knew firsthand that if you looked hard enough you could invent patterns and meaning in nearly anything. A bag in the wind became an omen from God. A blade of grass bent opposite those beside it could indicate a sea of change.

Just as Floyd was about to suggest that Happy Valley had made a mistake and that perhaps the reason why the email had been pulled was not because of Isaac Lomax but because it had been made in error, Will suddenly snapped his fingers.

"Check it out."

He'd stumbled upon a news telecast of Randy's death. It was fairly typical, with a blonde-haired woman—always blonde, always a woman—standing outside a large house speaking about how the police were still investigating the crime scene. Next, the news anchor interviewed a woman named Patricia Spitzer, who was an intern at PopTop Games. She uttered the typical rhetoric, mentioning how Randy was such a good boss, how she couldn't believe this had happened, how much she was going to miss him. But when they cut to the next person, Floyd felt his jaw hinge loosen so swiftly that his lower mandible nearly dislocated.

"It's tragic," the man said. "Randy was a pioneer."

That was it, just six simple words, of zero importance.

It was who had said them that mattered.

Unlike with Patricia Spitzer, there was no name tag at the bottom of the screen, nor was there a position listed. But the man, with long dark hair tucked behind his ears, a nose slightly too small for his face, and brown eyes, was recognizable. His teeth were average, if anything they were a little large, and unbroken.

But this was their man. This was the unsub.

"Dammit," Will grumbled. "Why don't they list his name?"

"It's him," Floyd said, more as an exhalation than revelation. They all knew it was him, this was the man who had attacked both Jake and Stu.

This was the man who had killed Jake and framed Stu.

Floyd surreptitiously looked over at Stu, trying to glean something, anything, from the man. But Stu was just staring at the frozen image, his expression emotionless.

Was he just numb? Is that why Stu has no reaction to seeing the face of the man, seeing him in the video?

Or is there something else?

Stu had someone following Isaac Lomax and he'd told nobody. Chase would have something to say about that, that was certain. But what else was Stu hiding?

"There's nothing here," Will said in a low voice. He'd scanned all the metadata from the video. "No mention of the guy's name anywhere."

Will managed to find a second version of the video, this one hosted by a sister station, but it was a carbon copy of the first.

"Can you call them?" Floyd asked. "Can you call the station, ask if the people they show on TV have to fill out a release form or something?"

"Unlikely," Will said. But he was grasping at straws, too. "But I'll give it a shot."

Stu was suddenly beside Floyd, and he realized that the man was no longer emotionless. Perhaps his action had been simply a delayed response. Floyd could smell the sourness of Stu's sweat and recognized it as fear induced.

"Do you think... do you think that this guy killed Randy, too?" The man's voice broke on 'too'.

Floyd instinctively thought of what Tate would say, about how his partner would analyze the situation and determine what Stu needed him to say in order to keep the man calm. After thirty seconds or so, he gave up.

He wasn't Tate. He didn't have Tate's skill nor his ability to compartmentalize and thinking that he had to do things the Chase and Tate way was what had gotten him into this mess in the first place.

Just keep moving forward, Floyd.

Choo-Choo.

"I have no idea," he replied honestly.

Stu looked on the verge of becoming physically ill. Even though it seemed that the man had everything, unlimited wealth, good looks, health, house, car, Floyd had to remind himself that none of this mattered if he was found guilty and they stuck a needle in his arm. Floyd also thought, oddly for the first time, that even with all of these things, even in the absence of his pending capital charges, Stu seemed alone. The man had no wife, no kids, and no girlfriend, so far as he knew. No friends had come by either, other than Will who was technically an employee. And when Stu had found himself embroiled in this murderous mess, he'd called Chase. Not a friend, but someone who owed him a favor.

It was incredibly sad. Perhaps being wealthy beyond belief was more alienating than anything else.

Floyd, feeling his emotions begin to well, cleared his throat. *Choo-Choo.*

"It's possible," he admitted, then pointed at the screen. "We won't know until we have a little chat with whoever *that* is."

Chapter 58

"THE METAVERSE... IT WASN'T DOING so well. It was doing well but not so well, you know what I mean? People were calling it the 'Sims' and were getting bored. The initial rush of players that came to it because it was so realistic had died down as had average time played. We thought it was the rules—no breaking character, no killing others, that sort of thing that annoyed people. Sure, they might want to be a bartender in the metaverse for a day or two but to be stuck as one for a week? A month? It was too much like real life. You couldn't get out of whatever life you had dropped into. Even programmers at Happy Valley were getting bored—myself and Jake included. Others were quitting. We knew that we were going to start having a real problem when the streamers, the people who play online for others to watch, started losing interest. They're the ones who really drive in-game purchases from their viewers. And once they, who play for hours every day have accomplished everything, stopped running into real players because they were leaving and instead just dealt with NPCs? That was going to be the end.

"As VP of Software, it was my job to keep everyone at HVG happy. I had to offer larger and larger packages to get programmers to stay. That's when Stu came along, or at least one of his representatives. We told him that things were going great, that the metaverse was growing, but that was..." Isaac paused and took a sip of water. Chase, wanting to keep the pressure on, leaned forward on her elbows. "The thing is what made our metaverse special wasn't just the realism, but that there were so few NPCs. So, yeah, our numbers looked good, but it was going to come crumbling down and we all knew it."

"You keep saying that—NPCs. What the hell does that mean?" Tate asked from behind Isaac.

When he started to turn, Chase repeated the question, wanting to keep Isaac's eyes on her. Let Tate be the authoritative figure, the almighty voice from above. Let her ask the questions.

"What's an NPC?"

"Non-playable character. Same as a bot."

Chase stared and Isaac elaborated.

"You know when you're playing multiplayer games, right?"

"Not much time for games when we're tracking down murderers across the country," Tate said in a voice that was slightly more baritone than his usual.

"Right, of course. Well, in multiplayer games, you have other players, right? Like other people at home on their Xbox or PC?"

Chase shrugged.

"Sure."

"Well, in many of the MMORPGs—*uhh*, the really big online games where the universe is huge? There aren't enough actual people playing, especially when a game first comes out, and the world is practically empty. So, there are computer players, I guess you could call them, NPCs, that stand in. They mostly suck and players don't like interacting with them. The conversations are unnatural, clunky, etc, and they're really only a stopgap measure."

"So, you cheated," Tate remarked. "You pretended that these NPCs were real players, is that it? To make the metaverse look appealing to an investor like Stu Barnes?"

Isaac's eyes went wide.

"It was—it was only temporary," he whined. "Just until we worked out—"

"Do I work for the IRS?" Tate asked.

"Wh-what?"

Isaac glanced over his shoulder and Chase let him this time. Tate looked fierce.

"Do myself or Agent Adams work for the IRS or the SEC?" Isaac blubbered.

"Wh-wh-what?"

"It's not a rhetorical question, Isaac! Do me and my partner look like we work for the fucking IRS or the SEC?"

"N-n-no," Isaac managed at last.

"Right, because we already told you that we're in the FBI and our job is to track murderers. I don't give a flying fuck about NPCs in the metaverse or you trying to make your little game look better than it is."

"I'm sorry—it's-it's-it's, I-I-I don't—"

"We want to know about Cerberus," Chase said, easing the man's attention back in her direction.

"Ce-Ce-Ce-Cerberus?"

"Isaac," Tate warned, and the man stiffened.

"O-o-okay. But I have to tell you about the HVG m-metaverse first. Y-you're right, we cheated, and we fudged the numbers with the NPCs, just like you said—to get Stu to buy us out. But s-s-something strange happened right around the time he bought it. We think by accident, a player killed an NPC. Here's the thing, our metaverse has very strict rules. You kill another player, and your account is shut down. But when someone killed an NPC? The software didn't flag it. This player, who went by the name Cerberus, told two of his friends. That's what we think happened, anyway. Then the three of them started hunting the NPCs—they aren't that hard to find— and they acted like, I dunno, some sort of digital hit squad. They were dressed all in black, had the face paint, everything. They played for hours, these three, logging the most time of any other players. And it didn't even go on that long, less than a week, before Jake realized what was happening."

Chase was admittedly getting bored of Isaac's long-winded explanations, but this last part brought her attention back.

"What happened to these players?" she asked.

Isaac blinked.

"Jake booted them, of course. Fixed the code so that you couldn't kill NPCs—or, if you did, you got kicked just like a real player. He even tried banning them, but Cerberus found their way back into the game, used someone else's credit card, that sort of thing—sorry, that's not really important. The important thing is, when they realized they couldn't kill NPCs, they just logged off. They weren't interested. That's when Jake came up with the idea."

A light bulb suddenly went off in Chase's head.

"Cerberus," she mumbled. "A new metaverse."

Despite everything that had happened to Isaac, the fact that he'd tried to run and Big Roddy had stopped him, and now he was being grilled by FBI Agents, he still smiled a proud little smile.

"Exactly. Cerberus: a new type of metaverse, one where killing others doesn't result in a ban, but is encouraged. It's like the opposite of the real world. It's anarchy, it's chaos, it's what the people wanted. And it's why Jake was killed."

Chapter 59

"IT STARTED AS A FUN side project," Isaac continued after another glass of water. "And I was on board. Happy Valley not only allowed but encouraged the programmers to spend a portion of their day on something not related to our work, which was the main HVG metaverse. But Jake... Jake saw Cerberus as something different. Something more important and more popular than the metaverse. He pictured something like Dante's circles of Hell, with different types of, I dunno, torture, I guess, at each level. But instead of starting small, Jake wanted to go big right away. He was terrified that someone was going to scoop the idea. But to get to the size he wanted, we needed NPCs."

"I thought you said that—" Chase began, but Isaac, on a roll now, cut her off.

"Yeah, when the game really gets going, when it gets popular, you don't want NPCs. But when you first start a universe, you need them. Not only do they give the early adopters someone to interact with, it helps you test different things. But we couldn't just use the metaverse NPCs in Cerberus. We needed a different kind of NPC. Jake wanted them to be mean, to be as brutal as he expected the players to be, the way the original Cerberus player and his posse had been in the HVG metaverse. But that was hard—real hard." Isaac sighed. "The thing is, Jake was a nice guy, you know? Yeah, he could be a bit manic and when he had an idea there was no talking him out of it. That's what made him so good. And I'm... well, I'm what you see here. We don't know how to be mean—like, mean mean? Every time we tried to make NPCs that were evil, they just ended up being laughably fake. We needed data, we needed input. If Cerberus was going to work, it had to be real. Jake was adamant about that."

Chase leaned back in her chair.

"So, what did you guys do? Make surveys? Put up a poll online?"

"Surveys? Polls?" Isaac repeated hesitantly before shaking his head. "No, you don't understand. We needed people to play the game, to be in the game. Jake had the idea that if we took data from Cerberus itself during beta testing then we could make NPCs feel more real. Only, that wouldn't work because we didn't have any beta testers. Oh, we enlisted some staff to try it out, but… well, it didn't work. Programmers aren't really the target market. They either got scared or just laughed at what they saw. It was like a little kid watching a horror movie for the first time. Their emotions were all out of whack, and instead of giving us data that would make the NPCs more real, it just made them worse. I was about to throw in the towel—at this point, Cerberus was taking up as much as if not more of my time than the metaverse, which, may I remind you was my actual job—but Jake was obsessed. He said that we needed to think outside the box, that we had to look for something different. We needed people with… trauma."

Chase squinted at the man accusatorially and he looked down at his fingers.

"Yeah, I know. Stupid, right? It's just a game. But the metaverse was going to collapse. We both knew it. Jake thought that Cerberus could save us but in order for that to happen he wanted to make the most realistic and sadistic game possible. That's what people want, believe it or not. They don't want movies with jump scares anymore, they want movies with decapitations and people sewn together ass to mouth. To make our universe believable, we needed to research people with real trauma. And that's where Jake's brother came in." Isaac finished this last part with a sigh.

"Jake's brother?" Chase asked.

She wasn't sure what was more alarming, the direction that this layered tale was taking or the fact that she'd spoken with Isaac already and none of this, not even a hint of this level of deception, had come to mind.

Chase debated reaching over the table and grasping the man's hands, touching his skin, seeing his story from a first-person perspective. The only thing that stopped her was knowing that Tate was there, watching.

And explaining to him what she was doing might require a more extensive narrative than the one they were already being subjected to.

Chase shook her head and regained her focus.

"Yeah, Jake's brother. He was in the military, a veteran. He did two tours in Iraq and when he came back the second time, the VA recommended a psychotherapist for him to see, to help him deal with his PTSD. Jake suggested that we could use them. He said that if we took these soldiers with PTSD and threw them into combat scenarios inside the metaverse, scenarios similar to the ones that triggered them, we would be able to see how they reacted. It was a gold mine for honest, terrified reactions and behaviors... at least, that's what Jake said."

Isaac reached for his water and Chase looked at Tate. The man was staring so intently at the back of Isaac's head that he didn't notice her stare.

"This is where I drew the line," Isaac said after a heavy swallow. "I mean, this was just a pet project, you know? But soldiers with PTSD? And that was just the start. Jake wanted to use the psychotherapist to gain access to all sorts of different people with trauma. But even if you ignored the ethical consequences of triggering these people, this would never get approved."

"So, you shut it down?" Chase asked. "Stopped Cerberus?"

Isaac did that thing with his top lip again.

"Yeah, I told Jake to shelve it. To focus on the HVG metaverse. That's the last I heard of it."

Chase frowned.

"You're kidding."

"No, I did," Isaac pleaded. "I told him—"

"Let me get this straight, you had what Jake—what you both thought—was a goldmine, a new, more popular virtual reality game but because it dealt with soldiers with PTSD you just... what? Told Jake to delete it?"

"Do you think we're stupid, Isaac?" Tate interjected.

"No—no, but that's the truth! It was so long ago... like three or four years?"

"And you just forgot about it?" Chase asked, incredulous.

"Well, yeah. I mean, shortly afterward, we were being sold and there were audits going on all the time. I had my hands full trying to hide our tracks about juicing the player numbers with NPCs. And Jake was a good worker. Like, he worked long hours. And honestly? I completely forgot about Cerberus until—"

"Jake was murdered?" Tate asked quickly.

Isaac looked over his shoulder at Tate, a curious expression on his face, and then slowly shook his head.

"Until the email."

"The one about Jake selling 'C' to some investor?" Chase elucidated.

"Yeah, that one."

Chase scowled.

"The one you told me you didn't see until after Jake was dead?"

"I mean, like, well—I-I-I might have seen it before but didn't know what it meant."

This was a lie. Chase didn't know if Isaac was aware that Jake had continued to work on Cerberus after he'd been told to stop or if he'd only found out when he'd intercepted the email about the sale. But did it matter? Chase didn't think so. It did, however, make Isaac their prime suspect, mangled teeth man notwithstanding. Isaac had told her himself that he was capable of doctoring the video of the shooting. Was it any more difficult to doctor HVG security footage? Who was to say that it wasn't him attacking Stu and Jake and he'd just superimposed some greasy meth head in his place?

In her periphery, Chase saw that Tate was about to speak, but she discouraged him with a subtle head shake. It was time to enact something out of Stitts' playbook. And it worked. Eventually, Isaac couldn't help himself.

"You have to believe me—it was Jake's project, not mine. I was just helping and-and-and I told him to stop."

"I bet you did," Tate said sarcastically.

"No-no, I did! I-I swear!"

"Right."

"Who else was involved in Cerberus, Isaac?" Chase asked, steering the discussion elsewhere.

"No one. At least not when I was helping him. It was just me and him. And then it was just him."

Chase looked down for a moment, and then slowly raised her eyes.

"Why did you lie to me, Isaac?"

"Lie?"

"Yeah, you know, when you don't tell the truth?" Tate was mocking him again and it was making Isaac even more uncomfortable.

"I told you everything."

"Except in the diner. You said you didn't know what 'C' meant."

Isaac cringed.

"Yeah—I knew, I-I knew. But I wasn't sure—"

"Sure, of what, Isaac? An FBI Agent comes to you and asks you about Jake, your dead colleague, and you lie to her face. Lying to a federal agent? That carries jail time, Isaac," Tate said. This wasn't exactly true, but Isaac didn't know differently.

"Look, I-I-I-I thought I was meeting Stu, okay? I was nervous and-and anxious and I—"

"Why did you delete our email?" Chase asked.

Isaac's eyes bulged.

"What?"

"Our email. We hired Happy Valley for some facial recognition work, and they sent an email with the results. Seconds later, it was gone—deleted. And our account was effectively closed. What did you think we were going to find?" Chase demanded.

"What?"

Tate took over what had now become a grilling.

"You were worried that we'd find out that you were pissed at Jake, that he was selling Cerberus and you wanted a piece. Isn't that right?"

"N-no. I thought Cerberus was dead."

"I don't believe you," Tate said.

"Well-w-well, it's the truth! I-I had nothing to do with it!"

"But you had something to do with Jake's death, didn't you?" Chase said.

"No!" Isaac suddenly started to rise but Tate put a hand on his shoulder and forced him back down. "No, no, no! I-I-I want a lawyer!"

Well, Chase thought, *that took much longer than I expected.*

"Won't be necessary. We're done here." Tate signaled toward the door and Chase got up.

"One more thing, Isaac, and we'll be out of here."

Isaac said nothing but his face suggested that he was amenable—anything to get the two agents out of his home.

"Jake's brother..."

"Dwight."

"Dwight," Chase repeated with a nod. "You said that he was seeing a psychotherapist and that you were going to go through them? I mean, before you shut Cerberus down, of course?"

"Yeah."

"What's his name?"

Isaac shook his head and for an instant Chase thought he wasn't going to answer, or, at best, he was going to lie and say he didn't remember.

Isaac surprised her.

"Not m-man but woman."

"What was her name?"

"Christina. Her name is Christina Bunting."

"Thanks, Isaac." Tate slapped the man on the back, nearly sending him sprawling across the antique table. "Oh, and if you're thinking of going anywhere, like on a trip? Be sure to let us know well in advance. If you forget, we'll just have to have our pal Big Roddy check in on you. How does that sound?"

Chapter 60

CHRISTINA BUNTING WASN'T DIFFICULT TO find. As soon as Tate began to look up her name and psychiatry, he was hit by an ad for her services, promising safe, effective, and reasonably priced assistance specializing in veterans with PTSD. This happened so quickly that he considered that his phone had been listening in on their conversation with Isaac. It wouldn't be the first time that something like this had happened. Once, he and Floyd were having a discussion about tequila of all things, with both of them saying that they were not big fans. Prior to this discussion, Tate couldn't remember ever seeing an ad for tequila on his phone, but sure enough, the very next time he logged into Instagram, he was served not just one, but three.

Tate relayed Dr. Bunting's office address to Chase and she plugged it into the car's GPS. Tate was glad to see that the route took them away from the Strip. He wasn't a fan of Las Vegas. It wasn't the gambling, or the drinking, or the sheer debauchery of the city, it was the fucking lights. Everything was always so bright, even at night, and it gave him a headache. Now, in the middle of the day, the sun was scorching. Even with the Maybach's AC blasting cold air the heat and sun were barely tolerable.

If Jake Hollister wanted to create hell with his Cerberus game, then he could have at least used Las Vegas weather as inspiration.

Tate looked over at Chase, who was focused on the road and lost in thought. He wanted to talk to her about last night. *Really* wanted to.

Chase… is this over?

Tate hoped not. The more time he spent with the woman the more time he wanted to spend with her. And this was something of an anomaly for him. Normally, Tate was wary of spending too much time with any one individual. It wasn't that he was worried he'd break character, it was more that it was an exhausting practice. Especially for a man who didn't sleep.

Once more, Tate let his eyes drift to Chase. It wasn't just her good looks, those blazing eyes, the small, delicate features of her face, or even her body, which she clearly took care of... now, anyway. It was her hair. The way that it was gray bordering on white. Not the color itself—in all honesty, Tate thought raven black would suit her better—but the fact that there was a story behind it. That's what Chase was: a book of infinite stories. Some bad, some good, some absolutely brutal like a Kristopher Triana novel.

But that's what made her so interesting and so appealing.

And the sex. My god, Chase was good in bed. She knew what she wanted and how and was not shy to ask.

Stay away, Floyd had warned him. *She's bad news.*

Rather than deter his interest, his partner's warning had piqued his interest.

"What do you think about this metaverse shit, anyway?" he asked, looking to open a dialog.

While Tate felt comfortable being himself, his vulnerable self, in front of Chase, he respected her dedication to the job, unofficial or not. They'd have the talk that he wanted—that they both wanted—to have soon.

But not now.

Chase shrugged.

"Doesn't really interest me."

"No?" Tate pulled the visor down to try to block out some of the infernal sun. "That's what I thought, too. But it was so real. I was in there for, what? An hour? Two?"

"More like ten."

Tate chuckled. It couldn't have possibly been that long.

"Sure, well, I didn't even leave that security room where I was watching the tapes, but after a while, I just kinda forgot that it was a game. "

After getting over the initial sensation of vertigo, the immersiveness of the HVG metaverse had become indistinguishable from reality.

Almost.

"Just seems like another lie to me."

Tate couldn't disagree. It was a lie—it was fake.

"True, but you know what they say, this whole world," he gestured grandiosely in the car, "could just be a simulation."

"Not this again," Chase said with an eyeroll.

"I'm just sayin'! This could be—"

"What does it matter?"

The question confused Tate.

"What do you mean?"

"I mean, what does it matter? Simulation or no simulation, I can't do anything about it. I'm still stuck here, living by their rules. No resets, no do-overs."

Tate's mind immediately went to the accident.

If I had only been there. If only I hadn't been working, if I only had been the one driving…

"Tate? You okay?"

Tate shivered.

"Sorry, the matrix just glitched. But, yeah, I know what you mean. There are no do-overs in this life, simulation or not. No do-overs at all."

The unintended ominous nature of the comment ushered them into silence until they arrived outside of a small medical arts building. The sign listed a dentist, a lawyer, and Christine Bunting, Ph.D.

Chase parked and stared up at the sign.

"What are the chances that Jake actually went ahead with this? With his plan to recruit these veterans with PTSD?"

"Not sure. But three years... if you believe Isaac Lomax, which I don't, then that's a lot of time to be refining the product," Tate said. "And if it was good enough for someone to want to buy it..."

"But I'm not sure anyone did. I mean, that Thuring guy was a fake, right?"

"Right," Tate said reluctantly. "Why was Jake suddenly eager to sell? I mean, if we assume he kept on working on Cerberus, and he was convinced that it would be even more popular than the HVG metaverse, why sell now?"

Chase chewed on her bottom lip.

"Maybe he got scared. Maybe that crazy guy who came to his work spooked him."

"You think that the two things are related? The attack and Cerberus?"

"I do," Chase admitted as she got out of the car. Tate followed. "I think he was scared and just wanted to get rid of it. You saw Isaac. These computer guys are generally averse to conflict."

Tate chuckled.

"Now, now, Chase, that would be what, in industry parlance, we call a generalization."

Tate felt sweat break out on his forehead during the short walk to the front door of the medical arts building.

"You know what they say about generalizations."

"What's that?"

"They're generally true."

Chase pulled the door to the building open. They found the suite number for Christina Bunting's office on the digital display board and then made their way to the stairs.

"You know how many psychiatrists it takes to change a light bulb?" Tate asked as they arrived on the second-floor landing.

"I'm not sure I—"

"One, but it really has to want to change."

Chase groaned and stopped in front of the door with the Christina Bunting, Ph.D. placard on the front. She raised her hand to knock but Tate grabbed her wrist.

She looked at him, and close as they were, he saw that pain in her eyes again. That deep, familiar hurt.

Tate was tempted to spin her all the way around, press her against the door and take her right there.

"What?" Chase asked.

"Nothing." He cleared his throat. "It's just—how badly do you want to keep Stu out of prison?"

Chase's thin eyebrows knitted.

"He didn't do it."

The question that Tate had asked but not asked was, How hard do you want to play this?

The answer that Chase had given but not given was, As hard as it takes.

Tate grinned.

"That's what I thought."

He let go of Chase's wrist and grasped the doorknob. He turned it and shoved the door open.

In a loud, booming voice, he shouted, "FBI—where's Christina Bunting?"

Chapter 61

NOT MUCH SURPRISED OR IMPRESSED Chase Adams these days. But what Tate just did was impressive.

It wasn't just that his voice changed, or even his posture. It was as if, by crossing the threshold into Christina Bunting's office, Tate Abernathy became a completely different person. His face hardened, his eyes narrowed, and even his gait altered. And while these physical changes were apparent, there were other changes, too. Ones that didn't go unnoticed but were harder for her to describe.

Christina Bunting, a plump woman with doughy features and shoulder-length brown hair tucked behind her ears, was sitting behind her desk when Tate blew through the door and bellowed.

She nearly toppled out of her chair.

"Are you Christina Bunting?" Tate accused.

The woman's thin lips opened but no words came out. She looked so frightened that Chase suspected had she been capable of speech she would have denied this claim, no matter the cost.

With great strides, Tate traversed the small office, which consisted of the woman, her desk, and two comfortable-looking suede chairs off to one side. He towered over her and then slapped his badge on the desk.

"FBI Special Agent Abernathy, and my partner, Agent Mulva."

Chase, who required a much less dramatic change, nearly broke character.

Agent Mulva?

"Are you Christina Bunting?" Tate asked again.

The woman continued to gape, but now there was a look in her hazel eyes that suggested to Chase that she knew exactly why they were there.

Tate's tactics, as melodramatic as they were, seemed to have worked.

"The questions are only going to get harder," Tate threatened. "Are you Christina Bunting?"

The woman finally came to her senses.

"Y-y-yes, it's me—I-I-I'm Dr. Christina Bunting. What's this about?"

Tate just glared at her.

"Am I—"

"You know what this is about, *Christina.*"

"I'm sorry, I just—"

Feeling that Tate might be pushing too hard, Chase stepped forward.

"Christina, we're investigating Jake Hollister's murder. I believe you know the man's brother?"

Christina glanced at Chase, eyes still wide.

"Yes, I—" she hesitated. "W-well, I can't really discuss patients."

Tate made a face, which perfectly relayed his previous comment: *The questions are only going to get harder.*

"Can you discuss Cerberus?"

Something dark flashed over Dr. Bunting's eyes.

"I don't—"

"Yeah, you do. You know about Cerberus, because you recommended your patients for the pilot project, didn't you?" Tate interrupted. "Patients like Dwight Hollister."

Fear.

Chase had mistaken the dark shadow as anger at first, but now she recognized it as fear.

In a matter of moments, they'd confirmed that Christina not only knew about Cerberus but that she had, in fact, recommended her patients. It was all in her face.

"Christina, we think that Cerberus might have something to do with Jake's death," Chase said, her tone deliberately soft.

"Wh-what? How? Isn't that billionaire Stu something or other the one who killed Jake?"

Genuine surprise and confusion.

"He'll be cleared tomorrow," Tate lied. If only it were that easy. "It was Cerberus."

"Wh-wh-wh-" Christina sounded like a helicopter starting up. "Wh-what? It was just a game. It can't hurt anyone. And it-it-it was supposed to help them. It was supposed to help my patients."

Chase was taken aback. Dealing with Stu had apparently changed her perspective on things. All the talk about buying and selling companies and salary packages for software engineers had conditioned her to believe that everyone's motive was financial in nature. The idea of using Cerberus to help patients hadn't even occurred to her.

"We're still trying to iron out the details. But here's the thing, Christina," Chase said, "we need to know who entered the program."

Christina appeared torn and Tate stepped up.

"I'm going to make you a deal, Christina. One deal, that's it. No negotiations."

The woman leaned forward, her posture confirming her amenability even if her words did not.

"You tell me the names of every single patient you referred to Jake, and I'll forget all about your involvement in Cerberus. If not, I'll be forced to report to the APA and TTYL that you used an untested, unapproved program for your patient therapy. And let's not forget that you shared confidential—"

"Okay," Christina threw her hands up. "Okay, okay." She grabbed a piece of paper from her desk and with a shaking hand, started to write. "I really did think it was going to help them."

"I'm guessing you didn't do it for free, though, did you?" Tate pressed.

Christina's hand froze and now it was her turn to change. She no longer appeared frightened or shocked.

She looked angry.

"I didn't take a cent. I just listened to Jake and what he proposed. Well, I thought it would help them. Mild exposure therapy has proven effective for many patients."

Mild?

Chase recalled what Isaac had told them about deliberately triggering these veterans to ensure realistic, and potentially violent, reactions.

"The names," Chase instructed, but she was ignored.

"You think that I did this for money?" The word money came out of Christina's mouth like a vile curse. "I didn't take a cent. Not a cent."

Shit, this is going downhill fast.

"Christina, we need the names," she said sternly.

The woman pursed her lips and then angrily scratched at the pad of paper. When she was done, she tore a sheet off and held it out, not to Tate, who was closer to her, but to Chase. Concerned that the doctor might change her mind, Chase quickly grabbed the paper and tucked it into her pocket without looking at it.

"Thank you." Chase took Tate's arm and yanked him into the hall. She waited until they were on the ground floor before turning to him. "That was fucking good," she remarked. "What the hell is the APA?"

Tate shrugged.

"American Psychiatric Association."

"Nice touch. And TTYL?"

Tate grinned.

"Talk to you later."

He wriggled free and strutted toward the Maybach like he was the king of the world.

"Wait! Mulva? Agent Mulva? Seriously?"

Tate laughed and kept on walking.

"Hey, it was either that or Dolores," he said over his shoulder and now Chase laughed, too.

Chapter 62

"YOU SURE?" FLOYD ASKED.

Will made a face.

"I'm not sure, no, but you saw the pictures. There's nobody working at HVG that looks like our guy."

"Then why would he be interviewed for the newscast? Was he a neighbor, maybe?" Floyd shook his head in frustration. "No, that doesn't make sense. He said, 'Randy was a pioneer.' That implies a working relationship, d-doesn't it?" Will seemingly had nothing to offer in this regard. "What about the news anchor? She call back yet?"

Will blinked.

"Right, sorry." They'd reached out to the news station, and the producer had agreed to look through their files to see if they had a name for the mysterious man on the telecast. They said they'd call back if they found anything, and Floyd had been standing beside Will the entire time. The lawyer's phone had remained silent. "It's just—"

The door opened and Chase and Tate entered looking surprisingly fresh. In Chase's raised hand was a piece of paper.

"Got something?" he asked desperately.

Chase nodded.

"A list of names." She handed the paper over to Stu. "You recognize any of them?"

As Stu squinted and read the names, Floyd said, "Where's the list from?"

Chase exchanged a look with Tate, which annoyed Floyd, but eventually, she told them all what they'd learned.

"And you think that one of the guys that enrolled in this... what did you call it? 'Cerberus' PTSD treatment killed Jake?" Floyd couldn't help the incredulity that crept into his voice.

Chase nodded, but it wasn't a confident motion. It was more a *Yeah, I guess* than a *That's exactly it.*

"Okay… why? Why kill Jake and why kill Stu?"

In the back of his mind, Floyd replayed what he'd lip-read from the security footage outside HVG.

There was no code. Cerberus isn't about code—never was. It's about you!

But before he could verbalize this, Tate answered his question.

"The psychiatrist said that the program, Cerberus, was supposed to be some sort of exposure therapy. That reminds me of this Maury Povich episode." Tate ignored the queer looks that others, particularly Will Porter, were shooting in his direction. "Maury was doing an episode on strange phobias and was using exposure therapy. There was this woman who, I shit you not, was terrified of pickles. When she's not looking, some cameraman put a giant ass dill pickle behind her chair. When she spotted it, she absolutely freaked. Jumped out of her skin. I don't know if it was an act or not, but she looked just terrified. And she ran. Ran right out of the fucking studio. This happened with some of the other guests on the show, but they came back and worked through their fear. Not pickle girl. She was gone gone."

"What the fuck are you talking about?" Floyd blurted.

Tate shrugged.

"I'm just saying that sometimes exposure therapy can make things worse."

"Let me get this straight," Floyd said. "You're comparing PTSD from the Iraq war to someone being afraid of pickles?"

"No," Tate replied, "of course not. But—"

"Okay, stop fighting you two," Chase intervened. "Tate might be onto something. Maybe someone entered Cerberus and went postal."

Floyd was pissed that Chase was taking Tate's side, especially after his insane story, but framed this way it made some sense.

"In the se-security video, Jake says to the guy with the teeth that Cerberus isn't about code, that it's about him."

Tate snapped his fingers as if he'd come up with something himself and Floyd glowered.

"Right. What if our guy got pissed off," Tate indicated Chase. "You heard Isaac, he said there were rules in the metaverse. What if our guy broke some rule and got kicked out? What if he wanted to get back into Cerberus but Jake wouldn't let him?"

"You think that that could piss someone off enough to make them kill?" Stu asked.

Tate shrugged.

"I dunno. That shit seems hella real when you're in there."

Stu tried to hand the list of names back to Chase but Floyd intercepted it.

"Well, if these are all the people that went into this game or whatever, I'm sorry to say that I don't recognize any of them."

Floyd didn't recognize them either. But there was one name that he didn't see that raised an alarm.

"Where's Jake's brother? Didn't you say that he was the reason why Jake had the idea to use vets with PTSD?"

Chase pursed her lips and took the paper back from Floyd.

"Yeah, he's not there—Dwight Hollister is his name. I don't know why he's not on the list. Maybe Jake didn't want to expose him to this? I mean, it was designed to trigger, no matter what Dr. Christina Bunting says."

"I don't understand any of this," Stu grumbled. "I don't fucking understand."

To be fair, Floyd didn't think any of them really understood. Not yet, maybe not ever. It just wasn't their world.

"Will, show the video we found," he said.

Will played the newscast, skipping to the part with the man they all recognized.

"That's him," Chase confirmed. "But no name?"

"No," Will replied, dejected.

Chase wagged the paper with the names on it.

"You think he's one of these guys? Can you look up these names?"

Now the paper was passed to Will.

"I'll try, but this is literally the only image of this guy we could find on the Internet. Only image that Happy Valley sent us, too, before our account was locked."

As Will set about this task, Tate addressed Stu.

"This is the mechanic? The guy in the video is the same man who pretended to change your oil?"

Floyd suspected that if this hadn't been the case the man would have said something already, but Tate was right in confirming this fact given Stu's suspect memory.

"Yeah, that's him."

"What about the Randy Milligan guy?" Tate continued. "The CEO who committed suicide. You know him?"

"No... no, I don't..." Stu's sentence trailed off and his knees buckled.

Floyd, being closest to the man, managed to grab him before he toppled and guided him toward an empty chair. Tate got him a glass of water.

"I'm sorry," Stu said when color started to return to his face.

"It's fine," Chase said. "Take a break. You should really rest."

"I'll be okay."

Floyd was doubtful, but he was in no position to say differently.

"There are six names," Chase said. "Tate, you take three, I'll take the other three. Floyd, if you—"

"N-no," he said.

"What?"

"S-six names. We each take two."

This was where Chase was going to say it was better if he stayed here, helped Will search the names on the 'net. And Floyd would reluctantly back down.

But not today.

Choo-Choo.

"I'll take two names," he said forcefully. "Will can use the computer on his own."

Chase was conflicted but Floyd held his ground. He was tempted to glance over at Tate but thought that if he did, his resolve might crumble.

After a good ten seconds, Chase finally relented.

"Fine, two each."

"But you get the rental," Tate chimed in. "I'm borrowing one of Stu's cars."

Chapter 63

UNLIKE CHASE, TATE ACTUALLY THOUGHT it was a good idea for them all to split up.

Especially Floyd.

He hadn't been joking about the Maury Povich episode. Well, he had, but he hadn't. There was something about exposure therapy that she found redeeming in a simplistic sort of way. Floyd had gone to see Dr. Matteo and while Tate didn't think that a single one-hour session was long enough to cure anything, not even a pickle phobia, his partner had to be tested.

And visiting a bunch of soldiers who played video games seemed rather benign compared to telling a mother that their child had committed suicide.

Besides, Floyd himself had insisted. If that wasn't evidence that he was on the road to recovery, then what was?

The pickle girl…

Yeah, there was the pickle girl to consider. She'd just snapped and left. Vanished, destined to live in perpetual fear of baby cucumbers mixed with salt and vinegar.

Tate couldn't ignore the possibility that, no matter how hard he tried to convince himself that sending Floyd off on his own was a good thing, this could backfire.

Agents could snap, and their first instinct was rarely to just run away.

He'd seen it before. Twice, actually. Tate's first partner, Constantine Striker, had been an absolute rock, but when they'd found The Sandman, a man who, at the time, had been suspected of murdering a dozen women, including Con's sister? Con had lost it. He'd come within a fraction of an inch of murdering an unarmed man.

The outcome of the second instance Tate had seen a member of law enforcement snap had been less than desirable. Three years into his FBI career, Tate had been called in to help investigate a rash of break-ins in Virginia. But it had been a beat cop who picked up the man he thought responsible, a man with a history of escalating crimes who had just gotten out of jail for breaking and entering. Tate had been there for the arrest as had the media. Even though he'd advised against it, the media had done a piece on the man they'd locked up and the cop, telling the public that they could sleep easier.

They couldn't.

The number of break-ins actually increased and the cop, embarrassed, went to visit the man he'd arrested in prison. No one knows exactly what happened next, but rumor had it that the perp had mocked the officer, told him he had the wrong man, and that the media would smear his name.

The cop lost it. Bludgeoned the man to death in the jail cell.

Floyd wasn't prone to violence, but Tate knew that snapping didn't always involve beatings or murder.

"Can I help you?"

Tate had been working on autopilot and hadn't even realized that he'd knocked on Jonathan Sillinger's door.

"Ahem," he coughed into his hand. "Jon Sillinger?"

This man looked nothing like the person who had attacked Jake. And when he opened his mouth to answer, revealing two normal-sized, albeit, nicotine and coffee-stained front teeth, Tate knew without a doubt that this wasn't who they were looking for.

"Yeah, who're you?"

Tate was tempted to say, *sorry, wrong door,* and move on, but he was driven by due diligence.

"I'm just following up on a service that you were provided with a number of months—maybe even a year or two back?"

The man's lips vanished, revealing a set of bottom teeth that perfectly matched the top with respect to color.

"Service?"

"Yes. It was called Cerberus, and I believe that you were—"

"Oh, that piece of shit. Game sucked. Tried to tell you guys that I wanted a new level or whatever, but nobody answered the damn emails. I hope you don't want it back because—"

"No, no, keep it. I just wanted to know what you thought of the game?"

"I told you. It was garbage. It was always the same: I was a kid, and my dad came home drunk and hit me. I kept trying to fight back, but no matter what I did I just got the shit kicked out of me. Played the game like fifty fucking times, but it never changed. Over and over again, the same thing."

"Really?"

Tate was surprised. Based on what Isaac had told them, he'd expected Jonathan to be immersed in a guerrilla warfare-style simulation. Had Dr. Bunting messed up? Or was this man's real trauma rooted in childhood abuse?

"Yeah, really."

"Well, then, on behalf of—" Tate hesitated, trying to come up with a name, "Gamers Anonymous, thank you for trying our product."

Tate, desperate to move on to the next name on the list, turned and walked down the broken path toward Stu's car.

"Hey, computer man, I'll sell this hunk of shit back to you, if you want? A hundred bucks? Game sucks, but the gear is good! Goggles, controllers, everything!"

"No thanks," Tate yelled over his shoulder.

"Fifty? C'mon, it's worth at least fifty! Look at the car you got! You can afford it."

"I'm good."

As Tate collapsed into the supple leather seat behind the wheel, he considered that this might, like pretty much everything else they'd done since arriving in Las Vegas, be a waste of time.

And why were they spread out across the city, interviewing people about a game of all things?

Because of one person: Isaac Lomax.

The man had been convincing at the house—nervous, bug-eyed, dehydrated.

But what if he was lying? What if everything about Isaac Lomax was a lie?

What if he was the one who killed Jake Hollister?

Tate wiped the sweat from his eyes, pulled out his phone, and dialed Stu's number.

Deep down, he had the gnawing feeling that he was being duped.

And what did born liars hate more than anything?

Being lied to, of course.

Chapter 64

THE FRONT DOOR TO PAUL Wenkler's house hung open when Floyd arrived. The screen was closed, however, and Floyd had a hard time seeing inside on account of all of the blinds being closed and the lights off.

"Mr. Wenkler?" Floyd hollered. He knocked on the screen frame, which rattled loudly. "Mr. Wenkler?"

There was no reply, but he caught a shadow of movement somewhere near the back of the house.

"Hello? Mr. Wenkler?"

This time there was an answer. And the voice that spoke—dry and hoarse—sent a chill up Floyd's spine despite the Vegas heat.

"It wasn't me!"

"Mr. Wenkler, I just wanted to ask you—"

"It wasn't me! I didn't kill him! I didn't kill *hiiiim!*"

The shadow lunged. At first, Floyd nonsensically thought that the owner of the desiccated voice was coming at him, but that was just one of the darkness' many tricks. The shadow was at least twenty feet away, near the back of the modest house, and it was moving laterally, not toward the screen door.

But there was something wrong with the way the shadow hitched jerkily that made Floyd's natural instinct take over.

His instinct to freeze.

It started with an icy chill on his brow and a thickening of his lower intestines. Soon, if he did nothing, it would spread to his limbs, turning his feet into poached elephant hooves, thick and incapable of movement.

No.

Floyd pictured a train in his mind. Not Thomas the Tank Engine, but a big, black locomotive like the one in The Polar Express, a Finnish double-decker night train. One that had to continue forward, had to reach the North Pole—one that could not be stopped.

Choo-fucking-Choo.

"Mr. Wenkler!"

Floyd saw a flash of greasy hair through the screen and knew that this was their guy. It had to be.

"I didn't kill him!" the man screamed.

Floyd grabbed the screen and wrenched it open so violently that the worn wooden frame smashed into the exterior clapboard wall. Then it was he lunging into the dark.

His nose was immediately accosted by the sour stench of old and new sweat, but this didn't slow him down.

Nothing could slow him down.

Floyd could see the man with the stringy hair now. Paul Wenkler was in the kitchen, a straight shot from the front door, and was staggering as if drunk toward a rear exit. Floyd pulled his gun out and raised it, surprised at how steady his aim was.

"Paul, don't move!"

The man hesitated but, as usual, Floyd's commands, even those issued with a pistol for moral support, went ignored.

Paul turned, staggered once more, and then slammed hard into the wall beside the back door.

"I didn't—"

"I just want to talk, Paul. That's it."

The man was wearing clothes that were far too thick for the weather. They were pale beige or gray. Floyd's first thought was that he was wearing a tracksuit of sorts, but the material seemed too coarse for this to be the case.

"I'm going to turn on the lights now, okay, Paul? I just want to talk. Please."

The man shook his head, flinging his greasy hair flying in front of his face.

"You can't! You *can't!*"

Floyd tried the light switch, but nothing happened.

Paul had said *can't* not *don't*—the man probably hadn't paid his electrical bill.

"Okay, that's okay. So, what I'm going to do is just slowly back up. I want you to come with me. Together, we're going to step outside into the sun. Just to talk."

There was a pause then Paul did something with his head that Floyd interpreted as a nod. Floyd, confident now that the man would listen, took one small step backward, followed by another. Paul moved forward in a less coordinated manner.

"Good. Now—" Floyd's elbow knocked something from the mantle—a metal pot, most likely, based on the vibrating crescendo it made once it struck the linoleum floor—at the same time he realized what the man was wearing.

Not a tracksuit but army fatigues.

Paul Wenkler snatched something off the kitchen table.

"Paul!"

"*I didn't kill him!*"

Before Floyd could so much as blink, Paul Wenkler's house was suddenly filled with the brightness of a muzzle flash, the crack of thunder, and the smell of gunpowder.

Chapter 65

CHASE AVOIDED TOUCHING ANYTHING ON the way down the stairs leading to Tony Metcalfe's half-basement apartment. The man lived in a veritable slum and the staircase was a reflection of this. The walls were covered in brown streaks the origin of which Chase didn't even want to contemplate, and what paint there was had mostly peeled away to reveal concrete beneath. The handrail had countless holes from cigarettes and there was a section that was completely missing—not broken off but it appeared to have been sawed free.

Chase had only seen two people in the complex, even though it had a maximum capacity of probably around forty. One had been a homeless man wrapped in a blanket despite the hundred-plus-degree heat, the only exposed areas were jaundiced eyes and part of a gray mustache. Two, an obese man in a Disney T-shirt that didn't cover half of his burgeoning belly, who was counting the tiles in what counted as a lobby, at least in technical terms.

All of the doors Chase passed in the half-basement were closed and apartment 017B was no exception. Despite the feeling that she would need a tetanus shot afterward, Chase found a relatively clean spot on the warped wood and knocked. The door, like the thick carpeting underfoot, was mushy and she felt her lips curl downward.

Jesus Christ, why did I get stuck with this place?

After a ten count, she knocked again. When there was still no sound inside, Chase looked up and down the hallway.

There was no one leaning out of their apartments to see who she was, no nosy neighbor taking notes of who was coming and going.

In this kind of place, people minded their own business.

If the place hadn't been so destitute, Chase would have considered investigating the second name on her list—Geoffrey Fixman—with the intention of returning later. But the last thing she wanted to do was come back here.

Awkwardly wrapping her hand in the front of her T-shirt, Chase grabbed the door handle and turned.

To her surprise, it moved freely and then the door opened without any further provocation. It almost seemed to pop open.

How inviting, she thought glumly.

"Hell—" the word caught in her throat, aptly after the first syllable of hello. The smell that exuded from the apartment was so foul, that it was unholy.

Chase gagged.

Fearing that perhaps Tony Metcalfe had died and no one had come to check on him, Chase now pulled her shirt over her mouth and nose and leaned into apartment 017B.

"Tony?" Her voice was muffled by her shirt. "Tony Metcalfe? You in here?"

Chase backed out of the apartment to take a breath of fresher air and used the opportunity to once again observe the hallway.

Still no movement other than a rather disturbing lump in the carpet that she could have sworn had previously been three feet to the left.

Fuck it.

Chase pulled her shirt up again and stepped inside.

She had been in dilapidated places before—hell, Chase had lived in a trap house when she'd been addicted to heroin, selling her body for the next hit.

But there was something about this apartment that was somehow worse.

The air was so hot and humid that sweat seemed to bead on all of her skin at once. In some ways, Tony's apartment reminded her of the trap house, only instead of the prevalent odors being burnt plastic and the sickly-sweet smell of burning heroin, she inhaled human feces and rot. Instead of hearing cocaine crackling in a frying pan, she heard the buzzing of flies that were gorging themselves on dishes piled so high that they rather effectively camouflaged a galley kitchen.

But as bad as these things were, they were nothing compared to what she found in the 'living' room.

This is where the real smell came from.

The centerpiece was a chair with tufts of cotton coming out of the armrests and a seat cushion that had been flattened to the width of a piece of cardboard. Resting on this chair was the only clean thing in the entire apartment: a VR helmet and handles, which looked similar to what Stu had back in his house. On the floor were perhaps a hundred empty tins of what could have been either SpaghettiOs or cat food. Interspersed amongst these fallen soldiers were larger buckets and containers.

Chase didn't need to look inside to know what they contained: human feces and urine.

Fitting.

This was Las Vegas, after all. Home of the blue-haired ladies who, fearful that if they left their slot machine for a single moment would lose their destined jackpot to some weary passerby, wore adult diapers to ensure that they never had to get up.

But this was taking it to the next level.

Chase felt bile rise in her throat and she reached for her cell phone. Before she could pull it out, a fly the size of her thumb buzzed by her face, and she swatted at it. Despite its sickeningly engorged body, it somehow managed to avoid the strike and cut a new path to her right. It was mesmerizing—how can an insect that fat actually maintain flight?—and Chase followed it with her eyes.

Clearly exhausted, the fly landed on the wall opposite the chair, and Chase, shocked by what she saw, inhaled sharply.

Her eyes started to water.

"Oh God," she moaned, the words equally inspired by the nausea in the pit of her stomach and what she saw through soggy vision.

The wall was covered from top to bottom with printouts and newspaper articles. There were so many of them that Chase had a difficult time focusing. She spotted some articles related to Happy Valley as well as others about a company she'd never heard of. Near the center of the wall, at what she suspected was eye level from the chair, were two prominent photographs: one of Jake Hollister and one of Stu Barnes.

She could tell it was them despite the large Xs that had been scratched with red pen over the images.

It's him. Tony Metcalfe is the one who killed Jake.

Chase dug her hand into her pocket for her phone again but once more she stopped, frozen by what she saw: another photo.

It wasn't nearly as large as Jake's or Stu's and instead of being Xed out, this one was circled dozens of times.

It was her.

It was Chase.

The photograph was a few years old, and while she recognized it, she couldn't exactly remember where it had been taken.

"…What the fuck?"

Chase finally managed to free her phone from her jeans but that's far as she got. There was a sound from behind her, a can falling, or being kicked, and she started to turn.

Something struck her behind her right temple, wreaking havoc with her equilibrium. She staggered and stumbled, but still somehow had the presence of mind to avoid crashing into several buckets brimming with human waste as she went down.

As darkness began to close in, she heard a syrupy voice whisper in her ear, "You're even prettier in person, Chase."

Chapter 66

"**WHERE ARE YOU NOW?**" TATE yelled into his phone. "Floyd? Don't stay in the house. Whatever you do, get the fuck out of the house!"

He swerved through traffic, trying to navigate his way through this foreign city and get to his partner.

"Floyd? You hear me? Floyd!"

"Y-y-yes," Floyd stuttered. "Tate, it has to be him. I-i-i-i-it has to."

"Don't worry about that now. Just get the fuck out of there!" Tate leaned on his horn, cursed, then pumped the gas.

"But it's him, right? It's over now?" Floyd whispered in a voice that made it clear this was an internal query.

Tate answered anyway.

"Yeah, sure. Just keep it together."

"Keep the train moving. Choo… *chooooooo.*"

Jesus, he's lost his fucking mind, Tate thought. Two minutes ago, Floyd had called him, but it had taken a good five to figure out why.

Eventually, Floyd admitted that the man he'd been visiting, Paul Wenkler, had shot himself in the head.

Fast forward ten minutes, and Tate, exhausting the full capabilities of one of Stu's supercars, arrived at Paul's house. But, despite his urgings, Floyd was still standing on the front walkway.

He was also still holding his gun.

Tate parked and leaped out of his car. So far, no sirens infiltrated the sweltering air. But while the neighborhood wasn't exactly upper crust, somebody heard. Some stay-at-home mom or housewife. The cops would be here soon.

Tate grabbed Floyd by the shoulders and spun him around. The man's eyes were wide and his face pale, but he didn't resist.

"C'mon, Floyd, let's go. Let's get out of here."

Tate dumped Floyd into the passenger seat of his car. Then he looked around, trying to locate their rental. He found it a half block over, parked on a side street. It was barely visible from the front of Paul's house. This wasn't ideal—hopefully, no one noticed it and they could pick it up later—but it wasn't the worst thing either. At least Floyd hadn't parked in the driveway.

Tate locked the car with Floyd in it and then walked briskly, not quite a jog, up to Paul's home, glancing in all directions to make sure no one saw him.

At this point, it didn't really matter, though.

He found Paul in the kitchen where Floyd had said he would be. The man crumpled on the floor, his back partially pressed up against a table, was dressed in desert fatigues.

There was no doubt that he was dead. Even if it hadn't been for the bullet hole in his left temple and the surprisingly minimal amount of blood, just a thin stream that dripped down the side of the man's face and neck, his open eyes and slacked jaw were telling.

Tate grimaced as he instantly understood why Floyd had been desperately asking or telling him that this was the guy. Because even at three feet from the man, he knew that this wasn't who they were looking for. To be absolutely certain, Tate got closer still, leaned down and peered into the man's mouth.

His front teeth were intact.

"Fuck."

Tate made sure that Floyd hadn't left anything in the house—his badge or a card—and then quickly returned to the car. On the way back to Stu's house, he called Chase.

She didn't answer.

Floyd didn't utter a single word until they pulled into Stu's driveway.

"W-w-was it him? T-T-Tate, tell me it was h-h-him."

Tate parked and then stared at his hands as he wrenched the steering wheel.

"No," he said flatly. "No, Floyd, it wasn't him."

When his partner didn't reply, he turned his head. Tate expected the man to break down, to weep, to bury his face in his hands, or simply turn to dust. But the man did none of these things.

Floyd just nodded.

"What are we going to do?"

Tate's eyes narrowed. He wanted to ask if Floyd was okay, he wanted to tell him that they could talk about it, but the man's grasp on reality seemed tenuous at best.

"I'm going to take Will with me and go back to get the rental," Tate said, speaking slowly and clearly. "Then I'm going to place an anonymous call about a gunshot."

Tate got out of the car and then went around and opened Floyd's door for him.

"I'll go with you. No need to get Will involved. I'm okay, Tate. Really."

Tate believed this like he believed Isaac Lomax had no idea Jake had continued to work on Cerberus after he'd told to drop the project. But Floyd had made a miraculous recovery, going from a mannequin standing with his gun out—now holstered, thankfully—to looking and acting like a hardened FBI veteran.

But Tate wasn't buying it.

"Will is just going to drop me off at the rental—I'll make up an excuse. He doesn't need to know anything. Floyd, you're not going anywhere. Sit tight, talk to Stu. If he asks, tell him that you found nothing. That neither of the guys you visited knew anything about Cerberus. Me and Chase will finish the list. Just…" Tate hesitated. "Just take it easy, okay?"

If Floyd heard this last part, he didn't acknowledge it.

"Did you get a hold of Chase?"

Tate frowned.

"No, I'm beginning to think that she's not a huge fan of cell phones. Either that or she just doesn't like us. Probably both."

Tate was trying to elicit a laugh, at worst a smirk, from Floyd but it didn't work.

Something wasn't right with him, and Tate couldn't help but think that it was all his fault.

Chapter 67

"THIS IS NOT A GOOD idea," Will stated for the sixth or seventh time. "Not a good idea at all." Eight now.

Stu didn't stop frantically texting.

"What do you mean?"

Will rubbed his eyes. Stu hadn't slept at all since making bail and even though he'd told—forced—his lawyer to go home yesterday, at least for a few hours, he didn't think that the man had gotten much shut eye either. Stu was grateful for his help, however. Pretty much everyone had abandoned him the second he'd been arrested: his company's board of directors, his colleagues, the few 'friends' he had.

So much for innocent until proven guilty.

But Will had stuck by him. Will, who was his corporate lawyer and friend, was doing yeoman's work while his crack team of criminal attorneys was... where were they, exactly? Last he'd heard, Colin Sachs and Mike Portnoy were sifting through the minutia of disclosure and analyzing the chain of evidence.

They wanted to get him off on a technicality.

They didn't give a shit if he'd killed Jake or not.

In essence, they were doing nothing.

The ragtag group of off-duty FBI Agents led by Chase Adams were the only ones really accomplishing anything.

And maybe a select few others, like Big Roddy.

"It's just—anything they find is going to be inadmissible. You know that, right?"

Stu nodded.

"I know, but I don't care. We need to find the guy who killed Jake—the guy with the teeth."

"Stu, I know you think that finding this guy will solve everything, but if there's evidence that—"

"I don't care," Stu repeated sternly. He knew that he was being stubborn but couldn't help it. He also knew that his attitude was bordering on Pollyanna, thinking that if they simply found the man who had actually committed the crime then he'd be instantly exonerated. Except, that wasn't the way the legal system worked, and he knew it. Stu wouldn't be the first person to be imprisoned even after exculpatory evidence came to light. American justice was often as much about saving face as it was about making sure the right man was behind bars.

Or strapped to a chair.

Yet, there was an intensely personal motivation at play that Stu was desperate to understand. If not understand, then at least know.

"Did you find out anything about the men on the list?"

Will made no effort to hide his displeasure, but he knew better than to argue with Stu when he got like this.

He pulled up a Word document.

"Five of the six people on the list are army veterans, just like Chase said. And the army is pretty tight-lipped when it comes to discharge, honorable or not, so I couldn't really tell why they left or what was the nature of their dismissal. Except for Paul Wenkler. Apparently, he was at the heart of a controversy involving a civilian death in Afghanistan. Paul and his crew were clearing a house when someone burst through the front door. The soldiers, including Paul, claimed that the man was armed. Only, an investigation concluded that he was a civilian and had no weapons on him. He was shot and killed, and Paul was discharged."

Stu had no idea how this related to him as he had nothing to do with the military.

"Who was visiting this Paul guy?"

Will cocked his head.

"Floyd."

"Hmm. I'll give him a heads up."

Stu had known Floyd for some time, known him back before he was an Agent and was just Chase and Stitts' driver. He was caring and kind, maybe a little naive. Probably not the best personality traits for an FBI Agent. The way that Chase and Tate, Chase in particular, babied him likely wasn't helping, either.

"Good idea," Will said. "While you're at it, give Chase a call, too."

Stu raised an eyebrow.

"Why's that?"

Floyd might be the least experienced, but Chase was definitely the most volatile.

"The guy that she was going to visit? Tony Metcalfe?"

"Yeah?" The name meant nothing to him. "What about him?"

"He's not like the others—I can't find any evidence that he was ever in the army, navy, anything like that. Can't really find out anything about him at all."

A strange expression crossed Will's face.

"And?"

"Nothing," the lawyer said, shaking his head.

"No, not nothing. What is it? What's bothering you?"

"I just have a bad feeling about this one, that's all."

Stu stared at his friend for a few seconds before addressing his phone again. He'd already pulled up Floyd's contact but instead of clicking send, he scrolled to Chase's name and called her. When it rang and rang and rang without her picking up, Stu started to share Will's feeling of discomfort.

When Chase didn't answer on his third attempt, discomfort transitioned into something more sinister.

Chapter 68

CHASE'S HEAD THROBBED, A DRUM roll of pain emanating from the side of her skull and spreading around to her forehead. She opened her eyes and found herself in foreign surroundings. The ground beneath was earthen, brown soil, but she didn't remember going outside, didn't remember anything after—

Chase scrambled to her feet. Her equilibrium was still off and that, coupled with the soft ground beneath her shoes, caused her to stumble forward. Her vision was still blurry and that didn't help either; she didn't see the bars right in front of her. Her left elbow and chin banged off the metal and she cried out. The pain in her skull and face balanced each other but now her elbow throbbed.

"Hello? *Hello?*" Her words echoed back to her, earthy and moist.

It was the familiarity of this sound, this echo, which made Chase lose what little composure she had left.

Her entire body was suddenly and inextricably frozen… except for her eyes. While they weren't quite immune to the fear-induced frost that gripped her—they moved in their sockets as if shivering—Chase could at least take in her surroundings, which she immediately recognized as Brian Jalston's dungeon.

She was back in the place where she and her sister had been brought after they'd been kidnapped from the fair.

"Hello?" she whined.

Chase thawed in a flurry of pins and needles.

"Louisa?"

She managed to turn her head and look into the cage next to her. Chase staggered again but this time she was too far from the bars to break her fall. Her knee dug into the dirt, sending a small, almost pathetic puff of dust into the air.

She was floored.

It was Louisa.

"Chase?"

"What's happening?" Chase gasped.

"He—Bryan got me," Louisa said, her voice wavering. "He got me again and he brought me back here. To this place. What—how did he get you?"

Tears streamed down Chase's cheeks.

"I don't—I don't know," she admitted. Tony Metcalfe—the name appeared in her mind out of nowhere. As did a photograph taped to the wall and roughly circled dozens of times with a red pen. "I was hunting for a—wait, where's Georgina? Where's Georgina?" Desperation fueled her movements and Chase wrenched her aching body up off the ground. She grasped the bars and pressed her face between them. "Georgina? Georgina!"

Louisa stared, dumbfounded, and Chase asked again.

"Where's Georgina?"

Louisa licked her lips.

"She's—she's dead."

Chase felt her vision narrowing, and her grip on the bars loosened.

It was too much. It was all too much.

"How?" she croaked. This was her penance, knowing every detail of how Bryan murdered her niece. To relive every moment until she either exacted her revenge or succumbed to her sorrow. "His own daughter..."

"Georgina was killed by Mark Kruk, Chase. You know that."

"What?" Chase clenched her jaw, which sent shooting pain around her head like motorcycles in a sphere of death. "No, not my sister... my niece. What happened to my niece, Georgina?"

Louisa's expression remained blank.

"Georgina was killed by Mark Kruk, Chase. You know that." The same words, the same intonation.

What the fuck is going on?

Chase's upper lip curled, and she pulled back just a little.

"Louisa, I'm not talking about my sister, I'm talking about my niece! What happened to my niece?"

Something happened then, something that made Chase queasy. Louisa seemed to glitch. There was no other way to describe it. The woman's round face seemed to disassociate into two-inch horizontal strips that didn't quite line up.

Chase gagged and moved backward, almost falling for a third time.

Something was wrong. Something was very wrong. Chase examined her cell. It was the way she remembered it—the ground, the cage, the bars, they were the same as in Brian's underground dungeon. Chase looked past glitchy Louisa and into the next cage. It was there, it was real, but beyond that, everything blurred a little.

"No, no, no," Chase said, shaking her head. "This isn't real, none of this is—"

"Chase!" a voice boomed. Like her earlier shouts, Chase's name bounced off the earthen walls making it difficult to determine where it originated.

But Chase found the source in a thick figure approaching from the hallway that ran between the two rows of cages dug out of the dirt. Backlighting made it impossible to make out his features, but she didn't back down.

"Where's Georgina? Where's my niece?" she demanded.

The man finally got close enough for her to see him clearly.

It wasn't Brian Jalston. It was Tony Metcalfe. But unlike in the security video, his teeth weren't broken in half. His face was smoother somehow, too, as if he'd expertly applied coverup.

"Hello, Chase. My name's Tony and welcome to Cerberus."

Chapter 69

TATE SHOVED THE DOOR TO Stu's mansion open and guided Floyd inside. One look at them, and both Stu and Will knew something was wrong. The latter opened his mouth to ask as much, but Tate shook his head.

"Long story. Haven't found our man yet. Will, I need you to come with me." Will made a face but didn't protest. Tate offered a surreptitious glance at Floyd and then mouthed to Stu, Don't let him leave.

"Is it Chase?" Stu asked.

Once again, Tate shook his head.

"No—wait, why would you ask that?"

Now it was Stu and Will's turn to exchange glances.

"What?" Tate wasn't in the mood and didn't have time for this. They needed to retrieve Floyd's rental before someone noticed it.

"It's just—Tony Metcalfe isn't a veteran," Will said. His intonation suggested that Tate was supposed to know who the hell that was. He didn't.

"Who?"

"A man on the list, one that Chase was visiting," Stu clarified. "He wasn't a veteran. Never was in the army."

Tate shrugged, not seeing the significance.

"So?"

"So, it makes him an outlier."

"Okay, fine, I'll call her," Tate said, formulating a plan in his head. "Come on, Will. Let's go." And then, just in case Stu hadn't gotten the idea before, he added, "Stu, stay with Floyd. Please."

On the way back to Paul Wenkler's place, a silent ride with Will the lawyer clearly exercising his right to plausible deniability, Tate tried reaching Chase several more times.

No dice.

Where the fuck are you, Chase?

The one item of good news for the day was that the cops had yet to arrive on the scene. Tate pulled up beside their rental and pointed at the Nissan through the window.

"That's our rental." Tate passed the keys to Will. "Bring it back to Stu's house."

Will took the keys but didn't get out.

"What? Don't act like—"

"The GPS," Will said. "All rentals have GPS trackers built in. We're going to need to wipe it. Should I ask Stu to find someone?"

The question from the straight-edged lawyer surprised Tate and he didn't answer right away. He also wasn't sure how much Stu might be able to help, given his ineptitude when it came to all things computers.

It was still the middle of the afternoon, which meant that if Paul was expecting someone they might not arrive until the evening—a wife or girlfriend, perhaps. That was the worst-case scenario—best case, no one would come until the smell polluted the streets.

It was also a clear suicide, especially given the man's history of PTSD. If someone happened to see either him or Floyd, well, depending on how much time passed between Paul's death and the discovery of his body, they might not even associate the two.

"No, don't do anything for now. Just take the car back to Stu's and wait for my call."

"Where are you going?"

"To find Chase."

Tate ushered Will out of the car and then sped off, heading toward Tony Metcalfe's house.

***

Tate had been uneasy before but glimpsing Tony Metcalfe's place—apartment, not house, it turned out—intensified the feeling. The apartment building was in a state of disrepair, seconds from becoming condemned. Tate kept his hand on his gun as he walked into the half-basement. His heart was thudding in his chest, and it rattled against his ribcage when he saw that the door to 017B hung ajar.

Out of habit, Tate checked the hallway corners for surveillance cameras but, of course, a place that was unlikely to have running water didn't have anything worth protecting.

Tate pulled his gun as he approached the door. And then he almost dropped it.

The stench coming from the gap in the door was strong enough to curdle his stomach.

"Fucking hell."

Tate used the barrel of the gun to push the door wide.

"Chase?"

Against his better judgment, and to the dismay of his olfactory glands, Tate stepped into the apartment. He moved quickly, leading with the gun.

The pictures on the wall told him all he needed to know. Images of Randy Milligan, Stu Barnes, Jake Hollister, and, of course, Chase Adams. The were many of her, different poses, older ones, ones in which she had dark brown hair, others with make-up on looking like a corpse.

But it was the large headshot, the one circled many times, that *really* bothered Tate. Moreso even than the pictures he saw of himself and Floyd.

He took a step backward and his heel collided with a bucket, which toppled. A warm, thick liquid sloshed forth, soaking his shoe.

"Chase? You here?" Tate shouted into the thick air. He shook his foot, flinging human waste onto the filthy linoleum. "Chase, if you're in here, for God's sake, say something!"

Chapter 70

CHASE TORE THE MASK OFF her head, assuming that she would find herself back in Tony's disgusting apartment. The place had the same decor or lack thereof, and the same poor lighting. But three things tipped her off that she wasn't at the man's domicile: the first was that the walls were peeling, but there were no photographs or articles taped to them. The second was that she wasn't sitting on the floor, but on a mattress. Third, while this place didn't smell great, it wasn't nearly as foul as 017B.

Confused and disoriented, Chase got off the mattress and inspected her surroundings more thoroughly. In addition to her own, there were more mattresses thrown haphazardly on what appeared to be a plywood floor. All of them were heavily soiled. Littered between the mattresses, Chase spotted discarded drug paraphernalia: syringes, crumpled aluminum foil, lighters, bongs, rubber tubing. A hand-held mirror. An empty vial.

In an instant, Chase knew where she was. But unlike when she'd awoken trapped beneath Brian Jalston's house, this element of her past wasn't so startling that she lost her footing. Perhaps it was because she knew that Tyler Tisdale was dead, or maybe it was just that this part of her life, as malignant as it had been, was submerged at the bottom of a bog, forced down by more recent tragedies that floated to the surface. This understanding felt odd, considering how her heroin addiction had shaped her life, but that probably made it true. After decades of searching, Chase had finally found her sister, alive and—mostly—well. Only, Georgina wasn't the same person. And then she'd died in Chase's arms. Not by Brian Jalston's hand, but he was the architect.

And now he was out of prison and gunning for Chase's niece.

So, yeah, heroin addiction was near the bottom of transformative life events.

Live in the moment, right, Dr. Matteo?

Except she couldn't live here because here wasn't real. Despite the convincing atmosphere—it wasn't just any American trap house; this was *the* Seattle trap house—Chase knew that this was not reality. The scent of burnt plastic invading her nostrils wasn't real. The texture of the mattress, coarse and pliable, beneath her bare feet, wasn't real. The sight of the thirty gage, half-inch insulin syringe, the pin so used that it was bent at a fifteen-degree angle, was not real.

A scrambling sound—also not real—from her left drew Chase's gaze. There was a man lying on his back, hands over his heart, the top of his head covered in a mop of dark hair directed toward her, who hadn't been there moments before.

Tyler.

He was thin, sporting a slightly yellowed muscle shirt. To their credit, the orchestrator of this fake world had gotten nearly every detail correct, down to the tear-away Adidas track pants that Tyler always wore. Chase instinctively glanced up to the ceiling, a ceiling that she used to stare at after injecting heroin and collapsing onto her back, eyelids fluttering.

It was the same, or near enough the same: warped, rotting floor joists, gaps in the wooden floor above allowing just a few dancing slivers of light through.

This version of Tyler grunted and rolled onto his stomach, rotating his head so that he could look at her.

It was Tony, of course, not Tyler. But this seemed strangely irrelevant. This was about the effort that Tony had put into recreating aspects of Chase's life. The attention to detail.

After faking her death to catch Mark Kruk, her past had been scrubbed. But Tony had uncovered it. She didn't know how, or why, but he had.

And it was all for her.

Chase suddenly remembered something that Stitts had said when she'd called him for a consult on the case: their unsub likely suffered from paranoid schizophrenia and exhibited classic signs of fixation. First ideas, then things, then people. In a way, this was analogous to the natural progression of addiction and trying to recreate your first hit.

But with Tony Metcalfe, black tar heroin wasn't his drug of choice. It was her.

Chase Adams.

She was his drug.

"Hello, Chase," Tony said. Like in the previous world, this wasn't quite the version of Tony that she'd seen in the frozen security footage—filthy, greasy, tired, and broken. This was an optimized version, this was the version that someone envisioned for themselves, the social media filter version.

"Hi," Chase said. She wasn't sure why she was playing this out, why she didn't rip off the head gear as she had back in the dirt dungeon, but she didn't. What was even more alarming was the fact that she really had no desire to leave this place.

"You… you look stressed," Tony said slowly. "Would you like something to take the edge off?"

I can make you forget, Chase. I can make you forget everything.

Tony produced a syringe, pre-loaded with a mustard-colored substance, and offered it to her.

Chase took it.

And why not? After all, this wasn't real so what harm could it do?

Chapter 71

"SHE'S GONE," TATE YELLED. "SHE'S fucking gone."

Floyd, Stu, and Will all looked at him with alarm.

"Who's gone?" Floyd demanded.

"Chase!" Tate glared at his partner, then turned his attention to Will. "You were right, it's this fucking Tony Metcalfe guy. It's *him*. His apartment—" Tate looked at his brown shoe and shuddered. "—it's a fucking nightmare. Shit everywhere—literally, shit *everywhere*. And he has pictures—pictures of me," he pointed at Floyd, "pictures of you, and pictures of Chase."

Tate was the veteran here, the one who should remain cool, especially because that was what they needed him to be at this moment—the voice of reason and master of rational action. But he couldn't pretend anymore.

Not while this psychopath had *her*.

"I think Chase went to talk to this guy and he got her. Grabbed her and took her somewhere. No security cameras and every toothless fuck I encountered wouldn't say shit." He looked at Floyd, recalling their experience at Junkie's Row back in Columbus. "I tried to fucking pay them, but they said nothing. *Nothing*."

Tate, baring his teeth now, grabbed the back of an empty chair. Nobody said anything for three beats until Floyd opened his mouth.

"We have to find her."

"Yes, we have to fucking find her!" Tate shouted. "But how? *How?* Wait, does the FBI track her phone?"

Floyd grimaced.

"The FBI has trackers in all their agents' phones, but Chase isn't technically in the FBI. Her phone is personal."

Tate threw his hands up and the chair toppled.

"Fuck!"

"Wait—wait a second." Stu shoved a pile of notes off the counter, revealing his cell phone. "I've been working with a hacker, some guy named Kendrick Deetle. Maybe he can track Chase's phone, personal or not."

Tate was incredulous.

"What? A hacker?"

What the fuck is going on here?

Stu's eyes were locked on his phone as he searched for this Kendrick's number.

"Yeah, a hacker... what do you call them? White hat? White hat hacker? Whatever, I hired him as soon as I saw the video of—of *me* killing Jake. He was supposed to find out how that video was made, who made it, but he hasn't—"

Tate walked over to Stu and grabbed him by the collar. The man was so startled that he nearly dropped his phone.

"First, you have this fucking thug following Isaac, now you hired a hacker?" Spit flew from his lips and speckled Stu's face. "What the fuck else aren't you telling us?"

The corners of Stu's lips dropped and with one, violent chop, he slapped Tate's hands-free of his shirt.

"It's my life!" he shouted. The man's anger, repressed since the arrest, now came out in full force. "It's my *fucking* life! So, yeah, I have other people trying to keep me out of prison!" He paused to catch his breath. His face had turned a deep crimson. "And I didn't tell you because you didn't *fucking* need to know! Alright? And before you start yelling at me for keeping secrets, why don't you tell everyone why you're really here? What you're avoiding back home?"

Tate was shell-shocked. He saw Floyd, staring at his toes, unable to even glance in his direction.

"Fuck you," he hissed.

"No, *fuck you.* You think that I was going to put my freedom into your hands without doing a little research first? Huh?"

That's when it dawned on Tate that, like him, Stu was also playing a role. And he was pissed at himself for not seeing it earlier. Stu portrayed himself as a meek, mild-mannered individual, a victim of a horrible crime who was helpless to do anything for themselves.

But he wasn't helpless.

Stu probably had an entire team of people, an entire legion, looking for the man who framed him. They—himself, Floyd, Chase, maybe even Will—were but a cog in the wheel.

Tate was simultaneously impressed and repulsed.

"We have to stop fighting," Floyd intoned. "We have to find her. This guy—he's unstable. He could—he-he could do anything."

Tate's mustache bristled. As incensed as he was, Floyd was right. They had to find Chase. Their timeline had been compressed before, but this was different. They weren't preparing for a trial that might happen six or eight months from now.

Chase had hours, if that, before this psychopath got bored and moved onto something or someone else.

Tate saw the man grinning in his mind, showing off his cracked teeth.

"Your phone," he said.

Stu, as if only now just realizing that it was in his hand and that he'd completed a call, put it to his ear.

"Not answering."

"Call him back, then!"

Stu shook his head.

"He hasn't answered in days. Kendrick called me, told me that he thought he found the man behind all of this. Said he was 'going in' but wouldn't say anything else. I haven't heard from him since."

Tate felt his anger mounting again and maybe Floyd saw it too because he spoke up first.

"Why didn't you tell us this?"

"Tell you what?" Stu snapped. "There was nothing to tell. I just assumed that, like everyone else, he just took my money and left me to *rot*."

Tate squeezed his eyes closed so tightly that he saw stars.

"Okay, *fuck*, okay! Where is this guy? Where did Tony Metcalfe take Chase?" Tate opened his eyes. There was no response, and he threw his hands up again. "Well, I'm not sitting around here while a man who shits in buckets and plays video games twenty-four hours a day does whatever he wants with Chase."

Tate, scowling so deeply that his neck was starting to ache, whipped around and strode to the door.

"Where are you going?" Floyd yelled after him.

Tate didn't know. He just knew that he couldn't stay here. He'd either murder someone or maybe this new version of Stu Barnes would murder him.

"Isaac's? The shrink's? I don't know, Floyd! I don't *fucking* know!"

Chapter 72

TONY HAD DONE HIS RESEARCH, alright, whether firsthand or not, Chase couldn't tell. Injecting herself with… *something*… in the metaverse, in *Cerberus*, wasn't that far off from a real-world high. Her senses were numbed, her vision languidly saccadic, her ability to smell muted but paradoxically enhanced for certain particles.

Chase was no longer separate from the world but had become an integral part of its fabric.

"Come on, I want to show you something," Tony said. His voice was low and slow, almost dreamlike in nature. This illusion extended to his movements, which involved him standing and holding out a hand. Chase took said offering and together they walked out of the trap house.

Chase was greeted by a spectacular sight, and the name Cerberus suddenly made sense. Tate—or had it been Floyd? Stu, perhaps?—had told her that Cerberus was a three-headed dog that prevented souls from trying to flee Hell.

This was Hell. And it was surprisingly beautiful.

The trap house didn't exit onto a seedy neighborhood, with crack addicts and homeless, the lesser dead, slumped on the sidewalk as it did in Seattle. Instead, it led to a double-wide street, concrete, maybe, but shinier. Almost reflective. Lining the streets were massive, twenty-foot-high poles, and on top of these, open flames. It was this fire, flickering by unseen and unfelt breeze, which caused the mirror-like street to seem alive.

There were other houses flanking the trap house, but they seemed less interesting, less developed, even. They reminded Chase of the buildings that had been used to test the effects of an atomic blast, ironically right here—there?—in Nevada. These houses were more than set pieces, more than just painted sections of plywood supported by two-by-fours, but they were still shells.

"Come on," Tony urged.

They walked down the slick street toward the horizon, which seemed infinite.

"Howdy," someone on their left said.

Chase turned and saw three young British police officers — Bobbies? They were giggling and horsing around, and after observing them for a few moments, she thought she recognized them.

"Are those — "

"Yeah," Tony said with a chuckle. "From A Clockwork Orange. My favorite film."

One of them saluted Tony.

It was them, Chase saw, the actors that played them, anyway. Including a young Malcolm McDowell.

And they were staring at Tony with something akin to reverence.

"Come on," Tony said, pulling her along. "There's so much I need to show you!"

He was like a child, giddy and proud of his first drawing that could actually be mistaken for a dog or a house or a family.

Up ahead, a fantastic building loomed. It was massive and even more reflective than the street. Rising so high that the top few floors disappeared into the clouds, the building still managed to hold a striking resemblance to its inspiration: Happy Valley Gaming.

"Beautiful, isn't it?" Tony asked.

It was gaudy, extreme, something that belonged in Dubai or UAE and not... Seattle?

Where the fuck are you, Chase? And what the fuck are you doing? Take the mask off. Take the mask off and grab this fucking sicko.

That definitely didn't sound like Dr. Matteo's voice of reason. It belonged to someone she didn't recognize.

"Yes," she found herself saying. "Beautiful."

Impressive would have been more accurate.

Leading up to the building was a set of stairs that even Rocky wouldn't have been able to sprint up without becoming exhausted. At the top of those was a giant throne made of swords.

"Is that—"

"Yes!" Tony proclaimed gleefully. "That's the Iron Throne from Game of Thrones. I love that show."

Tony ran up the first three steps and then spun around, holding his hands out at his sides in an expansive gesture.

"What do you think? This is all ours, Chase. All *ours*. Take a look around!"

And Chase did, which brought the real horror of Hell to light.

More poles lined the entrance to this malignant version of Happy Valley, only they weren't topped by flames.

They were topped by heads.

"Jesus," Chase gasped. This may have all been fake, the construct of an obsessed madman, but the emotions evoked by the decapitated heads were very much real. If she hadn't been high, Chase's bladder might have even let go.

The first head belonged to Stu. His eyes were open, his tongue lolled out of his mouth. His skin had an unusually vivid pallor for a dead man. Next to Stu was Jake. There were two bullet holes in his skull in the exact locations where real-world Jake had been shot. She didn't recognize the third head.

Tony followed her gaze.

"Randy Milligan. Randy *fucking* Milligan."

The name was tangentially familiar.

"He… he committed suicide, didn't he?" Chase's tongue was thick, which made her words equally dense.

Tony's face grew hard and part of the veneer finish on his face shimmered. For a split second, Chase saw his teeth as she knew them to be: broken halfway to the gums.

"No—he's a fucking lying, thieving prick. And he paid for it." Tony prodded his chest. "Captive Carnage? That was *my* game. I made the code! *I* made it. I made the code for Happy Valley, too. I broke the uncanny valley. Everything you see here, this *genius*, is my doing." Tony cackled. *"Tony Metcalfe is the best computer programmer in the whole world!"*

There were more heads set back from the prominent displays, a dozen in total, but she didn't know these people. There were probably others who had crossed Tony. Chase wondered if, in real life, they'd met the same fate as Jake and Randy.

Tony continued up the steps and eventually took a seat upon his throne.

"Join me," he said. "Come on, Chase, *join me.*"

Three men stepped from the shadows and flanked Tony. They were wearing uniforms, black slacks, black turtlenecks, white Converse sneakers.

"Chase, meet Geoffrey Fixman, Mark Dyson, and Fred Marquette," Tony said. "Friends of mine."

Geoffrey, Mark, and Fred…

A lightbulb went off inside Chase's head.

These were the last three names on the list. The final three war veterans who Christina Bunting had referred to the Cerberus program.

And now they were, what? Tony's protection? Were these men really in the metaverse, in Cerberus? Or were they, like Stu and Jake's heads… NPCs?

"Join me, Chase."

Chase felt her stomach twist into knots.

"Up here," Tony said, grinning now. "Join me up here."

All Chase had to do was reach up and take the goggles off. That was it. Such an easy solution to a hard problem.

But she wasn't ready to leave Hell. Because she belonged here.

It was a fitting location for her. For the pain she'd caused, for the people she'd hurt.

For the people she'd killed and for the deaths she was responsible for.

So, Chase did—she walked up those magnificent steps and took her rightful place beside the throne in Hell.

Chapter 73

"**KENDRICK STILL ISN'T ANSWERING.**"

"Fuck Kendrick," Floyd blurted. "Where can this Tony guy be? If his apartment is as bad as Tate says, it's not like he has a summer home in Martha's Vineyard. So, where is he?"

"I can call a friend in the LVPD," Will offered. "If Tony's a got a record, we might be able to—"

"He doesn't," Stu said. "If he did, the facial scan would have picked up his mug shot. He doesn't have a record."

"I'll check property records, just in case," Will said, likely just feeling a need to do something.

Floyd turned his thoughts inward. They were missing something. The beginning... what had started the entire case? There was the body, Jake's corpse, the video, the GSR, the Bluetooth scrambler on Stu's car.

"Any word on that TV station? The reporter?" Stu asked. "If Tony was just a neighbor and the station can tell us where the video was shot, we might have a starting point to look for his guy."

The video...

Floyd snapped his fingers.

"The fucking video!" Will and Stu stared at Floyd while he frantically searched his pockets. He'd gone to *U-Lock-it* yesterday and come back with a list of renters' names. He'd passed it off to Will and then when he'd gotten it back, he'd put it in his pocket... and then he'd fallen asleep in his pants. "Got it."

Floyd pulled the paper out and went over the names again. No Tony Metcalfe. Nor did he identify any of the other Cerberus participants on that list.

"Fuck."

"What is it?" Will asked.

Floyd ignored the lawyer.

It has to be here. U-Lock-it is the key, he thought, realizing how stupid that sounded even in his own head.

Stu leaned over Floyd and scanned the list.

"Do you mind if I look?"

Floyd shrugged and the gray-haired man took the sheet of paper.

The location of Jake's murder had been no accident. Tony had picked that place because he had easy access to the *U-Lock-it* security footage through the metaverse. And he had driven there, or walked, probably walked, but he hadn't left on the bridge.

He had to have a locker there.

That was the only thing that made sense. Tony Metcalfe, name on the manifest or not, rented a unit at *U-Lock-it.*

"Fuck it, I'm going," Floyd said.

Will's phone rang and he answered.

"Hello? Yeah, this is Will Porter." The serious expression on the lawyer's face kept Floyd from leaving. "You've got a name, yeah?" Pause. "Wait, *what?*" Floyd straightened and he subconsciously leaned toward Will. "Are you sure? *Absolutely* sure? Thank you. Yeah, thanks."

He hung up and stared blankly into space for a moment.

"Well?" Stu asked desperately. "Who was it? Your cop buddy?"

"No, that was—that was the news station," Will said absently.

"And? What did they say?" Floyd demanded, his patience completely shot. "What the fuck did they say?"

"They said that the man in the video… they-they found the release form. I don't even know why they have one but… it wasn't Tony Metcalfe, in the video. They said — they said it was Isaac… Isaac Lomax."

Floyd's eyes bulged.

"What? That's gotta be a mistake, right?"

Will shrugged, looking bewildered.

"I don't know. She said it was clear: *Isaac Lomax*, name and signature. She's going to email me the original video. They did a video release form as well."

Floyd felt something behind his right eye twitch.

"How can it be Isaac? The man in the news video was Tony… right? I mean, we all saw him and — "

"J. Turing," Stu interrupted, his voice strangely distant.

"What?" The parallel vein or capillary or muscle behind his left eye went off now, too. "What the hell are you talking about?"

"Here, on the list — J. Thuring. The same guy who — "

" —sent the email to Jake Hollister to meet him outside *U-Lock-it* and buy 'C', buy Cerberus," Floyd finished for Stu. "What unit number?"

Floyd grabbed his keys and bolted to the door.

"Let Will go," Stu protested. "You stay here, Floyd. Tate told me to make sure that you stay here."

"Fuck Tate. Tell me the unit number!"

Stu's eyes narrowed and he licked his lips.

"Tell me the fucking number! Unless you want me to go door-to-door while Tony slices up — "

"Four-twelve," Stu said. "J. Thuring is renting unit four-twelve."

But Floyd was already gone.

Chapter 74

TATE SLAMMED ON THE BRAKES a second too late and Stu's Maybach collided with the rear bumper of Isaac's car. His body hadn't even stopped rocking in his seat before he was out and sprinting toward the house. He didn't bother knocking this time; Tate just barreled through the front door.

"Isaac! Isaac!" he yelled, his chest heaving, his hands balled into fists.

Tate wasn't acting now, wasn't thinking about how to act, he was just doing. It so happened that his behavior coincided with the roles that he and Chase had initially enacted in this house.

Tate was the big bad tough guy, Chase was the voice, or ear, of reason.

"Hello?" a timid voice called from the kitchen.

Isaac Lomax was wearing a pale blue sweater and khakis. His hair, thin as it was, was slicked back. On the table in front of him was a VR set.

"Fucking metaverse, bullshit," Tate swore, slapping at the goggles and sending them scattering to the floor.

"Hey! *Hey!* What the hell—"

"Where is she!" Tate roared and then he lunged.

Isaac sidestepped the sloppy attack, but Tate pivoted and managed to grab a handful of blue sweater.

"Where is she?" he demanded again.

"Who?" Isaac gasped. He tried to spin away from Tate, but all this accomplished was stretching his shirt.

"Chase!" Tate bellowed. "Where the fuck is Chase?"

"I-I-I—"

Tate hit him. He hadn't planned on striking the man—his intention, so much as he had one, was just to scare the man.

But he'd lost all control.

Tate's knuckles struck Isaac directly on the forehead. Pain radiated up from his knuckles to his wrist, and while the man's head rocketed backward, he suspected that the hard bone had absorbed most of the damage.

"Where is Chase?" he demanded a third time, still holding the man by the shirt that was more poncho than sweater now.

"Jesus—fuck!" the man held his forehead in one hand. "I don't know! I swear, I don't know!"

"Then where is Tony!"

When Isaac answered with the same refrain, Tate struck him again this time in the jaw. Isaac's eyes rolled back, and his consciousness waned.

Tate shook him until lucidity fleetingly returned.

"Where the fuck is Tony Metcalfe!"

"I... don't... *knooooow*."

As the man moaned and continued to teeter on the edge of consciousness, Tate realized that this wasn't Isaac. Not anymore. This was a metaverse trick, and the man he was striking was Marco, the big Serbian bastard who had slugged him. It was also the judge, who had convicted his wife when the accident wasn't her fault, when she wasn't the one to blame, it was—

Someone grabbed the back of his arm, someone strong, and yanked him off Isaac Lomax with ease. Before turning to look at who held him back, Tate got a glimpse of Isaac's face.

It was a bloody, pulpy mess. The man's nose was angled to one side and his lips were swollen and coated in blood.

"Fuck!" Tate yelled, shaking out his bruised hand. "*Fuck!*"

"You gotta go," a deep voice told him. "You gotta get out of here."

It was Big Roddy. Big Roddy who had evidently still been watching Isaac's home and when Tate had arrived, he'd intervened.

A little too late but maybe that was on purpose.

"Go!" Roddy urged. "Get out of here!"

Tate grimaced, not at the pain in his knuckles, one or two of which were probably broken, but at his own lack of restraint. He'd just beaten the shit out of a man. A more-or-less innocent man. It wasn't the first time he'd broken a man's nose and bloodied their face, and it wouldn't be the last.

But it was the first time he'd completely lost it.

"Fuck."

Tate slid past Roddy.

"What are you going to do with him?" he asked.

Roddy's huge shoulders rose and fell.

"I can't stay here—on probation. Tell Stu I did what I could."

Behind the big man, Isaac blubbered something thick and wet as he rolled onto his side.

"I will."

Tate ran to Stu's car and backed out of the driveway.

Isaac might be a liar, but Tate didn't think that he knew where Tony was, where the man was keeping Chase. That was what he hoped, anyway. Because if Isaac knew, then he'd ruined any chance of getting the information out of him.

And in a matter of hours, Tate suspected that he would be in a similar spot as Stu, hiring a cracked team to prepare for his own trial. Not for murder, but assault and battery.

At least, assault and battery.

But that was fine. So long as he found Chase, then Tate didn't care about what happened to him.

Visiting Isaac Lomax had been an unmitigated disaster, but he promised himself that he would stay in control for his next stop: Christine Bunting's.

He was halfway to the psychiatrist's office when his phone rang.

"What?"

"Tate? It's Will, I just got a call from the TV station. The man in the video... it's not Tony. It's Isaac."

Tate's eyes reflexively shot up to the rearview mirror.

"What? What are you talking about?"

"Remember the newscast? The one of Randy Milligan's suicide? The one—"

"What?" Tate squeezed his fist and winced. "What are you talking about? What do you mean it's not Tony?"

"They sent over the original video... it isn't Tony who says that Randy is a true pioneer, but *Isaac*. Somebody changed the video to make it look like Tony. Just like Jake's murder."

Blood trickled from Tate's knuckles and into his palm.

"Why? Why would Tony do that?"

"I don't know. But it is Isaac."

Tate tried to make sense of this, but he couldn't.

"I was just there—I just—"

"Wait, there's one more thing."

"Yeah?"

"Floyd thinks that Tony is holding Chase at *U-Lock-it*. Somebody going by J. Thuring rents a unit there. He's on his way there now."

Tate yanked the steering wheel so hard that even the Maybach, with its racing suspension, had a hard time gripping the asphalt.

"Fucking hell, Will! You could have led with that!"

Chapter 75

"YOU... YOU MADE ALL OF this?" Chase asked. There was awe in her voice, and while she'd planned to feign the emotion, some of it was legitimate. What Tony had created was impressive.

"Yes, all of this," Tony gestured grandly, and the three army veterans bowed their heads. "It's all for you, and it's all real."

He's obsessed. He's completely obsessed. With me, with Cerberus.

This is what everything is about, Chase realized. Tony had entered into the Cerberus pilot program through his therapist, Christina Bunting. For some reason, maybe the trial had expired, or Isaac had made Jake shut Cerberus down if only for a little while, Tony had been booted.

And everything the twisted man had done since was about getting back here.

About getting the keys to Hell from Jake.

"No," Chase whispered. "No, it's not real."

"Is it not?" Tony asked. "What makes you say that this isn't real? Does the air not feel warm to you? Do you dare touch the flames?"

Chase's eyes inadvertently darted upward, finding the flames of which Tony spoke. In her mind, she knew that this was just a simulation, but Tony's question made her think.

Would she dare touch those flames? She wasn't so sure.

Chase was reminded of a video she'd stumbled across years ago: the rubber hand illusion. It was an experiment involving a seated man with both of his arms and hands laid across a desk in front of him. A wooden divider was then placed in front of one of his arms and hands, blocking it from view. Next, a rubber hand looking much like their own was placed in front of them, giving them the illusion that this was their actual hand.

The experimenter would then use two feathers to tickle both the real, hidden hand and the rubber hand at the same time. Then, without warning, they would bring a hammer down on the rubber hand.

The participants would cry out in pain and pull their real arm back even though they were never actually struck.

Would she shriek if she touched the fiery hot torches?

"Right," Tony continued with a grin. "These stairs? You can walk on them. This throne?" he laughed. "Not comfortable. Not at all. So, what *is* real, Chase? The world out there, outside of Cerberus, that's what you think is real, right? But how can you be sure?" Tony tapped a temple as he said this next part. "Everything you see—everything you feel, hear, smell, touch—*everything* is interpreted by your brain. That's not reality. It's an interpretation. And this here, is *my* interpretation."

The madman's words, while not as eloquently spoken, oddly mimicked something that Tate had said when he was discussing his experience in the metaverse with her.

"But this is just your interpretation," Chase countered for both of their benefits. "The real world is open for everyone to interpret."

Tony laughed again. It was an unsettling sound, and Chase wondered if he'd messed with that, too, if Tony had changed it to be more maniacal, more menacing.

"Oh, so you mean to say that we all interpret the world the same, Chase? Really? You can't possibly believe that. Muslims, Jews, Christians… blacks, whites, whatever? We all interpret the same world in the same way? What about addicts? *Hmm*? They see the world very differently, but what they see is real, isn't it?"

There was truth to what Tony was saying. That was the most disturbing part of his rant.

In the Academy, Chase had been warned about the unpredictable and unreliable nature of first-person accounts of crimes. Memories weren't like video recordings, and as she'd recently found out, even those were far from reliable.

No, memories can be warped, influenced, erased, or completely fabricated.

This, she knew better than most.

So, what *was* reality? Was it the planet? The sun? The universe? Or was it ones and zeros? Were they all just stuck inside a giant quantum computer, one of an infinite number of alternate realities?

Was her voodoo real? She'd lived with it, off and on, for years now. It was something that Chase couldn't touch or share or even explain, really. But it felt real. When she was inside a victim's head, seeing through their eyes, reliving their last moments on this Earth, that was real. It had to be.

But, at the same time, it wasn't. It was an illusion, a hallucination, fabricated by her subconscious.

Chase's scrambled thoughts threatened to overwhelm her, and she shook her head.

"It's not real," she said weakly.

"What's not real? Those heads you see? They're not real? They don't make you feel repulsed?"

Chase swallowed hard, ignoring the urge to look up at the decapitated heads, to stare into their hollow eyes.

"No, they're—"

"You're wrong, Chase. These heads *are* real. Look at Randy here... he's dead. *Really* dead. But do you know what the real difference between Cerberus and that simulation you call the real world is?"

Chase didn't want to know—she was suddenly feeling nauseous. Was it because of the vertigo Tate had mentioned that can happen when dropping in? Or was it the heroin that Tony had injected her with clearing her system?

"Oh, I'm going to show you the difference." Tony's grin spread from ear to ear. This, Chase decided, had to have been modified. "The difference is... wait for it... wait for it..."

Tony held both hands out to one side and his army bodyguards separated, revealing the outline of a woman. Chase squinted, trying to get a better look as the figure came forward. Her long, white dress reflected the flickering flames, making it seem as if she was a phoenix rising from the ashes.

"...the difference is that here in Cerberus, in my world, in *our* world, Chase, what's dead doesn't have to stay dead."

That's when Chase's sister stepped in front of Tony and her face came fully into view.

"Georgina?" Chase gasped. "Is that—"

"Chase, oh God, Chase, I've missed you so much."

Chapter 76

IT WAS HER SISTER. SHE had the same red hair, same green eyes, same… *everything*.

And it was terrifying.

Chase took two awkward steps down the concrete stairs, but Georgina kept coming. She passed in front of Tony on the throne, then began to descend.

Chase was torn. She wanted to run from the apparition because she knew that her sister, her *real* sister was dead, but she also wanted to run *to* her.

Because this *was* Georgina.

Wasn't it?

"Chase?" the woman said in Georgina's voice.

"What the fuck—what the fuck is this, Tony?" Chase begged, her eyes not leaving her sister's.

"I told you, this is real, Chase. This is *real*. This is your sister, the one who was murdered. But she's still here. She's always been here, waiting for you to arrive."

"I've missed you, Chase."

This broke the spell. Georgina would never say something like, *I've missed you*. And was it Georgina? Or Riley? Does she go by Riley? Or does she go by something else here in this Hellish place? Lilith, perhaps?

The three veterans, Geoff, Mark, and Fred, spread out and followed Georgina, staying roughly five feet back from her at all times.

"It's not perfect, I know," Tony admitted. "But here's the thing, Chase you can help with that. You can help make her… better."

More real.

That's what Tony wanted to say, Chase knew.

"But—"

That wouldn't be real.

And that's what *Chase* wanted to say. Tony had a response for that, too, even though her words went unspoken.

"That's the beauty of this world—" *of Hell,* "—it learns. I programmed it to learn, to grow, to *breathe*." Tony grinned with his perfect teeth. "It's a living place, Chase."

Georgina continued down the steps with the vets in tow. Chase stopped backing up and eventually, they found themselves within inches of each other.

Chase's mind had become fractured, incongruous.

Run.

Stay.

It's not your sister.

Riley wasn't your sister either.

This is Georgina.

This is real.

This is a simulation.

When Georgina extended her arms, Chase couldn't resist.

Real or not, one last chance at embracing her sister was something she couldn't turn down in Heaven or Hell.

Chase hugged Georgina, expecting her to be completely without form or, at the very least, be cold to the touch, but she wasn't. Georgina was full and warm and... Chase closed her eyes and breathed deeply.

It even smelled like her sister, which was impossible. With Tony's computer prowess, he'd have no problem digging up images, even long-buried ones, of Georgina Adams aka Riley Jalston. Thanks to Drake and Sergeant Yasiv, her sister's death in the Butterfly Gardens was a distant memory and news coverage had been deliberately scant. But if you looked hard enough...

The smell? How could Tony know that her sister smelled faintly of vanilla and lilac?

As Chase inhaled again, she began to wonder if this really was her sister's smell. After all, the most poignant memories she had, ones that hadn't been stripped from her mind, were of them as children. Georgina didn't smell like vanilla and lilac back then, did she?

It's just your mind projecting what you think *Georgina smells like.*

This realization did not affect her in any compelling way.

Chase adjusted her grip and her forearms made skin-on-skin contact with Georgina's shoulders.

It happened instantly; Chase saw through her sister's eyes. She saw herself in a field, her fingertips brushing the tops of the daisies. They were both singing, singing Ring-around-the-Rosie.

Tears flowed and Chase let them streak her warm cheeks.

"Chase," Georgina whispered.

"Georgina."

They embraced, in this world, in the other, in the vision.

"Chase, look after my daughter. *Please.*"

Chase froze. This was too much. She slowly peeled her arms away from her sister and when she opened her eyes, she found herself back on the steps in Cerberus.

Tony was staring at her, still smiling that Cheshire grin.

"No," Chase said.

Too much... too much.

She angrily swiped the tears from her face.

"No," Chase repeated more aggressively this time. Georgina reached for her and hugged her again. Chase tried to push her away, but the woman's grip was strong, and she squeezed her tightly.

"Stop," she insisted, wriggling to try and break free. "This is… wrong. It's fucked up. It's not real."

"Doesn't it feel real?" Tony asked.

It did. That was the worst of it. It felt so *fucking* real. All of it.

"Doesn't it look real to you? Smell real?"

Chase felt like she was reliving the same moment over and over again, a macabre Groundhog Day.

But was that such a bad thing?

"I—I can't," she whimpered. At last, Georgina let go.

"Why not? You can stay here with me." Georgina gestured toward the heads on spikes. "We can do whatever you want. We can make up for all that lost time, all those lost years."

That's when Chase noticed him for the first time. She wasn't sure if the head had been mounted on a spike all this time and she hadn't noticed it, or if Tony had placed it there when she'd been using her voodoo to see through her sister's eyes.

Brian Jalston's head. The attention to detail was incredible. Whatever template Tony had used, it wasn't from an archived photo. It was recent. The man's hair was gray, his jaw more chiseled, less flabby skin on his cheeks.

Chase started to smile.

This is what she wanted. Brian's head on a spike.

And now she had it.

"You see?" Tony bellowed, his voice coming from everywhere now. "Anything you want, Chase. If you can dream it, in Cerberus, you can have it."

Chase stared into Brian's lifeless eyes.

Tony was right, she *really* wanted this.

There was just one thing that he had missed in his bid to have her join him in Hell.

Her niece.

Perhaps this had been a tactical move by the man, thinking that it would be overwhelming for her. Or maybe he just didn't want to remind her of little Georgina.

But he could conjure her. There was no doubt in her mind that Tony could replicate the little girl's orange hair, the freckles on the bridge of her nose, her bright green eyes—brighter even than her sister's. Except that wouldn't change the fact that she was still out there. Deep down, Chase knew that Louisa would end up being a better mother to the girl than she ever would, and would have no problems with being the surrogate, either.

Chase could just stay here, in Hell, and leave her body back wherever Tony had put it.

Look after my daughter.

That's what Georgina had said.

And everything Chase did now was for her, for little Georgina.

"No." It wasn't a question now, but a statement. "I can't stay here. And neither can you."

Tony's smile faltered.

"This is my home, I run this place."

"You killed Jake, Tony. You set up Stu. You need to pay for what you did."

Tony laughed maniacally, the sound amplified by the invisible speakers.

"You have no power here, no authority," he said. "I am God and I am the Devil all in one. I am the creator."

"Maybe here," Chase admitted with a condescending shrug. "But not out there. Not in the real world."

Thinking that this was a good time as any, she raised her arms, intent on removing the VR helmet.

The veterans were on her instantly, holding her arms out to her sides.

"Let go!" Chase shouted, trying desperately to break free. But there were three of them.

How is this possible? Is someone holding my arms in real life, too?

Chase didn't know but figured that this had to be the case. Otherwise... otherwise, what did that mean?

"No, no, no, you're not going to be doing that. But that pose... that gives me an idea. Maybe beheading isn't the way to go with you. I like you better as a martyr—maybe I'll crucify you." Tony laughed again. "I was really hoping that you would join me here because I like you, Chase. I do. But no one, not even you, are worth what I've created. And no one is going to take it away from me."

Chapter 77

FLOYD MADE IT TO *U-LOCK-IT* in record time. He drove up to the barricade and leaned on the horn, flashing his badge in the vicinity of the camera.

C'mon, c'mon, hurry the fuck up!

Seconds ticked by and then there was a buzz, and the mechanical arm began to lift. It moved painfully slowly, and Floyd drove Stu's car beneath it before it was all the way up. There was a horrible scratching sound as the bar scraped across the roof, but he barely noticed.

The aisles between the rows of storage lockers, which were like individual car garages, were too narrow for the car so Floyd parked it as close as he could get before leaping out.

412... I need unit 412...

It took him all of thirty seconds to figure out how the units were arranged—the first number representing the row, starting with 0, and across from that, the next number in the sequence, while the last two digits indicated the individual units—and Floyd sprinted down the third row.

He had no problem finding the locker, but when he arrived in front of unit 412, he realized that he'd made a fatal error. The orange, accordion-style garage door wasn't just closed but there was a large padlock on the ground, looped through an impressive metal ring embedded in the concrete floor.

"Shit!" Floyd dropped onto his hands and knees and tried to open the locker anyway. It lifted about four inches off the ground but then the slack caught. He pressed his ear to the concrete slab and peered beneath with one eye. The smell was bad down here, the air still and stagnant. "Chase?" he yelled. There was no reply. "Chase!"

He couldn't see much—it was too dark and the opening too narrow to angle his eye upward. Even using the flashlight on his phone revealed little.

"Chase!"

Movement. Just a blurring of shadows but unmistakable, nonetheless.

Floyd rocketed to his feet and tried to wrench the door open, all the while shouting Chase's name. The lock held fast, and Floyd quickly gave up, his fingers aching. After kicking the door twice, more out of frustration than a reasonable attempt to get inside, Floyd ran back down the aisle.

The man that he recognized from the last time he was here was in the small office waiting for him.

"I need the keys!" Floyd shouted, flinging the door wide. "I need the fucking keys to unit 412!"

The man shook his head, his open mouth flapping.

"We don't have keys. People bring their own locks. The only person who has the key is the—"

"But you have something to open the locks, right?" Floyd interrupted. "You must! On those shows, the ones where people don't pay their fees and you auction off what's in their lockers you cut the locks off. You must have a saw or some big fucking snips." When the man just stared, dumbfounded, Floyd slapped the counter. "There's someone trapped in unit 412! There's a fucking FBI Agent in there!"

The man's eyes bulged.

"We have…" he reached beneath the counter and pulled out a pair of massive bolt cutters. "…these."

Floyd didn't hesitate. He snatched the snips from the man's hands and sprinted back to the locked storage unit.

***

"Let go of me!" Chase shouted. But no matter how hard she struggled, she failed to break free from the iron grip of the men holding her. One of the army veterans had released her arm and instead clutched her around the waist. Chase bucked wildly, but she was still rather effortlessly carried up the steps to Tony's throne. As a last-ditch effort, she looked back over her shoulder at Georgina. "Please, help me. Make him stop."

Georgina looked away. Chase should have expected this reaction, as it was in character for her sister, considering how the woman had once bowed down and offered servitude to the man whose head was rammed on a spike beside Stu's and Jake's.

"Chase! *Chase!*"

This new voice, familiar, came from nowhere and everywhere and her first thought was that it was Tony.

But even the king himself looked surprised by the interruption, his wide grin contracting a smidge.

"Nobody leaves Hell, Chase. *Nobody.*" Tony nearly shouted his words, clearly trying to drown out the mysterious interloper.

But even he couldn't speak loud enough to cover two distinct bangs, like massive rumbles of thunder, even though the texture or color of the sky did not change.

"I make sure of it."

The final two words of Tony's sentence degenerated into something akin to a snarl.

Then the man's face began to change. His nose elongated, becoming feral, snout-like, and his ears migrated from the sides of his face to closer to the top of his head. If this hadn't been so… natural, like the metamorphosis of a caterpillar to a butterfly, it would have been far less terrifying.

A shudder ran through the man's entire body, and he flopped out of the throne, landing on his hands. These, too, started to change, to morph, the fingers shortening, becoming paw-like.

The sound made everything worse. A wheezing punctuated by staccato wails. Two buds appeared on Tony's shoulders, mounds like tumors having gone unchecked. These grew at a phenomenal rate, darkening, molding themselves into the heads of snarling dogs.

In less than a minute, Tony had become completely unrecognizable, his humanoid form replaced by that of a snapping, drooling, three-headed dog.

When the unholy beast spoke, the words came from the air itself.

"I'm Cerberus and nobody escapes Hell."

***

Floyd squeezed the handles of the bolt cutters as hard as possible. The padlock clasp was indifferent—it didn't even yield.

"C'mon!" he screamed. "*C'mon!*"

Floyd pressed one of the handles against his inner thigh and the other to his belly. Using all 173 pounds of him, Floyd squeezed with all his might.

Nothing other than pain and instant bruising.

Floyd adjusted his grip again and then grunted with exertion. Just as he thought it was a loss cause, he felt the handles come a little closer together. Not much, just an inch, maybe two. But it was enough to inspire him to squeeze harder still.

The sound of the razor-sharp blades snapping together was perhaps the most satisfying thing Floyd had ever heard. But he wasted no time reveling in it. Floyd dropped the cutters and finagled the split clasp through the loop in the concrete. Once free, he didn't hesitate in flinging the door upward with both hands. The orange slats made a characteristic *frrrrrrp* sound as they accordioned upward and back.

Light spilled into the garage, as did fresh air, which forced its stale counterpart in Floyd's direction. It was foul and fetid but the scene inside the locker, equally as disturbing as the air was odiferous, was what took Floyd's breath away.

There were buckets on the ground, some already brimming with human waste, others empty, waiting to be filled. There were also cases of water stacked against one wall, nearly to the ceiling.

This was no temporary set-up; Tony was planning to be here for some time.

Floyd spotted two chairs in the locker, one near the entrance, one further back. Both were occupied.

The first by a man, although it was difficult to determine gender from features alone. The figure's hair was filthy, hanging in ratty, dreadlocked clumps that cascaded over the goggles that covered most of his face.

It was Tony. The man's lips were pulled back in a half-sneer, revealing those broken front teeth. Floyd saw Chase next.

She was seated in a similar chair to her captor, a soiled gaming chair, and, like Tony, she had a VR mask over her eyes. But whereas Tony held controllers that he moved freely in his hands, Chase's hands were taped and then her wrists zip-tied to the arms of her chair so that she couldn't move.

Keep the train going.

"Choo-Choo," Floyd whispered as he bent down to pick up the snips again, took a deep breath, and then rushed toward Chase.

Chapter 78

CHASE SCREAMED. TONY, NOW COMPLETELY canine, bounded toward her. She turned her head away, but he pressed the moist, warm snout of one of his three heads against her cheek, forcing her straight.

The vets were still holding her tightly, making it impossible for her to move.

This is fake… so why can't I just take the fucking mask off? All I have to do is take the goggles off and the nightmare will be over.

But Chase couldn't raise her arms.

Was this just a case of twisted art imitating life? Was the fact that her arms were immobilized here, in Hell, the reason that she couldn't move them back… wherever she was?

Cerberus' breath was hot on her cheek and the animal stared at her with six oddly human eyes.

"Nobody leaves, Chase."

The words didn't come from any of the dog's mouths, which would have broken the spell, but seemed to echo inside Chase's head.

When the refrain was repeated, however, first by the veterans, then by someone with a softer voice, Chase could easily recognize the sources.

"Stay with me, Chase," her sister pleaded. *"Please, Chase."*

"I—I can't…" Chase whispered.

Georgina pleaded again this time only using her beautiful green eyes.

"Last chance," Tony warned. "Last—"

The man holding Chase's right hand, Geoffrey or Fred, she didn't know which, suddenly just… let go. And with the tension gone, her arm shot forward, inadvertently smacking one of Tony's three muzzles.

He pulled back, snarling, but Chase was only interested in one thing.

"Georgina…"

***

As soon as Floyd severed the zip-tie holding Chase's wrist to the chair, her hand launched upward. The controller that was still taped to her hand collided with the underside of Floyd's jaw. The blow was more jarring than actually painful, and he was forced to take two steps back.

"Georgina…" The word out of Chase's mouth was haunting and Floyd didn't want to even consider what she was viewing inside Tony's twisted metaverse.

He collected himself and cut the other zip-tie, careful to lean backward this time to avoid being struck again.

***

The vet holding her left arm let go now, too. And with her hands free, Chase shoved Tony backward. The three-headed dog, surprised and confused by what was happening, by why his minions were releasing her without his command, scurried backward.

Chase spun around.

"Nobody leaves Hell, Chase!" Tony screamed behind her, his voice taking on the characteristics of a petulant child more than that of a malevolent leader.

Chase stared into her sister's eyes. NPC or not, there was something cathartic about being able to speak to her sister one final time. To say what she should have said when Georgina lay dying in her arms.

"I'll look after her," Chase promised. "I'll look after your daughter, Georgina. I swear. I won't let anything happen to her. I may have failed my own family, but I won't fail her, and I won't fail you."

Chase sobbed and Georgina's eyes started to become wet.

"I—"

***

"No!" Chase screamed.

Floyd jumped back a good two feet, his heel colliding with thankfully one of the empty buckets. It rattled loudly, but he couldn't look away from Chase. The goggles that he had started to remove still hung awkwardly on her head, half on, half off, and to his surprise, and equal horror, she wasn't grateful for having been rescued. Chase didn't even seem to recognize him. All she was concerned with was trying to put the goggles back on.

But that didn't make sense.

"Chase?" Floyd's words went ignored.

"Fucking thing," she grumbled. Her hands still being taped to the controllers made what she was trying to do nearly impossible. "Please," she nearly wept, "C'mon, *please*."

"Chase, it's me, it's Floyd," he said tentatively.

I'm too late. Her mind… her mind's gone.

He cautiously stepped forward, trying to cross her monocular vision.

"Chase?"

She finally acknowledged Floyd, the one eye not in the visor finally focusing on him.

"She's in here, Floyd," Chase whispered. "She's in *here*." She indicated the goggles by tapping them with the controller in her right hand. "I have to go back. I *have* to."

"What? Who?" Floyd asked. He knew that if there ever was a time to keep on rolling, to ignore whatever Chase was saying and completely remove her from the VR world, it was now. But there was something in her tone, in her eye, in *her* that made this impossible. Floyd could only stand there. "Who's in there, Chase?"

Chase lowered her gaze and said something too softly for Floyd to hear.

"What?" He stepped forward. "What did you say?"

"Georgina—she's in here. I need to go back... I *have* to, I *have* to go back to—"

Someone else finished the sentence for her.

"*Hell.*"

Floyd, having completely forgotten about Tony until this moment, swiveled. The man had since removed his goggles and in place of a controller in his right hand, he held a gun.

And it was aimed directly at Chase's forehead.

"The thing about Hell, Chase," Tony said, his voice lisping and cracked due to his mangled teeth. "Is that nobody *ever* leaves. Not while I'm in charge."

And then, before Floyd could pull his own gun free, Tony Metcalfe fired a single shot.

Chapter 79

TATE WAS JUST PULLING UP to the gate outside *U-Lock-it* when he heard the shot ring out. Cursing, he pumped the gas, ramming the Maybach through the barricade, which smashed into a dozen pieces. He slammed on the brakes behind the car Floyd had borrowed from Stu and got out.

Peering down the rows of lockers, he only saw one whose door was open.

Tate sprinted toward it.

***

"Georgina!" Chase screamed. Having the goggles wrenched from her face was not just disorienting, but nauseating. One eye was stuck in Cerberus, in the metaverse, while the other was—where? Some sort of dark, stinking room.

Chase was caught in two places at once, in two worlds.

And she had to go back.

She tried desperately to put the goggles back on both eyes, mumbling incoherently as she did.

She needed to see her sister again, just one more time. She had to hear Georgina say that she trusted her, that she knew Chase would look after her daughter.

That she would do a good job.

"Please," Chase moaned.

Her hands were like stumps and she couldn't manage.

One of her eyes picked up someone standing near her.

He could help her. This man, this stranger—*it's not a stranger, it's Floyd*—he could put the mask back on. Why wouldn't he?

"Chase, it's me, Floyd."

Floyd? I know a Floyd.

"Chase?"

It didn't matter who he was.

"She's in here, Floyd. She's in here. I have to go back. I *have* to."

"What? Who? Who's in there, Chase?"

"My sister—my sister is in here. And she's *real*."

"What?" The man stepped forward. "What did you say?"

"Georgina—she's in here. I need to go back... I *have* to, I *have* to go back to—"

"Hell."

It wasn't Floyd this time, but someone else.

Chase saw Tony Metcalfe, standing in the entrance of the garage, a gun in his filthy hand.

"The thing about Hell, Chase," Tony said. "Is that nobody *ever* leaves. Not while I'm in charge."

And then the gun went off.

Chase instinctively closed her eyes, waiting for the searing pain as the bullet tore through her skull.

But it never came, and Chase had a disturbing thought: what if this was actually the metaverse? What if this... garage or whatever it was... is Cerberus?

I have to go back... I have to go back... I have to go—

Floyd grunted and collapsed on the ground, sending buckets scattering.

"No!" Chase screamed.

The bullet had been meant for her, there was no question about that. But Floyd had put himself in its path.

This is real.

But rather than an exalted revelation this thought was met with sheer horror.

Chase didn't want this to be real. Real meant pain, real meant consequences.

Real meant that Floyd had been shot.

Tony, also surprised by Floyd's actions, adjusted his aim. Chase knocked the mask completely off her face and held her taped hands up in front of her.

"I told you, Chase," Tony said, repeating what had clearly been a planned diatribe. While in this world, the man was all human, there was still something feral about the way his lips twisted, and he snarled. "I'm Cerberus and nobody leaves Hell."

"This isn't fucking hell!" Chase shouted. "This is real! This is fucking *real!*"

"Everything's real."

Tony closed one eye and extended the hand with the gun.

Time seemed to slow down and somewhere the sound of a car approaching registered with Chase.

As did Floyd's breathing.

It was labored and irregular, punctuated by the occasional wet plop like a drop of water falling into a foamy sink.

"No, no, it's not. Cerberus isn't real. My sister isn't real."

Tony opened his other eye.

"Really? That wasn't your sister?"

"No!" Chase exclaimed emphatically. "My real sister is dead."

"But you saw her, you held her. You—"

"Yeah, I held her," she countered. "I held her in my arms when she *died.*"

"You're telling me that you felt nothing in Cerberus when you hugged your sister? Don't lie to me, Chase."

Chase had felt something. There was no denying that.

And she'd wanted to go back. But that was selfish, that was only for her. Most of what Chase had done over the past few years had been selfish—she knew that.

Shooting up, having sex with countless suspects and colleagues alike. That was all for her.

Going back to speak with fake Georgina was also for her.

She had to stop—Floyd was lying on the floor dying. *Really* dying.

Behind Tony, Chase caught sight of a man running toward them. Tony must have noticed her shifting gaze because he started to turn.

"Yes!" Chase shouted. "Yes, I felt something! And what I felt was real. Tony… I want—I want to go back. I want to see her again. I *need* to." Her intention was to distract but Chase could not deny the truth of her words. "Can I go back?"

Tony's lecherous grin returned.

"We can do whatever—"

"Put the fucking gun down!" Tate shouted. "Dickhead, put the fucking gun down before I blow a hole in your skull!"

Chapter 80

THE SCENE BEFORE TATE ABERNATHY was as confusing as it was heart-wrenching. Tony Metcalfe, his back to the locker opening, had a gun trained on Chase.

The woman looked terrible, beaten, downtrodden, and oddly sad. Her hands were taped to hunks of plastic, and she was saying something as tears streaked her red cheeks.

And then there was Floyd. Tate didn't notice him at first, didn't recognize the prone body on the ground as being a person at all. But then light shimmered off a dark liquid pooling next to his body and drew his eye. With all the buckets, a handful of which had toppled, Tate initially thought that this fluid was shit, like back at Tony's apartment. But this wasn't coming from a bucket.

It was coming from Floyd. And it was blood, not shit.

Tate moved his finger from the trigger guard to the trigger proper.

Tony had shot Floyd. Floyd, who had been the one to figure out what the hell was going on in this case. Floyd, who was only here because Tate had gone to bat for him.

And now the man was dead.

Tate saw red.

"Put the fucking gun down! Dickhead, put the fucking gun down before I blow a hole in your skull!"

Despite his words, Tate didn't want Tony to lower the gun. It would make explaining what happened next easier.

He was going to kill Tony Metcalfe. Even if the man chucked the gun into a dark corner of the garage and jumped to his knees, hands together, and begged for his life, he was going to die.

Tate didn't just see Tony, but he saw Marco, too. And his anger was bubbling over as it had back at Isaac's.

"No!" Chase yelled, and this stayed his finger.

The FBI-issued Glock 9mm had a trigger weight of 5.5 pounds. Tate was fairly certain that the tension he'd applied had come close to 5 pounds.

No? Why did she shout, no?

"Don't shoot him."

But this time, Chase's plea fell on deaf ears.

Tate had reached the point of no return.

He squeezed just a little more and a shot rang out.

***

Killing Tony Metcalfe would be a mistake. Not because it was inherently wrong, but because the man deserved to suffer.

And death would be a release for Tony.

The real horror for the man wasn't the Hell that he'd created in Cerberus, Chase realized. It was the real world. Tony ruled hell. Back on earth, however, he was a nobody. A programmer who may or may not have had his code stolen and had committed murder, probably twice. A twisted man who had framed an innocent one. Here, on earth, Tony was just a common criminal.

And that was his hell. The three-headed dog that made sure Tony didn't escape was a judge, a jury, and a jail cell.

But the look on Tate's face…

Chase had seen this expression before and knew that he was going to pull the trigger. She also knew that there was nothing that she could say that would prevent this from happening.

Tate fired.

The sound was deafening, and the seismic pop confused Chase's senses. Like when Tony had fired, she had no idea where the bullet went. With zero concern for her own safety, Chase leaped out of the chair, the cables going from her controllers to the goggles tearing free.

Her intention had nothing to do with Tony and everything to do with Floyd. She blanketed his body with her own.

"Nobody gets out of—"

Tate lunged, too, leading not with the barrel but the butt of his gun.

"Shut the fuck up."

The violent blow to the back of Tony's unsuspecting head was so forceful that he pitched forward and collided with Chase's controller-bundled fist. There was a satisfying crunch as the hard plastic broke Tony's nose, followed by an equally satisfying grunt from the man's broken mouth. He collapsed on top of Floyd, and Chase had time for one inane thought—*is that real enough for you?*—before she shoved the unconscious man off her friend. Tony's arm knocked over a full bucket of piss and shit and the foul liquid began to swirl about his head.

One more thought: *Is he going to drown?*

Tate was at her side now, helping roll Floyd onto his back.

"Where's he shot?" Tate shouted, searching the man's body for the entrance wound.

"I don't—I don't know!"

It didn't take them long to find the source of the blood. There was a hole in Floyd's chest, just beneath his right collarbone.

Instinct took over and Chase applied pressure to the wound, trying to stem the slow trickle of blood.

"Call someone! Tate, we need an ambulance, *now!*"

Chapter 81

CHASE LEFT THE HOSPITAL ROOM with her head low. Tate followed closely behind and while she couldn't see him, she could tell from his breathing pattern that the man felt the same as she did.

He's stable. We can airlift Floyd back to Virginia in the morning. He's lost a lot of blood. For now, he'll stay in an induced coma. As for a full recovery? I can't say for sure. No one can.

Chase walked down the hall, not saying a word to Tate. They approached the police officer stationed outside another room. He saw them coming, nodded, and then stood. Chase watched him go to the coffee machine and start to fiddle absently with it.

There was a full cup of coffee on the ground just beneath his chair.

She didn't want to go inside, didn't have a need for it. There was nothing that Tony Metcalfe could say or do that would offer any insight into his actions, or anything of value at all.

But she felt compelled to look at him.

He was lying on his back, his hands tucked beneath the blankets. Chase caught a glint of the handcuff chained to the thick metal bed.

Tony's head was covered in a thick bandage, hiding the wound that had required the doctors to shave his hair before putting a stent in to relieve the pressure. In the movies, the butt end of a gun to the back of the skull made you sleep for a few hours. In the better production, you woke up with a headache.

In real life, such a blow was often deadly. In this case, Tate had eased up just enough and the doctors were certain that, unlike Floyd, Tony would make a full recovery. But for now, he too was in a medically induced coma.

The bullet Tate had fired missed entirely, although Chase would never know if this had been deliberate.

"Where do you think he is right now?" Tate asked.

Under other circumstances, the question might have been considered bizarre.

But not here.

Chase stared at Tony through the thick, reinforced glass.

"None of what I've been through, or the places I've visited, the metaverse or Cerberus, has turned me into a believer," Chase said absently. "But I'll tell you this... I really hope Tony's in hell. Not *his* hell, but a place where he has zero control over anything."

With this, Chase grabbed Tate by the arm and pulled him away from the glass. This was the last time she ever wanted to see Tony Metcalfe, in this world or others.

***

"What's he doing here?" Will Porter asked, hooking a chin toward the surly detective standing at the back of the room with his arms crossed over his chest.

"Don't worry about him," Assistant District Attorney Matthew Lombardi said. "You should be more concerned about them."

He didn't indicate Chase and Tate, but they were the only two other people in the room. Will had advised against them joining him, just as he'd advised Stu to stay home, as well. But only Stu had taken the advice to heart.

Chase wanted to be there when the ADA uttered those magical words, "We're going to drop the charges."

"Why don't we just sit down and chat," Will suggested.

Matthew shook his head.

"No need to sit, this will be brief. We compared the bullet markings from the round taken out of Jake Hollister to the barrel of the gun found in Tony Metcalfe's garage. It was a match." Chase suppressed a smile. "Based on this and other information that has since come to light, we are—" *Here it comes,* Chase thought. *Here it comes.* "—prepared to drop the charges against your client Stu Barnes."

Detective Tolliver grunted and Chase glared at him, daring him to say something.

The man refrained.

"What about Randy Milligan?" Chase asked.

"We're taking a deeper look into his case. But for now, Mr. Milligan's death will remain a suicide."

"What about Stu? You guys ran his name through the mud. Everyone—"

Will stopped Chase midsentence by raising his hand.

"We," the ADA continued. He looked like a man trying to swallow a cactus. "Are willing to overlook the FBI's unsanctioned involvement in this case, if Stu is willing to go on the record praising the LVPD. And he will, of course, be required to waive his right to any legal action against the department."

Chase scoffed even though Will had prepared them for this possibility. If it had been her, she would tell the ADA to fuck off and sue the pants off them. After what Stu had been through? Being locked up and then on house arrest, Chase would have sued the LVPD for an incomprehensible sum.

But Stu didn't need or want the money—he only wanted to put this all behind him.

"I'll discuss this proposal with my client, but I'm sure he'll be amenable."

"Good." The ADA clearly expected this to be the end of the discussion, but Chase had other ideas.

"What about Isaac Lomax?"

Chase was tempted to inquire about Geoffrey Fixman, Mark Dyson, and Fred Marquette, as well, but this was something that Will had strongly advised against.

Asking about the three vets and what their involvement in Cerberus was would inevitably link them to Paul Wenkler, whose body had been discovered shortly after what went down at *U-Lock-it*. The coroner had marked the man's cause of death as a suicide.

They wanted to keep it that way.

But Isaac Lomax? That lying asshole was fair game.

"We are evaluating what you told us, Agent Adams, but for now, we have no plans to pursue Isaac Lomax."

Chase shook her head.

"He's the one who—"

Will stopped her again.

"Thank you, DA Lombardo."

Tate gently turned Chase around and they left together before either of them could say something that they'd later regret.

Chapter 82

TATE AND CHASE DIDN'T GO back to Stu's house as planned. Will did, to pass along the good news, but Chase took them in the opposite direction.

They parked outside Christina Bunting's office building and together they walked to her office on the second floor. There was no need to exchange words. There were no words to exchange.

Chase entered without knocking. Christina was speaking to a client, and they waited off to one side. She noticed them and cut the meeting short. The man, who had thick muscles and was sporting a USA ball cap, tipped the brim to them as he passed. Chase waited until the door closed behind the veteran before addressing Christina.

She led with, "Paul Wenkler is dead. Suicide."

Back with the ADA, the veterans had been off limits. Not so here.

"I know," Christina said, head bowed.

"Tony Metcalfe murdered Jake Hollister."

This, unlike Chase's previous comment, came as a surprise to the psychologist.

"What? Tony?"

"Yeah. Just got back from the DA's office," Tate clarified. "He's going to be charged with first-degree murder, among other things."

Christina shook her head in disbelief.

"No, that's not right. Tony... he—he did *what*?"

Chase repeated what she'd said earlier, and Christina remained incredulous.

"He—*really*?"

This time Chase didn't react at all, didn't so much as nod.

"You want to know the common denominator between Paul and Tony?" Chase asked, unable to keep the venom from her voice.

"Cerberus," Christina said quietly.

"Yep. Cerberus."

Silence.

Chase could see the machinations in Christina's head working and could literally feel the weight of her dismay. She still couldn't get a good read on the woman—Chase didn't know if Christina truly thought Cerberus would help her patients or if she had ulterior motives.

But she wanted the woman to hurt.

Would Tony have done what he did without Cerberus? Maybe. Probably. But Chase didn't work in what-ifs. She dealt with cold, hard facts. Tony had been recruited to join Cerberus and then following a series of insane events he'd shot Floyd.

"Tony Metcalfe," Chase said. "Paranoid schizophrenic, fixated on computers and the metaverse? I'm no psychiatrist, Dr. Bunting, but perhaps exposure therapy wasn't the best idea for someone like him."

"I'm sorry," Christina said, sounding genuine. "I was trying to help the man. I had no idea he would turn violent."

"I was thinking about that," Tate said. "Why were you treating Tony anyway? Everyone else was a veteran suffering from PTSD. But so far as we can tell, Tony was never in the military."

"No, he wasn't," Christina confirmed. "But Isaac recommended him—for both my help and the program, for Cerberus."

Chase wasn't sure she'd heard correctly.

"Come again?"

"Yeah, Isaac Lomax. I worked with him briefly when he was employed at PopTop Games. Tony used to work there, too. Before switching over to veterans, I used to consult for tech. Tried to get their programmers' heads in the right space to maximize returns. Typical corporate stuff. Anyway, Isaac came to me and asked me to help out his friend."

Chase could barely believe her ears. Isaac had set Tony up. She looked at Tate. He too appeared shocked by this claim.

We're going to need to go have another chat with Isaac, Chase thought. Obviously thinking the same thing, Tate had already started toward the door.

"When's the last time you heard from Isaac?" Chase asked.

"I haven't seen him—well, since he asked me to enroll Tony in Cerberus."

Chase cursed and hurried out of the office, but not without a parting shot.

"You're not Maury Povich," she hollered over her shoulder. "No more exposure therapy, Dr. Bunting, or we'll be back. And, trust me, you don't want us to come back here."

***

He wasn't there, of course. Isaac Lomax was long gone. He'd lied to them on multiple occasions. He said he'd bowed out of Cerberus when Jake wanted to recruit veterans with PTSD. But that had been a lie—*Isaac* was the one who had recommended Tony, not Jake.

"I warned you," Tate said as they stared into Isaac's dark house through the front window. The man's car was gone and while the place still had furniture, there didn't appear to be any personal effects anywhere. No pictures, no wall art, nothing.

"Things got twisted last time I was here. Probably scared him off."

Tate looked down at his still swollen hand.

Scared him off and then some.

"What about Stu's friend? Big Rod or whatever?"

He made a face, remembering what the man had told him about not being around in case the cops showed up.

"I think he's gone, too."

"Fuck."

Tate had hoped that catching Tony Metcalfe would provide answers. But like everything else, it only raised more questions.

What, exactly, was Isaac Lomax's plan?

The man had the means and the capability to change his identity, which was for certain. Hell, he'd even demonstrated as much, changing his appearance in the telecast to look like Tony.

But why? What was his end game?

"Let's go," Chase said backing away from the house. "Tate?"

"Sorry."

Tate followed her to the car.

"Where to?" he asked.

"Stu's."

Tate nodded. He had a feeling that Chase wanted to stay here in Las Vegas for as long as he did.

And he suspected that their reasons were the same: to avoid going back to the real world.

Chapter 83

"**WHO THE FUCK IS THIS** guy?" Tate demanded.

"This is Kendrick Deetle," Stu said, indicating the diminutive man with a thin blond mustache. "He's the hacker—"

"Do I know you?" Chase asked. He looked familiar, but she couldn't place him.

"I-I-I don't think so."

"Hmm."

"Anyways, Kendrick, please tell him what you found out," Stu insisted.

Kendrick licked his lips nervously.

"Well, uhh, Tony Metcalfe used to work for PopTop Games. He was a junior programmer, spent most of his time on a game called Captive Carnage." Chase shrugged, indicating she didn't know it. "Very popular a couple of years back. Made a shit ton of money for the company and the company's owner, Randy Milligan. HR ended up firing Tony. Not exactly sure why. Best I could find was the formal release papers that stated Tony had exhibited inexcusable conduct while at work."

Things started to fall into place now.

"So, Tony killed Randy because he thought the man stole some game from him." Chase's comment was met with a series of nods. "Let me ask you something, did Christina Bunting work at PopTop Games?"

Kendrick nodded.

"She was the in-house psychiatrist. Having one was the trend for a while. Her files, though? Even I couldn't get in."

"At the same time that Tony was there?"

"Yes," Kendrick confirmed.

"What are the chances they knew each other?" Chase asked.

"Well, I was unable to get into her files, but I know how these things work. Usually, every employee has time with the psychiatrist, even junior programmers. So, yeah, I'd say there is an excellent chance they got to know each other. Why?"

Why? Because Dr. Bunting said that Isaac had recommended Tony. She made no mention of knowing him beforehand.

"Never mind."

"Shit, we gotta go back," Tate grumbled. "We need to have *another* chat with Christina."

Chase sighed and rubbed her temples, picturing Isaac's empty home.

"She's not going to be there."

"You think that she and Isaac fucked off together?" Tate asked.

That was exactly what Chase thought. Just like Isaac, Dr. Bunting had been lying to them since the beginning.

"Yeah, probably. What else did you find?" Chase asked Kendrick.

"Well, Cerberus? Initially, it wasn't just one program."

"What do you mean?" Tate inquired.

"What I mean is that each of the participants in the Cerberus study or program or whatever all had different scenarios. For instance, Paul Wenkler was trapped in a house—"

"What about Tony?" Chase said, still uncomfortable discussing Paul, especially with Floyd in the hospital.

"Here's the thing: Tony's scenario was very different than the others. It had nothing to do with the army and it was also the most realistic. In Tony's Cerberus, Jake hired him as a programmer at Happy Valley and he made some big discovery, wrote some special code."

"Shit," Chase cursed. "So let me get this straight, Tony had PTSD from his time at PopTop where he thought that Randy stole his code, and Jake put him in a scenario where they actually stole his code?"

"Something like that," Kendrick said. "It wasn't real, though. There was no code."

Everything's real.

"It was real enough for him to believe it happened," Tate remarked.

Real enough for him to kill Jake and frame Stu.

"Which means that Christina was definitely involved," Chase said. "The psychiatrist would have known about Tony's issues at PopTop from working there and used that to help Jake make the world as realistic as possible for him. Jake and Isaac. Why, Stu, though? Why was he framed? Why was he involved at all?"

"Well, because he was there."

"What do you mean I was there?" Stu chimed in.

"Jake wanted to make Cerberus as real as possible, so he made you Happy Valley's CEO. I'm guessing that Tony harbored anger toward you when he was fired in the metaverse, and you made off with his code."

"But I didn't actually do anything. I even tried to help him when he came up to me in the lobby that day."

"*You* didn't do anything, but your digital version in Cerberus sure did," Kendrick said.

"And for that, he wanted to frame me for murder?" Stu asked, clearly not believing the motivation.

"Actually," Kendrick smirked, "it was quite genius the way that Jake and Isaac designed Tony's Cerberus. They made it so that Tony never knew what the real world was. It was a meta-metaverse, if you will, with him constantly putting on goggles and taking them off. After a while, I think his mind snapped and he just believed everything was real."

"Alright, enough fanboying," Chase barked.

Kendrick's mouth fell open, and she suddenly knew where she recognized the man from.

He had been one of the lolling heads that had been mounted behind Tony's throne in Hell.

Kendrick Deetle had been there.

"Right, sorry."

Chase nearly called the man out but bit her tongue at the last second. Dead or not, if Kendrick had been there, he might have seen her.

He saw her with her sister.

Chase wanted to keep that bit to herself.

"Okay, but why? If Isaac and Christina were behind this, which it looks like they were and Jake was maybe just a pawn, what was the point?" she asked.

"Oh, that's the easy part," Kendrick said. "For the code. For Cerberus."

Chase squinted at the man.

"What do you mean?"

"Well, this is going to be huge. Cerberus, the hell that Tony created, it's going to be worth... it's going to be worth your kind of money, Stu."

And you'd only know that if you were there.

"Wait—*will be?*" In her mind, Chase just imagined that when Tony had been pulled out of the matrix, it went with him. But even if this wasn't the case, it shouldn't matter because Jake had given Tony the master password before he'd been shot and killed. Unless... "There was someone else there, wasn't there? In Cerberus, watching?"

"That's right," Kendrick confirmed. "After Tony managed to get inside the master Cerberus program and create his version of hell, someone followed him and observed everything."

"Isaac Lomax."

"Shit, he had his VR gear on the table when I went to visit him," Tate informed them. "I bet he'd just taken it off when he heard me pull up."

Why didn't I see this sooner? It was about the money. It was always about the money.

"The real value is in what Tony created. He was... twisted. And he was in there all the time. The amount of data..." Kendrick was bordering on admiration again, but he caught Chase's look and stopped himself. "Let's just say this, when Cerberus 2.0 becomes available it's going to be huge."

As much as she wanted to deny it, Chase knew that Kendrick was right. She'd been there. Being able to talk to a deceased loved one a final time? Priceless.

And then there were the other types of users. People like Tony who got pushed around in the real world and wanted to exact their revenge in Cerberus. Do horrible, despicable things with no repercussions.

Yeah, it was going to be huge.

"Can you track Isaac through the metaverse?" Tate asked.

"Unfortunately, not. He is good. *Very* good. Hid his tracks."

The group fell into silence, with Kendrick doing his best to avoid Chase's stare as he awaited more questions. None came.

"Thank you, Kendrick."

Stu dismissed him and when the door closed and they were finally alone, the man let out a huge sigh.

"Tate, Chase, I'm so sorry about Floyd. I've already reached out to the hospital. I'm flying a specialist in from Boston to look at him. He will have the absolute best care possible. I mean that, no hyperbole. And it probably means nothing, and I doubt that what you've been through was worth it, but thank you. Anything you need, name it, it's yours."

Chapter 84

TWO DAYS LATER

By nature, Tate was not a nervous man. If, on the rare occasion, he felt an uneasiness in his stomach or tightness in his throat, he simply adopted a new persona.

But he couldn't do that here. Not with her.

Prisons didn't typically make him uncomfortable, either. As an FBI Agent, he'd spent time speaking to inmates behind bars, although, admittedly, not nearly as much as his previous partner, Constantine Striker.

Yet, as he sat in the visitor area, amongst dozens of others, mostly bleary-eyed wives waiting to see their incarcerated husbands, Tate felt more than uncomfortable. He felt downright anxious.

His eyes kept darting to the clock, which seemed to have slowed to the point of moving imperceptibly, even the second hand.

Why does this always take so long? He wondered. This was quickly followed by, *Does it usually take this long?*

Normally, when he visited his wife, Tate would have mapped out what he was going to say, what he would tell her about Rachel.

She's doing well, he'd say. *More talkative, actually making friends, although mostly online. Her sleeping? It's not great. Night terrors happen less frequently and they're less intense. But, yeah, they still happen. Her sessions with the psychiatrist have been helping, though. He says she's making real progress. Can't give us an exact timeline, of course—and why would he, with the money we're paying him, he's probably enjoying his time in his beach house—but things are getting better.*

But today wasn't about Rachel. It was about an even more difficult subject. Impossible, even. And as time ticked by, Tate started to reconsider his decision to tell Robyn about what had happened.

Ironically, despite portraying a fraudulent self on pretty much every occasion—professionally and personally—he considered himself an honest person.

Not for the first time, Tate wondered if it had just been a one-night stand if he would tell Robyn. Probably not.

The real issue was that it was more than that. And she deserved to know.

A door opened, loud, never lubricated hinges screeching like dueling banshees, announcing yet another inmate entering the visitor area, pulling Tate out of his head.

Robyn Abernathy looked tired. Her blonde hair was pulled into a lazy ponytail and her eyelids, shrouding hazel eyes, were heavy.

Even before the accident, nobody considered Robyn a striking beauty. She had an incredible figure, with large, firm breasts, a tight waist, and shapely legs. But her face had just been cute.

But not here, not now.

Her body was hidden by an ill-fitting jumpsuit and her face was worn.

Once, Tate had brought Rachel with him to visit Robyn. That had proven a terrible mistake. The trek alone had been incredibly uncomfortable and just getting inside the prison was an ordeal—prisons weren't generally suited for those in wheelchairs.

Not a huge priority for them.

The real implications of the visit didn't come until later.

Rachel's night terrors had escalated, and it took the girl weeks to recover.

That had been her first and only visit.

Despite this mutual decision, every time Robyn stepped through that horrible, squeaking door and her eyes met Tate's, she looked around as if expecting to see her daughter.

It nearly broke Tate's heart.

Robyn slowly walked over and slid into the metal seat across from him.

"Is she okay?" the woman said, fear in her eyes.

"She's fine," Tate said. "She's doing fine, really."

Robyn just stared and Tate felt his discomfort growing like a tumor deep inside his belly. And the way that she just continued to look at him with her tired eyes made things even worse. She'd always been incredibly perceptive, but this was bordering on clairvoyance. It was as if she already knew.

Spit it out, pussy, he chided himself, as he had Floyd many times. *Just fucking say it.*

"I need to be honest with you," Tate began. "Before you came here…" he paused. *Before you came here? What is this, a beach resort?* "Before you were locked up, you tried to talk to me about… about what I should do on the outside. Do you remember that?"

Great, obtuse. Way to make things clear, Tate.

But Robyn, perceptive as she was, caught on to what he was saying and nodded.

"I didn't want to talk about it, told you no way… there was no chance. But—"

"It's okay, Tate. It's okay."

This stung even more. He'd dealt with irate suspects, people who swore, spat, and fought, and he had experience with them. But this… this was new.

Understanding? Compassion? Empathy?

He hated all of it.

"It's not okay," he said forcefully. "It's not. But I don't want to lie to you. I met someone. I didn't mean for it to happen, but—"

"Tate, take a breath," Robyn said. "I just want you to be happy. You and Rachel."

Happy? Yeah, I don't think so.

"I'm so sorry, Robyn. I didn't know if I should tell you, and maybe I wouldn't have if it wasn't—if it wasn't—"

"I understand. As long as she's good for you and for Rachel, then I'm okay with it. Really, I am."

Tate looked away, his vision becoming cloudy.

"She's really good for Rachel. And," his voice hitched, "I think she's good for me, too."

When Tate looked back at his wife, he saw tears spill onto her cheeks.

"I won't—I'll tell her no," he backtracked. "I'm sorry, I—"

"No, Tate. Don't do that. You have to do what's best for the family and what's best for you."

Tate ground his teeth.

Why did she have to be so understanding? Why can't she yell at me? Tell me that I'm a cheating asshole?

Tate reached across the table and hugged her tightly.

"No touching the inmates," a loud voice boomed.

Tate ignored the guard until Robyn hugged him back.

"No touching—"

Tate released his wife.

"I love you," he said.

"I love you, too, Tate."

By some miracle, Tate managed to hold back his own tears until he made it to the safety of his car. But when they came, they came the same way he lived his life: hard and fast.

Chapter 85

CHASE HELD FLOYD'S HAND FOR so long, her skin became clammy. Eventually, her fingers went numb.

She watched his chest rise and fall hundreds of times and with each breath, she urged him to open his eyes.

He never did.

Stu had gone above and beyond, paying for a private helicopter, fully staffed with two nurses and one doctor, to bring Floyd from Las Vegas to Virginia. There, he'd been put up in a private institution, much better than the one that even the FBI's insurance would have covered, which they probably wouldn't have given the fact that they were never officially on duty.

And now she was playing the waiting game. There was no outward change in Floyd's condition. The doctors all said that his vitals were improving, but he'd lost blood and oxygen to his brain.

That was the most frustrating part. Nobody could tell Chase definitively when he was going to wake up.

Or *if*.

Chase banished the thought from her head.

He would get better. He had to.

The only reason she let go of his hand was because her phone started to ring. Hoping that it was Louisa or her niece, Chase backed out of the room before answering.

"Hello?"

"Chase?"

It was neither Louisa nor Georgina.

"Terrence? What happened?" Chase demanded, alarm in her voice. "What's going on?"

There was a hesitation.

"What? What is it? He won't have her. I promise—"

Terrence sighed.

"You're going to tell me that you don't know? That you had nothing to do with this?"

"Terrence, I'm not in the mood for games."

"Games? I'm not the one playing games here, Chase. You mean to tell me that you had nothing to do with the six pounds of coke that a 'random' check uncovered in Brian's house?"

"*What*? What the hell are you talking about?" A nurse who was passing by gave her a disapproving look. "Six pounds of coke? Six *pounds*?"

"Brian's back in jail, Chase. His parole has been revoked and he's facing another ten to twenty."

"This… this has to be a joke."

But deep down, Chase knew that it wasn't.

It was Stu.

Chase hadn't asked him to do anything, hadn't asked for a cent for keeping him out of prison.

But Stu knew. Stu knew because Kendrick knew. If she had to guess, Stu had asked Kendrick to look into Chase, like he had Tate. Just to be sure.

And she knew what the man had uncovered.

"No joke, Chase. Brian's back in jail. He's not coming for Georgina anymore."

Chase should have been elated but standing outside of Floyd's room, she couldn't help but feel that she'd given up a potential catastrophe for an actual one.

"Chase? I don't think—"

"Thank you for calling, Terrence. I won't—I won't bother you again."

And Chase knew that this was what *he* wanted, without him saying so: distance between them. She was foul, a poison, a cancer to anyone who came near.

Chase hung up the phone and stared at Floyd through the observation window.

She could leave now. Could take Georgina, go anywhere, do anything. She could permanently sever her link to the FBI.

Never take a case again for friend or foe.

But Floyd wouldn't want that, she knew. Floyd, who at one point had been driven to near catatonia by his PTSD, had continued to press onward. He came back, despite everything, despite how easy it would have been for him to just pack things, Floyd had persevered.

And that was inspirational.

No, she wasn't leaving.

Chase was back.

***

"Chase?" Director Hampton, who was known for having the world's greatest poker face, or an affect that prevented him from showing as basic an emotion as surprise, let his mask slip. "What are you—what are you doing here?"

Chase closed the office door behind her.

"Floyd's been in an accident," she said bluntly.

Director Hampton stopped sifting the papers on his desk.

"An accident?"

"He was shot. Right now, he's in a coma."

Hampton had recovered from the initial shock of her intrusion and her comment raised no expression on his face.

"What happened?"

"He was shot protecting me."

This was a wholly inadequate answer, but Hampton knew better than to press. In time, she would tell him. Pushing her now would just cause her to clam up for good.

"I'm sorry to hear that," Hampton said flatly. He was back to his automaton self. Chase didn't know which version was better. "What can I do for you, Chase?"

When Chase had initially retired from the FBI, they'd been on good terms and Hampton had made it no secret that he wanted one of his top agents back. But that had been a long time ago.

Since that day, Chase had caused numerous problems, which had ensnared Hampton in more than one tricky legal situation.

"I'm going to replace him."

"Excuse me?"

Chase stiffened and stared the Director straight in the eyes.

"I want back in. I'm coming back to the FBI as Floyd's replacement."

Chapter 86

TATE HADN'T EVEN TAKEN HIS coffee from Tabir when he heard heavy footsteps approach from behind. This time, he spun before Marco could grab his wallet or arm.

The man had other intentions. His right hand was buried deep into the pocket of his cheap leather overcoat.

"Tate, you ran out on me again," Marco stated as fact.

Tate swallowed hard. Any man who had no issue assaulting an FBI Agent in the middle of the sidewalk in broad daylight would have no problem killing them, either. That, Tate was certain of. His plan? Not so much.

"Work."

Marco stepped forward and his right hand started to lift from his pocket.

"But I have your money. All of it."

Marco stopped and Tate, very slowly, reached into the inside pocket of his own jacket. He pulled out a roll of bills, collected with an elastic band.

"Ten thousand. All of it." Tate tossed the money and Marco caught it—with his left hand. He held the roll up, stared at it, then tucked it away.

"You win the lottery, or something?"

Tate was pleased to see that Marco removed both hands—empty—out of his pockets.

"Something like that."

"Right, well, you owe us more than just ten grand." Marco started to smile. "You owe us interest on your loan. You—"

"I thought you'd say that." Tate reached into his jeans pocket this time and removed a flattened wad of bills. "Two grand. More than enough to cover any interest."

He tossed the bills, Marco caught them, and put them away with the rest of the cash.

"Tate, you owe us more than this. You need to pay us every week. That was the deal."

Tate's expression soured.

"I paid you back with interest. *That* was the deal," he countered.

Marco offered a humorless laugh.

"That's not how it works."

Tate looked over his shoulder at Tabir. The pale man was doing his best to pretend he wasn't listening—cleaning the shiny aluminum countertop, moving a metal napkin dispenser four inches to the left—but he'd clearly overheard everything.

"Tabir, maybe you should go take a walk?"

Tabir didn't need to be asked twice. He nodded and ducked away.

"Tate, I want you to think very carefully about what you do next," Marco warned. His hand was back in his pocket, gripping a familiar bulge. "You pay every week. *Every* week."

Tate stared into Marco's wide eyes. He made no move for his own weapon, which was holstered at his hip.

"You understand?"

Tate nodded.

"Oh, I understand. I also figured this would happen, so I decided to call one of my friends."

Marco didn't take the bait—his eyes remained fixed on Tate.

"You bring FBI into this? This not going to end well for you, Tate. You or your daughter."

"Yeah," Tate said, a grin forming on his lips. "I thought you'd say that, too. But, no, I didn't involve the FBI."

"Then who—"

"Man's paid you already, nigga."

Three people suddenly appeared behind Marco. Big Roddy was in the middle, and he was flanked by two men who were nearly as intimidating and as large as he was.

"Take a walk," Big Roddy ordered.

Marco's right arm flexed.

"You best think twice 'fore you pull that peashooter out," the man on the left said. He was wearing pale jeans that hung low on his hips and an LA Laker's T-shirt. He teased the shirt up just a little to reveal the chrome handle of a gun.

Marco took his hands out of his pockets.

"We Gucci?" Big Roddy asked. "Or we goin' have a problem? I don't like problems."

Marco scowled.

"No problem, no problem."

"The ways I sees it, man's paid you and his debt is gone. That work for you?"

Marco hesitated.

"That work."

"Good. What about you?" The question was posed to Tate.

"Works for me."

"Good. Best you take off then, nigga," Big Roddy told Marco.

Marco, still fuming, walked away.

He didn't look back.

"Thanks," Tate said.

"No problem. Take care o' yerself, Tate. And best you ice that hand."

The three men left in the opposite direction Marco had gone.

"Mr. Abernathy, you want your coffee now?"

Tate jumped.

Tabir was back behind his cart, smiling as if nothing had happened. As if there hadn't nearly been a shootout in downtown Virginia between the Serbian mob and some Crips... with FBI not just looking on but having orchestrated the conflict.

"You... you have something stronger under there?"

Epilogue

Tate exhaled loudly and rolled onto his back. Chase, her naked body covered in a sheen of sweat, struggled to catch her breath.

The sex, charged with a volatile mix of emotions, was even better this time around. After their hearts stopped racing, Tate leaned over and gently caressed her face. His fingers eventually found the wound just below her collarbone. While it was no longer visibly scabbed, it had become a keloid mass.

"What did it feel like?" Tate asked as he gently rubbed the spot. Initially, Chase wanted to pull away from his touch, but the man's two-finger massage actually felt good.

"We're not going to do this, are we?"

Tate's brow furrowed.

"Do what?"

"Tell stories about our wounds like bored American soldiers."

Tate chuckled.

"Oh, I've got many of those, but no, that's not what I meant. I meant, how did it feel coming so close to death?"

If anyone else had asked this question, Chase would have, at best, ignored it, at worst, told them off. But this wasn't anyone else.

This was Tate. When she touched his bare skin, this was a man whose pain she felt, pain she lived and experienced, pain that was so similar to her own.

"I've been closer," Chase said, removing his hand from her collarbone.

He seemed to understand and didn't press.

The two of them stared at the ceiling, reveling in the comfortable silence. It was nearly three in the afternoon, and they'd spent the entire day in bed. Chase had wanted to go for a run, get some air back in her lungs, and then go check on Floyd again, but Tate, who had stayed over in her hotel for the past few days, had other ideas.

And Chase was glad.

But now things were getting a little out of control. They were enjoying themselves, but Chase didn't want it to come to a point where they were together simply because they were avoiding reality.

She rolled out of bed and slipped on her tracksuit.

"Where you going?"

Chase, her back to Tate, replied, "I told Georgina I'd be home tomorrow. Have some stuff to do before I fly back to New York."

When Tate didn't answer, she turned to look at him. He was giving her puppy dog eyes.

"Can't you push it one more day?"

"No can do. Louisa has looked after her for long enough."

Tate nodded.

"But hey," Chase said with a grin, "you'll see me again soon. Don't miss me too much."

Tate flipped the script.

"A little presumptive of you, isn't it?"

Chase lifted her shoulders to her ears.

"No, not really. I mean, given that we're partners now we're going to be seeing a lot of each other."

"Well, maybe I'll—wait, *what?*"

Chase smiled broadly.

"I'm back, Tate. I'm back and I'm your partner."

There was something about this statement that made her nervous, and a little sad. Last time she'd been officially with the FBI, Floyd had been her partner. And then he had been Tate's.

Now, he was in a coma.

"You're lying."

"Sure, but not about this."

Tate sat upright.

"That's amaz—"

He was interrupted by a knock at the door.

Tate started to get up, but Chase indicated for him to lie back down. Louisa knew that she was staying here, Chase had given her the room number just in case, but no one else had it.

And nobody at all knew that Tate was here.

Chase wanted to keep it that way.

She walked over to the door and peered through the peephole.

"What?" The word just fell out of her mouth, and she was suddenly incapable of generating any others.

Chase didn't even think she could breathe.

"Who is it?" Tate, who had ignored her indication to stay in bed, asked.

Chase looked through the peephole again to make sure she hadn't imagined it. And then she tried to take off VR goggles that she wasn't wearing.

This wasn't real. It couldn't be.

"Chase?" Tate's voice was dripping with concern now.

She cleared her throat.

"It's Felix... Felix and Brad."

"Who?"

Chase somehow managed to turn and stared at the man who was wearing only his boxers.

"Tate... it's my son. My son and ex-husband."

***

Floyd gasped and his eyes snapped open.

"Woah, big fella, no need to sit up."

He saw a vision of Tony Metcalfe, grinning, showing off his busted teeth, and aiming a pistol at Chase.

"Chase!"

"She's fine," the voice replied. "She's fine. You saved her, Floyd."

Floyd breathed a sigh of relief. He didn't recognize the voice and he wanted to turn his head in the direction of the speaker, to find out who it was, but stopped.

Panic and pain filled his left side.

"Who—"

"Relax, you're in the hospital—you're going to be okay, Floyd. You saved Chase and you guys brought down Tony."

"I can't—I can't see you," Floyd said, panicking.

The man rose and slowly filled his field of view.

"Not much to look at, I'm afraid," Jeremy Stitts said. "Just me."

Floyd smiled and relaxed. He liked Stitts—he liked Stitts a lot.

"What are you doing here, Stitts?"

"I had to see you. After all, I have to approve before you join the club."

"The... club?"

"Yeah," Stitts said, pointing at Floyd's bandaged chest. "The *I got shot while working with Chase Adams Club.*"

Floyd wanted to laugh but feared the inevitable pain that would come with it. He did, however, smile.

"Thanks for coming."

Stitts took his hand and squeezed it.

"Wouldn't miss it. But you should probably go back to sleep. You're going to need your energy."

"Yeah?" Floyd coughed dryly. Pain spread across his chest and now he squeezed Stitts' hand. "For what?"

"Well, to keep up with your new partner, for starters. He has a bit of a limp, but his energy is unmatched."

Floyd stared blankly at the man with the perfect hair.

"New... new partner? I'm sorry, S-Stitts, I don't r-r-really—"

"Yeah, spoiler alert, it's me. I just got approval from the FBI—me and you, two wounded Agents are going to form our own team. We're going to be investigating cold cases together. So, rest up, my man, I want to get started *yesterday*."

Choo-Choo, Floyd thought, his smile returning. *Choo-Choo*.

END

Author's Note

IT'S BEEN A WHILE SINCE we've ventured into Chase's world, and it feels *fantastic* to finally be back. This was, by far, one of the most complicated books I've ever written. It's also been one of the most rewarding. Timely, too, given the recent explosion of AI tools available on the Internet.

The concept of reality has always been a fascinating one to me. The truth, as I attempted to explain it in this book, is that everything we experience is interpreted by our brains. There is no one true experience, therefore, there can never be one true reality. Everyone's experience is slightly different, influenced by their specific biology and psychology. I explored these constructs in Direct Evidence (even the title is a play on this) with the obvious Chase Adams-*esque* background of mayhem and murder and a little sex tossed in because, well, because it's Chase.

Do I think that we live in a simulation? Maybe. Actually, I'll go with *probably*.

But as Chase so eloquently put it, "I mean, what does it matter? Simulation or no simulation, I can't do anything about it. I'm still stuck here, living by their rules. No resets, no do-overs."

No one's going to write these books for me. At least not yet, anyway.

A couple of brief notes before I go: one, thank you for your patience with this book. As I mentioned, in addition to being complicated, and it is also the longest I've ever written. I hope it was worth the wait. Two, I have previously mentioned in the backs of other books that Tainted Blood is up next in the

Chase series after Direct Evidence. I'm pretty sure that is going to change. Tainted Blood will come out, but it will most likely be the twelfth and not the eleventh book. The next book will be Filthy Secrets and should be out soon. I promise not to make you wait as long for this one as you did Direct Evidence.

Thanks again for all your support and if you have a moment, please leave this book a review and a rating.

You keep reading, I'll keep writing.

Best,
Pat
Montreal, 2023